THE
WHISPERING
BONES

ANDREW LOWE

VINCI
BOOKS

By Andrew Lowe

Lennox & Blackwood Crime Thrillers

The Whispering Bones
The Vanishing Room

For Tom and Josh

Vinci Books

vinci-books.com

Published by Vinci Books Ltd in 2025

1

A CIP catalogue record for this book is available from the British Library.
Paperback ISBN: 9781036709235
Printed and bound in Great Britain by 4edge Ltd.

Prologue

He stepped out into the North London twilight, into the human herd. Vendors, vapers, screamers, streamers. Elbowed by power walkers, grazed by e-scooters.

He glided over it all like a phantom.

He slid into the driver's seat of a black BMW 3 Series, the leather's texture sparking an orange flare in his mind's eye. He started the engine, its purr a soothing aquamarine that washed away the bar's lingering cacophony of reds and yellows.

He had drunk a bottle of lager, and his thinking was a little dampened. But he navigated the streets with care and grace, counting the turns, threading slowly through patches of congestion.

No drama.

That came later.

The city's rhythms conceded to the quieter pulse of the suburbs. Here, the street lights were sparse, the shadows deeper.

He lowered the driver's side window. The sound of the sliding glass was mint-green, sharp round the edges.

He crawled the car along the perimeter road of a new-build estate, past modular red-brick homes with baize-like lawns and upscale SUVs parked side by side in dual drive-ways. Further in, the houses tapered to scruffy development sites set in buffer zones: prepared foundations marked out with orange plastic fencing and half-finished timber frames.

He turned into an unmarked track that led to a row of private lock-up garages shaded by a canopy of oak and beech trees. He pulled up, killed the engine, and sat still for a while, basking in the silence, broken only by the fading tick of cooling metal.

He waited, watching the garages. Listening.

Nothing.

He raised the window and got out of the car, gravel crunching underfoot: a spark of white against the night's blackness. At the end garage, he pulled on a pair of nitrile gloves and swiped an access card over a wall pad, which issued a soft double bleep: a burst of lime green.

Inside, he flicked a switch and the dark gave way to low fluorescent light. He blinked, adjusting. A silver-grey Vauxhall Insignia sat waiting. He ran a hand along its metal flank, closed his eyes, savouring the familiar bloom of purple and vermillion.

He walked back out to the BMW and retrieved a small but heavy canvas holdall from the boot. The items in the bag clinked and rattled as he moved, setting off a psychedelic surge behind his eyes, strong enough to send him down to his haunches. He took a few slow breaths and rose again. Back inside the garage, he set the bag down carefully on the Insignia's back seat.

A smile tugged at the corners of his mouth. He was in

dire need of nourishment, but tomorrow the ritual would take place again. The prospect filled him with a warm pulse: honeyed gold.

He stood by the door, waiting.

A faint sound caught his attention.

A bump. Muffled, but distinct, from the Insignia's boot.

He paused, head tilted. Another bump followed, then silence.

He waited for a few moments, then switched off the light, stepped back out onto the gravel, and secured the door behind him.

PART ONE

SYNERGY

Chapter One

The command vehicle's interior lights cast a sallow glow across DCI Oswald Lennox's face as he hunched over the tactical display.

His voice crackled on the secure channel. 'Control to all units. Radio check.'

A chorus of affirmatives.

Lennox's eyes flicked to the dashboard clock. 4:55.

Five minutes to breach.

He lashed his tongue round his mouth, trying to mop away the tang of scorched coffee. 'Final confirmations. Team target is Keane residence on Finsbury Park Road. Suspected armed presence.' He winced, spat. 'Christ. You don't boil coffee water. A child would know it.'

'*Sir?*'

'Never mind. Alpha lead?'

'*Copy that, Control. Set for hard breach on your go.*'

Lennox ran through the brief in his mind.

Two teams. One front, one back...

'*Sir?*'

'Copy that, Alpha. Beta team, you're covering the rear. Stay lively.'

Beta acknowledged.

Alpha team to breach. All officers were aware of Keane's history of violence and the firearm threat.

It was his girlfriend's flat. Limited intelligence on her but not perceived to be—

'Sir. Beta lead.'

'Copy.'

'Increased activity at rear. Light on in the basement room. Suggest we expedite entry.'

4:57.

Lennox recalled the scene in the briefing room, observing as it unspooled in his memory. The three men in the Alpha team sat on the right-hand side of the second row. Their faces triggered their names, records, honours.

He switched to a new track: reading through the documents as the teams assembled. The words re-formed in his mind as clear as the images on the tactical display.

One man, Braybrook, had grown up in the US. He was comfortable with guns but hadn't applied for firearms teams. Level head. Not a cowboy.

Lennox slipped a pellet of chewing gum into his mouth. 'Negative. Alpha team lead?'

'Sir.'

'DC Braybrook to take rear. Beta team, join Alpha and breach on my signal.'

A pause.

'DC Braybrook solo at rear, sir?' said the Beta lead.

'That's my order. SCO19, this is Control. Status?'

Radio crackle.

'Sir. Armed assets standing by.'

Lennox chewed his gum, pondering.

4:58.

'Sir. Beta team in position.'

Something was loose, hanging. Keane was a career toerag who'd notched up a cumulative five years for GBH and drug supply before his twenty-first birthday. But now he'd evolved, leaving a DNA-soaked beanie next to the body of a rival dealer.

Slash wound to the vic's throat.

Fourteen stabs to the chest. Zombie knife.

T-shirt sleeves torn. Two others holding him.

4:59.

'All units,' said Lennox. 'Stand by.'

'Sir.' Alpha team lead again. *'Suggest we—'*

'Stand by.'

'Sir. DC Braybrook reporting. From the rear.'

Lennox smiled. *Reporting.*

'Copy.'

'Figure at rear basement window. Light off again.'

'Don't deviate. Stay focused.'

Lennox savoured the moment, rolling the gum around, freshening his mouth.

Keane was probably expecting the attention. He'd have his girlfriend on watch. Maybe swapping with her when the hour got more sociable. But probably not.

5:00.

'Execute.'

A crash. Shouts.

Lennox leaned in, squinting at the shaky bodycam footage.

'Alpha and Beta team. Entry successful. Hall and sitting room empty. Ground floor clear.'

'Copy that,' said Lennox. 'Split between first and basement. DC Braybrook. Update.'

More crashing and shouting from the Alpha and Beta teams as the bodycam footage showed them sweeping the rooms.

Lennox took the gum from his mouth and stuffed it into his empty coffee cup. 'DC Braybrook. Update.'

'First floor clear.' Alpha team lead.

A woman's voice. Squealing, berating.

'Sir.' Beta team lead. *'Basement clear. We have Keane's girlfriend, but no sign of Keane.'*

Lennox detached the radio. He slid open the side door of the command vehicle and barrelled out onto the pavement. He ran across the road, past the entry point, shouting into the radio. 'Beta team. Suspect is away. Rear exit. DC Braybrook, confirm your position.'

Radio crackle.

Braybrook's voice came through. *'Sir.'* He was panting, snatching at his words. *'Suspect is unarmed but mobile... In pursuit... Of suspect. Heading east down Stroud Green Road. Towards the estate. Came out of fucking nowhere!'* A clattering noise. *'Sir.'* He grunted, then cried out.

'DC Braybrook?' said Lennox. 'Report status.' He slowed and stopped at the far end of the road. He peered through the half-light, across the scrubland that separated the converted town houses from a low-rise cluster of crumbling flat blocks.

Braybrook was on the floor, trying to haul himself up. Three officers caught up to him. Two kept running, while one crouched, trying to help him to his feet.

Ahead of the two, a hefty man in underwear and T-shirt sprinted across the scrub at half the speed of the pursuing officers.

Lennox bent double, catching his breath. He watched as the officers gained on Keane. One got alongside and felled him with a side tackle. They wrestled for a few seconds, but the other officer suppressed and cuffed him, then hauled him upright.

Braybrook was up but needed support from the other officer as they shuffled back to the road.

Lennox lifted the radio to call for reports and stand down the AR team.

He hesitated. Hooked the handset into the clip on his vest and raised his right arm.

The hand was trembling.

He stepped forward, into a pool of light from a street lamp, and stared at the hand, splaying the fingers.

Not trembling.

Shaking.

Chapter Two

Olivia Blackwood was up and moving, lurching between dresser and wardrobe. She dived into a neutral blouse, tugged on a pair of fitted black trousers.

There was a body in the bed, half-covered by the duvet.

Blond, with a scruffy burst-fade haircut. Too young for him.

Arm hanging down, fingertips on his phone.

Nasty calf tattoo.

She shook him. 'You've got to go. Landlord's coming in half an hour.'

The window pane rattled with raindrops. Blackwood flung the curtain aside, unveiling a dirty-grey pall over the distant spire of Harrow School Chapel.

She stamped into a pair of low-heels, then kicked them away, peeled off the trousers. Replaced them with dark jeans, scuffed brown boots.

'Hey!' She yanked the man's foot. 'I need you gone.'

He groaned. 'No breakfast?'

Blackwood half-tucked the blouse. 'It's not included. I'm afraid you only booked the One-Time Hook-Up special. That's a cup of instant coffee, one round of vanilla sex and a bed for the night.' She checked the dresser mirror, smoothed down her hair, grabbed her phone. 'No eggs. No pancakes. No Coco Pops. And check-out time was fifteen minutes ago.'

She crashed out of the room and jogged across the landing into the poky bathroom. Sink, toilet, wash basin, narrow bath with detachable shower head over the taps.

Blackwood segued through the rituals, barely finishing the last before starting on the next: face-wash, moisturise, few dabs of make-up. She brushed her teeth—toothbrush in one hand, scrolling the socials with the other—then used the toilet. She washed her hands, then smoothed shea butter through her dark curls before pinning them up, revealing a subtle tattoo behind her left ear. She leaned in close to the mirror, eyeballing herself.

Already, the thoughts crowding in. Tumbling over each other like a scrum of toddlers.

She stared herself down, blinking slowly. Her thick lashes wiped then renewed the image: wide, upturned eyes; glossy hazel irises.

A shout from the bedroom. *'Where's my fucking trainers?'*

If only she had a bouncer trained to clear them out at daybreak. Soundlessly, without fuss. Without waking her.

Or a chute that slid down from the ceiling and sucked them up and far away.

Or they could turn into pumpkins at midnight.

Or, better still, pumpkin pie.

No.

Apple pie. With cinnamon...

'Fuck's sake.'

She jerked away from the mirror, back into the bedroom.

He was up at least, and dressed, sitting on the edge of the bed, hunting around underneath it.

'Out, out, out,' she said. 'I mean it. I'm late for work.'

He sniggered. 'Not so submissive now, eh?'

Blackwood glared out at the rain, then bent down to pick up her brown leather shoulder bag.

His hand slapped her hard on the arse and she cried out. It stung, even through the jeans.

She turned, found him grinning. 'Didn't notice the purple streak in your hair last night.'

Bad teeth.

Oily skin.

Horsey face.

She returned his grin, then swung her open hand round in a wide arc, slapping him across the cheek.

He reeled, holding his face. 'Jesus Christ! What the fuck is your problem?'

She pulled the door wide. 'I've told you my problem. My landlord is due. He gives us shit if guests stay over.' She reached for the far side of the dresser, threw his trainers onto the bed. 'Last night was wonderful. Together, we scaled the holiest heights of ecstasy. But now you're just my guest.'

He pulled on the trainers, scowling at her. 'An unwanted guest.'

Blackwood smiled. 'Now you're getting it.' She gestured to the open door. 'You have officially outstayed your welcome.'

The man got up. He was shorter than her by a few inches.

He stepped in close, his grin fading to a frown, trying to stare her out. She held his eye.

He cracked first, smirking, rubbing his reddened cheek. 'Gave me a proper knock. What the fuck do you do, anyway? You're not a cage fighter, are you?'

He hissed out a laugh, leaned in closer.

Morning breath.

Rancid, with a sickly undertone.

Vape or gum or—

'You know what?' he rasped into her ear. 'I don't mind it. I'm up for the rough stuff. But it goes both ways, eh? How about one for the road? Make it quick, like.'

Blackwood smiled. 'How rough are we talking?' She pivoted and pushed open the window. Rainwater splashed over the sill, into the room. The man stepped back. 'We're on the first floor, above the front garden. It's quite overgrown, so it'll be a soft landing. But you'll probably break something. Particularly if you go out head-first.' She nodded to the door. 'I'd take the smooth way out if I were you.'

Chapter Three

Lennox eased into the tilting backrest of his Herman Miller office chair. But after a night of patchy sleep, the incline was unwise, and he forced himself upright, tapping the base of his desk lamp to boost the brightness.

He'd stacked the report templates on his PC desktop in order of urgency: Incident, Use of Force, Post-Incident Procedure. There would be a formal debrief, and probably a Professional Standards interview.

Personal Statement.

Risk Assessment Review.

Possible IOPC referral.

Welfare Check.

Action Plan.

He sighed, then stood up and headed for a low shelf in the corner of his glass-walled office. He bent forward, pushing his face close to the chrome-fronted Jura coffee machine. His contorted reflection glared back.

Ambient 1: Music For Airports wafted around him as he pressed the power button. He lifted the lid, inhaled the aroma, then scooped out a measure of single-origin beans from an airtight ceramic container and poured them in. He closed the lid of the machine, set his favourite ultraviolet Le Creuset mug into the holder, and tapped the *ESPRESSO* icon on the colour touch screen.

Nothing.

Lennox turned away, gazing out at the vast, open-plan operational floor of the Hendon Major Investigation Team. One hundred and twenty-five souls. Sixty detectives. Twenty-five uniforms. Forty civilian staff: analysts, researchers, admin.

Rows of light grey desks sat in clusters, each equipped with dual-monitor computers and modesty panels.

Along the far wall, a series of plasma screens displayed real-time information—London crime maps and stats, key CCTV feeds—above a row of whiteboards with timelines, suspect photos, flowcharts. In the near corner, a group of detectives sat huddled in a glass-walled briefing room, viewing a projected presentation.

Still nothing from the machine.

Lennox studied the display. He tapped the *ESPRESSO* icon again, caught a movement at the office door.

A short middle-aged woman had entered without knocking. She wore an immaculately draped deep-teal *hijab*, the fabric complementing her complexion. DSI Aisha Khokhar closed the door behind her and strode over to Lennox with confident, measured steps. She tucked the loose edges of the hijab under her chin and smoothed the fabric over her shoulders, then rolled up the sleeves of her white shirt.

Khokhar studied the display, then reached out a finger and tapped the *BREW* icon. The machine whirred into action.

'User error.' She smiled and took a seat facing the desk.

Lennox opened an app on his phone and silenced the music.

Khokhar caught his eye, holding her smile.

'Coffee, ma'am?' said Lennox.

She shook her head. 'On the wagon at the moment. I was shifting my last cup further forward in the day, but still couldn't switch off for sleep. So I'm retraining myself with matcha latte. Apparently, it's rich in antioxidants.'

'And a more sustained energy boost,' said Lennox. He brought his cup over and sat down. 'Tastes awful, though. Like drinking a lawn.'

Khokhar laughed, then rolled her eyes in pleasure. 'My God, that smells so good.'

Lennox nodded, took a sip. 'Just a glitch, ma'am.'

'The coffee machine?'

'The Keane op.'

Khokhar crossed her legs. 'A glitch on your watch, Oz. Collector's item. A double-tick for the apprehension and appropriate force, but a big red *SEE ME* for stationing a single officer at the rear.'

Lennox smoothed out his closely trimmed salt-and-pepper beard with the palm of his hand. 'I'm struggling with sleep too at the moment. Judgement is off.' He forced a smile. 'Braybrook picked up a sprain. Nothing big.'

Khokhar fixed him with a searching stare. 'I hear you asked a DS to "refresh everyone's memory" at the briefing.'

Lennox drained his cup. 'My homework on Keane was shaky. That was lazy. Won't happen again.'

Khokhar gasped. 'Oh, Christ. This isn't a bollocking. Really. I was genuinely curious.' She left some space for him to speak; he didn't fill it. 'Do you need a break?'

'No,' said Lennox, too quickly. 'It's just... Maybe I'm human after all.'

'I wouldn't go that far.'

'The date's coming up.' His eyes drifted to the photo frame on his desk, but he dragged them back to Khokhar. 'That's probably getting into my head, too.'

She nodded. 'Of course.' She wagged a finger. 'Don't tough this out, though. If you need time, you need time.' She sat back. 'Any more thoughts on the thing I mentioned?'

Lennox wrinkled his nose. 'I'd rather focus on the current generation. I just need to pace myself better now I'm—'

'Don't you dare say "over the hill".' Khokhar stood.

He grimaced as he got to his feet. 'Feeling it today. I'll sharpen up.'

'Again, Oz. Not a bollocking. Just checking in. For most people, I'd wait for three or four glitches. But for you, I'm here at one.' She spun and headed for the door. 'Here to help. But I can't do much if I don't know what you need help with.'

Lennox lowered himself back into the seat. 'Appreciate the offer, but no help needed.'

She stopped, turned. 'Plenty of magic left in the wand yet, eh? What are you now? Sixty-odd? That's young, these days.'

He grinned. 'Fuck off. Ma'am.'

Chapter Four

The packed 183 to Hendon Central juddered through the North London suburbs. Blackwood had been forced to clamber over a middle-aged man in a crumpled grey suit to claim a window seat beside him, near the back of the top deck. The man was slumped forward, head down, elbows on knees. Asleep or unconscious or dead drunk or dead. Possibly an unnoticed refugee from the night shift. As the bus weaved along Wealdstone High Street, his shoulder repeatedly nudged Blackwood as he lolled left and right.

She rested her forehead against the cool window, trying to twist away from the man. Away from the swaying crush of standers, most with one hand gripping the overhead rail and the other thumbing through their phones.

Stale sweat from her companion.

A morning mulch from the others: sickly colognes, soapy shower gels, tobacco and vape.

She slid her forehead through the tepid condensation: a couple of inches left, then a pause, then the same distance right. Repeat for a group of four pairs, then another four.

Then another, until four fours. Then one more pair as a closer.

Then repeat the whole thing.

Outside, the crowds scurried through the downpour, slipping in and out of shop awnings. A clay-white sky loomed above, sealing them all in, stealing the light.

The bus swung round into Kingsbury, and she took a heavy barge from the barely conscious man. The contact disrupted her count, and she pulled away from the window, giving the man a petulant shove which caused him to collide with a woman standing in the aisle.

The woman sighed, then looked up from her Kindle and sent Blackwood a *was that necessary?* scowl. Blackwood stared her down and she returned to her reading.

Rows of Edwardian semis scrolled past, some backing onto estates with contemporary apartment blocks.

If she could make the step up, she would find somewhere closer to work. She might even stretch to a place of her own.

A tinny music beat struck up from the seat behind: plodding with a textured, chopping snare. Blackwood turned. A twentysomething man held his phone up close to his face, nodding to the music.

A languid rap came in: heavily accented London English.

She turned back to the window.

Kurta-style shirt. Charcoal.

Lightweight bomber.

Minimalist backpack on knees. Herschel, maybe.

Shaped beard, well groomed. Smartwatch.

IC3. Yo-Pro. Middle class. Low threat.

Blackwood reached into the side pocket of her shoulder bag.

No headphones.

Case on the bedroom window sill.

Knocked off by opening the window?

Another shoulder barge.

'Excuse me, mate?'

Blackwood turned again. An older man in the corresponding window seat waved a hand in the air, trying to get the music player's attention.

'Mate?'

The player turned his eyes to the window, head still nodding, making a point of ignoring the older man.

'Can you please switch the music off?'

'Yeah!' A woman standing further forward in the aisle spoke up. She leaned to the side, clearing her line of sight, and glared at the back of the music player's head.

The young man sucked his teeth and gave a dismissive little laugh. 'We're good, Karen. Getting off in a minute, yeah?'

The woman gaped, looked around for support. 'Karen?'

A solid-looking man in a tight blue beanie sitting a few rows ahead turned and leaned on the back of his seat. 'Yo! That's pretty rude, man. Yeah?'

The music player smiled: a borderline sneer. He shook his head. 'Nah, bro.'

He nodded harder to the rhythm as the track ramped up. A jagged synth line cut across the beat and a second voice joined the lead rapper in call and response.

The temperature dropped.

Blackwood faced the window again. She wiped away the condensation, glared out through the rain, into the gloom.

Mutterings all around.

Her hand wiping on her jeans.

Forehead against the window.

Head left, head right. For two. Then four.

Squeaking against the glass now.

Shoulder barge.

Sweat, like old soil. Like rotting soil.

The boom and chunk of the music. The overlapping flows of the rappers. Drowsy, sneering.

Shoulder barge.

Blackwood sucked in a deep breath. She tipped back her head and sang, full-throated, into the air.

'Oh! I do like to be beside the seaside. I do like to be beside the sea...'

The man beside Blackwood jerked his head up. He rubbed at his eyes and turned to stare at her.

She repeated the lines.

'Oh! I do like to be beside the seaside. I do like to be beside the sea...'

Blackwood paused, turned. The music player squinted at her in confusion.

Boom, click.

Synth riff.

Rappers overlapping.

A tall, late middle-aged man standing near the back caught Blackwood's eye. He smiled, tilted his head from side to side as he sang the next line in a halting, husky voice. *'I do like to stroll along the prom, prom, prom.'*

Another pause.

Cautious laughter from a few passengers.

The solid man raised his arms in a theatrical shrug. 'The fuck?'

A young couple in the seat ahead of Blackwood turned. The woman looked wary; the man was grinning. He raised his eyebrows in encouragement.

Blackwood struck up again. *'Where the brass bands play...
tiddly om-pom-pom.'*

More laughter.

The standing man continued. *'So, just let me be beside the
seaside...'* He thought for a moment. *'I'll be beside myself with
glee.'*

A head poked up out of the stairwell, curious.

The singing faltered. Blackwood couldn't remember the
next line, and nobody else volunteered it.

She turned to look at the man beside her.

Still staring.

Red eyes. Unshaven.

The sour sting of alcohol on his breath.

The music player hauled himself to his feet and pressed
the stop bell. As the bus slowed, he killed the music and
shoved his way through the bodies towards the stairwell.

A few ironic cheers went up.

The man sitting ahead of Blackwood applauded, but
nobody joined him and he turned away.

As the music player reached the top of the stairwell, he
jabbed a finger at Blackwood, then tapped it against the side
of his head and spun it around in a cranking motion.

Chapter Five

Lennox pushed through the double doors of the Monro Room and strode down the central aisle, his polished Oxfords clicking against the wooden floor. The chatter trailed off, and the brains trust of MIT 1 straightened in their tiered seating, cradling their reusable coffee cups.

The mostly male DIs owned the front and middle rows, all dressed in variations of the unofficial uniform: dark suit, white or light-blue dress shirt, a splash of colour in the tie. The unit's other DCI—Ian Rafferty—sat front and centre, facing Khokhar at the curved control desk beside a large wall-mounted screen. The Teacher's Pet slot.

Further back, the ranks descended to DS and DC, where the gender balance shifted, but the uniform principles held firm: dark skirt suits, pastel blouses, minimal jewellery. A couple of rebels had struck out on a knee-length dress with matching blazer. A gaggle of admin staff lurked at the back.

Lennox slowed his pace, steering his tall frame towards

the control desk. No rush, anyway. The party couldn't start without him.

The overhead lighting would expose the thinning spot in the centre of his neatly combed greying hair. Resistance, of course, was useless, but he wasn't yet ready to embrace the out-and-proud bald look favoured by Rafferty, four years his junior.

He set down his tablet on the desk and took a seat beside Khokhar. She raised her eyebrows at him and he nodded.

Khokhar got to her feet. 'Good morning, all. Another day in paradise.' She grinned.

Bleary acknowledgement. Muted. Matching the attire.

Lennox sat with hands clasped. He caught a glint from one of his silver cufflinks and looked down. The angle of the left zeppelin-style link was offset slightly from the right. He adjusted it and reclasped his hands.

'I know we're all busy,' continued Khokhar, 'and so I'd like this briefing to stay brief. I wanted to confirm last night's successful acquisition and arrest of Clayton Keane, suspect in the murder of Stefan Alexandru, whose body was found in the front garden of his mother's house in Totteridge last Tuesday.' She frowned. 'This was an ugly killing, which we believe is contained to local drug rivalry. But there are other individuals involved from other jurisdictions and DCI Rafferty is working with MIT 3 and 5 to bring them in. Hopefully, the intelligence from Keane will lubricate that process.'

She took a seat, touching a hand to Lennox's shoulder. He nodded and stood up, taking a moment to sweep his eyes over the audience, left to right.

Then right to left.

Expectant faces stared up at him.

A couple of coughs.

Left to right again.

Lennox searched himself. It was like plunging a hand into uncertain water, grasping for purchase, flailing for something sunken.

'And now to the main event,' he heard himself say.

His voice was rich and sonorous, easily carrying to the back of the room.

He craned his neck to one of the admin staff in the corner, and the lights dimmed.

Lennox picked up his tablet and navigated to the HOLMES case management system. He mirrored the output to the wall screen, glancing up as he broadcast the image files. 'I know you all have urgent casework, but I'd like you to do a refresh on an ongoing enquiry. You should already be familiar with this case. The details are in the system, so consider this a homework assignment. Actually, no. This is more like revising for an important exam. I'm calling a full briefing for next week. I expect you all to know the case back to front by then, and I'm expecting plenty of fresh ideas.' He glanced at the screen again. 'For now, though. A quick recap. This is a heavy load for this time of day, but I make no apologies.'

He swiped at his tablet, quickly cycling through a series of flashlit crime scene photos.

Close-up on the blood-caked face of a young male, eyes open and glassy.

Wide shot of a well-appointed home office room. The body lay sprawled at the foot of the desk, surrounded by a circular pattern of small items.

Close-up, revealing the items in detail. Rat or mouse skulls. Detached vertebrae aligned in a spine-like formation. Skeletal wing structures arranged in fan patterns. Precisely cut sections of femur or tibia acting as cornerstone pieces for the overall design.

'In a moment of deep inspiration, we came up with a nickname for the individual responsible for this. Internal use only.'

'The Bones Killer,' said a female detective on the front row.

Lennox nodded. 'It wasn't my choice, DI Whitmore.' He swiped again, and the screen shifted through similarly grisly shots from different crime scenes. 'We can speculate over the motive and the thinking behind the bizarre staging, but here's what we actually know. He, and it will likely be a he, has so far presented us with three victims, all male. The first was seven years ago. The second a year later. The third a year after that.'

Close-up of the bludgeoned face of a late middle-aged man, his upper head surrounded by a halo of delicate bird bones.

Ligature marks on the wrists and ankles. A deep red fissure across the centre of the neck.

'The first victim, Christian Kerrigan, was killed in his detached home office. Big house in Borehamwood. The second two, Duncan Langford and Robert Sinclair, were murdered in their living rooms in Radlett and Hadley Wood. All three were well-off. Nothing interesting or consistent in victimology. All deaths were due to exsanguination. Single incision to the jugular. Straight blade. Victims were heavily bound at the wrists and ankles with duct tape. Gagged with the same tape. Minor head wounds. Probably a suppressing blow from a blunt instrument. Limited signs of struggle. No forced entry.'

Mid-shot of an adult male body sprawled in a shallow lake of blood on a tiled bathroom floor.

Close-up of a linked necklace of animal teeth and small bones draped around the victim's neck.

'I welcome your thoughts and theories, but as you'll see from the file, they're hardly in short supply.'

Wide shot revealing bone arrangements extending from the bathtub across the bathroom floor, creating a path-like pattern.

Lennox killed the display and waved to the admin, who raised the lights. 'If Edmond Locard were alive today, these killings would cause him to rethink his ideas. We have no meaningful trace evidence. Whatever the person responsible is getting out of these killings, I believe he is highly forensically aware and scrupulous with clean-up.'

'All killed in private homes,' said DCI Rafferty. 'Plenty of time to cover his tracks.'

Lennox nodded. 'All we have is traces of nitrile on some of the animal bones, which only indicates he was wearing gloves. But there are also deep, finger-shaped impressions on two of the long bones. No prints. So far, we've kept the distinct nature of these killings out of the media. This gives us an advantage, in that the killer doesn't know how much we've pieced together, and we don't risk copycats or false confessions muddying the waters.' Lennox chopped his right hand into his left palm; the slapping sound echoed around the silent room. 'We've had some of the Met's keenest minds on this. Some of those minds are in this room. And I am not blowing smoke, because so far, those minds have drawn blanks. We have scoured the technology, consulted with multiple agencies and international experts, ran several national reviews, devoted hundreds of hours of police resource. Yet we have three people dead and not the faintest idea who killed them or why.' He tilted back his head and stared up at the dropped ceiling. 'Seven years.' He lingered, running his eyes along the rigorous geometry of the LED lighting.

'So, why the revision now, sir?' said DI Whitmore. 'What's the exam?'

Lennox looked at her. 'We have found nothing because we've been looking in the wrong places. This is about the gaps. The detail in this case is disturbing and distracting, but what has kept me awake at night, and I mean literally, is the space between the killings. Roughly a year each time. Are they cooling-off periods? Necessary for planning and victim selection? External factors in the killer's life that dictate his active periods?' He raised a finger, pointed into the air. 'I feel this is the key to finding him.'

Khokhar spoke up. 'Might be simple risk management. Spacing out the crimes makes it harder to make connections.'

Lennox ran both hands over his face. The skin was rough, borderline leathery. 'The killings have all happened in summer, which is where we are now. What really bothers me is that, for most killers, the gaps get shorter. They become emboldened, arrogant, need more frequent fuel for their cravings. We've had nothing new from the Bones Killer for five years. DI Whitmore, I want everyone to knuckle down with revision because the long gap doesn't mean he's finished, or tired of it, or incarcerated for something else, or dead. I think he's overdue.'

Chapter Six

Blackwood flooded the laptop screen with a solid block of unpunctuated, lower-case text. She tensed her right leg and bounced the knee up and down, as if the typing were powered by an unseen foot pump. Her section of desk vibrated with the movement, and her peripheral vision caught a scowl from her neighbour: a young male officer with his mock smartphone inches from his face.

DS Megan Reeves stood at the back wall, gazing into a glass case of vintage forensic tools. She turned, scanned the class for a moment, then prowled over to the whiteboard. 'Right. As I outlined earlier, you've each been provided with a phone containing data related to a series of burglaries in Kensington and Chelsea. The goal was to construct a time-line of the suspect's movements on the night of 15th March, using the phone's GPS data, call logs and social media activity. You were to pay particular attention to any anomalies or patterns that might indicate attempts to establish an alibi or mask criminal activity.' Reeves stopped at the board and turned. 'Incidentally, can anyone tell me why the room we're in is called Faulds Hall?'

Blackwood calmed the knee but kept typing.

A female officer at the desk in front waved a pen in the air. 'Henry Faulds, ma'am?'

Reeves smiled. 'Who was...?'

'Pioneer in fingerprint classification,' said Blackwood, still typing. 'He was a missionary in Japan. Late 1800s.' She stopped, looked up. 'He noticed fingertip impressions on some old pottery and wondered if the patterns were unique to each individual. He used his ideas to help a colleague wrongly accused of theft.'

The female officer turned and glowered at Blackwood.

'Sorry to interrupt,' said Blackwood, returning to her typing.

Reeves tilted her head. 'You seem busy, PC Blackwood. Doing your emails?'

Blackwood finished typing and looked up. Most of the heads were turned towards her, and she shifted her gaze to the view from the floor-to-ceiling windows that lined the back wall. Faulds Hall was a modest-sized lecture theatre on the second level of Hendon Police College, overlooking the landscaped front lawns. She watched a small group of uniformed trainees hurrying through the rain along a narrow path from the glass-and-steel forensic lab into the low-rise tactical training centre. A purpose-built suite of angular contemporary buildings stood at the far end of campus, their vast tinted windows reflecting the afternoon sun.

She turned back, focusing on Reeves, trying to screen out the faces. 'Uh, I was just laying out my thoughts on the burglaries, Sergeant Reeves.'

Reeves smiled, hitched herself up on the desk. 'That

was quick. Care to share? What can you tell us about the suspect's movements on the night in question?'

Blackwood's knee bounced again; she steadied it with her hand.

Her eyes darted around the room, catching the male officer beside her, who now wore a predatory smile.

'The suspect's GPS data shows regular stops at twenty-minute intervals along the North Circular. Each stop lasts exactly three minutes.'

DS Reeves raised an eyebrow. 'And the significance of this?'

Blackwood's words tumbled out. 'The stops correlate with the locations of traffic cameras. The timing suggests the suspect was using a device to interfere with the cameras' function. There's a small spike in data usage from the phone at each stop, possibly uploading a looped video feed.'

Reeves stepped off the desk. 'Excellent. That level of detail wasn't part of the original scenario. How did you spot that?' She wandered forward and stood near the students at the front, just out of Blackwood's eyeline.

Blackwood stood and held up her test phone, gesticulating as she spoke. 'I noticed a pattern in the data usage graph that lined up with the GPS stops. It seemed odd, so I cross-referenced it with a map of traffic camera locations I remembered from a previous exercise.'

The door opened and a uniformed female officer entered. She caught Reeves's eye and stood off to the side.

'Excuse me for a moment,' said Reeves.

Blackwood stood frozen as Reeves spoke to the officer. Most of the other students had lost interest in her and had returned to their laptops. She dropped back into her seat, eyes flashing from phone screen to laptop to Reeves's notes on the whiteboard. She glanced to the side; the male officer was still looking at her and she raised her eyebrows in challenge. His gaze shifted from anticipation to bemusement then mild disappointment as he focused back on his laptop.

She angled her chair away.

Closed her eyes.

Fluttered her fingertips across the back of her hand.

The sensation carried her to verdant woodland. A blazing summer day. Bicycles abandoned at the edge of a path. A blonde girl ahead: turning, smiling. Beckoning her into the trees.

'PC Blackwood,' said Reeves. 'You've been summoned.'

Chapter Seven

DCI Richard Mallory slid a document from a black vinyl folder and scribbled on the facing page with a stout fountain pen.

Scratchy.

He flipped it over, made another mark, and another, then pushed the document back into the folder and added it to a large pile on the other side of his capacious glass-topped desk.

'Won't be a moment.'

Posh. Faint West Country accent.

He took another folder and repeated the process, keeping his head down, never looking at Blackwood, perched in the facing chair set a few feet back from Mallory's desk.

Blackwood tensed her leg, which set her knee bouncing. She settled it and looked around the office.

Desk surface reflecting the fluorescent light in a uniform pattern.
Uneven carpet pile where the chair has worn a path.

Blinds closed on the glass front of the office but not the small open window on the side wall.

She glanced up at the academic plaques on the wall behind Mallory, then studied the framed poster on the opposite wall: a vintage Scotland Yard publicity campaign depicting crime prevention tips from the 1970s. The distressed look seemed retro-applied rather than authentic, and it had kinked to the right slightly, in need of a re-hang.

Blackwood blinked, tapped out the fingertip rhythm on the back of her hand. She refocused on Mallory, who had raised the latest document up in line with his face, reading with a doubtful sneer.

He was stocky, approaching heavy. Lightly tanned, bald, with a slight grey shadow. Good suit.

Mallory sighed, scribbled on the document, added it to the pile.

'PC Blackwood.' He pushed the chair back and reclined, lifting his feet onto the desk. He gave her a smile that was closer to a grimace. 'My apologies for the delay in the final assessment. We have a few borderline students.' He folded his arms. 'Now, I'm afraid I'm going to have to keep this meeting brisker than you might like, as I have to head into the city. We have several students who, like yourself, are attending for a second time, and I was determined to speak to you all this morning, although that's rather set my schedule back. But I feel second timers are special cases, and I wanted to pay you all the courtesy of a one-on-one.'

The smile again, drawing out a few wrinkles around the eyes. Mallory's stony features seemed uncomfortable with the adjustment, and the lines quickly re-blended as his expression darkened.

Blackwood nodded. 'Thank you, sir.'

Mallory clicked his tongue. 'This process wasn't

designed to be easy.' He slipped his feet off the desk and sat upright, taking a sip from a mug, then pulled up something on his computer. 'I've reviewed your performance across all modules of the development programme. You have strong investigative instincts, but there are still significant areas of concern over focus on procedure and overall conduct.' He tapped his pen on the desk three times.

Loose thread on his sleeve.

Mallory continued. 'Your written assignments show an uneven attention to process and the mock trial exercise revealed gaps in your understanding of PACE and some evidence-handling protocols.'

Blackwood felt her face flushing. She lowered her head, hoping it wasn't too obvious. 'Sir. I've had good feedback from—'

He held up a hand. 'I haven't finished. Your interruption is an illustration of one of the issues at hand.' He leaned forward, resting his elbows on the desk, then shook his head slowly. 'You're not quite there, Olivia. I'm sorry.'

The use of her first name jolted her.

Mallory tapped his pen on the glass desk again. 'I'm happy for you to take the rest of the day off, but you will return to your duties as normal tomorrow. Wood Green are aware. I appreciate you will be disappointed, but I recommend you spend at least another year addressing the areas of concern in my report before considering reapplication.' Mallory toyed with the pen, passing it from hand to hand. He sat back, hauled his feet up onto the desk again. 'Can I ask you a straight question?'

'Of course, sir.'

'Why are you so keen to move up? You're doing good work at Wood Green. Important work. Status isn't everything.'

Blackwood shifted in her chair and tucked a strand of hair behind her ear. She closed her eyes briefly, resetting, then opened them again. 'I believe others can do the work I do. But I feel I'm capable of more. Sir.'

'So, you think you're better than your colleagues?'

'Yes.'

Mallory surveyed her. 'Unfortunately, PC Blackwood, my role is about responsibility allocation, not your self-actualisation. This process is designed to ensure progress for only those fully prepared for the responsibilities of detective work. It's not just about your career. It's about justice for victims and the integrity of our investigations.'

Pompous twat.

'Yes, sir.'

The pen again. *Clang, clang, clang.*

Blackwood lowered her gaze, watched the rhythm of her fingers on the back of her hand. She counted out a set of three threes, with a final three to close.

'Come along.' Mallory softened his voice. It sounded like a bad impersonation of compassion. 'Don't beat yourself up. You've just set your sights too high, too soon. You'll come through in time. You have age and good looks on your side.'

Blackwood kept her eyes down, listening to Mallory's laboured breathing, feeling his phoney-sympathetic stare scorching the top of her head.

She looked up. 'Number one, sir. The way I look isn't relevant. Number two. I'm thirty-four years of age. This hardly feels "too soon".'

Mallory bristled, but shook it off. 'Your age isn't the issue. Your instincts tell me you'll make a fine detective one day. But today is not that day. Pushing back like this only confirms the decision is correct.' He stood, gestured to the door. 'Keep your open mindset. Work on your attention to process detail and tempering your impulses. It's a setback. We all have our frailties. Our failures. What matters is how we respond. Whether we see it as an opportunity for learning or a blow to the ego.'

Blackwood lingered for a moment, then leaned forward and pushed herself to her feet. 'How can I learn from failure if I'm not given the chance to fail?'

Chapter Eight

He eased the Insignia into the dusk-shrouded streets and lowered all his windows. He inhaled, flooding his lungs with the bristling air, and a Day-Glo indigo rippled through his veins. His hunger could no longer be denied. Tonight, he was its vessel.

He had starved his organic body, and his stomach was a hollow drum, amplifying his need.

As he navigated the arterial roads leading out of the city, his senses sharpened. Every headlight flare, every engine growl, every blink of shop-front neon sent sparks of colour cascading across his vision.

The suburbs of Edgware blended into the affluent rural enclaves. Radlett. Elstree. Borehamwood. Here, the houses stood further apart, shielded from the road behind looming hedgerows and wrought-iron gates.

He cruised, eyes roving. There had been nothing the previous night. But experience told him that prey would eventually emerge, if he could just comb his territory with poise and precision. If he could suppress his impatience.

He joined the middle line of traffic at a busy crossroads, preparing to turn left. He indicated to join the filter lane, but a white Tesla Model 3 shifted forwards, blocking his access, forcing him to wait for the line to open up again and the car behind to let him through. In front, the silhouette of the male Tesla driver gesticulated against the glow of a heads-up display, deep in conversation. The Tesla surged forward on the red-and-amber light and turned off the main road.

He followed, keeping a discreet distance as the Tesla powered ahead and veered into a low-lit side track flanked by dense woodland. He dimmed his headlamps, keeping the back lights of the Tesla in view as it made a sharp turn into a labyrinth of winding lanes.

He trailed behind for a few minutes, until the Tesla's brake lights flashed red, triggering a low-register humming sound that seemed to begin at the base of his neck and then resonate, almost muting his hearing. He slowed and passed by the Tesla as it crept off the road into the sweeping driveway of a substantial detached house. Ungated.

He eased the Insignia into a lay-by beside a low fence at the edge of an open field and killed the engine and lights. He turned, watching through the back windscreen as a lean, suited man walked from the parked Tesla up to the house front door, unlocked it, and disappeared inside.

He adjusted the rear-view mirror until it showed the front of the house, then sat in silence. In darkness.

A ground-floor light came on, followed soon after by a first-floor light.

On the ground floor, sharper light flickered behind drawn curtains. Television. He winced at the crackling sound, like water on hot fat. The association raised the hair on his neck, and he opened the passenger side window, steadying himself with a gulp of peaty air.

He watched and waited as the minutes ticked by. An hour. Two.

Occasional cars. First, the rising engine rumble, velvety blue, then a shock of acid yellow as the vehicle passed by.

Around midnight, he spotted movement on the verge at the other side of the road. He flicked on his side lights and caught the back end of a fox, darting into the undergrowth. The animal's russet fur ignited an aura of crimson in his peripheral vision.

He blinked, refocusing on the house, now dark and still.

He started the engine: a viscous purple. And as he pulled away, the molten gold of anticipation puddled in his core.

He would return soon.

The ritual could begin.

Chapter Nine

Lennox stood at the marble-topped sink. He washed his hands with precise, uniform strokes, then elbowed the dryer button and blasted them with warm air. The bathroom at Galvin la Chappelle echoed the restaurant's blend of modern luxury and historical elegance. Exposed brick arches framed bevelled mirrors, while sleek chrome fixtures contrasted with the weathered wood of the stall doors. The air was infused with a subtle vanilla fragrance.

As he reached for a monogrammed paper towel from the neatly stacked pile, Lennox caught sight of his reflection. Tired eyes stared from a face that seemed to have aged years in mere months. In this light, his hair looked bleached, and the white of his collar accentuated the pallor of his skin.

He raised his right hand, watching as it trembled. This was new and recurring. More than just an adrenaline response. He took a breath and waited for the tremor to subside. After a moment, it settled and he stepped out into the corridor.

He paused at the door that led back into the dining room, then edged into an alcove and pulled out his phone. He hesitated, then called up the number from his contacts.

'Oz?' The voice was warm, tinged with surprise.

'Hey, Martha. How are you?'

'I've been better.'

He sighed. 'Same. It's the second most wonderful time of the year.'

The door opened and a willowy male maître d' bustled into the corridor, then pivoted towards the kitchens. Lennox looked through into the restaurant. Vast circular chandeliers hung from an arched, chapel-like ceiling, casting a hazy glow over the dining space. A young woman with cropped auburn hair sat alone at a window table, scrolling through her phone.

The maître d' shouted to someone ahead as he scurried away.

'Sounds like you're having fun,' said Martha softly.

The auburn-haired woman turned and looked over to the door as it was easing shut.

Lennox ducked back into the alcove. 'Posh restaurant. My date is far from stimulating.'

'Oh dear. Are you fishing in a familiar pool?'

'She's not police. Publishing. I'm now fully informed on current trends in celebrity memoir.' He leaned against the wall. 'How's your domestics?'

Martha took a breath. 'Do you want to know or shall I tell you what I think you want to hear?'

'The first one.'

She made a noncommittal noise. 'He was widowed quite young. He has two teenage daughters but doesn't see them much. It's sad.' She took a drink of something. 'Unsolicited call, Oz. Not like you.'

'You always said I needed to be more spontaneous.'

A moment of silence. Lennox ran a finger down the rough grain of the alcove's wooden support pillar.

'Is there something wrong?' said Martha.

Again, the delve into himself. Sifting for connection.

'Just stress, I think. My thinking feels cloudy.'

'You get this when the date is coming up.'

He turned away from the corridor, nose close to the exposed brickwork. 'It's a bad one this time.'

'Don't go Googling.'

'That's all doctors do, these days. Then they print you out a fact sheet.' He caught her barely suppressed sigh. 'I'm joking. I know you didn't do that.'

'No, I didn't. But I'm safely downstream now. Look. Let's get through the meeting, yes? I'm sure things will settle for you after that. Breathe, then take the next step forward. We've learned this.'

A young mother burst through the dining room doors, shepherding an overdressed toddler towards the toilets.

'Remember how he used to lose spades?' said Lennox. 'On the beach.'

She gave a wistful laugh. 'Every time. On every beach. You told him the sand monsters were eating them. Then it was all we could do to get him anywhere near a beach.'

'Crazy to think of the journey taken by those bits of plastic. How someone else's child might have found them, cherished them, lost them.'

Martha was quiet for a few seconds. 'Only forward, Oz. There's no other path. We've been enriched by those times, but we can't relive them. That's where the pain lies.'

'Nostalgia,' said Lennox. '*Nostos, álgos.*'

'I know. Return and suffering.' Her voice dropped to an

almost-whisper. 'Next week will hurt enough. Let's not live in it before we have to. Try to enjoy your evening.'

Lennox turned back to the corridor. 'All we have is now.'

'Exactly. I have to go, Oz. Take care of yourself. We can get some dinner after the meeting.'

'Okay. Lots of love.'

'Bye-bye.'

She disconnected.

Chapter Ten

Blackwood set down a mug of tea on the windowsill and dragged over a bloated cardboard box.

She looked up at her mother. 'They're not marked.'

'Should they be?'

'Yes, Mum. They should.'

Angela Blackwood slumped into the restored patchwork armchair. She was late-fifties, with tinted ash hair cut into a tidy bob. She took off her reading glasses and twirled them by the arm. 'It's just a few boxes, Liv. Bits and pieces. I almost threw them away with the rest of the stuff, but there's a lot of your things in there.' She picked the lemon slice from her G&T. 'From when you went to uni.'

Blackwood rooted through the box. 'This is more than bits and pieces. And why are you even throwing stuff away? It's not like you need the space.'

Angela sucked on the lemon.

'Mother...' Blackwood covered her eyes.

'What?' She popped the slice back into the G&T.

Blackwood pointed. 'That. It's horrible.'

Angela waved a hand. 'It's not. Eating it would be horrible. Are you sure you won't have a drink with me?'

She sighed. 'I am having a drink with you. In my special receptacle.' She held up the mug: a cartoon image of a red blob in a green hat standing beneath the heading *LITTLE MISS SCATTERBRAIN*.

'One of my most inspired stocking fillers,' said Angela. 'I mean a real drink.'

Blackwood took out a pile of papers and cards wrapped in elastic bands. 'I'm on duty later.'

Angela sipped her drink. 'Oh, Livvy. I thought we could have some dinner. I don't see you that often.'

'Mother...' Blackwood ducked her head and raised her shoulders, mortified.

'Sorry. Liv. Not Livvy.' Angela stood up and opened a white plastic box with an interlocking lid.

Blackwood sighed. 'Don't say it again. I can't stay. Need to get back—'

'On the horse?'

Blackwood smiled. 'Yes.' She shuffled through the cards. 'I've been at Hendon. Training.'

'And you've only just thought to come and see me?'

She rolled her eyes. 'No. I just haven't had the chance.'

'Sorry, Livvy. Liv. I'm not being needy. I know that's cringe.'

'As is saying cringe. It's not being needy, Mum. Yes, I should come over more often. Yes, I love you. No, I don't hate you. It's just...' She waved the mug again.

Angela finished her drink and crouched by the box. 'Are you still on meds?'

'No. Mum, these are postcards I sent you from travelling. You've saved them all.'

'What would you want me to do with them?'

'They're not meant to be saved. Do you keep our text messages, too?'

'Of course. The past isn't all junk. Those cards are like little snapshots of you at different times. They're special.'

Blackwood pulled over another box and wrenched it open. 'The main thing I remember from Physics was that Stephen Hawking says time only goes forwards. There's real time and imaginary time. Humans experience real time and science is imaginary. Real time has direction, like an arrow. Things that are broken stay broken. You don't see them going from broken to unbroken.'

Angela nodded. 'I'm thinking of making the top floor an Airbnb.'

'Really? Who's coming for a weekend break in Brent Cross?'

'There's the shopping centre. We're good for Wembley, too. This is why I'm having a clear-out. Only a few years left on the mortgage and some Airbnb revenue will help me over the line.' She patted the plastic box. 'There's a few of your old books in here. Some lovely bird books. And a few of Abigail's. Her mother brought them over when you were in the third year. Doesn't look like you've read any.'

Blackwood paused her rummaging. 'Reading's hard for me. You know that.'

Angela went back to the chair. 'You still did it, though. If something grabbed you, it grabbed you hard. Like the birds.'

'That came from Abi.' Blackwood grimaced, rubbed at her eyes. 'I promised her mum I'd find her.'

'Your tea's going cold.'

Blackwood glanced up. 'Of course it is. Oh, my god. Mum, you've got my attestation certificate in here. And my CKP. Did you ever film me taking the oath?'

'No. Bloody Covid. No family allowed at the ceremony. Dad would have been so proud of you, Liv. He's up there somewhere, watching over you.'

'Maybe.' Blackwood closed up the box.

'Abigail, too.'

Blackwood glared at her. 'Mother.'

'Sorry. Will you come and stay soon?'

Blackwood sat back, took a sip of tepid tea. 'Course. I can help you clear more stuff. Take a few things with me.'

'That would be lovely. But don't you dare throw anything away today.'

'I won't.' She looked up to the ceiling. 'Dad would tell on me.'

Angela got up. 'When are you out?'

'Graveyard. Just a half shift because of the training. I don't mind it.'

'I'll make a nice *parmigiana*.' Blackwood opened her mouth to protest, but her mother silenced her. 'Yes. You do have time.'

She hurried out. Blackwood listened as her mother thudded down the narrow, uncarpeted stairs to the first floor.

Loud creak from the last but one.

Groans of exertion.

Blackwood lifted her eyes to the framed photo on the wall by the door. A sunny day on Hampstead Heath. A tall man in his early thirties stood behind a navy-blue pushchair. His deep brown skin glowed in the summer light, his close-cropped hair and uneven beard softening his angular features.

Smiling.

Eyes crinkled at the corners.

Her eyes.

The man wore a red-and-blue plaid shirt tied around his waist, and stone-washed jeans, slightly rolled up at the ankles.

1991. Maybe 1992.

The toddler Blackwood lay in the pushchair, covered by a yellow blanket, a dark curl peeking out from beneath a white sun hat.

Blackwood spoke out loud to herself. '*The past, like the future, is indefinite, and exists only as a spectrum of possibilities.*'

She shuffled over to the plastic box and rummaged through a few books. *The Secret Garden, The Borrowers, Sophie's World.*

She lifted out a paperback copy of *A Field Guide to the Birds of Britain and Europe.* The cover was a composite image of a pair of European robins, a blue tit, a barn owl and a peregrine falcon in its characteristic hunting stoop position. The spine was uncracked, the pages still crisp, untouched by time or hand. A faded price sticker from an independent bookshop in Islington clung to the back cover.

Blackwood flicked through the book and a thin sheet of lined paper fell out of the centre. She held it up to the fading light from the small spare room window.

A neat cluster of girlish handwriting sat in the top left corner.

LS.
Primrose Hill.
Ivory Room.
White Lion.
Mr Shade.

Chapter Eleven

Lennox stared down at his dessert: a perfect rectangle of tiramisu, barely two inches high, served on a matte black plate with a sprinkle of gold leaf.

'Everything okay?'

'Sorry?' He looked up at his date: Jennifer.

'I saw you on the phone.'

'Ah, yes. Just a work thing.'

'Can you talk about it?' She took up a long spoon and carved a shallow furrow into the top layer of tiramisu. 'Or would you then have to kill me?'

She slipped the spoonful into her mouth.

Lennox laughed. 'I'm a detective. Not a spy. But I wouldn't want to talk shop here, anyway.'

Jennifer rolled her eyes in ecstasy, pointing to her plate with the spoon. 'This is fucking incredible. Excuse the language.'

Raised voices from a nearby table.

'I've heard worse,' said Lennox, turning to the source of the commotion. A male diner was on his feet, gesticulating.

His female companion kept her head down, staring into her food.

Lennox turned back to Jennifer.

'I thought that since I'd shown you mine,' she said, 'then maybe you could do likewise. You know. Tell me more about what you do.' She dug out another spoonful, offered it across the table to Lennox.

He waved it away. 'No thanks.'

Cutlery clattered as the man thumped a fist down on the table.

Jennifer carried on eating. 'Someone didn't get his toast cut into soldiers.'

'Perhaps if you hired waiters who actually waited the tables instead of behaving like bloody hospital porters, we'd have been served sooner.'

The maître d' approached the table. 'Sir. I believe you have a grievance. I'd be happy to help.'

Jennifer leaned over to Lennox and spoke in a theatrical whisper. 'Heavily pregnant woman at the table behind you. The waiter helped her to the sofa on reception. Got her some water. I think she was feeling unwell.'

The maître d' pleaded with the man to keep his voice down, but he raised it further, slurring his words.

'No! He's a fucking simp.'

Lennox turned to see the man prodding a finger towards the reception area.

'That's not his job. His job is to wait tables. The clue is in the title. Okay?'

He was forty-odd, in good shape, well dressed and groomed. But also red-faced, puffed out, bolstered by a half-empty bottle of Dom Pérignon.

His companion touched a hand to his shoulder; he shrugged it away.

'Doesn't matter how good the food is, right? If you fill your restaurant with betas, then you get beta-quality service.'

Lennox tried the dessert. It was buoyant and creamy.

'His job is to wait, okay? Not to keep us waiting.'

'What's a simp?' whispered Jennifer, sniggering.

'Excuse me.' Lennox got up and raised a hand. He stepped towards the angry patron and stood in the spot between him and the maître d'. 'Sir, I understand you're frustrated and I hear you're upset. You came here for a nice evening and you clearly feel let down. I agree with you. We are paying for a fine dining experience here, and the service should be high quality. But perhaps we could take the temperature down a little? And the volume. How about we work together to resolve this? What would make you feel better about the situation?'

The man squinted at Lennox. 'My friend. This has got nothing to do with you. Whoever you are.'

Lennox smiled. 'I'm sitting close to your table with my companion. Like yourselves, we're also trying to enjoy a nice evening. But the situation is making that difficult. I suggest that this is the same for everyone here. So, it's in everyone's interest that we resolve this calmly and respectfully.'

The man lowered his head, nodding. He glanced across at his companion, then took a step closer.

Lennox caught a waft of alcohol breath.

The man looked up, smiling. He tapped a finger on his own chest. 'And I suggest...' He shifted the finger slowly away and tapped it on Lennox's chest. '...that you sit down and finish your pudding before you get yourself hurt.'

Lennox held his eye. 'I'd advise you not to make physical contact. I'm still hopeful we can keep this conversation civil and avoid any more actions that could be misconstrued as threatening.'

The man barked a laugh. He turned to his partner, then back again. 'He's finally getting the idea. Yes. I am threatening you. Unless you fucking well sit yourself back down and stay out of this, then you'll regret it. I'm at least ten years younger than you. If I were you, I wouldn't fancy my chances.'

Lennox sighed. '*De Minimis Non Curat Lex.*'

'What?'

'It's a legal principle. *The law does not care about the smallest things.*' He turned and took his seat, angling himself towards the man. 'It's used to argue that a minor mistake or violation shouldn't be subject to legal action.' He took another spoonful of tiramisu. 'It's what your defence brief will use if I pursue an assault case for the unlawful physical contact you've just applied. But under Section 4 of the Public Order Act 1986, it is an offence to use threatening, abusive or insulting words or behaviour with intent to cause a person to believe that immediate violence will be used against them. So, along with the physical contact, your clear threat of violence, overheard by several witnesses, has moved us out of the *de minimis* territory. This is now legally actionable.' Lennox took another spoon of tiramisu. 'You've confirmed the intent of the threat. You've told me I'm going to "regret" this conversation. You've referenced the difference in our ages and the reduced "chances" I would face in a physical confrontation.' Lennox waved his spoon. 'Also, if you carry out the threat and strike me, you would, at the very least, face a heavy fine or a community order, both of which would saddle you with a criminal record.'

Lennox's phone buzzed; he checked the screen.

'Finally,' he continued, 'if your attack inflicts bodily

harm, then you'd be looking at a minimum of six months in prison and a fine. Also, you might hit me and I could fall in such a way that causes grievous bodily harm. That happens more often than you might think. In that case, we're talking five years to life.' He waggled the phone at Jennifer. 'I'm so sorry, but I've been summoned. It's urgent.'

'Okay. But... Will you call me? Shall I call you?'

Lennox shrugged. 'If you like.' He got to his feet, then turned to the maître d'. 'My apologies, Theo.' He handed over his credit card. 'Please use this to settle the bill. I'll pick it up tomorrow.'

He swept away, heading for the door.

The angry patron watched the exchange with bewilderment. He touched a hand to a table, steadying himself. 'No tip?' he shouted.

Lennox waved over his shoulder. 'Don't drink so much.'

Chapter Twelve

Blackwood stepped out of the squad car passenger seat, her hand reaching to her radio as she surveyed the flat block. The building was modern: a blended facade of glass and pale brick that glimmered in the late-evening sunset. A Grade Two domestic incident call required attendance within the hour, and usually sent her to a rundown estate in Northumberland Park or Broadwater Farm. But this was Hale Wharf, a freshly built regeneration spot on the edge of the River Lea. Young professionals, small families, a few well-supported first-timers. Waterside living, only a forty-minute Brompton dash to The City.

'PC Blackwood to dispatch,' she reported into the radio. 'Arrived at the scene with PC Harris. Heading to flat 7B.'

'At least I can skip leg day.' Tom Harris looked up to the seventh floor. He was indecently young, with a pressed uniform that seemed a size too big for his angular frame, as if he was still growing into his role, into himself.

Blackwood caught his complexion in the light: the sprinkle of freckles across his nose and cheeks.

'The lifts will work here,' said Blackwood. 'There will still be money in the pot for maintenance. Probably cut corners on the cladding.' She strode past him into the building lobby.

Harris followed. 'Doesn't look like the *WET PAINT* signs have been down for long.'

Inside, tall windows flooded the space with natural light, reflecting off the polished marble floor. Blackwood pressed the lift call button and the doors slid open silently, revealing a spotless interior.

On the way up, the whir of the mechanism pulsed in Blackwood's ears, and she timed her breaths to match its rhythm.

Scuff mark on the floor, probably from a moving dolly or wheelchair.

Slight flicker in the ceiling light.

Faint fingerprint on the mirrored wall. Chest height.

She wrinkled her nose. 'Someone's had the Flash out.'

'I thought that was your perfume.'

Blackwood smiled, kept her gaze ahead. 'Says Mr Black Vanilla Lynx.'

He turned. 'It's Aqua Bergamot, actually.'

'Don't get metro on me now, Harris. It's time for your best big boy voice. We don't know what's waiting.'

He nodded. 'Access, de-escalate.'

'Yes. No forced entry unless absolutely necessary.'

The lift hissed to a halt and the doors slid open.

'Don't get seduced by the surroundings,' said Blackwood, stepping out first. 'The veneer might be different here, but people are people.'

The lift lobby window gave a panoramic view over the nearby Walthamstow Wetlands and the distant City skyline.

Harris followed her through a set of double doors, deeper into the building. 'Assume nothing. Believe nobody.'

'Question everything,' she finished. 'Just been on a course, then?'

'*Interviewing Techniques for Witness Statements.*'

'I've done that one. It was a thriller.'

Their movement triggered soft overhead lighting along the length of the carpeted corridor. At the end, they realised they'd taken a wrong turn and doubled back into an adjoining corridor marked 7A-7G.

'Don't take this the wrong way,' said Harris.

Blackwood laughed. 'This doesn't sound good.'

'How come you're still doing this?'

She stopped, faced him. 'You mean at my age?' She moved off again.

'No... I mean, you don't look—'

'My age?'

'Yes. No!'

Blackwood stopped at the door to Flat 7B and pressed the bell. 'Another one I remember from that course... Appearances can be deceptive.'

The door opened, revealing a slim man in his mid-thirties with neck-length sandy brown hair, lightly styled. He wore a dark-blue shirt with the sleeves rolled up to his elbows.

Tanned forearms. Muscular.

Breitling watch.

Leather loafers, indoors.

Blackwood showed her warrant card, as did Harris. 'Evening. Do you live here, sir?'

The man folded his arms, leaned on the door frame. 'Yes.'

Clean-shaven. Tightness around the eyes.

A touch of alcohol on his breath.

'We've received a call about a disturbance in your flat. I'm PC Blackwood. This is PC Harris. May I ask your name?'

He eyed them both. 'I'm under no legal obligation to give you my name.'

'Lewis?' A woman's voice from within.

Wavering.

The man smiled.

'Well, we've got your address,' said Blackwood, 'and half of your name. Might as well go all the way.'

'Lewis Hartley. You've had a call from where?'

'Do you mind if we come in for a few minutes?' said Harris.

Hartley looked back into the flat. 'What for? There's no "disturbance".'

Blackwood forced a smile. 'We need to gather information in response to the call. It's hard to do that standing out here.' She pointed inside. 'Is that your partner?'

He glanced at Harris. 'My girlfriend, yes.'

'We'd like a quick word with her, too. Then we can all get on with our evening.'

Hartley sighed and turned, leading the way. 'Make it quick.'

Blackwood and Harris moved down a short hallway into a spacious, well-furnished flat with an open-plan kitchen and living area.

'What do you do, Lewis?' said Harris.

'I'm a solicitor at Clifford Chance in the City. Multinational law firm.'

He stepped aside, gesturing towards the living area with a sweep of his arm. As the officers entered, he folded his arms across his chest and leaned against the kitchen island, standing with shoulders back, chin raised.

Blackwood's eyes flitted around the room.

Anthracite oven and hob. Gaggenau. Shard of glass on the floor at its base.

Half-empty bottle of Macallan whisky on a polished cabinet.

Phone on the sofa. Face down. Propped against a cushion, as if it's been thrown there.

Smudges on the pristine white wall near the hall doorway.

Framed photo on a side table, slightly askew.

A young woman with shoulder-length blonde hair and bright green eyes came out of a bedroom and hovered at the back of a handsome charcoal-grey sofa, her fingers gripping the upholstery.

'This is Sophie,' said Hartley.

She nodded. 'Sophie Lawson.'

Hartley squinted at Blackwood. 'I'm surprised you were allowed to join the police with purple hair.'

'My hair is black,' said Blackwood. 'With a light purple streak. I didn't style it for your approval.'

Hartley scoffed, then slumped forward over the kitchen island like a sulking teenager. 'This is all rather an over-reaction.'

'Hi, Sophie,' said Blackwood. 'I'm PC Blackwood. This is PC Harris. We've had a call about a disturbance. Can you tell us what happened?'

'We had a row, okay?' said Hartley. 'It happens. Couples argue.'

Blackwood kept her eyes on Lawson, who had turned to take in the view from a back wall window. 'According to the call, it sounded like a bit more than just a row.' She nodded to the glass shard. 'Did that happen recently?'

Hartley pushed off the island, paced. 'Okay. I lost it. Threw a glass onto the floor.'

'Lost it?' said Harris.

Hartley looked to Lawson.

Urging confirmation.

'So sorry for the trouble,' said Lawson. 'We had a bit of a disagreement. It wasn't just Lewis. I was shouting a lot, too.'

Blackwood walked to the window, closer to Lawson.

Fresh concealer around one eye.

Bruise on left cheekbone?

'Could we talk privately, Sophie? Out by the front door? PC Harris can take a few more details from you, Lewis.'

Hartley pivoted away, threw up his hands. 'For heaven's sake.'

Lawson flinched at the raised voice.

'It's standard procedure,' said Blackwood. 'Ensures unbiased accounts.'

Lawson nodded. 'Okay.'

Blackwood walked down the hall and waited outside by the door as Lawson exited and, hesitantly, stepped closer. At this range, the cheekbone bruising was unmistakable.

'Is everything okay, Sophie?' said Blackwood.

Lawson smiled. 'Really. Everything's fine. Things just got heated.' She held her hands down by her side, one caressing the other.

'Why did it get heated?'

She waved a hand. 'He saw something on my phone. Got the wrong idea. It was from a friend, Charlie.'

'A female friend?'

'Yeah. From work. He thought it was another man. She leaves kisses at the end of messages.'

'And how come he had access to your phone?'

Lawson looked away, then back at Blackwood. 'We agreed to keep our phones without passwords. So we can always check on each other.'

'And do you check on him?'

She laughed. 'He usually keeps his phone in his pocket.'

'Are you happy in the relationship, Sophie?'

'Yes, of course.'

Too quick.

'How long have you been together? How did you meet?'

'Almost a year. We met on a dating app. I was with someone who wasn't right for me and Lewis just—'

'Swept you off your feet?'

Lawson raised her eyebrows. 'Yes. I suppose so. He sent flowers to my office. Chocolates. He took me to Claridge's for dinner. He sent a car to pick me up from work.'

Smiling, but avoiding eye contact.

'Do you feel safe with Lewis, Sophie?'

She looked up, scowling. 'What kind of question is that? Of course I do. This was just a silly row over nothing. Really. Listen. I know you've probably seen my eye, right? And you're wondering how I did it.'

'No,' said Blackwood. 'I'm not. I'm wondering who did it to you. You've tried to cover it up, but you've used too much concealer. I can see the bruising has spread to your cheekbone.'

Her hand flew to her face. 'Yes. I've been doing that since it happened. Girls' night last week. I'm not great with heels. I fell. I know it sounds like a cliché, but I really did. I still don't know my limits.'

Blackwood tilted her head, smiling. 'I'm concerned about a few things, Sophie. The way Lewis speaks to you. The way he looks at you. The one-sided nature of your phone sharing. And smashing a glass in someone's presence isn't *losing it*. That's an act of intimidation and control. An act of abuse.' She stepped closer. 'If Lewis gave you that black eye because of his suspicions or his anger, it suggests he's feeling humiliated. That's a major risk factor. Particularly if he's concerned that you might want to leave the relationship.' Blackwood took a takeaway card out of her wallet and wrote her phone number on the back. 'We don't have many options tonight, I'm afraid. There's no evidence of a crime or imminent danger, so we can't make an arrest. And there are no grounds to issue a verbal warning.' She handed over the card. 'But this is my personal number. If you ever feel unsafe, day or night, I want you to call me, in absolute confidence. Okay?'

Lawson stared down at the card, nodding. As Blackwood headed back into the flat, she looked up and said something in a quiet, frail voice.

'What was that, Sophie?' said Blackwood.

Lawson gathered herself. 'Will you check in on me?'

Blackwood smiled. 'Of course.'

Chapter Thirteen

'Talk me through it,' said Lennox, snapping on a fresh pair of blue nitrile gloves. He caught DI Isaac Adeyemi exchange a glance with David Pearson, the Tyvek-suited Scenes of Crime Officer. 'Yes, I know I can see for myself, but I want to hear what's in your mind first.'

Adeyemi gave a nervous laugh as they stopped outside the open bathroom door. He pinned back his narrow shoulders and raised his head, as if about to break into song. 'Vic is Hamza Malik. Twenty years old. Second-year student at UCL. Flatmate Karl Prentice found him about two hours ago when he came home after a shift at Nando's in Edgware. Checks out. He's in the living room.'

Lennox fitted a pair of protective covers over his shoes. 'How's he doing?'

'Not well.'

'TOD?'

Adeyemi caught Pearson's eye again.

The SOCO cleared his throat. 'Based on body temp

and early rigor signs, I'd estimate between two and four hours ago.'

'Rigor just starting in the smaller muscle groups,' said Adeyemi.

Pearson nodded, with indulgence. 'I concur.'

'Last time Karl saw Hamza alive?' said Lennox.

'Mid-morning,' said Adeyemi. 'He says they had coffee in the kitchen before Karl went in for a seminar.'

'Just the two of them here?'

'There's a girl. But the term's only just started and she's not back from summer break yet.'

Lennox's eyebrow arched. 'A girl?'

Adeyemi consulted a notepad. 'Mia Chen.' He paused. 'Computer Science.'

'What's in your mind?'

'Early days, sir. I can give you a gut feeling.'

Lennox sidestepped into the cramped bathroom. The air was thick with a familiar coppery tang. 'Surely you've heard of the gut-brain axis.'

'Sort of, sir. Yes. The two are connected.'

The body of a young man, naked, lay slumped in the bathtub, in a puddle of sickly pink water.

'They certainly are,' said Lennox. 'The gut has its own nervous system. It's like a second brain.' He crouched by the bath and surveyed the body. The upper torso was doused in dried blood, the skin pale and waxy in the harsh overhead light. Multiple stab wounds peppered the lower abdomen. He reached in and lifted each arm, examined the hands. The joints offered light resistance.

'Scene is fully documented, sir,' said Pearson. 'Water level and temperature backs up TOD. Water drained and filtered. No foreign bodies. Samples taken for analysis.

Scrapings, hair and swabs. Weapon is untouched, awaiting your attendance.'

Lennox ran a finger over the tiled floor. 'Did you dry this?'

'Didn't need to,' said Pearson.

Lennox shuffled over to the large kitchen knife resting on the floor close to the bath. He picked it up by the wooden handle and turned it around. The blade was slick with blood, mostly dark and dry.

'It's from the kitchen block, sir,' said Adeyemi. 'Blade tip looks slightly bent to me.'

Lennox looked closer. 'Good spot. Thoughts?'

Adeyemi was silent.

'Hitting bone,' said Pearson.

Lennox nodded. He set down the knife and stood upright, then turned and scanned the room. 'Let's hear that gut, detective.'

Adeyemi ran a hand through his short afro. 'It's too early, really. Flatmate is the prime suspect. His prints and DNA will be everywhere, though, so further interview needed. Wait until full forensics for signs of third-party DNA. Scrub the phone for recent comms and movements. Run victimology and recent history to check for beefs and criminal associations. Tox for drugs. Chase the sources of anything illicit.'

Lennox twirled his horizontal index finger in a circle. 'Bottom line?'

Adeyemi looked up at the ceiling, then back at Lennox. 'No sign of forced entry in this room or at the front door. Hamza let someone in, he took a bath, didn't lock the door. They got the knife from the kitchen. Surprised him in here...'

Lennox walked out of the bathroom and lingered in the

connecting hallway where a corkboard hung askew on the wall. Postcards, photos, fast food menus, handwritten notes. The photos mainly featured Hamza, and another young man and woman, with various companions in different settings: bars, beaches, restaurants. He leaned in to a photo showing Hamza with a slightly older man. Both were grinning and raising a glass. The man's other arm was raised in a peace sign, while Hamza's wrapped around the man's torso, gripping him just above the waist.

Something about the expressions of wild joy in most of the photos sent a spike through him. These people were so light and unburdened. Soaring on a fleeting thermal. For the foreseeable future, it was their sole duty to be young and reckless.

He smiled. Jonah would have loved that. He would have been good at it.

'Flatmate?' said Lennox. He straightened out the corkboard.

'Sir?'

'You said it was a shared flat.'

Adeyemi looked at Pearson again, this time confused. 'We talked about that, sir. Karl Prentice. He's with an officer in the sitting room.'

Lennox nodded, staring at him. Staring through him.

'Whitechapel,' said Lennox. '2009. Brighton, 2015. Similar cases. Religious families.' He groped through the mist of his mind again, found a handhold. 'We need CCTV from the building entrance to confirm no one else entered the flat last night.'

Adeyemi narrowed his eyes. 'You think the killer was already here?'

'I don't think there is a killer. No defensive wounds. No forced entry. Shower curtain undisturbed and no sign of struggle in the bathroom. No water from the bath on the bathroom floor. Knife not brought in from the outside, left at the scene. Close to the body.' He headed for the door. 'Direction of blood spatter looks to be up towards the victim's body. Not a lot on the sides of the bath. Minimal cast-off from the weapon. Heavy concentration around the wound sites and on Hamza's hands and arms.' He pointed back to the corkboard. 'Look at the photos. When men embrace, they hang their arms around each other's shoulders. Hamza's is around his companion's waist. More intimate. That one's a reach, but it ties up with everything else. Concentrate on Hamza victimology and his social media and online activity. I expect you'll find issues with gender ID or sexuality. I think he was gay but couldn't come out. He would have been in unbearable distress, but self-harm is complex in Muslim culture. It's viewed as taking away the gift given by God. It brings shame on the family.' Lennox opened the door. 'These cases are rare, but they turn up from time to time. This is suicide staged as murder.'

Chapter Fourteen

Blackwood toggled between multiple windows on her dual monitors. The left screen displayed the Police National Computer record database, while the right showed the Metropolitan Police's Crimint Plus intelligence system and an overlapping window for a Multi-Agency Risk Assessment database. In another tab, she had Companies House open, scrutinising Lewis Hartley's business dealings and directorships. His role as solicitor at Clifford Chance checked out, but she was rooting for discrepancies or red flags in his financial history.

Her workstation was curated chaos. Tangled charger cables, fidget toys, case files and printouts, granola bar wrappers, a multi-tiered organiser overloaded with pens and highlighters. The monitor bezels were fringed with multi-coloured Post-it notes, scrawled with reminders, phone numbers, case detail, quotes and observations. To her colleagues, the notes were random, possibly even decorative. But for Blackwood, they were the colour-coded bedrock of her task priority system.

Several mugs of coffee lay around the desk, in various states of fullness. The nearest—hot pink with white writing —proclaimed, *I'M NOT ARGUING. I'M JUST EXPLAINING WHY I'M RIGHT.*

A small potted plant sat in one corner, miraculously alive. A framed photo of Blackwood with a group of friends leaned against it.

She pulled up the Electoral Register, confirmed Hartley's previous addresses, and cross-referenced them with the intelligence reports, making a note to check with neighbouring forces for any incidents that might not have made it into the Met's systems. As she worked, she scribbled on a pad beside the keyboard, creating a timeline of Hartley's known history.

Blackwood sat back, sighed. She picked up her phone and navigated to a WhatsApp chat. The profile picture of the blond guy with the calf tattoo stared out from the chat header. A gym selfie, naturally. She typed out a message— *free later?*—with a wink emoji and sent it, staring at the status tick as it turned from single to double grey. Sent and received.

'What's going on?' Harris popped up at her shoulder. He nodded at the screens. 'Dare I ask?'

'No financial flags,' said Blackwood, tapping a pen on the screen showing the Companies House info. Getting a blank from MARAC, but I need a pass from the co-ordinator, who isn't around.'

'To see if he's flagged as high risk?'

She nodded, looked between the screen and her notepad. 'PNC shows Hartley with an arrest for Common Assault on a previous girlfriend. No Further Action.'

Blackwood scowled at the screens, pondering for a micro-moment. She spun her chair round to face Harris and the rest of the Wood Green operations room. The place was lively for the late hour: uniforms swigging energy drinks, grinding through paperwork; a mini conference in the glass-walled meeting room; a steady flow of front desk visitors and custody suite guests. It smelt of feet and takeaways.

'Do you want to know what Hartley said to me?' said Harris, sitting on the desk.

Blackwood snuck a look at her phone. Still two grey ticks. Message unread. 'Go on.'

'He said they have a "turbulent" relationship.'

Blackwood peeled open a granola bar and took a bite. 'Standard abuser bullshit.' Her phone rang: Stephanie, one of her old uni friends. 'One second.' She tossed the bar aside and took the call. 'Hey, Stef.'

A moment's silence at the other end. 'Where were you, Liv?'

Calm, cordial. Undertone of irritation.

'When?' said Blackwood.

Stephanie sighed. 'Last night. Birthday drinks. My birthday drinks. At The Faltering Fullback.'

Blackwood's stomach dropped. 'Oh, fuck. *Fuck.* Stef, I'm so sorry.'

'Liv, you suggested the venue. You could have at least messaged me if you couldn't make it. That's what normal people do.'

'I'm sorry, I'm sorry. There's a lot going on here. I'll make it up to you.' Blackwood scrolled through Hartley's PNC record. 'I promise. Happy birthday. For yesterday.'

The silence again. 'Love you, Liv.' She disconnected.

Blackwood closed her eyes for a few seconds, opened them again.

'Everything alright?' said Harris.

She took a breath, checked WhatsApp. Two grey ticks. '*Turbulent relationship.* It's a euphemism abusers use to distance themselves from their actions. Taking themselves out of the conversation. Did you notice Sophie's black eye?'

'No. Didn't see that.'

At the far end of the squad room, a chunky man in a tight-fitting blue-and-white shirt opened his office door. He caught Blackwood's eye and beckoned her.

'She'd covered it with make-up,' continued Blackwood. 'Said she fell when she was drunk. And, of course, Hartley swept her off her feet. Flowers, chocolates, fancy dinners. Love-bombing.'

Harris waved a hand. 'That's not always sinister. Decent guys do that, too.'

'Yeah. Because they've seen it work in films. A shortcut to intimacy. But in the real world, relationships take time. You can't hack trust. I'm worried Sophie might be thinking of leaving him. That's when it gets really dangerous.'

She sprang up and headed over to the open office door.

The amber glow of Detective Inspector Greg Pollard's desk lamp was a pocket of ambience amid the institutional glare of the ops room. Pollard stood behind his desk, head slumped.

Trouble.

Phone. Two grey ticks.

Blackwood closed the door behind her and perched on the edge of a chair, her knee bouncing. 'What's up, sir?'

Pollard took a big breath, straining his shirt against his barrel chest. He was apparently neckless, with a flat head coated in a suspiciously consistent fuzz of evenly cropped greying hair. His face had weathered beyond his forty years, with deep creases running from his nose to the corners of his mouth, which was framed by a scruffy goatee.

Phone again.

Two grey ticks.

'PC Blackwood. What do we do in circumstances that raise concern for domestic abuse?' She opened her mouth to answer, but he interrupted with a raised hand. 'What does PACE say we do?'

'Risk-assess according to the DASH model, sir. Take evidence if necessary. Escalate to MARAC if appropriate. Consider arrest. Refer to safeguarding. In this case, the thresholds weren't met but I found some things concerning. I also committed to a follow-up visit for monitoring. I'm building my report—'

Pollard held up a meaty hand, palm out, silencing her. 'We also give the victim information about support services and let them know their rights. We don't give them personal numbers.' He wandered around the back of his desk, avoiding eye contact. 'Why don't we do this?'

'Impartiality.'

'Correct. A decent defence lawyer might argue that an officer sharing personal details is complicit in whatever happens next.'

'That's ridiculous, sir.' She drummed her fingers on the legs of the seat.

Phone.

Two blue ticks. Message read.

'You're a civil servant, Liv. Light touch. The support services go heavy when they feel it's necessary. They don't have the bodies to step in on every domestic.'

'Did Lewis Hartley complain?'

Pollard took his seat, looked at his computer screen. 'Yes.'

'I saw subtle things, sir. Evidence of coercive control. Domestic violence begins with subtle things that don't hit the thresholds. There are patterns. It's predictable. Preventable. Hartley has been accused of abuse before—'

'With no charge.'

She stared him down. Her eyes flicked up to the framed Chelsea FC home shirt, signed by ex-player and manager Gianluca Vialli. 'We should pay more attention to where the ball is going. Not where it is.'

He smiled. 'No. We shouldn't. As I've said, that's for the support services. Your intentions are good, but we know where that road leads.'

'The fact that Hartley found out that I gave Sophie my personal number is a red flag in itself.'

'Not all arseholes are potential murderers.'

She shook her head. 'Not all men, eh?'

'I'll have to log the complaint. Start the formal process. Professional Standards might want a word.'

Phone.

No reply yet.

She nodded, turned to go.

Pollard held up the hand again. 'We're not done here yet. I've had a message from the Hendon show-runner. Mallory. He wants to see you there first thing Monday.'

Blackwood frowned. 'Really? What's that about?'

'No clue. I just get told to tell you to be there. I don't get told why. I'm sure it'll all trickle down to me when they see fit.'

Blackwood spun and headed back to her desk.

She checked her phone.

Calf Tattoo Boy's profile pic had vanished, replaced by a generic head-and-shoulders icon. And the two blue ticks had turned to a single grey.

Blocked.

Chapter Fifteen

He sat motionless in the Insignia, cloaked in shadow. The street had long since fallen silent, but he kept his eyes locked on the house, scanning for any flicker of life behind the curtains.

The hunger had risen steadily, encroaching like a golden tide. He had wallowed, drifting in its currents. But now he needed to feed.

He stepped out of the car and opened the back door, retrieving the canvas holdall. Again, the clink and rattle of the contents detonated a starburst of psychedelia at the front of his roiling mind.

He paused, waited for the colours to fade, then closed his eyes and inhaled the night air: a banquet for his heightened senses. Petrichor. Cut grass. Damp earth. Decaying leaves. The sweet aroma of jasmine and honeysuckle. Distant woodsmoke.

A fresh lightshow fluttered behind his eyes. Pure technicolour: coral, cobalt, sapphire, cherry-red, shamrock-green.

He opened his eyes and caught a movement at the base

of the low wall at the front of the house. A tabby cat slinked past, hugging the wall. It prowled across the gate opening, casting a fleeting shadow. The animal's presence banished the colours invoked by the night scents, and a new symphony flared in his mind. Soft greens and golds, in contrast to the strident reds and blacks that humans often evoked.

He inhaled again and caught a prickle of the cat's musk, marvelling at the creature's efficiency and purity.

He pulled on a pair of nitrile gloves, and with measured, silent steps, moved round to the boot and popped it open. Inside, a man lay heavily bound and gagged with duct tape, eyes wide with terror.

He swept his gaze over the captive, ignoring the muffled whimpers. It was a practical assessment, without interest.

He took a wide belt from the back seat and fastened it around his waist, adjusting it until the long sheath hung snug against his thigh. He hefted the canvas holdall onto his shoulder and turned to face the still house.

With a slow, reverent motion, he slid a machete from the sheath. The blade flashed in the moonlight, its edge obscenely sharp. He tested its weight, then pushed it back into the sheath.

He reached into a side pocket on the holdall and took out a Glock 19 handgun, then crouched by the boot, level with the man's eyes.

'Ready.'

Chapter Sixteen

Lennox's eyes roamed over the room. Unlike the modular furnishings in most of the building, DSI Aisha Khokhar's office boasted a sleek, artisanal desk of glass and chrome, complemented by an upscale ergonomic chair. The walls were sparsely decorated with a balanced mix of professional accolades and abstract art. A bookshelf lined one wall, rammed with criminology texts, biographies, contemporary fiction.

A row of framed photos sat along one side of the desk: Khokhar in her graduation robes, another of her receiving an award, and a few family shots. A small prayer mat lay in the corner, neatly folded.

The door opened, and Khokhar strode in, her teal hijab a jolt of colour against her white shirt and dark suit. She flashed Lennox a smile as she took her seat.

'Oz. Thanks for coming to see me. How did the Malik scene wrap?'

'Strange one. Staged suicide. Adeyemi's enquiries back up my assertion. No evidence of external involvement.

Social media and phone shows Malik was struggling with coming out. He'd already made an attempt, six months ago, and he'd been stockpiling anti-depressants. In the end, he went with a more dramatic approach to soften the cultural shame for his family.'

Khokhar interlaced her fingers, and a delicate silver bracelet slid down her wrist. 'How dreadful.'

'Tough one for the FLOs.'

Khokhar took a breath. 'How are you managing?'

'I'm fine. I've been focusing on the Bones Killer specialist briefing. Hoping for some new ideas.'

'Maybe it's something to hand off to one of the DIs once you've set everything up? It's in danger of going cold.'

Lennox's hand moved to his tie, adjusting the knot unnecessarily. His fingers lingered there for a moment, as if seeking comfort in the familiar motion. 'I'm not stashing this one up in the five per cent loft. It's not an unsolved. There's an angle somewhere. Something we haven't seen or worked enough.'

Khokhar gave a grim smile. 'An unknown unknown. Always fun to justify on the budget review.'

'He's forensically aware. Maybe that's the line.'

'Oz, I'm not signing off internal witch hunts.' She leaned forward. 'I'd rather you focused on something more active. And it's not what you think. The regional detective training has been mothballed. I think you would have been excellent at running that show, but I want to try something that keeps you hands-on. And, given the recent...' She searched for the word.

Lennox raised an eyebrow. 'Glitches?'

'Yes. After the recent glitches, this might bring some new focus.'

'I'm not interested in overseeing training projects, ma'am.'

Khokhar's air turned steely. 'It's not that. Mallory is staying as the training lead. He's a touch unreconstructed, but there are sections of brass that are practically Jurassic compared to him. He's a bureaucrat, trying to fit people into a rigid template that, between you and me, is starting to feel outmoded. I've been reviewing his recruitment record. He's not a talent spotter. His net is way too fine. There's a shortage of good detectives, and he's failing people with potential because he doesn't like their handwriting.'

Lennox rested his elbows on his knees. 'Global poaching? I'll take a few months consulting in Sardinia. East coast, if you don't mind.'

Khokhar didn't smile. 'I don't want to shunt you onto any sidelines. I want you in the thick of something current and relevant. Something active that makes use of your talent and experience but might ease some of the pressure you're clearly feeling. We have some outstanding DIs here, and you should delegate more.' She sighed. 'We all pick up a little limescale over time, Oz. This initiative might remind you of first principles. And remember, it's purely a trial.'

Lennox's gaze flicked to the window for a moment, a brief loss of focus that he masked by clearing his throat. 'Ma'am. Really. I'm good. I'm sharp. I'm active. It's just the time of year. It's always a challenge for me, mentally. You know that. It'll settle. There's no need to do anything radical.'

Khokhar tilted her head slightly. 'I know about the personal challenge. And I'm sympathetic. But if you were in my chair, you'd see this as long-term strategy, not a knee-jerk.' She laid her hands flat on the desk. 'The force needs to evolve. Conduct scandals, abusive officers, corruption.

It'll take a generation for the IOPC to wash it all out. We need root-and-branch reform, and that starts with recruitment policy. At this stage in your career, you should be a part of making that happen.'

Lennox nodded. 'Representation.'

'Exactly. London has been minority white for fifteen years, and it's only going to get more diverse. The Met is sixty-five per cent male. We need a recruitment policy to shift that to fifty per cent, setting us up for the changes in the society we're policing.' She smiled. 'This is me putting you at the centre of this. It is not me setting you on the road to retirement. I want to make you more relevant, not less. It's a fact of life, Oz. No matter how good you are, eventually you have to shift from climbing the ladder to managing your legacy.'

Lennox's gaze drifted to a small imperfection in the chrome leg of Khokhar's desk. He blinked and turned his head away from the glare of morning sun spilling through the office's tall, thin windows. With one side of his peripheral vision obscured by light, his focus migrated, coalescing around the tiny scratch.

The silence stretched until Khokhar's voice cut through his reverie.

'Oz? Are you with us?'

Lennox blinked again, and the room snapped back into focus. He straightened in his chair, moving himself out of the sunlight, smoothing down his tie. 'Okay. So, you want me to offload more live investigation and get deeper into management?'

Khokhar smiled. 'Not managing. Mentoring.'

Chapter Seventeen

Blackwood burst through the door, her shoulder bag swinging. DCI Richard Mallory glanced up from his computer, his face a mask of practised indifference.

'Sorry I'm late, sir. There was an accident and the bus had to—'

'How long have you lived in London, PC Blackwood?'

'Years. I know. I should leave earlier, assume there'll be delays.'

Mallory turned back to his computer. 'So, why didn't you?'

Blackwood dropped into the chair opposite the desk. 'Time myopia.'

He laughed. 'Now, that is a new one.'

'It's an ADHD trait, sir. Sometimes you only sense the urgency when it's up close. By then it's too late.'

Mallory slowly pivoted his chair to face her. He managed a doubtful nod. 'Tell me. Is there anyone who doesn't have ADHD, these days?'

'Around ninety-five per cent of UK adults, sir. Although

a fair chunk of them will be undiagnosed, high-functioning. It's a neurodiversity suited to some jobs.'

He leaned back, folded his arms. 'Such as?'

'TV producer. Choreographer. Paramedic. Daycare worker. Journalist. It's not so great for librarians, though. Or accountants. Or retail workers. Or lab assistants.'

'How about police detectives?'

She smiled. 'Ideal. Many people with ADHD have scattered attention, but they can also be hyperfocused and highly observant with something they find interesting. And the ADHD brain craves the structure demanded by police work.'

Mallory turned back to his computer. 'Interesting.'

Blackwood looked around. There was a new addition to the office decor: a framed print of a mournful-looking bloodhound on the wall shelf behind Mallory. 'Is that your dog, sir?'

He nodded. 'Bruno. My daughter named him when she was a child. She's now a professional photographer. She took the picture.'

'People often choose dogs they feel mirror their personalities.' Mallory side-eyed her. 'Bloodhounds are easy-going, but they're stubborn when following a scent. They're terrible guard dogs, though. They like to be around people too much.'

'Are you a dog lover, Blackwood?'

'Yes. I prefer birds, though.'

Mallory pivoted again. 'I've just emailed your DI at Wood Green.' He checked the monitor. 'Pollard. I've reevaluated your performance across all the modules in more detail. But don't get excited about a closing door suddenly swinging open. I'm going with a third way.'

'Sir?'

He slid a document across the desk. Blackwood leaned forward and looked it over. The front page was covered in red ink, with annotations crowding the margins.

'You're closer than I thought in several areas,' said Mallory. 'But close only counts with hand grenades.'

Blackwood's knee bounced; she clamped a hand on it. 'So, why the email to Wood Green, sir?'

He took the document back and looked it over. 'Your written assignments show a keen analytical mind, but there's a tendency to leap to conclusions without fully tracking your reasoning. And while your investigative instincts are strong, you sometimes overlook crucial procedural steps in your eagerness to solve the puzzle.' He tapped a hand on the document, pondering. 'But I'm not here to go over old ground. I've decided to throw you a lifeline.'

Blackwood shifted in her chair, eyes flitting around.

The loose thread on Mallory's sleeve.

Slight misalignment of his pen holder.

Faint coffee ring on a coaster near his elbow.

'Before we get to that, though,' continued Mallory, 'I'm aware of the complaint you've picked up following a recent house call. It rather highlights the point I made last time about the rush to self-actualisation. But I'm sure you've had a similar lecture from Pollard.'

'I have, sir. I understand I have some learning to do.'

He grinned, without joy. 'That's correct. We're trialling something here at Hendon, in the Major Investigation Unit. It's based across the way.' He waved a hand towards the window.

'The big shiny buildings with the tinted windows, sir? At the far end of campus?'

'That's right. It's a mentoring scheme for trainees who are close to the line. To get them over it. You'll shadow a senior detective, which means you'll be based on this site for a while, effective immediately. Hence the email.'

Her heart raced. 'Is this part of the course, sir?'

He wrinkled his nose. 'Sort of.'

'Are any of the other students doing this?'

'Why does that concern you?'

'It's the first question my mother will ask.'

Mallory scoffed. 'Not from this intake. You should know, Blackwood, this isn't baby-minding. You'll be expected to follow all the usual protocols and will exercise your standard police powers. But this is quite the test for your approach to process and PACE regulations. It's also a rarefied learning opportunity. And you'll certainly find structure over there.'

Blackwood's fingers itched to fidget with the strap of her bag. She forced herself to keep still by focusing on the scent of Mallory's aftershave, then the musty smell of the old files in a bookshelf by the door.

Slight wobble of Mallory's desk lamp as he shifted in his chair.
Dust motes drifting in a shaft of sunlight.

'Can I give you a piece of advice?' said Mallory.

'Of course, sir.'

He tapped the back of his head. 'You might think about losing that hair colouring. I don't know many senior female detectives who've kept their old student style. And, let's be honest, in this job you don't want to stand out any more than you already do. Some things can't be helped. Others can.'

Blackwood's hands trembled as she gripped the arms of the chair, anchoring herself back in the moment.

Mallory turned back to the computer. 'Best get started, then.'

She stood up. 'Thank you for the opportunity, sir.'

He waved a hand. 'This isn't the bloody *Apprentice*.' He

glanced at his watch. 'You're expected at the unit's reception. Just head out front and stick to the central walkway. Aim for the big shiny buildings. DSI Aisha Khokhar is the unit lead. Her PA will greet you and introduce you to your mentor.'

She stood there. Frozen. Staring.

Mallory typed something. He side-eyed her again. 'Any reason you're still here?'

'Can you... give me any more, sir? Do you know anything about my mentor?'

Mallory kept typing. 'He's particular about his coffee.'

Chapter Eighteen

Blackwood approached the corner table, balancing a mug of coffee and a blueberry muffin on a small tray.

'Sure I can't get you anything?'

Lennox shook his head, kept typing on his laptop.

She set down the tray and took a seat opposite. At Wood Green, Blackwood shared an industrial-sized tin of Nescafé with colleagues in a box-room MDF kitchen. The Major Investigation Team cafeteria was all modern furnishings in washed-out greys and blues. Chrome-legged tables. Low-slung sofas in partitioned meeting areas. A few well-tended potted plants added splashes of green to the corners and dividers. Colossal windows stretched from floor to ceiling, overlooking the campus grounds: groomed lawns, paved paths with recessed uplighters.

'This is the first place I've worked that has an in-house bakery,' said Blackwood. She peeled a frosted chunk from the muffin's crust and popped it into her mouth. 'The custody desk sergeant at Wood Green does a run to Bean +

Brew on Monday and Friday morning. They do amazing cinnamon rolls.'

Lennox grunted an acknowledgement.

She sipped her coffee. 'This is good. Bean + Brew is slightly better, though.'

Lennox kept typing. 'I beg to differ.'

'Have you been to Bean + Brew?'

'I mean, I doubt it's good.'

Blackwood munched on the muffin, her eyes darting around, downloading details.

Tarnishing at the base of the table leg.

A tear in the upholstery at the back of Lennox's seat.

Ceiling patterns. Interlocking hexagons. Like honeycomb.

She pointed up. 'Are they special tiles?'

'Acoustic,' said Lennox. 'With integrated sound-absorbing panels. It means you can talk.' He glanced up. 'And concentrate.'

The air-conditioning whirred softly, swaying the leaves of a plant at the corner of their section.

'Well, this makes a change.' Blackwood clunked her mug down on the table.

Lennox stared at her. 'A change?'

'From sitting in a male superior's office while they list my shortcomings. That's a theme with me lately.'

'I won't waste energy on that, then.'

Back to typing.

Blackwood broke the muffin in two. It crumbled, with a few fragments spilling off the plate onto the table. She took another bite. 'I saw these buildings from my course. Is this exclusively Hendon MIT?'

Lennox looked up briefly, scowled at the crumbs. 'Yes.'

'Can you tell me more about the operation? I sort of got dropped in on this, out of the blue. Didn't have time to—'

'We have a DSI in overall command, supported by two DCIs, including myself, who oversee multiple investigation teams of DCs and DSs, each led by a DI. The numbers and make-up of teams vary according to ongoing enquiries. The hours are twenty-four-seven, with rotating shifts.'

Blackwood nodded. 'Any specialised units?'

'Digital Forensics. Financial. Family Liaison. Intelligence Cell with analysts and researchers. We also have a Major Incident Room for developing cases, dedicated IT support facilities, in-house forensics who coordinate with external services. And a Press Room.'

'For press conferences.'

Lennox narrowed his eyes. 'Correct.' He reached for a bottle of water.

Trembling hand.

'And you have access to all the major systems and databases?'

Lennox sipped from his bottle. 'Of course.'

Something about him seemed familiar, but she couldn't place it.

He closed his laptop. 'So, why do you want to be a detective, PC Blackwood?'

She finished her mouthful of muffin, wiped her mouth with a napkin. 'I suppose you could say I'm manifesting.'

His head dropped to one side. 'Manifesting?'

'Putting it out into the universe. Affirmations, positive vision, visualisation.'

'Is this a TikTok thing?'

She laughed. 'I hate TikTok. The boring answer is that I've wanted to do it since I was a little girl.'

'Why?'

She caught his tone: more curious than challenging.

'I like mysteries, sir. I call you that, right?'

'Right.'

That gaze. Icy blue eyes drilling into her.

Blackwood took a slug of coffee, studying Lennox over the rim of the mug. His silvery-grey hair was tidy, with a slight wave that hinted at a stubborn cowlick. The deep lines around his eyes spoke of years of intense focus and, perhaps, worry. His eyes, almost turquoise in this light, seemed to look through her rather than at her. A faded scar ran along his left jawline.

Lennox's posture was impeccable: spine straight against the chair back, shoulders squared. He wore a fitted white dress shirt—collar perfectly starched—under a charcoal-grey suit jacket, probably tailored. A royal blue tie with a subtle stripe added a faint suggestion of personality.

His hands rested on the closed laptop.

Long fingers, slightly calloused, with neatly trimmed nails.

He radiated competence, confidence, experience. But there was also a hint of weariness. Perhaps a guarded vulnerability.

The tremble again. Right hand, almost imperceptible.

Blackwood nodded to the lanyard around his neck. 'Oswald Lennox. That's a great name.'

A slight smile. 'Thank you. I didn't choose it.'

'Sounds like a fashion designer. Do people call you Ozzy?'

'Sometimes. Usually only once.'

She laughed, too loud.

'So, are you Olivia? Liv?'

She winced. 'Only my grandmother calls me Olivia. Although she takes a while to recognise me, these days. My mum calls me Livvy. Which I hate.'

Lennox's eyes glanced upward in thought. 'Sounds like *privy.*'

'Yeah, perfect. An old toilet. I prefer Liv. Sir.'

He drew in a long, slow breath.

Again, the gaze.

He opened the laptop, navigated to something. 'I've read your training report. Second time round. I hope I can help you avoid a third.'

'Thank you, sir.'

'I'm happy for you to stay close. Within reason. But please try to stick to observing unless I ask you direct questions. And we have a timescale. I'm due to report back to DCI Mallory in two weeks. So, what would you like to work on first?'

Blackwood smiled. 'What have you got?'

Lennox gave a quiet laugh. He pushed the open laptop to one side, half-exposing the screen. 'Are you a maverick, PC Blackwood?'

'You mean like the detective movies?' She put on a gravelly, movie trailer-type voice. *'Her methods are unorthodox. But she gets results.'*

He didn't smile. She cleared her throat, sat upright.

Blackwood nodded to the image on the laptop desktop: a young boy in ski gear, grinning, standing in front of a busy ski lift. 'Is he family?'

Lennox turned away and slowly closed the laptop. 'That's personal. You need to work on your boundaries, Liv.'

A jolt of mortification.

Then the flaring, like nausea.

It faded to the usual ache: a desire to rewind time a few seconds.

'I'm sorry, sir. He looks nice. Really happy.'

Stop.

Lennox turned back to her; she avoided his eye.

'I've never skied. I'm not sure it'd be my thing.'

Stop.

'I'm conducting a case review in the Monro Room,' said Lennox. 'Just down the corridor.'

'Like James Monro?'

Lennox arched an eyebrow. 'Yes.'

'Met commissioner during the time of Jack the Ripper. He was a reformer. A moderniser. Made the CID more professional and efficient.'

Lennox got to his feet. 'Gold star. Come and sit in. I hope you've got a strong stomach.'

Chapter Nineteen

Blackwood settled into a chair with a pull-down desk in the far corner of the top tier. Attendance was sparse at the back, but the front rows were filled with granite-faced men in good suits, and upright women in sharp business dress. A senior-looking male detective sat facing the group down front, at a curved control desk beneath a huge wall-mounted screen.

At the end of her row, two admin staff in casual dress poked at their tablets. One came over as she opened her laptop.

'PC Olivia Blackwood, right? I'm here to set you up with temporary HOLMES access.'

She nodded. 'Thank you. I appreciate that.'

'I'm Dom.' He took Blackwood's computer and sat in the seat beside her.

'Liv.' She leaned back and watched as he navigated to a secure intranet. He kept his eyes on her screen while rattling in passwords and access codes from memory.

Mid-to-late thirties.

Short, chestnut-brown hair.

Cologne. Woody with a whiff of spice.

Silver wedding ring with geometric pattern on the raised edge.

Nice nails. Manicured?

'Have you used HOLMES before?' said Dom.

'Yeah. Mainly for processing witness statements at crime scenes.'

'There's a lot more than that in there. Case files, evidence logs, profiles and addresses of every officer and detective in the unit.' He grinned, lowered his voice. 'There's also a secret coffee order database. Pretty hush-hush, that one. Do you want a quick refresher?'

'I'll be fine. I'm good with tech.'

'Okay. I'll set user as *pcblack*. Password? You can have anything you like. No need for exclams or squiggles or whatever.'

Blackwood thought for a moment. 'Abigail.'

He nodded, typed some more. 'Okay. You're set up. I've logged you in to the hub screen of the case under discussion.' He lifted the laptop onto her pull-down desk. 'Are you a CID trainee?'

'Yeah. Shadowing DCI Oswald Lennox.'

Dom whistled. 'Good luck with that.' He lowered his voice. 'Do you know what they call him? Not to his face, though.'

'No.'

'The Wizard. Y'know, as in Oz. He says he hates it, but I bet he secretly likes it.'

She nodded. 'Well, he's certainly made himself disappear.'

Dom chuckled. 'You have met him, right?'

'Yeah. He dropped me off in here and then said he had to check something.'

'He likes to make an entrance. Bit up himself, I think.' He headed back to his seat. 'Give me a shout if you need any help.'

Blackwood surveyed the HOLMES case management system hub screen. The interface was clean and intuitive, with a series of tabs across the top covering the key elements: Case Overview, Incident Reports, Victim Profiles, Exhibit Log.

The hub was tagged as *OPERATION OSSUARY*, with a sub-heading:

MULTIPLE HOMICIDES WITH DISTINCTIVE MO. NORTH LONDON/HERTFORDSHIRE. 2017-2019. SENIOR INVESTIGATING OFFICER: DETECTIVE CHIEF INSPECTOR OSWALD LENNOX.

Blackwood read the case summary, including the key dates and locations. She took out a stack of Post-it notes and wrote a few details, including the Crime Report Information System number, on an orange note. She clicked through the Incident Reports tab, which listed the murders chronologically. Each entry contained a synopsis, date, location, and links to associated files.

She switched to Victim Profiles and digested the detailed breakdowns of each victim's background: photographs, personal history, last known movements, daily routines and social circles.

The door swung open, and Lennox entered, quieting the bustle and chat. He walked at speed down the steps, nodded to the other senior detective, and stood before the curved desk.

'DCI Rafferty.' Lennox turned to the group. 'I hope everyone's done their homework. Thank you all for taking the time to review the case. Today, I want to focus on the gaps between the killings. All thoughts are welcome. Just raise a hand and I'll call on you.'

The second admin—a young woman with a braided ponytail—reached up to a dial and the lights dimmed. Lennox accessed his tablet and the screen showed a mirror of the HOLMES case hub. He pulled up a timeline and shifted through various documents and imagery to match his points.

Using the light from her phone screen, Blackwood separated her Post-it notes into individual colour piles and arranged them along the top of her desk. She navigated through the case files, photos, witness statements and forensic reports, and employed an attention-splitting method she'd developed at school: isolating Lennox's words and the contributions from the detectives into a dedicated audio head-space, freeing the rest of her focus onto her laptop screen.

She zoned into the Forensic Evidence section, with its subcategories for each crime scene: Photography, Ballistics, DNA Analysis, Trace Evidence, Toxicology, Pathology. The Photography folder featured high-resolution images of the victims, showing the gruesome tableaux of the bodies, surrounded by carefully arranged animal bones. She cycled through the photos, scribbling notes and sketches onto green Post-its: victim positions, precise bone placement, lack of struggle marks.

Blackwood navigated back to the main hub, switching to the Intelligence Reports section with its analyses of potential patterns, geographical profiling data, and links to similar cases from other jurisdictions. She added a few details to an orange note, then marked the Post-its with colour-coded topics: orange for high-level notes, yellow for victim details, green for forensics, pink for witness info, blue for investigative actions.

A male voice from the front desk cut through her concentration.

'He might take his time to rebuild his fantasy. Elaborating. He's got away with it for a long time, so he's allowing himself a refinement period.'

She looked up.

It was the male DCI at the top table. Rafferty.

Square jawline. Prominent brow. Shiny bald. Vaguely military.

Blackwood delved deeper into the system, opening multiple browser tabs, cross-referencing details from the case file with external sources: news reports, crime databases, academic journals on serial killer psychology. She filled her Post-its, copied web addresses into her laptop notes app, and bypassed paywalls with an archive snapshot service, saving journal articles to read later.

'Would he see it as refinement?'

Female voice, a few rows ahead.

'So far, he's barely elaborated. The consistency tells us something about him.'

As Blackwood burrowed deeper into the case file, her audio compartment grew more distant, degrading in quality, with only occasional comments breaking into her bubble of focus.

Lennox. *'If he's sticking to specific types, like high-status individuals, for a deeper reason, then victim selection could be more complex than we've considered.'*

Different female voice near the front. *'His last kill was before the Covid pandemic. Could that have disrupted him?'*

The discussion melted into a distant hum.

The room lights brightened slightly. Blackwood looked up to see the wall screen had glitched, freezing on a crime scene image. Dom hurried down to a control console at the front desk and fixed the issue. As he returned to his seat, he caught Blackwood's eye and smiled.

But the disruption was like a splash of icy water, jolting Blackwood from her multi-threaded reverie.

She closed her laptop and gathered the Post-its, trying to refocus as Lennox wound down the briefing.

He sat on the edge of the desk as the lights came up. DCI Rafferty half-rose but then sat again as he realised Lennox had final comments.

'I'm calling a final review briefing for next Tuesday, same time. Please bring some fresh ideas on the psychopathology. I'll do likewise. We still have no real understanding of the animal bones. Are they part of his signature? Distraction? Presentation? Why the arrangement? Is there something in his MO that could give us a new line?' He turned from the desk towards Rafferty, now standing. They spoke in low voices as the rest of the detectives stood and began filing towards the main doors.

'Maybe he's recharging,' said Blackwood, loud enough to carry across the room.

A few heads turned. The chatter softened.

At the front, Lennox looked over to her, shielding his eyes from the light.

'Sorry,' said Rafferty. 'Who are you?'

'This is PC Olivia Blackwood,' said Lennox. 'My CID mentee for the session.'

A female detective standing near Lennox raised her head. 'What do you mean by "recharging"?'

Most of the detectives had stopped and turned to watch. Blackwood collected her Post-it notes, stuffed them into her shoulder bag. A few spilled onto the floor and she gathered them up. She looked around at the faces, reading the expressions.

Curious. Pitying. Irritated. Amused. Confused.

She glanced at Dom, but he was staring into his tablet screen.

She took a steadying breath. 'It's like... energy levels. After intense activity, social, I feel overwhelmed. I have to mask. Put up a normal front. It can be tiring. I need to power down for a while. Get some alone time. Refill my tank. I feel sort of bloated. I thought maybe the killer could be feeling the same.'

Silence.

Rafferty cleared his throat. He glanced at Lennox, then up to Blackwood. 'Interesting.'

Chapter Twenty

He stepped out of the house into the leaden late-evening air. But he was lighter footed tonight, and the world seemed brighter, more vibrant. He felt renewed, invigorated. A kaleidoscope of primary colours swirled at the edge of his vision, pulsing with each heartbeat.

The drive in the BMW was a segue of familiar turns and traffic lights, and as he rumbled down the unmarked track, his mood blackened at the prospect of the unpleasant but necessary chore.

At the lock-up, he snapped on a pair of nitrile gloves and swiped his card, savouring the flash of acid green. He closed the door behind him, flicked on the light, and popped the boot of the Insignia.

The stench blew back his hair. Caustic urine: a murky, sulphurous amber. Rancid sweat: a sour off-white.

The unmistakable reek of fear.

The man lay curled in a foetal position, bound and gagged with fresh tape. His nostrils flared, gorging on the fresher air.

The captive's skin was sallow and greasy. Deep pits of bruised flesh underscored his sunken eyes.

He regarded the pitiful creature with a mix of irritation and detachment. If he could only press a button and erase this byproduct without fuss...

But he had a process to follow. It had kept him free for so long now. He would carry it through and then rest again.

He reached in to the back seat of the car and took out a roll of duct tape and the machete, holding its blade up to the light, where the man could see. His captive writhed and jerked like a beached fish, his muffled cries leaking around the edges of the tape.

He crouched at the boot. 'Water?'

The man nodded vigorously, hope flashing across his bloodshot eyes.

He leaned in to the back seat and lifted out four five-gallon plastic bottles of water, one by one, lining them up along the side of the car.

He walked to the far wall, slid open a low cupboard, and took out a medium-sized fish tank, setting it down near to the water bottles. He unscrewed the cap off the first bottle, then slowly poured its contents into the tank. He repeated with the other three bottles until the tank was almost full to the brim.

He reached into the boot and cut the tape binding the man's legs. He stepped back and held up the machete.

'Out.'

With difficulty, the captive scooped his legs over the rim of the boot and hitched himself over and out onto the garage's stone floor. He watched, appalled, as the man whimpered and keened beneath the gag, legs trembling with the effort of supporting his weight after days of confinement. He stepped back as the man buckled, dropping to his knees, then flopped onto his side.

He crouched and tried to tape the man's ankles again. But his captive resisted, kicking his legs. He dug the point of the machete into the side of the man's neck, and he froze, dropping his head in despair, silent but for the ragged whistle of air through his nostrils.

The man went limp, and he taped his legs. He threw the machete onto the car's back seat.

He dragged the man over to the fish tank and shifted him up onto his knees. He grabbed a fistful of his matted hair and plunged his head into the water.

The captive bucked and thrashed, his bound hands scrabbling uselessly behind his back. Water sloshed over the sides of the tank, spattering onto the floor. Bubbles erupted around the man's submerged face.

He straddled the man's back, holding his head with both hands, keeping it under the water until the resistance grew weaker, more sporadic. Thin jets of water spurted from the man's nostrils with each failed attempt to breathe, and he lurched into a final, desperate burst of thrashing, then seemed to give up.

He held the head under the water for a few more minutes until the tremors stopped. The body sagged and he had to support the man's torso with one hand while keeping his head under the water with the other.

With a grunt of effort, he dragged the sodden corpse out to the boot of the BMW, lifted it in head-first, then rolled its legs over the rim and closed the boot. He replaced the machete in its bag, emptied the fish tank into a corner sink, then returned it to the cupboard.

As he slid back behind the wheel, a sense of quiet triumph stole over him, rewarding him with a symphony of his favourites, intertwining in blissful harmony: rich indigo waves cresting into shimmering gold; soft tendrils of violet weaving through vivid emerald; warm orange, throbbing and cycling between cool azure.

He sank his head into the seat rest and settled his breathing, wallowing in the afterglow.

His hunger would rise again. But for now, he was sated.

PART TWO

DIVERGENCE

Chapter Twenty-One

'I nearly killed my mum once.'

Lennox stopped typing and looked up.

Blackwood leaned forward in the chair facing his desk. 'I was nearly two weeks overdue. She says I was too cosy. Didn't want to come out. So, they induced her. They had to go with Caesarean because of foetal distress. But she had an amniotic fluid embolism during the Caesarean.'

Lennox clasped his hands together on the desktop. 'That doesn't sound healthy.'

'Definitely not.' She crossed her legs. 'Amniotic fluid enters the mother's bloodstream. Triggers an allergic reaction. They noticed straight after they pulled me out. They put her under general, stabilised her. She was in Intensive Care after.' Blackwood spoke quickly, barely taking a breath between sentences. 'My poor dad. He just had to get on with it. It was a week before they let my mum hold me.'

Lennox leaned back in his chair and smoothed down his tie. 'That must have been awful.'

'Luckily, I was too young to remember.'

He raised an eyebrow. 'For your mother.'

She squinted at him. 'Obviously.'

Lennox glanced out of the window. The late afternoon sun had thrown long shadows across the campus lawns. He got up and went to the Jura machine. 'Coffee?'

'Please, yes. Just black, no sugar.'

He opened the machine lid and inhaled the waft of coffee beans. Earthy, with tangs of citrus, jasmine, dark chocolate. He measured out a precise amount of beans from the airtight container and poured them in, then slid a sky-blue Le Creuset mug into the holder and tapped the *AMERICANO* icon on the touch screen.

As the Jura whirred into life, he wiped down the steam wand, standing with his back to Blackwood. 'I'm revoking your access to the HOLMES system.'

'Right. I'm sorry about the briefing, sir. It just came out. I hope I didn't embarrass you.'

He waved a hand. 'This is not a punishment. I just felt—'

'I think it's a good idea.'

He turned. 'Really?'

She nodded. 'HOLMES is a distraction. I want to focus on ticking the boxes. Convincing Mallory... DCI Mallory to wave me through. I think the problem is that I've been trying too hard. Whenever I try to impress or go the extra mile, it never seems to help.'

'Remember, you're just jumping through hoops for now. There'll be time to impress later.' Lennox brought over the coffee, then sat on the edge of his desk and sipped from a bottle of Evian.

Blackwood raised the mug. 'You not partaking?'

He smiled. 'Not after 4pm.'

'That's when I need the pep.'

'Caffeine has a half-life of four to six hours. If I take coffee after four, it disrupts my sleep.'

'I use a sound effects app to sleep. Natural sounds. Waves on the shore, rain. It clears my head. You should try it. I'll send it to you.'

'Please do. Now, I'd like to establish a few rules of engagement. Give you an idea of how I think we can make this work.'

She nodded, took a tentative sip of her coffee.

Her eyes widened. 'Oh my god. This is so good. What is it?'

'How much do you want to know?'

'Everything. Always everything. Take that as my default setting.'

Lennox took another sip of water. 'You're drinking a single-origin coffee from the Yirgacheffe region of Ethiopia. It's grown at high altitudes, which contributes to its complex flavour profile. The beans are wet-processed, which helps preserve their natural acidity and results in a clean, bright cup. You're tasting notes of jasmine, bergamot, and perhaps a hint of lemon. The machine ensures optimal extraction, maintaining precise temperature control throughout the brewing process. This, combined with the freshness of the beans which I have delivered weekly, results in coffee that highlights its innate qualities with no bitterness or off-flavours.'

'I love it,' said Blackwood. She blew on the drink and took another sip, staring at Lennox over the rim of the cup. 'I switched off slightly during the part about optimal extraction, but I caught most of that. So, you're a coffee connoisseur?'

'It's kind of you to dress it up like that. I usually get "coffee nerd".'

He studied her for a moment. Her hazel eyes were alert and curious, casting around occasionally before settling back on him. She had gathered her dark curls into a messy bun, with a few stray tendrils framing her face. She dressed like a detective: off-white blouse under a charcoal blazer; indigo jeans and lived-in brown boots; a hint of individuality in the bird-shaped brooch on her lapel.

Blackwood's posture was a contradiction. She sat upright, clearly making an effort to appear composed and professional. But her left leg bounced nervously, and her fingers tapped a rhythmic pattern on the side of the coffee cup.

She drank more, smiled.

There was something he was supposed to say. It hovered close, but as he tried to pluck it out of the air, it flitted away, out of reach.

Blackwood watched him, her head angling.

Was the silence awkward yet?

He took another sip of water, hoping the distraction would bring clarity.

'You seem really familiar,' said Blackwood. 'I can't work out why, though.'

'I don't remember arresting you.'

She laughed. 'No, it's not that.'

He took a breath.

Still nothing.

Blackwood raised her eyebrows. 'So, what are these rules of engagement?'

'Ah, yes. We have a two-week window to work with. During that time, you'll be shadowing me on active cases, attending briefings and assisting with paperwork.'

'My favourite. I finished reviewing those witness reports, by the way.'

Lennox hitched off the desk and walked back to his chair. 'I can't imagine that was too taxing. But it helps me get a sense of your attention to detail. I'll also be looking for your ability to follow protocol.'

'Not the best start there.'

He sat down. 'I'm happy to hear your contributions, in context. Because I want to see how you interact with colleagues and witnesses. I need to see a rigorous approach to PACE guidelines. Maverick cops are for the movies. I'll be looking at how you apply PACE in practical situations. I'd also like a look at your interview technique, both witness and suspect. You could observe initially, then conduct some yourself under supervision. Basing at a hot-desk in the open-plan office is a good idea.'

'Cross-pollination?'

'Yes. You'll pick things up. Don't involve yourself in case conversations unless invited, though.'

She nodded. 'Interactions with colleagues.'

'Exactly. I've asked one of the DIs, Carla Whitmore, to assign you a few tasks. Talk to her if I'm not around. I have a private appointment this afternoon, so she'll fill in.'

Blackwood set down her mug on the desk. 'What about the shadowing?'

Lennox took a marble coaster from a stack and slipped it under the mug. 'You can accompany me to crime scenes, but unless I specifically request your input, it'll be observation only. And remember your obligations to ethics and confidentiality under the Official Secrets Act. You might need to sign more non-disclosure agreements specific to certain sensitive cases.'

Blackwood leaned forward. 'Can I ask you a question?'

'Of course.'

'You're pretty senior...' She smiled, held up a hand. 'Not in that way. It just makes me think, why would you do this?'

'You think it's some sort of test?'

'Or a reality show.'

Lennox laughed. 'I've been in policing for a long time. There isn't much I haven't seen repeatedly, both mundane and extreme.' He shrugged. 'It's something new.'

Chapter Twenty-Two

Dr Alistair Moorcroft's consulting room was more like a design showpiece, blending vintage charm with modern style. The centrepiece was a mahogany desk with a green leather inlay paired with a sleek white Eames executive chair and a brushed-aluminium Anglepoise lamp. A restored dark-wood apothecary cabinet stood in one corner, topped with a Bang & Olufsen sound system.

Lennox shifted in the upholstered patient chair facing the desk. He eyed the examination couch in the corner, beneath a widescreen abstract.

Krasner? De Kooning?

A framed monochrome photograph hung on the back wall behind the desk: a line of sea defence poles, standing vertically, extending out into still water.

John Lewis.

'Hello, hello.'

A trim man in his late fifties entered through the open door, carrying a laptop under his arm. 'Apologies for the delay, Mr Lennox. Our new encrypted result retrieval system decided to perform an unscheduled update. I had to get the IT chap on the line to push it through manually.'

Moorcroft closed the door behind him and took his seat. He had thin silvery hair and wore a navy waistcoat above a light-blue shirt. No tie. Circular, black-framed spectacles clung to the end of his aquiline nose. His complexion was flushed, as if he'd just bounded up a flight of stairs.

He opened the laptop, squinting at the screen. Lennox surveyed the row of initialisms in a framed certificate near the Anglepoise: MB ChB. MRCP. FRCP. PhD.

'I bring good and slightly concerning news,' said Moorcroft, a faint Welsh lilt in his accent. 'Blood tests are excellent. Liver and kidney function are normal, as are your thyroid hormone levels. B12 and B9 are optimal, and I would rule out any vitamin deficiency. Sodium, potassium, calcium... All good. No signs of diabetes. No inflammatory markers.' He frowned. 'Cortisol is a little high, but nothing significant. I'm seeing no abnormal autoimmune markers, so I'd rule out any contribution in that regard.'

Moorcroft sat back in his chair and pushed his glasses up his nose. He rested a hand on the desk, then placed the other on top.

'What's slightly concerning?' said Lennox.

The doctor raised both eyebrows. 'I was hoping to find a potential culprit,' he said brightly. 'Something that might speak to your symptoms. You said you were experiencing confusion. Is that right?'

'It's more like... moments of blankness. I know what I want to say, but I can't quite articulate it.'

'Has this been persistent? Getting worse recently?'

Lennox paused, looked up at the photograph: the rugged wooden poles receding to a vanishing point. 'I'd say so, yes. I noticed it first a few months ago, but it feels worse now.'

Moorcroft looked at his screen again. 'The cortisol level might be telling us something. Are you under more stress than usual at the moment? You're a policeman. Is that correct?'

'I'm a detective. I often deal with distressing cases, but I usually manage that well.'

'How do you do that?'

'I exercise. Walks in nature. Listen to music. I cook.'

Moorcroft observed him. 'Tell me more about the hand tremors.'

'Mostly my right hand. Comes and goes.'

The doctor typed something. 'And you feel these episodes are becoming more frequent?'

'Perhaps.'

'Recent head injury? Even minor.'

'No.'

'Change in sleep patterns?'

'My sleep is pretty broken at the moment, yes. And this time of year is never good.'

Moorcroft looked up. 'Why's that?'

Lennox took a long breath. 'I'm approaching the anniversary of a difficult bereavement.'

'I see.' Moorcroft rested his hands in a stack again. He tapped the bottom hand with the top. 'Before we go any further, I'd like to ask you a few basic questions, Mr Lennox. Standard cognitive screening. Nothing too taxing. I'm not trying to catch you out. I just want to get a quick overall impression. Please answer as briskly as you can.'

'Fire away.'

Moorcroft nodded. 'Your age?'

'Fifty-two.'

'And what time would you say it is now, roughly? Don't look at your watch.'

Lennox glanced back at the window on the wall behind, gauging the light. 'About quarter past three.'

Moorcroft typed something. 'I'm going to give you an address to remember. 42 West Street. Could you repeat that back?'

'42 West Street.'

'Good. Which month are we in?'

'June.'

'The year?'

'2024.'

'And where are we now, Mr Lennox?'

'Your private consulting rooms in Harley Street.'

Moorcroft typed something else. 'Your date of birth?'

'24th January 1972.'

'When did the First World War begin?'

'1914.'

'Who is the current monarch?'

'King Charles III.'

Moorcroft nodded, typed again. 'Could you count backwards from twenty to zero for me?'

Lennox did so, with little hesitation between the numbers.

'And that address I gave you earlier?'

'42 West Street.'

Moorcroft looked up from his computer and smiled.

'How did I do?' said Lennox.

Moorcroft shrugged. 'The test is just one tool among many, Mr Lennox. But I would like to conduct a couple of slightly deeper assessments before you leave today. No big panic. They might prove basic for someone of your mental acuity, but it won't take more than fifteen minutes and may provide some further insight. I'll also do a quick physical exam. And let's get you in the MRI tube further down the line. Belt and braces.'

The air seemed to thicken in Lennox's lungs. 'What are you thinking?'

Moorcroft pondered for a moment. 'Why don't you tell me what you're thinking? What are your fears?'

Lennox gazed at Moorcroft's busy hands. 'Any sort of cognitive impairment. My work demands focus, detail, perfect recall. I normally have an excellent memory. Highly specific.'

'You remember dates, times, sensations? Clear visuals?'

'Yes.'

'Given your work, I suspect you've developed some sophisticated recall techniques. Some you might not have even realised.'

Lennox looked up. 'Do you think that might be masking a deeper issue? If you were me, would you be worried?'

'Goodness. I could never be you. I can barely imagine the things you have to deal with. But as a detective, I'm sure you're familiar with deductive reasoning. You develop a theory about a crime and then look for evidence. You start with ideas and move towards observation. Medicine is more inductive. We start with observations and move towards ideas, ruling things out until we're left with the most likely solution.'

Lennox nodded. 'We do a bit of both.'

'Indeed. So, if I were you, I wouldn't worry at all. I would focus on those observations. Let them take the lead. You perhaps have some concern about the destination, but at this stage, we simply don't know. To find out, we need to keep our focus facing forward. Begin the journey.'

Chapter Twenty-Three

Blackwood's temporary workstation sat at the periphery of the Hendon MIT floor. It was well-fitted—spacious L-shaped desk with dual high-res monitors; ergonomic keyboard; high-end PC—but placed directly beneath a row of fluorescent strip lights, and in audible and olfactory range of the toilets. Her AirPods marked her rookie status, but it was the only way she could focus amid the persistent flushing, the drone of hand dryers and the squeak of the hinge on the men's toilet door.

She returned the handover admin from Lennox in an email and submitted the witness statement analyses set by his DI, then tilted herself back on the cheap chair with worn armrests.

It was after nine in the evening, but the activity in the twenty-four-hour office had barely thinned. Through her noise-cancelled bubble, Blackwood monitored the near-silent film: detectives slumped over case files, pacing their desk space, huddled in wilted conference.

She peeled open a Grenade Carb Killa protein bar and launched Microsoft Edge on her main monitor.

A strip light flickered above.

Blackwood stared at the Edge background image—a group of flamingos gathered at an expansive salt flat—and let the options cascade through her mind, momentarily frozen by the overwhelm.

She would get the least advisable out of the way first: Calf Tattoo Boy's socials. They'd been introduced via Harry Stanway, an actor acquaintance she'd known since uni second year. She could start with Facebook. Trawl Stanway's friends list, see if CTB popped up. Then, once she had a name...

She typed 'facebook' into the Edge search bar. It navigated to the platform's home page, but an overlaid message box prevented access.

SITE CATEGORY: Social Media.
You have attempted to access a website that is blocked by the IT security policy of the Metropolitan Police.

This site has been categorised as unauthorised or inappropriate for access from a work device.

If you believe this site should be accessible for work-related purposes, please contact the IT Helpdesk or submit a request through the appropriate channels.

Blackwood sighed. She took another bite of the protein bar and slid her iPad from her leather shoulder bag. She attached the portable keyboard and opened the Safari browser, enabling Private Browsing mode. Using the iPad's 5G connection, she accessed her VPN app and selected

Netherlands as the server location, encrypting and re-routing her iPad traffic.

Strip light flicker.

She opened Safari, navigated to Facebook. After a few minutes of rooting through Stanway's posts, friend list and photos, she spotted CTB in a group photo. She checked the profiles of the responses to the photo and, via a reply with nothing but a line of laugh emojis, found herself on the main profile page of Ryan Decker. CTB stared out from the profile pic: another gym selfie, flexing in front of a mirror, his calf tattoo just visible at the edge of the frame.

Lennox's DI, Carla Whitmore, approached the desk, holding up a hand in greeting. Whitmore was a slim woman in her late thirties, with close-cropped brown hair and cautious eyes.

Blackwood took out her AirPods.

Whitmore stopped at the front of the desk without looking at the monitors or iPad. But Blackwood clicked the iPad sleep button, blanking the screen.

'How are you getting on, Liv?'

'I sent over the witness statement analysis, ma'am. I'm just finishing up on the admin set by DCI Lennox.'

'What are you listening to?'

'Rain.' She checked her phone. 'Light rain. A bit of thunder. It's an app. Helps me concentrate.'

Whitmore smiled and pointed to the half-eaten protein bar. 'I hope that isn't your dinner.'

'No. Just a pep.'

'You are allowed to go home, you know. You're not under office arrest.'

Blackwood laughed. 'I know. Thank you, ma'am. Just a few more minutes.'

Whitmore turned and headed back to her desk.

Strip light flicker.

Blackwood slotted the AirPods back in. She took out a Post-it note and wrote 'Ryan Decker', then re-accessed Safari on her iPad and typed 'lewis hartley' into the Facebook search bar.

Hundreds of hits. She scrolled through a few, but none of the profile pics looked likely. She tried 'sophie lawson', to similar effect.

She opened a separate tab on the Safari browser, navigated to Google, and typed 'ivory room' into the search bar.

Bridal shop in Lincolnshire. Yarn shop and knitting studio in Chiswick. Spa in Woodhall. Various Instagrams and Etsy pages.

Strip light flicker.

Waft of air freshener from the women's toilet.

She opened another tab, searched for 'bones killer london'.

In the briefing, Lennox had said that the details of the killings had been kept out of the media to avoid copycats or false confessions.

She dug into the search results. Most were news reports with little she didn't already know about the murders: dates, general locations, and a few comments on the killings being connected. There were vague victim descriptions, including ages and genders, but little on crime scene detail, although a couple of reports mentioned potential 'ritualistic elements' to the killings. The rest were police appeals, news of increased policing in certain areas, and, from the social media search results, some speculation from true crime amateurs and former detectives. The killings were so spaced out in time, it was difficult to find any through lines in the reports.

Strip light flicker.

Blackwood sprang to her feet and clicked the wall switch near her desk. The row of strip lights on her side of the office floor extinguished. She took her charcoal blazer off the back of the chair and climbed up onto the desk. Several detectives, including Whitmore, turned to watch as Blackwood covered her hands with the fabric of the blazer sleeves. She reached up to the light fitting, gripped the warm fluorescent tube with both hands, and gently twisted it, feeling it lock into a tighter position.

She climbed down and turned the wall switch back on, then slipped her blazer back onto the chair as she stared up at the strip light. No sign of flicker.

Blackwood smiled at the detectives still watching. She sat down, squeezed the last chunk of protein bar from the wrapper into her mouth, and opened another tab on Safari.

She typed 'dci oswald lennox' into the Google search bar.

News articles quoted him on various cases. Press releases detailed his successful operations. She found academic papers co-authored by Lennox on modern investigative techniques, links to police department pages highlighting his career achievements.

She filtered the search results to video only and scrolled the page. A headline caught her eye:

DESPERATE PARENTS APPEAL FOR RETURN OF MISSING GIRL.

The timestamp read 15th August 2010.

The footage loaded, showing a middle-aged couple seated at a table in what appeared to be a hotel conference room, with the Metropolitan Police logo hung behind them and microphones arrayed before them.

The woman was openly weeping, comforted by the man who spoke in a juddering voice.

'Abigail, sweetheart. If you can hear this, please come home. We love you more than anything in this world. We miss you so much it hurts. Every day without you is agony.' He steeled himself, stared into the camera. 'If you're holding Abigail, then please let her go. She's nineteen years old. She still has so much life left to live.' He dropped his head, holding back tears. '*Please*. She's our little girl.' He looked up again, eyes red. 'Abi, darling. Please come back to us. If you're scared, I promise... We will never stop looking for you. We will never give up.'

He broke down, unable to continue. The woman pulled him close, both of them shaking with sobs.

Blackwood looked up at the strip light. Still no flicker.

On-screen, a hand reached over to the man and the camera panned slightly, then pulled out to reveal the comforter as a late-thirties man in a tailored grey suit and blue tie.

Lennox.

Chapter Twenty-Four

Lennox's eyes flicked open. Judging by the low light outside and the infrequent, isolated bird calls, he guessed the time around 4am. He checked the bedside clock. 4:28am.

He lay motionless for a while, poking through the embers of his dreams. Jonah was usually present: his finest moments, sharpest lines, fondest expressions. On bad nights, he was close but distant: avoiding Lennox's eye, strolling too close to some invisible edge with an infinite void beyond the boundary.

But at this time of year, Jonah was absent from the dreamworld. As if he were gifting Lennox respite, steeling him for the meeting.

The phone chirruped its alarm at 4:30. Lennox silenced it, took a few deep breaths, then swung his legs out of the bed. He padded across the cool hardwood floor to the chair by the window where he'd laid out his clothes for the day: white shirt, charcoal suit, navy tie, polished Oxfords lined up beneath. He opened the blind and gazed out at the tree-lined street in pre-dawn repose. If he squinted, he could make out the distant contours of Porter's Park Golf Course.

He unrolled the yoga mat onto the floor by the bed and ran through his morning press-ups and sit-ups. Fifty each, slow and deliberate, savouring the muscle burn.

In the en-suite, he stepped into the rainfall shower and turned the dial until the digital display read 38°C. He set the timer on his phone and propped it on the window shelf. He stood under the spray for two minutes, eyes closed, then lathered himself with body wash, rinsed. At the sink: teeth, exfoliant, moisturise. His phone popped up a reminder for a beard trim—every other morning—and he spent another two minutes in front of the magnifying mirror with a battery shaver.

Lennox dressed, then walked out across the landing, his footsteps muffled by the blue-and-gold Moroccan Azilal rug. Oversized art prints hung on the light grey walls: an orange-and-yellow Rothko colour field, a Mondrian, and a black-and-white Ansel Adams landscape of the Half Dome at Yosemite.

His office was a mid-sized room at the back of the house —Jonah's old room—with a glass-topped desk facing a small window, and a wall of bookshelves stuffed with law textbooks, hardback fiction, true crime.

He took out a notebook from the top drawer of his desk. The cover was worn, its gilded edges distressed by time. He sat down and smoothed it open to a fresh page, then uncapped his Meisterstück fountain pen and wrote.

I'm Oswald. My son, Jonah, was fifteen when...

He tore out the page and started a fresh one.

I've sat here many times listening to your stories without speaking. But now I'd like to share...

No.

He tore out the page again and retrieved a pre-written sheet from the notepad's inlay sleeve: his checklist for the evening.

Prepare statement.
Neutral clothing.
Packet of soft tissues.
Hydrate.
Leave in time to arrive fifteen minutes early.

He'd try again with the statement later.

As he left the room, his eyes lifted to the photo frame on the wall above the desk: a young Jonah crouched in the courtyard at the Islington house with their old cat, Bobby. Lennox had taken the picture, and the image took form in his memory, began to move, gather sound and sensory texture: the midday sun warming his skin; the scent of Martha's freshly baked fruit scones; Jonah's shout as Lennox walked away, asking to see the picture, insisting on no social media posting.

At 5:15, Lennox entered the kitchen. He took out his digital scale and measured fifteen grams of butter into a glass ramekin, then slipped two slices of sourdough into the toaster. The cooker's LED display read 5:18 as he set the pan on the hob. After one minute, he scraped in the butter, which sizzled as it slid into the pan.

The bread popped up. He turned up the pan heat and cracked in three eggs, carefully scrambling them together with a silicone spatula. He took long, light strokes, counting the seconds: thirty with the pan on the heat, thirty off, three minutes in total. As the eggs coalesced, he added a spoonful of Greek yoghurt, lowering their temperature, ensuring they didn't overcook. At 5:24, he buttered the toast, seasoned the eggs, and served them with snippings of fresh chives.

Lennox opened the wall cupboard and took out a glass tumbler. He set it on the granite kitchen island next to the plate of eggs and opened the fridge, pausing for a second as he surveyed the options in the door shelf.

He selected a carton of organic orange juice, closed the fridge door, then reached up to the wall cupboard and took out a glass tumbler.

As he pivoted to set the glass down next to the eggs, his arm swept the first glass over the edge of the island. It fell, and shattered across the slate-tiled floor, the height of the drop spreading the fragments wide.

Lennox stood frozen for a moment, stunned by the violence of the sound.

He squatted by the sink and took out a dustpan and brush, then swept the glass into the pan.

He'd need the vacuum to get it all.

Some might get caught in the brush.

But he could vacuum the brush.

His phone rang, vibrating on the kitchen island.

The cooker clock read 5:31.

Lennox checked the caller ID: Khokhar.

He set down the pan and brush, then tapped the answer button.

'Oz?' She sounded clipped, tense.

'I'm here.'

'How soon can you get to Harpenden?'

He stared at the mess on the floor, the untouched eggs. Order collapsed into chaos.

'About thirty minutes. Why?'

'You were right. He's back.'

Chapter Twenty-Five

Lennox parked his Volvo V60 Estate in a lay-by near a low hedge near the outer cordon. He took a lungful of sharp morning air and approached the cluster of marked and unmarked vehicles gathered at the end of the circular driveway. The house was red brick, Georgian style, with broad sash windows and a portico entrance.

As he signed in with the uniformed officer, DI Whitmore came out from the drive and lifted the bright yellow crime scene tape. 'Good morning, sir.'

'I'll reserve judgement,' said Lennox, ducking under the tape. 'Talk me through it.'

Whitmore led the way. 'Two vics. Daniel Foster, twenty-eight, and Lara Tanner, twenty-six. ID at scene. The place is owned by Malcolm Foster, Daniel's uncle. He's the CEO of a FinTech firm based in Shoreditch. Currently in Singapore, on his way back. Daniel was house-sitting, feeding Malcolm's two cats. We assume Lara is his girlfriend.'

'His first double kill,' said Lennox. 'And his first female. Is that the owner's car?' He pointed to a white Tesla Model

3 with all doors open, parked at the house end of the driveway. Two forensic officers in Tyvek suits inspected the exterior, while another leaned into the interior from the passenger door.

'Yes. Digital forensics say it was driven here around 10pm on the 14th, three nights ago. Key fob was with Daniel's belongings.'

As they reached the portico, Lennox nodded to a young male detective standing at a folding table beside a plastic crate.

Whitmore saw the nod. 'Scene manager is—'

'DS Walden,' said Lennox.

'Sir.' Walden nodded. He opened the crate and took out shoe covers and nitrile gloves. 'No need for mask. No biohazard.'

Lennox signed Walden's logbook and put on the shoe covers and gloves. He strode away towards the house. 'Who found them?'

Whitmore caught up. 'Daniel had pledged to check in every other day. When he missed two and didn't answer his phone, Malcolm asked the cleaner to come over late last night.'

'Entry?'

'Looks like an unlocked window around the back.' She shrugged. 'Consistent. He doesn't do force.'

Lennox nodded. 'Or he's just been lucky so far. All the previous killings happened during the summer.'

At the solid oak front door, Lennox leaned in close and slowly ran his eyes along the edge of the frame. SOCO David Pearson emerged from inside and stood watching.

'David,' said Lennox, keeping his focus on the frame.

'Sir.'

Lennox crouched as he reached the bottom of the frame. 'Where are the cats?'

'Fed and watered,' said Pearson. 'Fur samples and clippings taken. Currently at RSPCA Southridge.'

Lennox stood up. 'Does Lara have blonde hair?'

'Yes,' said Whitmore.

He pointed to a long strand caught in the weather stripping.

Pearson checked. 'Good spot.' He forced a grin. 'We haven't got to fibres yet, though.'

'Anything else?'

'Not so far.'

Lennox looked down the hall, through a window at the back of the house. A group of Tyvek-suited forensic officers stood in conference out in the garden. 'Vehicles?'

'Multiple tyre tracks at roadside. Erosion and waterlogging from rain early yesterday.' He winced, shook his head.

Lennox took a few steps into the hallway, looking up and around. The entrance hall was grand, with a high corniced ceiling and a central chandelier that projected prismatic reflections. The walls were hung with gilt-framed oil paintings and baroque mirrors, and a wide staircase with a polished mahogany banister curved up to the first floor.

The air was heavy with the mingled scents of expensive room fragrance and the taint of decay.

Whitmore showed her warrant card to a sentry officer outside the closed door. Lennox did likewise and followed Whitmore inside. The sitting room was deep and wide, with windows draped in heavy velvet curtains. A grand fireplace dominated one wall, its mantel loaded with ornamentation and family photographs in silver frames. The furniture had been pushed aside, creating a large open space in the centre where the bodies lay.

Lennox approached, scanning the scene. The two victims lay fully clothed on the dark hardwood floor, surrounded by an intricate array of small animal bones.

Daniel lay on his back, arms outstretched, his white T-shirt stained dark with dried blood. Lara lay beside him, her head angled towards his chest in a macabre parody of intimacy. Her blonde hair was matted with blood, spreading out across Daniel's torso like a gruesome fan.

Lennox squatted by the bodies, taking care not to step on the animal bones. The waxy, greenish tinge of Lara and Daniel's skin was consistent with several days' decomposition.

He sniffed the air. The subtle odour of initial putrefaction was giving way to a pungent, acidic smell. He caught notes of rotten eggs from the sulphur-based compounds; sickly-sweetness from the decaying flesh; a musty, compost-like scent from the protein breakdown; a sharp ammonia-like tang from the degrading urea.

Lennox could taste the stench, feel its weight on his tongue. But he found a queasy sense of comfort in the odour. It was the essence of transformation: an alert to the ecosystem, announcing the bounty of death; a complex organism reverting to its basic components, primed to fuel the next cycle of life. *Daniel* and *Lara* were labels, conceived by other similarly labelled organisms for convenience. Their brief lives were lived, and it was his job to find meaning in their deaths.

Both victims' throats bore deep, clean incisions, the edges of the wounds precise and unjagged. Their eyes were open, gazing sightlessly at the vaulted ceiling. Around them, the carefully arranged bones formed patterns: spirals, concentric circles, and what looked like crude representations of anatomical structures.

Lennox scrutinised the scene, turning his head slightly as he cycled through the details.

There were no defensive wounds on their hands and arms, and the fingernails looked clean and intact. Like the others, they were incapacitated before the killing blows.

Lividity was consistent with their current position. They hadn't been moved post-mortem.

Subtle differences in the depth and angle of the throat incisions.

The considered positioning of the bodies and the decorative bone arrangements spoke of an unrushed and meticulous post-slaughter procedure. As with the previous victims, the murders were clean, efficient. Nothing sadistic or overtly brutal. Was the killing a means to an end? Was it the ritual itself that fulfilled him?

Lennox expected little trace evidence to track the killer. They would find him by decoding his patterns, clarifying his needs.

'Reminds me of the Radlett murder,' said Whitmore.

Lennox pointed to a small cluster of vertebrae near Daniel's left hand. 'Avian?'

'I think so,' said Pearson.

Lennox stood, his knees cracking. He kept his eyes fixed on the bodies. 'Get the Intelligence Cell started on victimology. Fast-track PM. Same with forensics. Keep it in-house at Hendon for maximum confidentiality. Divert every available resource. Refer any stalling to me directly.' He angled his head towards Pearson. 'How long?'

The SOCO pondered. 'Late afternoon?'

'Briefing for midday. These two will be his last.'

Chapter Twenty-Six

Blackwood's desk vibrated with the increased activity on the MIT floor. Detectives stomped around, consulting, breaking away in twos and threes, hurrying in and out. She switched off noise-cancelling on her AirPods and tried to tune in to the chatter. But the row of temporary desks was too far from the nerve centre, and she could only catch the odd word from a raised voice.

One of the male DIs slammed down his phone, ending a call, and sprang to his feet. 'Harpenden,' he said to a colleague, and spun away, heading for the double doors leading to the lift corridor.

He stepped back as the doors opened and Lennox entered. The man tagged alongside Lennox as he strode along the central channel of desks, head down, then fell back as he accelerated into his office and closed the door behind him.

Blackwood waited for the male DI to leave, then headed over to Lennox's office. She tapped on the door and entered, hovering in the frame.

He was at his desk, eyes on his computer screen. 'Timing isn't great.'

'Sorry, sir. I've finished DI Whitmore's casework and emailed you the completed admin.'

He waved a hand. 'Ask around. Someone will give you something else.'

'This is starting to feel like work experience.'

Lennox looked up, scowling. 'What you feel like isn't my concern. I've been thrown into a major development and I need you to manage yourself. I'll check in later.'

Blackwood started to back out. 'Is it the Bones Killer?'

He sighed. 'Why do you say that?'

She eased in to the office, closed the door. 'I heard someone mention Harpenden. That fits with the geographical profile. It might tell us—'

'I appreciate your insight,' said Lennox, pushing back his chair. 'But this is a longstanding enquiry and there's plenty else for you to work on. Speak to one of the other DIs. Not Whitmore.'

Blackwood took a seat. 'Why not?'

'She's needed on this enquiry. We have to reshuffle.' He focused back on the screen. 'PC Blackwood, I welcome your enthusiasm, but I have a briefing to prepare.'

'What's this?' She reached over and picked up an item on Lennox's desk: a vintage-looking egg timer with a polished brass frame engraved with floral patterns. The curves of the design give it an organic, flowing appearance, contrasting with the precision of its function.

Blackwood held the timer up to the window, admiring its tinted blue glass bulbs and deep burgundy sand. She tipped it upside-down. The sand transferred smoothly into the bottom bulb.

'A gift from my father,' said Lennox. 'Apparently it's an antique. He cares about that kind of thing.'

Blackwood marvelled at the falling sand glittering in the light. 'What does he do?'

'He was a barrister. Retired now.'

She placed the timer back on the desk and tucked her hair behind her ear. 'I had an idea for a business once. Egg timers with the ashes of loved ones instead of sand. Keep them around after they're gone.' She grinned. 'They can help in the kitchen.'

Lennox laid his hands on the edge of the desk, palms down. 'What do you want?'

'A challenge.'

He gave a quizzical smile. 'The casework is too easy for you?'

'Yes. No... Not too easy. Just... It's not what my brain is good at.'

'And what is your brain good at?'

She took out a pen, twirled it across her fingers, left to right, then back again. 'Something live and moving. Something interesting and... peopley.'

Lennox angled his head. 'Peopley?'

'I'm not great with the documents, reports, spreadsheets.'

'Sadly, that's what gets you access to the peopley stuff.'

Blackwood's knee bounced. She stared for a moment, then shook herself out of the reverie. 'The work is okay, but I was hoping for something stronger.'

Lennox held her eye. 'You can help by rebuilding the Bones Killer casework based on the fresh development and evidence. Work with the Intelligence Cell. That's a group of specialist detectives processing evidence and reports.'

Blackwood tipped back her head, exasperated. She

twirled the pen. Left to right. Right to left. Repeat. 'With respect, sir. That sounds like more of the same.'

'No. It's not. It's working on an active enquiry. So far, you've been helping process admin for closed cases. I can't fast-track you because you're bored. This isn't the kind of work where you can learn on the job. You gather experience, bit by bit, and the experience moves you up, bit by bit.'

The pen spun faster. She stopped, pocketed it. 'Sorry. Stimming.'

He nodded. 'An ADHD trait.'

She looked at him, shocked.

'Self-soothing. You think I didn't bother to read up on you? When were you diagnosed?'

'A few years ago. It's the reason for the peopley bias. Some of us see numbers and columns of figures and statistics and they're in heaven. It makes me want to run and hide in a hole.'

Lennox got up, headed for the coffee machine. He took down the sky-blue Le Creuset mug. 'I knew a firearms officer with ADHD. You couldn't trust him to sign his name, but he was brilliant on operations.'

'He would have seen things before others. Been able to scatter his attention wider. Make super-quick decisions. Because he was engaged with the work. Sounds like he found his calling.'

Lennox poured in the beans. 'Americano?'

'Please.'

'Look,' said Lennox, standing with his back to her. 'Help with the Intelligence Cell. Try to see it as an opportunity. I need to re-galvanise the team. You can play a part, but it might not be as peopley as you'd like.' He looked over his shoulder. 'I might not be so available for you. DI Whitmore will fill the gap.'

She flashed him a wry smile. 'So, you're dumping me.'

'Don't be ridiculous. I'm just saying things are going to get busy. If you want to keep shadowing me, you'll need to be agile and lateral. You'll also need to learn to cope with process. And setbacks. Don't interpret non-contact as rejection. This is part of what's been holding you back.' He handed her the coffee.

Blackwood stared into the mug. 'It wouldn't be the first time you've rejected me.'

Lennox busied himself with setting up his own coffee. He turned. 'What do you mean?'

'I thought you might have realised by now. But I'm not so sure.' She tried a sip of coffee, winced at the heat. 'Abigail Ashbourne.'

A cloud passed over Lennox's features. He rubbed at his temple. 'What about her?'

'She was my best friend. We grew up together. We were practically sisters. When she disappeared, it was like a bereavement for me. Just after uni, before I joined the police, I started a podcast looking into it. I think I wanted to be a journalist then. So, I researched the detectives who'd worked on her case. You were the SIO. I sent you an interview request. You said no.'

Lennox turned again, took his ultraviolet mug and sat down. 'I was probably busy. It was a long time ago.'

She brightened. 'It's okay. It's probably not your fault.'

'What do you mean?'

'I can take knockbacks too personally. It's another ADHD trait. RSD. Rejection-Sensitive Dysphoria. Feeling deep pain when you sense rejection or failure or abandonment.'

Lennox swirled his coffee around. 'I was the official SIO on Abigail's case for three years until it wound down. You must realise by now, she hasn't moved to some secret island to start a new life. The files are full of people who disappeared without trace. The longer someone's missing, the less likely they'll be found.' His tone softened. 'I'm not rejecting you. I have to prioritise an active case. Abigail went missing fourteen years ago. I now have two people who were murdered this week.'

'Two people?' said Blackwood.

He nodded.

'Your instincts were right. He was overdue. But it's more data.'

Lennox took a drink. 'Yes. The more he kills, the easier it'll be to spot patterns.' He pondered. 'Come to the live briefing. Strictly a non-speaking role. Embrace the process. If you lose focus and take everything personally, you'll get left behind. I don't have the energy to carry you.'

'Have you ever come across the name *Mr Shade*?'

'No.'

'How about The Ivory Room? Something to do with Primrose Hill? A white lion?'

Lennox stared ahead, eyes narrowing.

Blackwood sprang to her feet. 'Oh, my god!'

'What?'

'Sir,' she breathed, pointing. 'There's a peregrine falcon on the roof across the way.'

Lennox walked over and followed Blackwood's finger to the blue-grey bird perched on the rooftop of an adjacent building. Its pointed wings and facial markings were unmistakable.

'They've adapted well to urban environments,' said

Blackwood, her voice hushed with excitement. 'They nest on tall buildings, hunting pigeons and other city birds.'

'They're apex predators,' said Lennox.

'They certainly are. Top of the food chain. Once they've locked on to their prey, it doesn't stand a chance. Their diving speed can reach over two hundred miles an hour. Fastest animal on the planet.'

Lennox looked out at the bird for a moment, seemingly rapt. Blackwood shifted her eyes towards him, ran them down to his right hand, which seemed steady enough, then up to his face. His blue eyes sparkled, but his gaze seemed unfocused, as if he were looking at a point beyond the bird rather than at it.

A knock on the door.

Blackwood pivoted as Whitmore entered.

'Sorry to interrupt, sir. I thought we could prep the briefing.' Lennox didn't turn. 'Sir?'

'Jonah loved birds,' he said.

Chapter Twenty-Seven

Blackwood slipped into a seat at the back of the Monro Room and took out her Post-it notes. The meeting was more select than last time, with plenty of space in the forward rows, and only a few detectives taking their place in the higher section.

'In with the big boys.'

She looked to the end of her row. Dom sat in his usual spot alongside the female admin assistant with the braided ponytail.

'Yeah,' said Blackwood. 'What's going on?'

He eyed her. 'Looks like a case update. Just the main bodies involved.' He pointed, smiled. 'But I think you knew that.'

'I don't know that much. Lennox kicked me out of HOLMES.'

Dom shook his head. 'He would have sent me a note on that. I didn't get anything.' He nodded to the Post-its. 'You going analogue, then?'

The chatter softened as Lennox entered and hurried down the steps to the front.

'It's a system I've had since uni,' said Blackwood. 'Helps me organise bitty information to analyse later. Is that the big boss?' She pointed to the elegant woman with a teal hijab, sitting beside DCI Rafferty at the curved desk.

Dom nodded. 'DSI Aisha Khokhar. She's okay. I don't deal with her much.'

Lennox took his place at the front, tablet in hand. The ponytailed admin dimmed the lights and the video screen fired up, showing a still from the HOLMES hub.

OPERATION OSSUARY
MULTIPLE HOMICIDES WITH DISTINCTIVE MO
NORTH LONDON/HERTFORDSHIRE
2017-2024

Blackwood shifted in her seat. Something on the back-rest was digging into her shoulder. She leaned forward suddenly, drawing an abrasive squeal from the seat support.

A few detectives turned their heads, frowning.

She glanced at Dom, who was wincing, eyes screwed up, covering his ears.

'Sorry,' she said, too loud.

Lennox swiped at his tablet. The screen cycled through scene photos: a young man and woman sprawled on a hard-wood floor; close-ups of throat injuries; detail of animal bone arrangements similar to the previous murders.

'I hate to say it,' said Lennox, 'but I told you so. After a five-year break, I believe this is the work of the offender we've dubbed the Bones Killer. This individual is now responsible for the murders of five people. Before we begin, I commend DI Whitmore and her team on the fast and efficient early intelligence and analysis. Also, David Pearson's scenes-of-crime work. It's too early for a full post-mortem, but we have some initial pathologist findings.'

Lennox looked up at the screen.

Time crawled, as he stood stationary, regarding a close-up of the young man's head with open eyes.

Blackwood caught a look between Khokhar and DCI Rafferty.

'Daniel Foster,' continued Lennox. 'Twenty-eight. Lara Tanner. Twenty-six. MO, staging and lack of forced entry as seen in the previous killings. Location is also consistent. South Hertfordshire, although this one just slips over the border into North London. So, we have a firmer idea of his geographical comfort zone. You could argue that he's expanding his hunting ground, but the difference is nominal. Details are in HOLMES. The house has no camera coverage, but I want a sweep for CCTV in the area and along all major routes.' He paced for a moment. 'I want you to focus on the differences, not the similarities. This time, there are three new factors. One. This is the first time he's killed two people. All the other murders were individuals. We have to call that a significant escalation and find out why. Has his appetite increased over the years? Was he targeting one, and the other just happened to be present? Two. It's the first time he's killed a woman. Lara and Daniel were in a relationship. Is that significant? Is he escalating to couples?'

He swiped his tablet and the screen showed a close-up image of a curved fragment of finger or toe nail presented in an evidence bag, labelled with a case number and scale bar for size reference. 'Three. He left us a present. Probably not intentional. The previous scenes have yielded no meaningful trace evidence. As I've said, I believe he is highly forensically aware and executes a meticulous post-killing clean-up. At this scene, as with the others, there is evidence of thorough sanitising, including the absence of fingerprints on high-touch surfaces, lack of hair or fibres in expected areas, and a complete absence of DNA. We've detected residue from high-end industrial strength cleaning products, specifically a hydrogen peroxide-based solution commonly used in crime scene clean-up.' He paused for effect. 'But I think, this time, he missed something. David's team found this fragment of nail in a groove between the sitting-room floorboards. We have a full DNA profile from keratin and skin cells.'

'On the database?' said a male detective on the front row.

'Sadly, no. It's not from Lara or Daniel and we'll be cross-checking with anyone else who might have been in the house lately, including the owner. But at least we may have something to back us up when we ID a suspect.'

Blackwood scribbled a note about the nail on a green Post-it, and a few general details on an orange. She turned her head to see the ponytailed admin leaving the room by a side entrance. Dom shifted over a seat, further away.

Lennox switched the images to show close-ups of the victims' neck wounds. 'Cause of death for both was exsanguination due to a deep incision in the jugular. They're clean cuts, likely made with a sharp, straight-edged blade. As before, no defensive wounds on either victim, suggesting they were incapacitated before the attack. Prelim pathology shows each received a heavy blow to the head, subduing them before incapacitation.' He switched again, cycling through close-ups of the animal bone arrangements. 'It's the same story. Rodents, small mammals, birds. We assume he acquires the animals over time and stores the bones.'

'There's another difference,' said Khokhar.

Blackwood scribbled a note on a yellow Post-it: *low-grade vics?*

'Victimology,' said Rafferty.

'Yes,' said Lennox. 'In the previous killings, the victims were high-status individuals. This represents a shift. Daniel was a mid-tier management consultant. Lara was a primary school teacher. The house belongs to a wealthy individual, but our victims don't measure up to the Bones Killer's usual metric of social standing.'

'It could be coincidental,' said DI Whitmore on the front row.

Lennox nodded. 'The Intelligence Cell is running background checks on both victims. We need to look at connections to high-status individuals, potential links to previous victims.'

'What's the background on their relationship?' said Rafferty. 'Deep checks on the house owner... Maybe he expected the owner and was surprised to find Daniel and Lara.'

'And why the extra-long gap?' said another detective a few seats along from Blackwood.

'That's a puzzle we probably won't answer until we have a suspect,' said Lennox. 'Maybe he's been out of the country, suffered an illness, received treatment.'

Blackwood wrote an orange note: *killer in prison?*

'The one thing that hasn't changed,' continued Lennox, 'is the animal bones. What are they for? What do they represent? What need do they fulfil? I called a legacy briefing on this, but now we have a new murder, let's dedicate a section of the Intelligence Cell to psychopathology. I have a private behaviour analysis contact, but I want DI Whitmore's team and the Intelligence Cell to focus on data-driven investigative psychology. And let's enhance our geographical profile. Also, consult with the NCA behaviour unit for related offender patterns, risk factors, victimology, similar unsolved cases. DI Whitmore will lead the main thrust of the investigation. She'll assign tasks, manage media strategy. I'll be overseeing, consulting at resource level, coordinating with other departments as needed.'

He held up a hand.

Nothing happened. A few heads turned.

Dom sprang up and raised the lights. 'Sorry.'

Blackwood looked over, hoping to express solidarity at the lapse of attention, but Dom buried his head back into his laptop.

Lennox continued. 'For me, our general profile still stands. Our offender is not impulsive. He's methodical, meticulous, patient. He's intelligent, educated, with a probable interest in anatomy and possibly archaeology or anthropology.'

Khokhar shifted in her seat. 'That doesn't sound too data-driven, Oz.' She gave an indulgent smile.

'It'll be broadly accurate, ma'am.'

Khokhar leaned forward, keeping her eyes fixed on Lennox. 'I think we need to adjust our approach slightly. Given the complexity of this case, I'd like to draw on your vast experience in the realm of consultancy and resource management. DI Whitmore and her team should drive the live investigation, reporting to you, and benefiting from your knowledge of the case history.' She clapped her hands together, beamed at him. 'That means I get the best value from two of our brightest brains.'

Lennox's posture stiffened slightly. He took his time covering the tablet with its screen protector, then turned to

Khokhar, smiling. 'Whatever you feel serves the investigation best, ma'am.'

'Marvellous. And let's put out an immediate call for witnesses. Someone must have seen something out there.'

She stood and walked up the steps to the exit alongside Lennox. Blackwood watched them all the way.

At the door, Lennox slowed, giving Khokhar space to leave before him. But she reached over and touched a hand to his elbow, ushering him out first.

Blackwood leaned to the right, towards Dom. 'Well, that was tense,' she whispered.

She turned. His seat was empty.

Chapter Twenty-Eight

'It's been three years since we lost Emily.' The middle-aged woman smoothed out her short dyed-blonde hair and drew in a wavering breath. 'I'm sorry... Even saying her name like that... I can feel it. Here.' She patted a hand on the left of her chest.

The facilitator, a thirtysomething man with a thick but tightly groomed dark beard, leaned forward and rested his elbows on his crossed leg. 'Take it at your own pace, Rebecca. You're sharing. It's not a performance.'

Lennox sat rigid in his chair, hands clasped on his lap. He usually travelled to the community centre in Golders Green straight from work, but this time he'd gone home, prepared, changed into a polo shirt and fitted chinos.

The group convened annually, courtesy of The Compassionate Friends, in a stuffy side room that smelt of cleaning supplies. Most TCF groups were general peer support for bereaved parents and grandparents. Some, like this one, covered a specific type of loss.

They sat slumped on moulded plastic chairs arranged in

a ragged circle. The scuffed off-white walls were plastered with posters for yoga sessions, children's art classes, coffee mornings. A corner table held a cheap kettle, a few mismatched mugs, and an unopened packet of Digestives.

Lennox glanced at the woman by his side. Martha sat tall but kept her gaze on the scratched linoleum floor. She looked older than her fifty years, with silver-streaked auburn hair and sharp lines around her eyes, softened by the light tint in her large-framed glasses. She cradled her coffee mug with slender, ringless fingers.

Rebecca took out a tissue. She dabbed at her eyes, then twisted the tissue in her hand as she addressed the circle. 'The last day plays over and over in my head. It's like that film.'

'*Groundhog Day*,' said the man next to her.

'Yes. I see it all. On good days, I imagine it not happening the way it did.' She faltered; the man reached over and squeezed her hand. 'We go out to the restaurant, we come home, and there she is, making her tea and toast. On bad days, I only notice all the things I could have done. Should have done.'

She lowered her head, faltering again.

'You're doing very well, Rebecca,' said the facilitator. 'Take all the time you need.'

She nodded, managed a smile. 'One of the hardest things is watching her friends grow up. One of them, Helen, got married a few weeks ago.' She sniffled. 'Helen used to come for play dates and now she's an adult with her own life.' Rebecca glanced at the man holding her hand. 'It's like a constant reminder of what we'll never have.' She wiped her eyes, rallied. 'But I'm learning to enjoy those memories for their preciousness. For how they made me feel. Rather than being sad because I'll never feel them in that way again.'

Rebecca dropped her head: a signal that she'd finished. The man slipped an arm around her shoulders.

'Thank you so much for sharing that, Rebecca,' said the facilitator. 'It takes a lot of courage to speak so openly about your child, and your words mean a lot to everyone here. Your memories keep Emily's spirit alive with us.'

Lennox watched as he dipped his head in a moment of silence, taking the opportunity to check his watch.

He looked up again. 'We have a few more minutes if anyone else would like to speak.'

'I'd like to say something,' said Lennox in a quiet but firm voice. 'Sorry it's taken me a while.' He saw Martha's head turn to him in his peripheral vision. Her hand came over, holding his, fingers warm from the coffee mug.

'It's wonderful to hear your voice, Oswald,' said the facilitator. 'Take all the time you need.'

Lennox kept his gaze fixed at a point just above the heads of the group members. 'Jonah Alexander Lennox. Born 17th September 1998 at 3:42am. Died 15th June 2014 at approximately 4:15pm.' He paused, swallowed. 'Those are the facts. The data points that bookend my son's life.' He unclenched his hands, spreading his fingers wide on his knees. Martha gently withdrew her hand. 'Jonah was funny. He was a fan of 1970s and 1980s British comedy, probably because I watched a lot with him when he was younger. You could hear it in his sense of humour. Sharp, articulate. He had great timing. I always thought he was going to be a stand-up comedian or a comedy writer. I taught him to cook, and he quickly started to teach me. He was a knowledge sponge.' Lennox smiled, looked at Martha. 'We don't know where he picked it all up from. He knew every country's flag, all the US states and their locations on a map. He wanted to visit the US to see for himself. He was obsessed with nature and developing an interest in ecology and climate issues, economics. But he was a teenager, so he was mostly into video games, football, girls, mates. He had a phase of learning to play drums. Then guitar. He had his sulky moments, but he could also hit you with this crooked smile. And it just lit you up inside.'

Lennox shifted his gaze to the facilitator, then looked around at the other parents in the circle, as if waiting for one of them to speak.

'You're doing well, Oswald,' said the facilitator, smiling.

Lennox darkened. 'But around two years before his death, Jonah became distant. He shut himself away, took food up to his room, only spoke to us when he really had to. We put it down to teenage hormones, but it felt much deeper. It was like a cloud had moved over him, blocking out his sun.' Lennox took a breath. 'I'm a detective. My ex-wife is a doctor. A cardiologist. We solve mysteries. We assess evidence and facts, then apply our knowledge to diagnose and demystify. With Jonah, we have so many facts. There is so much we know. But none of it helps to solve his mystery. We know the whats and whens, but we have no idea why our brilliant, loving young boy chose to end his life at the age of fifteen.'

Martha's hand gripped Lennox's fingers. He curled them into a fist.

'At first, it felt like a rejection. A brutal dismissal of all the love we'd poured into him. But now, my feelings have matured, and I understand that Jonah's pain was not about me or us. It is beyond anything we can reasonably comprehend. It remains a mystery, with no clues. He left us no explanation, no note. As if he was challenging us to work it out for ourselves.' Lennox took his hand away, covered his eyes with both palms. 'I used to wish I could wipe the entire experience of my son from my mind, just to escape that limbo. But lately, I feel the opposite. A desperation to hold on to every detail.' He took his hands away. 'I have an extremely good memory, which is a gift and a curse. I don't just remember events, I remember expressions. How I was feeling. Vivid sensory details. So I'm trying to use that, and project the fifteen-year-old Jonah into the present with me. I hear his voice speaking to me, comforting me. I never go to his grave because I don't feel I have to.' Tears came now, tracking down the grooves between his nose and cheeks, running into his mouth. The facilitator offered a box of tissues but he waved it away, savouring the sting in his eyes, the salty taste. 'Please don't misunderstand me. I accept Jonah is part of my history and he will never cook for me again. He will never go to the US, marry, grow old. But he is not lost. I don't believe that he is following me around or hovering over me, like some spirit. But he is in me. I don't see him, but I do feel him. And I hear him. Speaking to me calmly. Quietly. Without drama. A voice in my ear. The past inside the present. And I am terrified that the voice will fade away, fall silent. And those memories of him will degrade, and I will lose touch with him. And that will feel like him leaving me all over again.'

Chapter Twenty-Nine

Blackwood awoke, gently shaken by a hand on her shoulder.

'*Resting your eyes?*'

She lifted her head off her arms, looked up from the desk. Lennox gazed down at her, suppressing an indulgent smile. He'd swapped his usual charcoal suit for dove-grey with a light lavender shirt and plum tie.

Blackwood tidied her hair, reached for her Costa cup. 'My eyes are fine.' She took a sip: tepid but she drank anyway. 'Brain was running hot, though. You're looking sharp, sir.'

Lennox nodded. 'That was the idea.' He glanced at the wall clock. 'It's early.'

'Couldn't sleep.'

He turned, headed for his office. 'Join the club.'

Blackwood followed for a few steps, stopped, scurried back to her desk. She grabbed the coffee cup, then scooped up a pile of curling Post-it notes and jogged across the floor after Lennox.

The MIT office was quiet, with only a few detectives at their desks.

Lennox unlocked his office.

'One or two other early starters,' she said

'They're late finishers.' He stepped inside. 'I have an appointment first thing. What's your excuse?'

She followed. 'Racing thoughts. Lots of ideas after the briefing yesterday. Can I come in?'

'You're already in.' Lennox opened his blinds, went to the coffee machine. 'Let's hear these ideas. Let me guess... Colonel Mustard. Candlestick. Conservatory.'

Blackwood took the seat facing Lennox's desk. 'Is that Cluedo?'

He lifted the lid, inhaled the aroma. 'Yes.'

'You're being facetious.'

'I can see why you want to be a detective.' He poured in the beans.

'I can't do board games.' Blackwood slurped her coffee. 'Too much waiting for people to take their turn.'

'You use that time to plan your next move.'

'That takes a couple of seconds. Then it's just waiting.'

Lennox set the Jura brewing and turned. He took out his phone and navigated to something. Low-volume music drifted from a white Apple HomePod speaker in the corner: an elongated synth chord with a sparse and ethereal piano melody playing over the top.

'What's this?' said Blackwood.

'Nils Frahm. German.'

'Ambient.'

He tilted his head. 'Well, yes. Although that sounds like an insult.'

She took another gulp of coffee. 'No, no. I like it. I like music where nothing happens. It's soothing.'

Lennox turned back to the machine, gathered his mug. 'I hear a lot happening. Depending on my mood.'

'I remember my dad playing classical music a lot when I was little.'

'I'm making you a fresh coffee. It's turning my stomach seeing you drink that gunge.'

'Correction. Cold gunge.'

'What did your dad do?'

Blackwood sorted through her Post-it notes: orange, yellow, green. 'Architect. I don't remember him that much. He died when I was seven. Brain tumour. He was thirty-nine.'

'Sorry to hear that.' He handed her the sky-blue mug, then perched on the far edge of his desk, sipping his coffee, gazing out of the window at the low-rise Hendon suburbs, bleary in the dawn light.

'If you're looking for peregrines,' said Blackwood, 'it's too early. They're not active until later in the morning when the air warms up and creates thermals for them to ride.'

He nodded. 'Ideas.'

Blackwood took a sip of Lennox's coffee. 'Wow. Is this extra strong?'

'Death Wish. It's a blend of arabica and robusta beans. Chocolate, smoky wood, cherry. High caffeine content. It's my morning coffee. I get it from a specialist place in Covent Garden.'

'Well, I'm definitely awake now.'

'Caffeine doesn't really wake you up. It blocks the neurotransmitter that makes you feel drowsy. It's more like tricking your brain into thinking it's not tired.'

'But it stimulates dopamine, though, right?'

Lennox smiled. 'Yes.' He walked around his desk and sat down. 'Ideas.'

Blackwood sorted through the notes. 'I was looking through the Bones Killer file late last night, then more this morning. Once I get my head into something my brain is enjoying, I can lose track of time. Forget to drink or eat.' She looked up, saw that Lennox was scowling. 'Sorry, sir. Should I be speaking to DI Whitmore about this?'

He sighed, adjusted his tie. 'I'm the Senior Investigating Officer. The moment yesterday was simply DSI Khokhar directing me to give DI Whitmore more responsibility. I still own the case actions. Whitmore is good. You should see her as a model. I'm frowning because I'm confused. I thought I revoked your HOLMES access.'

'Actually, you didn't. Sir. I can still get in.'

A flicker of concern passed over Lennox. 'I'm sure I asked IT to revoke your access. Remember? You said it was probably a good thing.'

'I know, but it's still... Sorry, sir. I shouldn't have—'

He waved a hand. 'Never mind. Maybe I forgot. Ideas.'

'Okay.' Blackwood sat up. 'I noticed that the second and third victims used the same private city bank as the first.' She checked her notes. 'Handelsbanken. It's Swedish. Personalised banking services.'

Lennox sat back. 'We looked into that connection. Many firms use the bank, and it employs hundreds of people. The victims were high-earners, so it wouldn't be unusual for them to be customers. But good lateral thinking.'

She sifted through the Post-its. 'I also noticed the direction of the slash wounds on the previous victims were left to right, but on Lara and Daniel they were right to left.' Blackwood mimed the motion with the edge of her hand.

Lennox took a long drink of coffee. 'And what do you draw from that?'

'Maybe the killer injured his right hand subduing Lara and Daniel, and had to use his left?'

'And how does that help us?'

Blackwood faltered. She opened and closed her mouth without sound. Thoughts rolled through her mind like slot machine reels.

'I'm sure the pathologist will highlight the difference in his full PM,' said Lennox, keeping his tone measured. 'It's a good spot and I like the theory. But until we can find a suspect who matches the nail DNA and who has an injured right hand or who visited A&E with a right-hand injury, it doesn't help much.'

A silence lingered. Blackwood held Lennox's eye, waiting for more. But nothing came. Was he waiting for her to respond? His expression was benign, but he seemed momentarily suspended, stuck on stand-by.

She broke the moment by looking back down at her lap and shuffling through her Post-its. 'There was one more thing... I noted all the dates of the body discoveries along with estimated times of death, then cross-checked with records for unsolved regional crime a few days before and a few days after.' She glanced up at Lennox, then back down at her notes. 'I read something recently about how serious offenders often commit other offences in the build-up to main crimes, and sometimes after, as a sort of warm-down. I wondered if there could be any relevant unsolveds around the time of the bones killings. Mix and match trace evidence...'

Blackwood looked up at Lennox. He was smiling.

Intrigued or pitying?

She continued, studying her notes again. 'I couldn't find any potential in unsolved murders. But there were two drownings. One in June 2018, the other in August 2019.

Both just after the second and third bones killings. The first was found in the River Lea. The second in the Grand Union Canal, Rickmansworth. The first body was spotted by cyclists riding through Tottenham Marshes. It was caught on a submerged tree branch near a footbridge. The second was found by a barge owner. Something snagged on his rudder.' She looked up again. 'Divers found the body.'

Lennox gave a slow nod. 'Keep going. What do you suggest we do with this information?'

Blackwood shrugged. 'Exhume the bodies. Check for trace evidence that matches the second and third scenes. Look deeper into victimology for connections. The post-mortems concluded death by drowning. Do them again, to see if—'

'It sounds to me,' said Lennox gently, 'like you've found something you were looking for, and then exaggerated the significance. How many drownings occur in the Greater London area over the course of a year?'

Blackwood bit her lip.

Slow it down.

'Ten to fifteen. I checked it. Around five are unexplained or marked by the coroner as open verdict. That's the case with both these deaths.'

Lennox stared into his mug. 'That's low, yes, but the most likely explanation is suicide or difficult swimming conditions or intoxication. And both deaths occurred in summer, when people often drown trying to cool off.'

Breathe.

Blackwood tried to reset with a quick look out of the window. She turned back to Lennox. 'I found another drowning, still under investigation. A man named Derek Simmons. He became homeless two months ago after losing his job.' Her voice softened. 'He was found by a park ranger in the River Colne, near Watford, two days after the estimated time of death for Lara and Daniel. Maybe the killer is taking easy prey as a chaser or dessert after the main course?'

Lennox barked an unkind laugh. 'This is pure speculation.'

Blackwood floundered. 'I'm just saying... Since the Simmons death is fresh and matches the patterns associated with the second and third bones killings, we could prime the pathologist to—'

'But why would the killer bother with this?'

A rush of irritation flared through Blackwood. 'We still don't know why he kills the primary victims.' She lowered her voice. 'So this is only as speculative as everything else. There is a pattern, sir.'

Lennox held up a hand. 'Okay. Check in with DI Whitmore. Get acquainted with the Intelligence Cell. I'm happy for you to look deeper into the drowning victims, but I doubt you'll find any connection to the bones killings.' He took a breath, eased off the edge in his voice. 'PC Blackwood. I worry that, again, you're trying too hard to impress. Remember what we talked about? Follow the process. Don't get distracted by—'

'Side quests? Like in video games.'

'Or sub-plots.' He finished his coffee. 'Let's get back to the main thrust. I'm due to see an expert today, to consult on the psychopathology.'

She pointed. 'So, that's why you've scrubbed up.' He raised an eyebrow. 'Sorry.'

Lennox rose to his feet. 'Now we have a fresh killing, insight into psychopathology is more urgent. I'm happy for you to come along. I think you'll like him.'

Chapter Thirty

Blackwood hurried to keep pace with Lennox as he marched past the shuttered nightclubs of Old Compton Street. She followed him into Greek Street, shielding her eyes from the morning sun seeping into the narrow lanes.

He stopped at the blue-and-white awning of the Maison Bertaux patisserie and studied the rack of freshly baked cakes and pastries.

'Is this a tailing test?' said Blackwood.

Lennox kept his eyes on the window. 'What do you mean?'

'I get the feeling you're trying to lose me.'

'Sorry. I'm not much of a stroller. Not out here, anyway.'

Blackwood swooned at the scents wafting from the café: zesty citrus from the fruit in the cooling tarts, caramelised sugar from their crusts; the buttery, golden layers of baking croissants.

'Breakfast?' she said.

'I lost my sweet tooth a long time ago. I need to get our host something. He's a treat fiend.' Lennox disappeared inside.

Blackwood hung back and marvelled at Soho in limbo: delivery drivers hefting fresh produce over stacked seating; jaded hedonists surfacing from basement bars, shambling home to their unmade beds.

Lennox emerged and hurried past, holding a large brown paper bag in both hands, keeping it flat. 'Frangipane.'

She tagged along. 'I used to come here a lot when I moved to London. Feels so different these days.'

'Where are you from?'

'Ware.'

Lennox glanced at her. 'Yes.'

Blackwood smiled. 'This is the joke of my life. Ware is where I'm from. *W, A, R, E*. It's a tiny town in the middle of nowhere. Well, Hertfordshire. Mobility scooters and charity shops. You?'

'Richmond.'

They crossed the main road and turned into Dean Street.

'Oh,' she said. 'So you are quite posh.'

'Genetically speaking.' Lennox looked around at the weathered Georgian facades. 'Complaining that Soho has gone downhill is a London cliché. But it's true.'

'Rising rents.'

He nodded. 'Pricing out indie businesses. Then you get tighter licensing regulations. Everything gets sanitised, homogenised. It was fun while it lasted. But money has a habit of spoiling fun. Even the LGBT crowd is leaving.'

'LGBTQ+,' said Blackwood.

He side-eyed her. 'Technically, LGBTQIA+. But by the time you've said that, the bad guys are long gone.'

'The fringes are being pushed out to the fringes,' said Blackwood. 'Vauxhall is the new Soho. And Shoreditch, Peckham.'

They stopped outside a converted Georgian townhouse with tall windows covered by wrought-iron railings.

'When I was a DS,' said Lennox, 'I attended a call in Peckham about a noisy gathering. Turned out to be a group of elderly naturists who had locked themselves out of their meeting hall. I had to arrange their re-entry.'

'That sounds like a dad joke. You had them covered.'

Lennox gave her a dim look, then stepped up to the black front door, beside a discreet metal wall plate with buttons and intercom. A set of narrow stone steps led down to a basement flat. 'I think you'll like Guillermo, but he can be challenging. He loves his sugar, but he's not all sweet.'

Dr Guillermo Cabrera's office was larger than Blackwood expected. The low ceiling extended under the pavement, with exposed pipes painted black. A panelled corner desk sat at the far end, beneath a slim horizontal window that drew meagre light from street level. The walls were almost completely obscured by oversized posters and original artworks—Dalí, Munch, Magritte—and a series of smaller prints depicting a nightmarish fusion of flesh and machine. A beautiful charcoal sketch of a decaying high-rise cityscape overlooked the desk.

'Those are original Gigers,' said Cabrera, standing behind the desk. 'The sketch is Beksiński. Polish. A fascinating character. Rather jovial, despite these testaments to human frailty. Riddled with neuroses, though. He was murdered by his caretaker's son. Stabbed seventeen times.'

Cabrera was a tall, twiggy man in his early seventies, with a bald head and fulsome white beard and moustache. His heavily lined skin was the colour of burnished gold, and he wore a vibrant tomato-red jacket and trousers with a thin black polo-neck.

He flopped into his seat and gestured to a Chesterfield sofa at the foot of an overstuffed bookcase.

Blackwood sat, but Lennox browsed the stack of vinyl records on a shelf above a custom hi-fi system while Cabrera tore open Lennox's brown paper package. The pastry was a rich brown, lightly scorched, with crimped edges and a fan of pear slices in the centre.

'*¡Qué alegría!*' said Cabrera. 'You bring me such delight, Oswald. I only hope I can return the favour.'

He spun his chair and faced a vintage drinks trolley wedged into the corner, stocked with an eclectic mix of spirits and mixers. 'It's a bit early for a proper drink, but perhaps a mineral water?'

'I'm fine, thanks,' said Lennox, taking a seat beside Blackwood.

Cabrera poured himself a glass, then spun back to face them. He flashed a set of porcelain-white teeth at Blackwood. 'How about you, my dear?'

'No, thank you.'

The desk held a slim orange iMac beside a stack of folders and a small rainbow flag tucked into a pen holder.

Cabrera drank, then clunked the glass down on the desk. 'So, you're a trainee.'

Blackwood glanced at Lennox; he stared ahead. 'Mentee.'

Cabrera beamed, unfurled a hand theatrically towards

Lennox. 'And this is your mentor. How wonderful. Sharing that brilliant mind at last. You don't know how lucky you are. But you will, as long as you're not into real music.'

Lennox looked at her. 'That's a point of contention.'

'Yes,' said Cabrera. 'I know I am old-fashioned, but for me, an instrument requires physical contact. Intimacy, dexterity. Piano. Guitar.' He waved his arms in the air. 'A comb with a piece of paper would work. Oswald is more of a muzak man.' He regarded Lennox with a roguish smile, braced for a response. Nothing came. 'But I'm a forensic psychiatrist, not a music critic.' He pointed at Blackwood. 'I see you're on the team.'

'Sorry?'

'The hair. The purple streak.'

She laughed. 'Well... Fluid, I suppose.'

His eyes widened. 'Ah! Best way to be. To sup from both cups. A wider playing field.' He turned to Lennox. 'So, is this an open discussion, Oswald?'

'PC Blackwood knows the case, yes. But, as ever, we're off the record.'

Cabrera clapped his hands, then rubbed them together. 'Excellent. I know police brass think of me as a pseud. They like to follow their trails, like dogs.' He touched his trackpad and the Mac screen came to life. 'Now, I feel great sadness for the new victims, but I can't deny a certain excitement. It's public-spirited of your friend to update the file after such a hiatus. What on earth could he have been up to for five years?'

'Are you seeing anything interesting in the new scene?' said Lennox.

'Oh, many things. Yes. I still feel that you're looking for someone who was terribly warped by something beyond our imagining. Those bone arrangements speak of a profound inner chaos. I think perhaps the decorative presentation shows a compulsion to impose order. It may be how he finds respite from his turmoil. He was grown in rotten soil rather than planted from a bad seed.'

Blackwood frowned. 'You mean trauma?'

'Of course. My thinking used to run against the grain of the accepted origins of psychopathology. I tended towards nature over nurture. But now I believe that aberrant behaviour of this type is a maladaptive trauma response. When you grow up feeling secure and loved and attached, you learn that life is about connection. If you do not, you learn that life is about survival.' He tilted his screen towards Lennox and Blackwood, then scrolled through the most recent scene photos. 'Here, we have part of your friend's survival mechanism. When we know who he is, and the nature of his early experiences, it will all make sense. But we don't know who he is yet. So we have to interpret, decode.'

Blackwood shifted along the sofa, getting a better angle on the screen. 'What do you think the bones represent?'

Cabrera flashed Lennox a look. 'Well, this is my point. If I could tell you that, you could narrow it all down significantly.' He took a drink. 'Listen. I know the scepticism you face over profiling. You have your MMO lines to follow.'

'Means, motive, opportunity,' said Blackwood.

Cabrera grinned. 'Indeed. And I'm sure your Hendon tutors told you that you find criminals by focusing on opportunity. How they gained access to the victims. Then, once you have your suspect, you work on the two M's. I agree, to a degree. If you can find a route to go further back, and you can decipher the signature, you can apprehend more quickly and prevent further killing.' He switched the images to scenes from the previous murders. 'What does he need? What is the fantasy that the killer has about his victims? What has happened to him, usually in early childhood, that has embedded that need, that fantasy?'

'It's his first female victim,' said Lennox. 'And his first double killing.'

Cabrera pondered, covering his top lip with his bottom. He leaned in close to the screen and spoke in a hushed voice. 'External stressors progressing his self-narrative, pushing a drive for more intense experience. It could be a critical moment in his evolution. It could be nothing.' He spied Blackwood reaching into her shoulder bag. 'Yes, I do mind if you vape.'

Lennox chuckled.

'I was going to make notes,' said Blackwood. She set down the bag. 'But I forgot my Post-its.'

Cabrera turned his chair towards them. 'We are blessed. A millennial who can still use a pen.'

'What about the shift from high-status individuals to low status?' said Lennox.

'Your two victims were house-sitting, correct?' Lennox nodded. 'It's a very nice house to sit.'

'Did he make a mistake?' said Blackwood.

'I suggest you look closely at victim acquisition. Are there any similarities with how he selected the previous victims? This feels like a radical departure. More arbitrary. I agree he is forensically aware but he might also have realised that he's leaving a pattern, so this is about breaking that pattern, rather than the victims fulfilling a specific need. But if the killer is becoming more opportunistic, that might signal instability. Perhaps he is suffering a crisis of purpose or his role in his self-constructed narrative is evolving.'

'This all feels pretty devious,' said Lennox. 'Could he really be such a deep thinker?'

Cabrera took a glug of water. 'Oh, goodness me. Oswald. I know you're not really that naive. This is an exceptionally intelligent and organised individual. Methodical, precise. That he leaves so little behind implies he is someone who deeply understands forensic techniques and may have experience in evading the law. But you already know this.' He opened a drawer and took out a stack of paper plates and a bag of plastic knives and forks, then reached to the drinks cabinet and retrieved a small paring knife. He wiped the knife down with a tissue. 'It's only been used for chopping olives. Would either of you like a slice of tart?'

Lennox shook his head.

'Could I have a small one?' said Blackwood.

Cabrera cut into the tart with the knife and transferred a slice to a paper plate. He added a plastic fork and handed it all to Blackwood. 'Why small? It is an indulgence. An act of self-allowance. Not a time for compromise.'

She took the plate. 'I get bored with food quickly.'

Cabrera studied her, amused. He cut himself a large slice. 'Our friend's killing blows have remained the same. Swift, efficient.' He tore off a chunk of tart with his hands and popped it into his mouth. 'I feel he doesn't like to kill.'

'So, why do it?' said Lennox.

'Well...' Cabrera smiled. 'That is the question.' He turned to his screen, scrolled through the scene photos as he chewed. 'These people are objects to him. There is little pleasure in their dispatch. I don't detect any sexual sadism. No semen found at any of the scenes. No sexual violation.' Cabrera took another mouthful of tart. 'If he draws no pleasure from their suffering, what need does the death fulfil?'

'Could it be ritualistic?' said Lennox.

Cabrera grimaced. 'No, no. They are not sacrifices. At least not in the dreary old demonic sense.' He leaned in close to the screen. 'But there is a grand design here.'

Blackwood cut away a forkful of tart. 'Why does he leave such a long time between the killings?'

'Liv had an idea that he was recharging,' said Lennox.

Liv.

'I mean recharging his energy,' said Blackwood. 'Like he's suffered a sort of burnout. I get it after too much social-ising.' She took a bite of tart. It was soft and velvety: vanilla and cinnamon in the crust, sweet juice from the pear.

Cabrera waved a hand. 'Ugh. Energy. No, no.' He brightened, looked at Blackwood. 'Ah! You have ADHD, yes?'

She glanced at Lennox; he shrugged. 'Yes. I was diag-nosed at twenty-seven.'

Cabrera slowly turned his chair back to face them. 'I like your idea, Liv. But the scenes are so elaborate, perhaps it's the other way round. What if the gaps drain him and the killings are his recharge?'

'So, a refuelling,' said Lennox.

'Perhaps that's why he killed two people this time,' said Blackwood. 'To compensate for the long gap.'

Cabrera beamed at her. 'This works for me. Yes. The killings are swift and precise, but together with the bones, they give him what he needs. They nourish him. Maybe the bones aren't just ritualistic or for display. They might mean something deeper to him. He is getting something out of them. Something essential. Perhaps even spiritual. I feel they are the path into his mind.'

'Forensics found deep nitrile impressions in two of the bones,' said Lennox. 'Like he's holding them tight.'

Cabrera nodded, thought for a moment. 'As I said, there is a compulsion for order. For control. It soothes him. Calms his inner chaos, whatever its nature might be. There is no intimacy in the death blows, but he is tactile with the animal bones. They are not just there to be laid out into pretty patterns. They are there to hold close, to be communed with.' He steepled his palms, scrubbed at his beard with his fingertips. 'The bones are non-human. So, could there be an animal fetish? Could his trauma involve animals?' He turned to his computer, pulled up a scene photo of the bones arrangement at the latest scene. 'The victims hold no thrill for him. They are tools to serve his fantasy. I feel the key to his mystery is in the bones. They connect to his trauma. And, of course, there is the question of how he acquires them. Does he capture and kill the animals himself?'

'Maybe that explains the gaps,' said Blackwood. 'It takes time to prepare.'

Cabrera nodded as he cycled through the images. 'Giger saw bones as symbols of mortality, blurring the line between life and death. And in the Tibetan Buddhist tradition, there is the ritual use of *kapala*, skull cups, and *kangling*, trumpets made from human thigh bones. They serve as conduits for spiritual transformation.' He glanced at Lennox, then Blackwood. 'As I'm sure you both know, there are also cases of killers who kept bones as trophies, believing them to hold mystical power.'

'Maybe look into historical incidents of animal mutilation or similar?' said Lennox.

Cabrera made a face, not convinced. He stared down at his desktop. 'There could be live animals involved, but I don't think mutilation is his bag.' He shut down the image application and shovelled in another forkful of tart. 'The deep impressions in the bones...' He chewed, pondering. 'Do we not hold on tightest to the things we love the most? In fear of losing them?' He looked up. 'The bones are speaking to us. But we can't hear what they are saying yet.'

Chapter Thirty-One

He stepped out into the bristling night air. He stayed close to the buildings, holding a singular line, eager to avoid unexpected physical contact. The lurid street lighting triggered discordant ripples of white noise that scraped over his teeth like steel wire. As they dissipated, he caught their necrotic aftertaste: sour milk, stale ash.

As ever, the alcohol blunted the edges. But after learning of his mistake, he had been sputtering, running on fumes. The fury had fortified him, but now it was draining away, and he needed to mask just to get by.

Day to day. Hour to hour.

A passing ambulance turned on its siren, showering him with crimson shards.

He ducked into the BMW and closed the door, pressing the cool metal of the key to his forehead, savouring the sheen of ice-blue. The texture of the leather seat doused him in shit-brown and he pulled away slowly, fearing a tyre squeal might finish him.

A sickly bile—grimy chartreuse—rose and receded in

his throat as he breathed, like tidewater. He focused on the navigation, cruising through the streets of Colindale and Kingsbury at a steady pace.

Timely indication. Smooth braking.

Nothing jarring. Nothing memorable.

He had been greedy. Blinded by the improvised thrill. He had overestimated the worth of his target, and his core ached from the empty calories: a maw gaping for nourishment.

But he had a new goal: more substantial and prestigious. The process took time, patience. But he couldn't afford to wait. The void inside him was opening, threatening to rip him apart.

He pulled away from Kenton Road and checked his rear-view mirror. The tarmac snaked away behind him. He breathed, slow and deep, and the flashes dimmed to flickers.

He turned into Vaughan Road and parked the car in a side street that led to West Harrow Park. He got out and walked, wincing at the electrical crackle across his back as he passed through the light pools from the street lamps.

At the corner of the target road, he lingered, wallowing in the baking air. The house was a modest Edwardian semi. Two storeys, small front garden. But this time he had scoped, completed the pre-work. Status wasn't always about grand facades.

As he walked down a side alley alongside the property, a first-floor light came on and he froze, gazing up, buried in the shadows. His pulse quickened, sending a scurry of white dots across his vision. A female silhouette opened the window, reaching out to secure the casement bar. She turned, disappeared from view.

Footsteps on the main street, as a second woman approached the front of the house with a tall, broad-shouldered man in tow. The man said something as the woman let herself into the front door, and she laughed: a searing glare of magenta and olive.

A shared house. He would have to adapt, change his approach. And he couldn't take his time, couldn't follow his carefully crafted routines. The hunger was too demanding.

Tonight, he would drive to the garage, begin his final preparations.

First, the bones.

Chapter Thirty-Two

Lennox sat on the doorstep, beneath the porch light, staring out across the buzz-cut lawn. The red-brick facade of his home loomed behind him, its vast bay windows dark and lifeless. A late-night breeze jostled the trimmed hedges lining the driveway.

'Stupid,' he hissed to himself. *'Stupid, stupid, stupid.'*

A plasma-blue Audi e-tron turned into the drive and glided to a stop. Martha stepped out. Her compact frame seemed smaller than usual, dwarfed by the bulk of the car. As she approached, Lennox noted something new: a slight stoop in her shoulders.

'You're a lifesaver,' he said, rising to his feet.

She smiled, a little pained. 'It's fine. I was on a late shift. Although I'm not sure I should enable this behaviour.' She walked over, hugged him, then studied his face. 'Have you been—'

'No. But I might take a nightcap to bring me down after this. I was at the Barbican. Eno show with a live orchestra.'

'Good?'

'Incredible. I realised I'd lost my door key on the drive home. Maybe at the show.'

Martha produced a key on a silver heart-shaped fob. 'Gift from a patient's family.' She handed it to Lennox. 'Get two new ones cut and give me this one back when you see me again. Put one under a plant pot or something. Next time, you're getting a hotel. You're lucky I wasn't on call tonight.' She kissed him lightly on the cheek. 'I do have to get back, though.'

He looked down at the key. 'Thank you for doing this.'

She hovered for a moment, studying his eyes. 'Try to get some rest, Oz. I do still worry about you. I don't want to see you on my list.'

He watched her walk back to the car, thought about waving as she backed out of the drive, but turned and let himself into the house.

He flicked on the hall table lamp and stood there for a few minutes, staring at the front door key in the cobalt-blue bowl, hand-crafted from hammered brass. Martha had bought the bowl on his insistence at the Jemaa el-Fna, a thousand years ago. He saw a flash of the moment: the contours of her cheekbones in the stallholder's hanging lamp as she haggled him down from a hundred pounds to seventy-five.

Why was that detail so vivid, but his routine this morning such a fog? In the twelve years he had lived at the house, he had never once walked out in the morning without taking the key from the bowl. Was muscle memory something you lost, too?

He walked into the kitchen and poured a generous measure of Talisker into a heavy Waterford tumbler, then retreated to the bedroom. He lay on the bed in the dark, fully clothed, and cued up *Ambient 1: Music for Airports* on his phone. The notes hung in the air, shimmering like dewdrops, before dissolving into the ambient wash.

Lennox sipped his drink, closed his eyes, and synchronised his breathing to the languid pace of the music. The undulating tones seeped into him like anaesthetic, slowing his marching thoughts.

In the en-suite, he brushed his teeth by the ambient mirror light, cringing at the memory of Martha's visit. It was the first time he'd locked himself out since they had separated eight years earlier. Was this now his fate? Diminishing returns. Lagging further and further behind his baseline. A slide into obsolescence, then dependency.

He walked back into the bedroom, undressed, and slid beneath the duvet, burying his face in the cool Egyptian cotton pillow case. He navigated to Blackwood's sound-effect app and tapped the icon of a cloud with two droplets underneath. He lay back, tuned in to the monotone static of heavy rainwater, and stared into the dark void above, his eyes drooping.

Soon, he was crouched on a tall, grassy headland, pummelled from all directions by stinging wind and rain. Jonah stood ahead, with his back to Lennox, close to the edge, staring out at the rolling sky, the seething waves.

Lennox called out to his son, but the wind stole his words. Jonah turned and shouted something, also swallowed by the storm.

He walked towards Jonah with heavy legs, leaning into the wind like a mime. As he reached the cliff edge, Jonah leaned forward and spoke into Lennox's ear. But again, his voice was smothered by swirling, hissing wind.

'I don't understand,' said Lennox.

Jonah nodded and stood up straight. He gave his father

a sad smile, then let himself topple backwards, over the cliff. Lennox tried to grab him, but his hands flailed at nothing.

Lennox's eyes opened wide. The bedroom ceiling was just visible now, behind a layer of gloom. A faint aura of dawn light had gathered around the edge of the window blind.

He turned his head. The bedside clock read 5:17am.

His phone was ringing.

Whitmore.

He connected the call. 'Lennox.'

'Sir. Sorry it's early. But we have a potential witness for the Harpenden murders.'

He cleared his throat. 'Go on.'

'Brandon Chambers. Says he was walking his dog near the Foster house on the night of the murders and saw a man behaving strangely, walking up and down the road outside, like he was staking out the place.'

'Description?'

'Nothing yet. He says he can come in at half-six but can't spare much time.'

'On my way.'

Whitmore paused. 'Shall I get Blackwood to sit in on the interview? Good experience.'

He sat up. 'Yes. Not in the room, though.'

Chapter Thirty-Three

The man sat alone, his chair pulled up close to the round table. He kept his eyes on the far wall, nodding his head to an imaginary beat. He was late middle-aged, with a low, furrowed brow and ruddy skin that spoke of a life lived hard. Dark bags hung beneath his narrow eyes.

Blackwood leaned in close to the one-way glass in the dimly lit viewing room. The man's light T-shirt and shorts didn't match his demeanour. He took frequent short sips from his Starbucks cup, checked his phone, glanced up at the camera in the corner. The witness interview room was brighter and more relaxing than the typical interrogation cell—padded chairs, soft blue ceiling, natural light—and the man was in voluntary attendance. Not a suspect. But he seemed ready to leap out of the frosted window at any moment.

He tilted his head from side to side, and Blackwood flinched as the room's sensitive intercom relayed the crack of his neck muscles.

The door opened, and DI Whitmore entered with Lennox behind.

'Good morning,' said Whitmore. 'Appreciate you coming in so early. Brandon Chambers?'

The man sniffed, nodded.

'I'm Detective Inspector Whitmore. This is Detective Chief Inspector Lennox. I believe you have some information about the incident that occurred in Harpenden earlier this week.'

'Yeah,' said Chambers, keeping his eyes on Lennox as he took a seat beside Whitmore.

Blackwood pulled up a chair close to the viewing glass and took out a pen and a stack of orange Post-its. 'Can I make notes?'

The male DS—Willoughby—sitting in the far corner of the viewing room, glanced up from his laptop. 'Sure.'

She scribbled a few quotes as Whitmore laid out the situation to Chambers. He wasn't under investigation or caution… They were simply asking for his help about the case… He could take a break at any point.

Blackwood squinted at Chambers as he placed his clasped hands on the table, keeping his head held high. Lennox flicked his eyes briefly towards the glass.

'Can you tell us what you saw that evening, Mr Chambers?' said Whitmore, her tone warm and welcoming.

He gave a slow, formal nod, took a deep breath.

He's looking at Lennox more than Whitmore.

'There was a thing on the news,' he said, finally focusing on Whitmore. 'You asking for witnesses and that.'

Whitmore nodded. 'Take your time. What exactly did you see?'

He cleared his throat. 'I was walking the dog. Quite late.

About ten. He's getting on a bit and if I don't take him out, I have to clean up the mess first thing. So, up by the house on the news, I seen this bloke walking up and down the other side of the road. He was taking pictures of the place on his phone.'

'You say the "house on the news",' said Lennox. 'Are you familiar with that area?'

Chambers grinned. 'Oh, yeah. We go there all the time. My place isn't far. And there's a wood nearby. It's good for the dog.'

Ask him the dog's name.

'Can you describe the man?' said Whitmore.

Chambers cleared his throat again, hesitated. 'Tall.' He held his hand up a couple of feet above his head. 'I think he was wearing walking boots. But there was a car parked further down and I think he might have seen me because he got in quickly and drove off.'

He lowered his gaze, exposing a bald patch on the crown of his head.

Whitmore glanced at Lennox. 'Did you see the man's face at all? Did he look at you? What makes you think he saw you?'

Chambers was silent for a long time, his shoulders rising and falling, his breaths growing shorter and more frequent.

He whipped up his head and pointed to the corner camera. 'You filming this?'

'Yes,' said Lennox. 'But it's just procedure. For accuracy.'

'You're not under suspicion,' said Whitmore.

Chambers' expression hardened. He shifted his eyes back to Lennox. 'Can I get a drink of water?' He leaned forward. 'It's my throat.' He reached a hand up to his neck. 'Bit dry. I can hardly breathe.'

'Of course.' Whitmore got up and walked to a corner table with a jug of water and a stack of plastic glasses.

Chambers stared at Lennox, rocking slightly. 'He said you'd be here.'

'Something isn't right,' said Blackwood.

DS Willoughby looked up. 'What do you mean?'

Chambers leaned in closer to Lennox, standing up slowly. He was tall, heavyset. 'He said to remind you.' He reached into his pocket and pulled out a shabby length of thin rope, a sinister grin spreading across his face.

Whitmore strode to the door and threw it open, shouting. *'Officer help in here.'*

Willoughby crashed out of the viewing room.

Chambers opened out the rope; it had already been fashioned into a rough noose. He slipped it around his neck and held it upright by the open end, yanking gently, making an exaggerated choking sound, opening and closing his mouth and sticking out his tongue.

Lennox jumped up and lunged for him, but Chambers staggered back into the wall, holding the noose aloft.

'Shame on you,' shouted Chambers, scurrying backwards as Lennox rounded the table, his face red with rage. 'Couldn't even keep your own boy safe.' Lennox was on him now, forcing him against the wall.

Willoughby ran in.

Chambers sneered and pointed at Lennox as Willoughby grabbed him by the shoulders and hauled him away. 'What kind of father lets his son swing while he's out playing detective?'

'Custody desk,' Whitmore shouted at Willoughby. 'I'll be there shortly.' She turned to Lennox. 'Are you okay?'

Blackwood stepped closer to the viewing window, pressed her fingertips against the glass.

Lennox gathered himself. His eyes flicked to the window as he walked out of the room. 'I'm fine.'

Chapter Thirty-Four

'Chambers was a Trojan horse,' said Lennox, sitting back in his corner seat at the Hendon cafeteria. 'A lackey sent in to troll me. I'm sure he was paid well.'

Blackwood picked at her blueberry muffin, waiting for a pair of detectives to pass by and slip into a booth. 'Who by?'

He sighed. 'I arrested a cocaine dealer named Ewan Vance in Harlesden a few years ago. A seriously nasty bastard. Saw himself as the Escobar of Edgware Road. But he was loaded. He'd won a big prize on the EuroMillions lottery a couple of weeks before the arrest. Vance hired top lawyers and put in an early guilty plea for intent to supply. He shifted most of the blame onto a couple of his street dealers and his lawyers pushed his own drug issues as mitigation. He could have got life, but the judge gave him five years. He was out in four. And ever since, he's been harassing me anonymously around this time of year. He usually just sends foul things in the post. Sometimes emails. This is a new low.'

He sipped from a bottle of mineral water.

Blackwood took a mouthful of muffin, washed it down with coffee.

'Do you want to know more?' said Lennox.

'Only if you want to tell me.'

Lennox looked around the cafeteria, as if searching for something. 'My son died. It was the tenth anniversary two days ago.' He took a long drink of water. 'He was fifteen.' He wavered. 'He ended his own life.'

Blackwood slumped back, suddenly appalled at the banality of the crumbled muffin. 'My god. Sir. I'm so sorry. Did he leave—'

'No, he didn't. There was no warning. Nothing I noticed, at least. My wife Martha was a GP.' Lennox zoned out, staring at a spot just beyond Blackwood's shoulder. 'She's now a cardiology consultant. We both found him after we came home following a night out. It was our last night out. We didn't survive it.' His eyes drifted to Blackwood's. 'Vance has done his homework. He knows what hurts. There's no point pursuing Chambers. He's probably been forced into it. Maybe owes Vance money he doesn't have.'

Blackwood frowned. 'But... Public Order Act? Causing harassment, alarm, or distress. It's definitely Criminal Law Act. Wasting police time.'

'Of course. But the CPS won't be interested. He might put in a complaint of assault, but it won't stick. The point was to cause me pain.' He shrugged. 'I can take it.'

Blackwood squeezed her eyes shut, opened them again. 'It's not often I'm speechless.'

Lennox gave a grim laugh. 'Let's talk about something else. That was quite a first experience in the viewing room.'

She set down her coffee. 'Okay. Here's something else. Abigail left me a note.'

Lennox narrowed his eyes. 'What kind of note?'

'In a book. A bird field guide. It was in a box her mother brought over for me after she disappeared. I opened it for the first time at my mum's house last week. It said, "LS. Primrose Hill. Ivory Room. White Lion. Mr Shade." She would have written that in spring 2010. By the end of that summer she'd gone.' She leaned forward. 'I wanted to ask you. Could I take a look at Abigail's file? You worked on the case and—'

'No.' He took a breath. 'We don't revive cold cases unless there's compelling new evidence. A cryptic note isn't compelling new evidence.'

'But if we could work out what it all means, it wouldn't be cryptic.'

Lennox held up a hand. 'This is what we talked about.' He softened his voice. 'Not getting distracted. Following process. Keeping focused on one thing at a time. Not trying too hard to impress. I'm sorry you had to see that little episode, but it's done now. I have a live case to pursue. Speak to Whitmore. Have a full day with the Intelligence Cell. There's plenty of work you can cover or witness and there may be forensic or pathology updates to come. I'll keep you informed.'

He got up and walked away from the corner table, towards the door leading to the main MIT office.

Blackwood took her phone out of her shoulder bag and navigated to email. She read through her messages, then sprang to her feet and hurried after Lennox, walking alongside him.

He eyed her. 'Shadowing me doesn't mean literally standing in my shadow.'

She waved her phone at him as they passed through onto the MIT floor. 'You know when we talked about the drownings? The ones that happened a couple of days after three of the bones killings?'

Lennox kept moving, aiming at his office. 'What about them?'

'Derek Simmons. The homeless guy they found in the River Colne two days after Lara and Daniel's time of death? I asked DI Whitmore if I could expedite a DNA cross-check, via the in-house lab, on Simmons and the nail found at the Harpenden house.'

Lennox stopped, turned to her. 'What did we say about side quests?'

'Sir. I've covered DNA checks at Wood Green, but they usually take a few days. The lab here did this one quickly because of the case priority and your sign-off—'

'What do you mean? My sign-off? I didn't give permission for you to do this.' His voice was raised now, and the two of them stood in the middle of the busy MIT floor, face to face.

Blackwood took a moment. 'You did, sir. You said you were happy for me to look into the drownings, but that I probably wouldn't find anything—'

'I did not,' said Lennox, louder.

'Sir, you did. In your office the morning we saw Cabrera.'

'I don't remember that.'

Blackwood grimaced. 'Although I submitted the request the day before. Better to apologise than ask for permission, right?' Lennox glared at her. She looked around. Several detectives had half-turned their chairs to watch.

Lennox pulled away and stomped into his office. Blackwood followed, and he slammed the door behind her as she entered.

'Sir, I followed the process. Please give me a moment.'

Lennox looked over her shoulder through the window, distracted.

She turned. DI Whitmore was hurrying across the MIT floor towards the office.

Lennox headed for his desk. 'PC Blackwood…'

'Sir! They have a preliminary match.' She checked her phone. 'Full confirmation pending further analysis. I was on a task force at Wood Green last year and worked on some of the DNA elements. I also took an online course.'

A knock at the door. Lennox waved Whitmore in and sat down.

She closed the door behind her, looked from Lennox to Blackwood. 'Is this about the DNA hit with Simmons?' No answer from either. Lennox lowered his head, staring down at the desktop. 'It poses a big question.'

'Preliminaries aren't admissible,' said Lennox. 'This isn't evidence yet.'

Whitmore nodded. 'We would need to confirm, sir. But both samples are good quality. Blood from Simmons. Nail material plus soft tissue under the nail. I'd expect the prelim to stand up to further analysis. It's Simmons' nail. We have no DNA from the previous scenes, so there's nothing to cross-check. But we have a concrete connection to the Harpenden scene with Simmons. We could deep-dive into his background, and his movements around the time of the Harpenden murders.'

'We could also do victimology on the other two drownings,' said Blackwood. 'June 2018, River Lea. August 2019, Grand Union Canal. All three were soon after bones killings.'

Whitmore nodded but kept her eyes on Lennox. He still hadn't lifted his head. 'I also suggest doing an in-house PM on Simmons, check for further connections to the Harpenden scene. He's in the morgue at Hemel. With your sign-off, I should be able to get the body transported today. PM by tomorrow.'

'Sir,' said Blackwood carefully. 'There's been nothing for eight years. This is something.'

'The nail could be contamination,' said Lennox, raising his eyes to them. 'Simmons might have known Lara or Daniel. The other two drownings might be unrelated.'

Whitmore took a step towards his desk. 'Yes, but there's also a chance he could have been the Bones Killer.'

Chapter Thirty-Five

Blackwood dug out a forkful of chicken salad and held it up to the light.

'I think it's safe,' said Whitmore. She raised her soup spoon, paused. 'Don't quote me, though.'

Blackwood surveyed the MIT cafeteria. The lunchtime crowd was sparse: mostly cliques of detectives she recognised from the briefings and a window table of dressed-down support staff, including Dom.

'I'm not very foodie,' said Blackwood, taking a mouthful. 'It's just fuel to me.'

'This is hardly Michelin-star fare.'

Blackwood's gaze fell on a group of heavyset detectives planting stacked trays of food on a nearby table. 'More Michelin Man than Michelin star.'

Whitmore laughed. 'I might have to report the fat-shaming. Remember your DEI training?'

'Yeah,' said Blackwood. 'Not fat person. Obese person.'

Whitmore slurped her soup, shook her head. 'Person with obesity.'

They ate in silence for a while. Every time Blackwood looked towards Dom's table, she caught him shifting his gaze to his food, slightly too late to go unnoticed. Intentional?

'It was a nice idea to check unexplained deaths before and after the bones killings,' said Whitmore. 'The DNA cross-checking was smart, too. Be careful, though. This isn't a world that favours mavericks or people who don't rigidly follow process. You might find that Lennox sells it as his own work if it leads somewhere.'

'Success has many fathers.'

'Oh, yes. Rarely mothers.'

Smear of soup at the side of Whitmore's mouth.

Blackwood shook her head. 'I hear that word a lot. *Process.*'

'From what I can see, you have good instincts. But even if you make DC, you'll still be a slave to PACE. Everything goes on the record, gathered with the correct protocols, or it didn't happen.'

A companion of Dom's showed him something on a phone screen and he laughed. His eyes flicked up in Blackwood's direction. He spotted her watching and averted his gaze.

'It's a world where men set the rules,' said Blackwood.

'Yes. For men to follow. But women, doubly so. The Met is about sixty-five per cent men. Closer to eighty at the top of the chain. It's one reason why it's so hard to get domestic violence and coercive control taken seriously.' She wiped her mouth with a napkin.

Blackwood nodded. 'I had a case recently. I felt there were red flags, but it didn't hit the threshold. But by then it might be too late.' She sighed. 'Plus, he put in a complaint about me giving her my private number.'

Whitmore winced. 'Yes, but again... Process. You can only be a wild card for so long until you get shut out of the game. I learned that. The way to progress is to play it clever. Manage upwards.'

'Manage the men.'

Distant PA announcement. Tinny voice, words indistinct.

'Coercive control and domestic abuse are often predictors for future escalation,' said Whitmore.

'Yes. Past behaviour is the best indication of future behaviour.'

Whitmore tore apart her bread roll. 'Exactly. And so coercive control and domestic violence should be taken more seriously. But as long as it's men making the rules... They're too busy with the "not all men" nonsense to see the root of the problem. That's the way men are raised and nurtured. A lot of women drop claims of domestic abuse because there are so few convictions.'

'It makes me wonder if I'm choosing the right career,' said Blackwood. 'If I can really do anything about that.'

Squeak of chair legs on floor. Sharp. Grating.

Whitmore's expression softened. 'You have lucked out here, though. Lennox is well respected. They wouldn't have put you with him if they didn't think you were close to getting over the line. How are you finding him?'

Blackwood hesitated. 'He seems very good, but he's obviously under a lot of stress. His hand shakes sometimes. And he zones out, like he's somewhere else.'

Whitmore chewed her food, pondering. 'It's been noticed. It's a tough time of the year for him. But I wouldn't go there. He's very private.' She leaned back. 'Just try to hit the marks and don't undermine him. I learned a lot from him when I was a DS. We'll pursue the Chambers harassment, but it'll probably end up in a fine or low-level community order.'

'But there was intent to cause distress.'

'Lennox grabbing him complicates that legally. If he was Batman, Ewan Vance would be the Joker. You might get to meet him one day, if you're unlucky.'

Dom looking over.

'Do they really call Lennox "The Wizard"?'

Whitmore rolled her eyes. 'They used to. Back when he was a DI. Not so much, these days. He has an insanely precise memory. He seems to recall specific moments and scenes when most people have to keep referring to notes. It taught me I could never do that. I notice you write a lot down, too.'

'It's an ADHD thing. Helps me organise my thoughts. Otherwise, they just bounce around off each other, like a room full of ping-pong balls.'

'Do you take meds?'

'I used to. But I'd rather just accept it and work on self-management. It's a neurodiversity, not a disease.'

'Part of who you are.'

She nodded. 'I overthink, therefore I am.'

Whitmore smiled. 'I heard Lennox took you to see Cabrera.'

'Yes. I liked him.'

'He's good, but the brass look at profiler psychologist types as old-school.'

'Cabrera said it was interesting that the Bones Killer had gripped the bones so tightly, and we should try to find out why.'

'We won't get anywhere near the whys until we have him in custody. We follow the evidence. We don't try to read the killer's mind. That's for the movies. Look for questions instead of answers.'

She finished her soup.

Blackwood ate more, her thoughts fluttering around: scene photos, Cabrera's Giger sketches, Lennox's shaking hand, the peregrine. 'So, what questions are you asking?'

'We believe we have five confirmed victims.' Whitmore lowered her voice. 'Including the double murder in Harpenden. I'm interested in the five-year gap between the third and fourth killings when it was only one year between the first three. I'm keen to understand why he might have gone dormant for so long. Maybe he was out of the country. Or in prison.'

'I thought that. What about the DNA match with Simmons and the nail?'

'We're confirming the hit.' Whitmore took a slow drink from a glass of water, as if considering how much to share. 'Lennox has signed off on transferring Simmons' body here for a second post-mortem. We should get something from that within forty-eight hours. We're also doing a deep dive into Simmons' background and recent movements. CCTV. Dash and doorbell cams from around Harpenden.'

'What about the previous victims?' Blackwood asked.

'Still working on connecting the dots there. The shift from high-status victims to Lara and Daniel is puzzling. We're re-examining everything, looking for patterns we might have missed before.' Whitmore sighed. 'It's a lot of moving parts. Lennox wants daily briefings with me from now on to keep everything aligned.'

Dom's wedding ring. Silver.

'Are you listening?' said Whitmore.

Blackwood blinked. 'Sorry. Sort of.'

Whitmore followed her line of sight. 'That's Dominic.' She gave a sly smile. 'I shouldn't say this, but he is available. He got married to one of the admin staff here a few years ago, but I think they divorced recently.'

'He's still wearing his wedding ring.'

'Some men do that out of pride. Men do a lot of things for that.'

'Or he might want to keep wearing it to show he's not on the market.' She shook her head, resetting. 'I'm not looking for that kind of thing, anyway.'

'Follow the process,' said Whitmore. 'Focus on getting that DC card before you think about...'

'Self-gratification? I have a question.'

'Go on,' said Whitmore, checking her phone.

'The direction of the slash wounds on the previous victims were left to right, but on Lara and Daniel, they ran right to left.'

Whitmore scrolled on her phone. 'Mm-hmm. That's been noted. No explanation yet.'

'Who noted it?'

Whitmore looked up, thought for a moment. 'Lennox mentioned it in a one-to-one brief with me.' She held up a hand. 'More importantly, Intelligence has confirmed the drowning victims you highlighted were all homeless.' She looked up. 'And they all stayed at the same shelter in Watford. A place called The New Hope.'

Blackwood perked up. 'Maybe the killer works there?'

'You're getting ahead of yourself,' said Whitmore, laughing. 'I'll pass this on to Lennox, suggest he pay the shelter a visit.'

'Will you go with him?'

'I have another case to catch up on this afternoon. Ask

him if you can tag along, though. See how he works in the field. It is what you're supposed to be doing as his mentee. Let me know how it goes later.'

'Managing upwards.'

Whitmore stood to leave. 'Now you're getting it.'

Chapter Thirty-Six

Lennox strode across the polished floor, Oxfords clicking, and took the chair next to DCI Richard Mallory. He pivoted away from the shaft of sunlight beaming in from Khokhar's window and reflecting off her glass-topped desk.

Mallory nodded to Lennox and shifted in his seat, the leather creaking under his bulk.

Khokhar's emerald hijab shimmered as she leaned back in her seat and smiled at them both.

'My ears are burning,' said Lennox.

Khokhar waved a hand. 'Oh, no. We weren't talking about you, Oz. Well, sort of. Richard was wondering how things are going with your...'

'Apprentice,' said Mallory.

'Protégé.'

Mallory cleared his throat with a phlegmy rattle. 'Her boss at Wood Green, DI Pollard, wants her back. Absences. Resource.'

'I need more time with her. She's rough round the edges, but she's doing well. A good brain.'

Mallory's lips curled into a smirk. 'Spotting the talent. There's life in the old dog yet, eh?'

'If she doesn't make DC, she could work in intelligence,' said Khokhar. 'Report to Whitmore.' Her phone buzzed on the desk. 'Excuse me for a moment.'

She turned away from the desk and took the call, speaking in a low voice.

Mallory leaned over to Lennox. 'I wouldn't get any ideas about an interracial conquest, Oz,' he hissed. 'I'm pretty sure she's gay or bi or queer or whatever they want us to call them these days.'

Lennox's gaze shifted to the window.

Khokhar ended the call. 'Sorry about that.'

Lennox turned back to Mallory and hit him with a frosty glare. 'I don't think they care what you call them, DCI Whitmore.'

Mallory sniggered, exchanged a look with Khokhar. He studied Lennox, jaw clenched. 'I care what people call me, though.'

'What?' Lennox frowned, his brow furrowing.

'You said "Whitmore".'

'Anyway,' said Khokhar. 'Anything new from the Harpenden scene?'

Lennox tipped back his head, adjusted his tie knot. 'We're looking into a DNA hit on a homeless man pulled out of the River Colne, two days after the couple's time of death. I've had the body moved to the in-house lab for a deeper post-mortem. See if we get any other connections to the scene.'

'Could it be the killer?' said Mallory. 'And he's offed himself?'

'It's possible.'

Mallory nodded. 'We live in hope.' He took out a hand-kerchief and mopped his bald head, clammy from the heat.

'Victimology?' said Khokhar.

'Unlike the previous vics, Lara and Daniel were both low status. So, either he made a mistake in acquisition or he's changed his priority. Both would be interesting.'

'But we don't know which it is?'

'Not yet. DI Whitmore has been liaising with the NCA, cross-checking with other offender patterns. I'm hopeful that will turn up something now we have more data.'

'Fresh bodies,' said Mallory.

'If you like. I've been reviewing the offender's MO with my psychology contact.'

Khokhar's eyes flicked to Mallory. 'Cabrera.'

'Yes.'

Mallory puffed out a theatrical sigh. 'He's a loony loner with some pretty medieval ideas about rehab.'

Lennox kept his eyes on Khokhar. 'His views have softened lately, and his work on offender psychopathology is peerless. It's judicious to pursue lateral methods alongside the usual data-based analysis. I believe Cabrera's insights helped catch an unusual killer up in Derbyshire recently.'

'Oh, the stiff-shagger?' said Mallory.

'Necrophile.'

Mallory scoffed. 'I thought they were into sheep up there.'

'Pot, kettle,' said Lennox, turning to him.

Mallory gave a mock recoil. 'What do you mean?'

'Aren't you from the West Country, Richard?'

'Boys, boys...' Khokhar got to her feet; Mallory and Lennox did likewise. 'Richard. Stall Wood Green. Oswald. I'll give you more time with your...'

'Wing-woman,' said Mallory.

Khokhar eyed him. 'Student.' She hurried for the door; Mallory slipped in ahead and opened it for her. 'I can open my own doors, DCI Mallory.' She stopped in the frame, turned. 'Oz. One more week of mentoring. Then I need you fully focused on the bones case now it's moving again. Alongside DI Whitmore.'

They filed out of the office.

Lennox paused in the corridor and looked up into the overhead fluorescent lights. Their buzz seemed louder than usual.

Mallory brushed past without a word and disappeared around the corner.

Lennox put a hand to the wall. His breath came in short, ragged gasps. The world tilted, his familiar surroundings taking on a distant, dreamlike quality. He closed his eyes and counted to ten under his breath.

'Sir?'

He opened his eyes. Blackwood stood at the other side of the corridor.

'You okay, sir?'

Lennox nodded. 'Just a headache. Let's go for a drive.'

Chapter Thirty-Seven

Lennox tucked his Volvo Estate behind the bollards at the end of a side street of Victorian semis.

'We're on double yellows,' said Blackwood.

He took a blue-and-white laminated badge from the glove box and handed it to her. 'Put this on the dash.'

The badge had a Met insignia with *POLICE: OPERA-TIONAL USE* across the centre.

'Isn't this a bit entitled?' said Blackwood.

'Active enquiry. Justifiable. We can take our chances with the multi-storey if it makes you feel better.'

Blackwood slid the badge onto the dash and followed Lennox outside. 'We have to rely on squad cars.'

'Sometimes you don't want people to know you're coming.'

The New Hope Shelter was a weather-beaten converted chapel overlooking the Watford ring road. Tall, arched windows ran up the front end, with a vast curved door beneath a modest awning.

'I once spent time at a place like this in Tenby,' said Blackwood.

'You were homeless?'

'For a night, yes. My mum took me there on a whim for a summer break and we couldn't find anywhere to stay. All the guest houses had *NO VACANCY* signs in the window. They set us up with sleeping bags on the floor of a church, along with a bunch of others in the same boat, and local homeless. It was too noisy to sleep. Stank, as well. I just lay there all night, staring up at the bible quotes and stained-glass windows, listening to the coughing and spluttering. Put me right off religion.'

Lennox pushed through the door into a roomy hall with a reception kiosk. A bulletin board announced job postings and support group flyers, and a group of people clustered around a door labelled *CLOTHING DONATIONS*. Food smells and music drifted through the open door of a crowded kitchen.

Tyler, the Creator.

Beef. Onion. Something cheesy.

Sign above kiosk: HOPE STARTS HERE.

A short, brisk woman in her mid-forties came out of a side door in the reception kiosk. She wore a simple navy-blue cardigan over a white blouse and held her greying hair in a taut ponytail.

She stuck out a hand. 'Detective Lennox?'

'Is it that obvious?' He shook. 'This is PC Blackwood.'

The woman smiled, shook Blackwood's hand.

Cold. Poor circulation.

Pale skin. Anaemia?

'I'm Emma Cook. I'm the Shelter Director. Pleased to meet you.'

Cook stood there for a moment, smile wavering.

'Could we talk somewhere private?' said Lennox. 'It won't take long.'

'Of course. If you'd like to follow me...' She used a pass to open a door at the back of reception, and Lennox and Blackwood followed her into a shadowy corridor that led along the side of the building.

'So, do you run the show, Ms Cook?' said Blackwood.

'I oversee all the main operations, yes. I've taken the liberty of inviting Mark Jenkins, our night supervisor, and Samira Kapur, one of our case workers, to join us. Our provision begins with intervention services, building relationships and offering support to people who are street homeless. We have secure rehab and recovery accommodation for ten people and thirty-five overnight beds on a first come, first served basis.'

'How do you allocate them?' said Lennox.

'The British way.' Cook opened a door at the far end and ushered them through. 'They queue.'

Lennox and Blackwood walked into a cramped utility room with just enough space for a desk, corner filing cabinet and cheap sofa.

Stale coffee. Bleach. Soapy perfume.

A chunky middle-aged man and a slender thirtysomething woman stood up from the sofa as they entered.

'Our aim is not just to provide a bed for the night,' continued Cook, 'we're about rebuilding lives, offering a pathway back to society. Mark, Samira. Detective Lennox, Detective Blackwood.'

Detective.

Blackwood side-eyed Lennox with a smile as everyone shook hands.

Cook fell into a squeaky seat at her desk, while Jenkins

pulled up two mismatched chairs for Lennox and Black-wood before sitting back onto the sofa alongside Kapur.

'Now,' said Cook, 'we're gearing up for the dinner run, so I hope you don't mind if we make it quick. How can we help?'

'I'm interested in three male individuals who stayed overnight at the shelter,' said Lennox. 'The most recent user, Derek Simmons, has only been homeless for a few months.'

'Guests,' she corrected gently. 'That's our preferred term for those who take overnight shelter. Residents for those in longer-term rehab and recovery and Service Users in general. Also, I hope you understand, we have strict confi-dentiality policies.'

'Of course. I appreciate you sharing the sign-in sheets with my team. Our enquiry is more about your experience of these three, who I'm sorry to say are all now deceased.'

Cook glanced over at Jenkins and Kapur. 'Is this a murder enquiry?'

Lennox shook his head. 'I'm afraid I can't say any more. But it is a serious and ongoing investigation, yes. Could you please walk me through the process for your overnight guests?'

Jenkins leaned forward, hands on knees. 'We open the doors at 7pm.' *Slight lisp.* 'It's first come, first served for the thirty-five beds. People start lining up around four or five.' He checked his watch. 'Won't be long now. Sometimes earlier if the weather's bad. We do a quick assessment, make sure they're not visibly under the influence, check if they've been here before. Once they're in, they get a bed assignment, access to showers, a hot meal. Lights out is ten, and everyone has to be gone by 8am the next morning.'

Blackwood scrolled through her phone as he spoke, pulling up a line of headshots showing the three men. She held it up to Lennox, who nodded. She handed the phone to Cook. 'Do you recognise any of these guests? From left to right, Peter Kensington and Jamie Farrell. The man on the far right is Derek Simmons, who was here most recently.'

Cook slipped on a pair of glasses and squinted at the screen. 'I'm sorry. I don't. We see so many faces.' She handed the phone to Jenkins and Kapur.

'Ah!' said Kapur. 'I recognise the guy on the right. He was here a week or so ago. I work more directly with the guests, helping with housing and employment. I remember he came two nights running. He got a bed the first night, but we had to turn him away the second.' She looked up. 'Is he okay?'

Blackwood looked at Lennox, but he was keeping his eyes on the floor. 'How was he, Samira? Derek. Did he make you feel uncomfortable in any way? Did he mention anyone else here who was troubling him?'

Kapur shook her head slowly. 'Not that I recall.'

'Where did he go on the night he couldn't get a bed?' said Lennox.

'Most of them head along St Mary's Road,' said Jenkins, 'then down to Cassiobury Park, which stays open twenty-four hours. That's why it's popular with rough sleepers.'

'There are other shelters, though,' said Cook. 'It's a transient culture. Those three probably stayed in many other places.'

Jenkins handed back the phone. 'If you send me the images, I can ask around.'

'That would be perfect,' said Blackwood. 'Thank you.'

'Do you ever have issues with criminality?' said Lennox.

Kapur shrugged. 'You get some antisocial behaviour, but there's a general vibe of solidarity.'

'Homelessness and crime aren't always linked,' said

Cook, her tone sharpening. 'These people are vulnerable unfortunates, not dangerous outsiders. If anything, it's you lot making rough sleeping a public order offence that contributes to the problem. Fining people for not being able to house themselves.' She gave a bitter laugh.

'We're civil servants,' said Lennox. 'We don't fine people.'

Cook scoffed. 'Ah. You don't make the rules, right?' She gave an exaggerated, sarcastic smile.

Yellow-stained teeth. Receding gums.

'Ms Cook,' said Blackwood. 'We're not here to vilify the people you're trying to help. Yes, most homeless people are victims, and the link between homelessness and crime is complex, often rooted in survival needs and systemic failures.'

Lennox turned his head slowly to Blackwood.

'Our goal is justice and prevention,' she continued. 'Not persecution. So, how about working with us, instead of assuming we're the enemy?'

Cook raised her eyebrows, her smile thawing. 'Yes, of course. I'm sorry. But do you know how hard it is to not be able to step in and help someone in terrible need? To walk away from them because they're somehow out of your jurisdiction. You're right. We need to work together for these people. They leave here with nowhere to go. No one to turn to. And that's when the real dangers come for them.'

Chapter Thirty-Eight

A cavernous bass note fluttered and throbbed around Blackwood's candlelit bedroom. It faded, then surged, launching a jittery breakbeat. A distorted voice intoned, *'Breathe.'*

The young woman raised her head and rested it on top of Blackwood's leg. 'What's this?'

Blackwood looked down at her.

Honey-blonde hair. Ruffled with sweat.

'Jamie xx,' said Blackwood.

The woman nodded, then sank back between her legs.

Black bra. Why is she still wearing it?

Blackwood arched her back as the woman's tongue swept along the top of her inner thigh. The evening heat prickled across her neck and chest, clinging to her skin.

The woman's right hand rested on Blackwood's thigh while her left worked the centre, gently parting her.

Blackwood gasped and pushed the top of her head into the pillow. She closed her eyes.

Cabrera at his desk. The prints on his wall. Skeletal, depraved.

She grabbed a fistful of the woman's hair, held her firm as she worked.

'Giger saw bones as symbols of mortality.'

'Conduits for spiritual transformation.'

The woman pulled back, mumbled something about her tasting good. She paused, as if waiting for a response, then gripped the fleshy undersides of Blackwood's thighs with both hands, and dived back in.

Hair tickling her stomach.

A cycle of scenes blending into each other.

Cook warning about the dangers outside the shelter.

The strip light flickering.

Abigail's mother at the press conference. 'Please come back to us...'

Blackwood drummed on the back of her hand with three fingertips.

Abigail turning, smiling, beckoning her into the trees, blonde hair whipping as she turned.

Three right to left. Then three left to right.

Three times. Then six from right to left.

The woman stopped again. Blackwood shifted, gripped her hair, pushing her back down.

Sophie Lawson's bruised cheekbone.

The breakbeat cut out, hovering in the background at a low volume, building to a drop.

Cabrera again. 'The bones are speaking to us.'

Blackwood's hips rose as the woman found her target. She tried to focus on the sensation, but her thoughts raced on.

'But we can't hear what they are saying yet.'

The breakbeat steadily rose in volume.

Blackwood pictured a hand on a mixing desk fader, easing it upward.

The flickering strip light.

Her father, in his red-and-blue plaid shirt.

Her mother. 'He's up there somewhere, watching over you.'

'I fucking hope not,' hissed Blackwood.

The woman lifted her head. 'You okay?'

'Yes,' said Blackwood. 'Don't stop.' She gripped the woman's hair with both hands this time.

The breakbeat lurched in again.

Her breathing quickened, and a switch tripped in her core. As the wave crested, her thoughts at last surrendered to the physical.

She cried out—too loud, performative—and lay back, panting, as the woman withdrew and flopped into a chair below the window.

Blackwood reached for her phone, silenced the music. She stared up at the ceiling, as the flickering dark clouded with sweet-smelling vapour.

She looked over at the woman lounging in the chair, sucking on her vape.

'You remind me of someone I once knew,' said Blackwood, staring back at the ceiling.

'In the biblical sense?'

Blackwood laughed. 'I never have much luck on dating apps.' She reached for her phone. 'You're a rare treat.'

Missed call from an unknown number.

'Who do I remind you of, then?' said the woman. 'Someone famous and utterly desirable, I hope.'

Blackwood's eyes drifted to the bright pink folder lying on its side at the top of her bookshelf. 'Her name was Abigail.'

The woman nodded, blew out more vape smoke. 'Do you remember my name?'

Blackwood studied her. 'Daisy?'

She sat up abruptly and gathered her clothes. 'It's Rosie.'

Blackwood turned on a dim table lamp. 'We met on a hook-up app and you're leaving because I don't remember your real name?'

Rosie tugged on her underwear, hitched herself into a floral summer dress.

Powder blue?

Cornflower.

She glared at Blackwood. 'I'm leaving because you're barely here.'

Blackwood sat up. 'What do you mean?'

Rosie found her shoes.

High-heeled wedges. I need those.

Different colour, though.

She slipped them on, stood up. 'Like everyone else on that fucking app, I'm looking for thrills, intimacy, connection. And I'm not getting much of that here.' She paused. 'Look. I've had a nice night, but it's like you're somewhere else.' She headed for the door. '*With* someone else. Maybe this Abigail?' She jabbed a finger at Blackwood. 'Why not see if she'll have you back? Good fucking luck to her.'

Blackwood flopped back on the bed and listened as Rosie hurried down the stairs and slammed the front door. She braced for the familiar rejection pangs, but nothing came. Was she getting used to it, or training herself to not care?

She got up and pulled down the pink folder with *WHAT HAPPENED TO... ABIGAIL ASHBOURNE?* slashed on the front in heavy black marker. The folder was stuffed with printouts, handwritten notes on various paper sizes and types, press cuttings, and, taped onto the inside of the front flap, a USB drive of audio files from the few interviews she'd conducted. She'd told herself she would call the podcast *What Happened To...* and devote each series to a different missing person. But after researching a couple of other cases, she realised she was only interested in Abigail.

It was a familiar theme: initial dopamine rush at a big, ambitious idea, then waning enthusiasm as the logistics and drudgery kicked in.

Was she thinking too big, hoping to make detective? As she'd seen from her time at Hendon, she'd mainly be working on intelligence and admin for the higher ranks. And, as the Bones Killer case was proving, even the glamorous work was high effort, low excitement. Maybe Mallory was right and she'd found her level. At least PC work was honest and changeable, and it would give her the time to revisit the podcast in earnest.

Blackwood took out the note she'd transferred from the copy of *A Field Guide to the Birds of Britain and Europe.*

LS. Primrose Hill. Ivory Room. White Lion. Mr Shade.

She could have Abigail's handwriting analysed. No. That was all bullshit.

She'd ran through all permutations of people and locations and companies whose initials might be 'LS' and come up blank.

She'd found nothing related to 'Mr Shade'. There was a pub in Covent Garden called The White Lion, but she could hardly ask the punters if they'd seen someone matching Abigail's description fourteen years ago.

All she could find on 'Ivory Room' was a few random bridal shops and knitting studios.

If she could leverage her growing relationship with Lennox and get him to agree to that interview, he might finally give her access to Abigail's case materials, and all the work he'd done himself. Surely something would join up if they could get their heads together.

It might help if she learned more about him, beyond his love for coffee and German ambient music.

'You mean stalk him online,' she said out loud.

Blackwood reached under her bed and pulled out her laptop. She navigated to Google and typed in 'oswald lennox son suicide'.

Chapter Thirty-Nine

Blackwood's fingers pattered against her thigh as she leaned forward on the edge of the chair facing Lennox's desk. He walked over from the coffee machine in silence and handed her the sky-blue mug, then sat down with his ultraviolet.

She inhaled the rich aroma.

Lennox sat there in silence, surveying his computer screen.

Something is coming.

He sipped his coffee, sniffed, then looked at Blackwood. 'We have less than a week left together.'

She nodded, settled back in the chair, her gaze switching between Lennox and the mug. She blew on the coffee, sipped. 'So, how am I doing?'

He hesitated. 'You're doing well. Your moment with the shelter manager showed maturity, empathy.'

Blackwood's shoulders relaxed. 'I did a lot of research on homelessness a few years ago when I was planning another series of my podcast.'

'Did you ever publish it? Release? Broadcast?'

'I'd say publish. And no. That's one of my patterns. I get deep into something when I'm feeling passionate about it, but then my interest fades when the less interesting stuff kicks in.'

Lennox smiled. 'The hard work.'

'Well...'

He turned his chair to her. 'Tell me about it. The podcast.'

'I started the project after working in print magazine journalism, post-uni. I was bored by all the puff pieces and jollies managed by PRs. I became obsessed with Sarah Koenig's *Serial* and thought producing my own podcast might be a way in to investigative journalism. Something more meaningful.' She shrugged. 'Then I hit a few dead ends, got frustrated, and joined the police.'

'Quite the journey,' said Lennox.

Blackwood leaned forward. 'Can I show you something?' She pulled out her phone and tapped the screen a few times. Lennox's phone buzzed softly on his desk. 'I've AirDropped you an image,' she said, her eyes bright with excitement. 'It's a picture of the note I mentioned. From Abigail. The one she would have written in 2010, before she went missing.'

Lennox picked up the phone, his expression hardening. 'We've discussed this. We don't revive cold cases unless there's compelling new evidence.'

'I know, sir,' she said quickly, 'but I was wondering... Could you at least look back at the file and see if there's anything that relates to the note? It is new, and if we can connect it with something, it would be compelling. But if we just leave it unexplored, we'll never know.'

Lennox studied his phone. 'Alright. I have a lot going on at the moment. But once things settle, I'll take a look.'

'Thank you, sir. Abi and I were very close, growing up. She lived in this big house in Hertford Heath. She was always trying to get me to go into the woods nearby. I was scared of nature, but she was so confident and knowledgeable. She had her own horse. I couldn't believe that. We'd get to the trees and she'd see me hesitate and then urge me to follow. She had this look. So sure of herself. It was hard to resist.'

Slow down.

She took a sip of coffee. 'We had this little private detective agency.'

Lennox smiled. 'How old were you, then?'

'Nine or ten. Don't laugh. We ran pretend investigations into local village people, or if we found dead sheep or whatever. To make sure the adults didn't find out about our cases, we made up a coded language. It was pretty basic, but we thought it was worthy of the Enigma or something.'

A sharp knock at the door. Whitmore entered.

'Sorry to interrupt, sir. We have new post-mortem detail on Simmons.'

Lennox straightened in his chair. 'Go on.'

'The diatom test shows different species in the lungs compared to the River Colne. Water in the sinuses doesn't match the river. There's evidence of finger-shaped bruises consistent with being held underwater. Nothing we can get prints off now, though.' She checked a note. 'Two types of plant matter in the lungs, one not native to the Colne. Traces of a sedative in his system. Chlorinated water in the stomach. Particulate matter on skin and clothing is inconsistent with the river environment. Insect activity suggests the body was elsewhere before being dumped. Forensics estimate Simmons died approximately forty-eight hours after Foster and Tanner, but the body wasn't discovered until days later. The timeline and evidence are inconsistent with accidental drowning.'

'He was murdered somewhere else,' said Blackwood. 'Drowned. Then dumped in the river to make it look like he drowned there.' She stood up, waving her arms. 'Maybe the Bones Killer kept his body somewhere, then killed Lara and Daniel, but he had Simmons' fingernail on his clothes and it came loose at the scene...'

Lennox held up a hand. 'This is speculation. All we really have is a suspicious death. Possibly a murder. The fingernail at the scene might have been from Simmons visiting the house earlier. We should look deeper into his links with Daniel, Lara, or Malcolm Foster, Daniel's uncle.'

Blackwood's mind raced away, hurrying down several dead ends, returning, trying other routes...

Whitmore came over. 'Could the Bones Killer have murdered Simmons, then left his fingernail at the scene, to throw us off the scent?'

'Or Simmons himself was the Bones Killer,' said Lennox, 'and someone else got to him after he'd killed Lara and Daniel.'

'No!' said Blackwood, way too loud. 'Remember what the shelter manager said? The guests are most vulnerable when they're turned away from the bed queue.' She sat down again, gathering her thoughts. 'What if Simmons isn't the Bones Killer but he was present on the night of the Harpenden murders, and for some reason, the Bones Killer didn't want to leave his body at the house?' She pointed, wide-eyed. 'Maybe Simmons was procuring the animal bones for him? But this time the killer had to kill him, too.'

Blackwood paced over to the window.

'We know Simmons was at the Watford shelter a few days before the Harpenden murders,' said Lennox. 'He had a bed there for the first night but was turned away on the second.'

Whitmore nodded. 'So, how did he go from being turned away from the shelter, to being present at the Harpenden scene, to being murdered himself, either at the scene or elsewhere, and then dumped in the River Colne?'

Blackwood gazed out of the window, across the rooftops. A slate-grey peregrine falcon stood on the edge of an adjacent building's air-conditioning unit. 'He leaves the shelter, then in the next day or so, he takes the bones to the BK, who murders him to keep him quiet. Maybe it's a long-standing arrangement that he wants to end.' She waved a hand. 'Don't know why... And then... He kills Lara and Daniel, tidies up by dumping Simmons in the river... The fingernail finds its way to the scene via the BK's clothing...'

Whitmore frowned. 'There are a lot of unknowns in here.'

'Yes,' said Lennox. 'We're just speculating.'

Blackwood watched as the peregrine opened its wings and launched into space, dropping away from the building before catching an updraft. It banked sharply as it disappeared between the buildings.

Must have spotted a pigeon.

She turned and headed back to the desk. 'Doctor Cabrera said the bones "give him what he needs". The killings are almost incidental. They don't seem to nourish in themselves. So, what if Simmons did the killing for him? And... he wasn't expecting two people at the Harpenden scene. That made him sloppy and he didn't clean thoroughly like he'd done at the other scenes, which left the fingernail...'

Whitmore narrowed her eyes. 'So, he's been in this

killing partnership with Simmons for seven years and decided to end it by drowning him?'

Blackwood sat down. 'Maybe Simmons also sourced the victims for the BK. But he messed up this time, leading the BK to two instead of one, which angered him...'

Lennox gave a hollow laugh. 'And the other two drownings after the second and third scenes?'

Blackwood thought for a second. 'Not related. That's why there wasn't one after the first killing.'

Lennox shook his head. 'Now you're just twisting ideas to fit your theory, instead of—'

'Or,' Blackwood continued, 'he didn't use an accomplice the first time. And Simmons is the last of three.'

'That's a hell of a lot of work and risk just to avoid getting hands-on with the killings,' said Whitmore. 'And how does he convince the accomplices to do this?'

'Money?' said Blackwood, her mind now a runaway horse. 'He has it. They don't. Drugs? Maybe that explains the gaps between the killings. He takes time to find the right opportunity to get his accomplices. Then, once he has one, he can plan the killing. They're homeless. Desperate. Lost. Addicted. Easy prey. Maybe he threatens someone they love, on top of a money offer.' She turned to Lennox. 'It's like Chambers. Vance manipulated him, too. Paid him to come in and troll you over Jonah hanging himself.'

Blackwood inhaled sharply, as if trying to suck the words back into her mouth.

A frost settled over the room.

Lennox's face reddened. His right hand trembled as he placed it on the desk.

'Give us a minute, DI Whitmore,' he said in a tight voice.

'Sir.' Whitmore turned and left the office, closing the door softly behind her.

Lennox skewered Blackwood with a withering look. 'One more week.'

'Sir... I'm so sorry. It just... I didn't mean—'

'You have qualities, Liv. Some interesting ideas. Excellent mental agility. But as things stand, I will have to confirm to DCI Mallory that his suspicions are correct, and you're simply not ready to make the step up.' He paused, his gaze unwavering. 'Between stimulus and response, there is a space. Try to lengthen that space. That gap.'

She bristled. 'That's like telling a depressive to cheer up.'

He pivoted to his computer. 'I'm revoking your HOLMES access. And I'll remember this time. Not as a punishment, but because I'm not sure it's helping you to hit the marks. Giving someone like you access to such depth of detail is like handing the keys of a sports car to a driver who's just passed their test.'

'"Someone like you"?' said Blackwood. She stood. 'You've been stealing my interesting ideas, anyway. Passing them off as your own.'

'What do you mean?' said Lennox quietly, keeping focus on his computer.

'The different direction of the slash wounds. That was something I raised. Whitmore said you mentioned it in a one-to-one brief, without crediting me.'

Lennox nodded, typed. 'This has turned into quite the moment for you, PC Blackwood. Crass insensitivity. Breaching DI Whitmore's confidentiality. If you were a real detective on my team, then I'd be scheduling a formal disciplinary hearing.' He turned to her with a pained smile. 'DI Whitmore will assign you casework duties. If I hear good things from her, then I'll be happy to relay positive comments to DCI Mallory, which should help if you decide to attempt the course again.' He leaned back. 'Stick to the process, shut down your tendency for side quests, and you might have a good career ahead of you.' He held up his index finger. 'One week. Knuckle down and use it wisely. Busy yourself with the here and now. Don't waste it on snooping on colleagues or digging up the past. Yours or mine.'

Chapter Forty

Lennox lay on the narrow bed of the MRI machine and nestled his head into a cushioned cradle.

A male technician, Yuri, appeared at Lennox's side and gently tilted his head each way as he inserted a pair of soft ear plugs.

On his right, the young female clinician, Naomi, moved in and turned his right arm palm upwards. 'Just relax your arms flat, Mr Lennox. And please don't cross your legs.'

He moved his legs off the cushion and lay them side by side.

'I'm just going to insert a canula for your contrast dye,' said Naomi. She palpated his arm. 'You have excellent veins.'

'I'll take that as a compliment.'

She smiled, rubbed an alcohol wipe over the crook of his arm. 'Sharp scratch...'

Lennox winced as she inserted the needle.

Yuri slipped a pair of padded headphones over the ear plugs, and the ambient sound dropped to a distant fuzz. He fitted a plastic cage with intersecting bars onto the head cradle, a few inches in front of Lennox's face.

'This is a coil,' said Yuri, loud but muffled. 'It improves the radio frequency from the brain tissue. Gives us clearer images.'

'Try to keep your head perfectly still,' said Naomi. 'Use the button if you're feeling unwell or anxious.'

Yuri handed him a squeeze ball with a panic button on top.

The cage bars over Lennox's head triggered a flare of claustrophobia, and he closed his eyes.

'Okay,' said Naomi. 'We'll get started.'

The bed slowly slid backwards into the tubular scanner. Lennox kept his eyes firmly closed as the surroundings darkened. He had soothed his anxiety by reading a detailed report on the scan process, but he knew he would need to divert his thoughts away from the confinement. Transport himself from reality to imagination. Escape the present and live in the past.

Naomi's voice came over an intercom. 'Okay, Mr Lennox. Try to relax. I'll keep talking to you and let you know where we are with the scan.'

After a moment's silence, the machine emitted a soft whirring and humming.

Powering up.

Then a burst of rhythmic thumping sounds.

Localiser scan to calibrate positioning.

Lennox steered his mind away from his temporary tomb to happier times, calling up the images and sensory detail as vividly as if he were watching bodycam footage.

Strolling along the shore of Lake Garda with Martha, eating pistachio ice-cream, a few days after their marriage.

He inspected the memory. All was intact: the jade-green

cypress trees silhouetted against a pastel sky; the lemon grove terraces; the wet slap of the waves against the rocks; the Monte Baldo mountain range shimmering in the heat haze.

Intermittent buzzing. Sharp, descending, laser-gun chirps.

Tissue protons aligning to the magnetic field.

At home, with Martha and baby Jonah. Encased in a hormonal cocoon. The rapture and terror of new parenthood.

He could smell it all: the sour-milk nappies; the lavender tang of Sudocrem; the velvety warmth of talcum powder.

Rapid-fire knocking, jackhammer-like.

The MRI detecting and processing its signals from the tissues. Constructing the images.

Standing at the door of pre-teen Jonah's bedroom, as he hammered his drum kit, then paused, offering a toothy smile as he waited for applause.

But then the images shifted to Moorcroft's office.

The doctor's stacked hands, fidgeting.

The sea defence poles in the black-and-white photograph, shrinking away to an unknowable horizon.

'We start with observations and move towards ideas, ruling things out until we're left with the most likely solution.'

Rapid staccato knocking and clicking.

Diffusion of water molecules in tissues.

After a brief silence, Naomi came over the intercom. 'Everything okay, Mr Lennox?'

'Yes, thank you.'

'We'll just put in the contrast dye.'

The bed slid forwards and a chill ran through Lennox's arm as the dye seeped into his veins.

'Only a few more minutes now,' said Naomi, as the bed slid back into the tube.

The earlier sound sequences repeated as the scanner scrutinised the enhanced tissue.

Moorcroft's physical exam had been fine, but his deeper assessments were inconclusive.

'I was hoping to find a potential culprit. Something that might speak to your symptoms.'

Lennox switched away from the doctor's office.

Back to the house, at the top of the stairs. Legs buckling.

Jonah's bare feet, impossibly still, far from the landing floor.

Martha's mindbending scream announcing the end of their world.

If only he could select the memories to forget. Empty himself of the pain. Keep only the pleasure.

Amorphous green blobs—phosphenes—swam across his vision.

Rapid switching of magnetic gradients inducing electrical current in the retina and optic nerve, creating the perception of light flashes.

Moorcroft had told him the MRI was precautionary: to rule out structural abnormalities. Identify patterns consistent with neurodegenerative conditions. Seek signs of atrophy in the hippocampus and medial temporal lobes.

White matter lesions.

Ventricular enlargement.

The scanner wound down until all Lennox could hear was the underlying hum from the cryogenic pumps.

The intercom crackled. 'You did really well, Mr Lennox,' said Naomi. 'It's all over.'

Chapter Forty-One

Blackwood looked up from her table in a shady corner of the Faltering Fullback. Mid-Friday evening, and the pub was bursting: a three-deep brawl for the bar, mini-scrums of drinkers blocking the spaces between tables, groups squeezed into booths designed for half their number.

Blending conversations, clinking glasses, scraping chairs.

She had bought herself three gin and tonics and was halfway through the third.

Alcohol scattered her attention wider than usual, and she absorbed the chaos with the usual lack of filter. Noise from a crowd of pavement drinkers leaked in through the open window above her table: a steady clamour of yelping and hooting and bellowing and shrieking.

It was all too loud, all too much. But for now, it was helping. Blocking the frequencies of regret and self-flagellation.

Football on the wall-mounted TV.

Fairy lights around the ceiling beams.

Flashing phone screens.

Scurrying bar staff. Opening bottles, shaking shakers.

Sweat. Beer. Fried food. Table polish. Cologne. Perfume. Flatulence. Smoke from outside.

Faces: leering, gaping, grinning.

Heavy-lidded eyes flicking to her: some briefly curious, some lingering, most unseeing.

She finished her drink and got up, shoving her way into an adjoining room that led to the toilets.

Three young men with smart shirts and square shoulders were huddled around a central table, heads close to hear each other over the music.

'The Sound' by The 1975.

As Blackwood passed, one of the men leaned back to laugh and take a swig from his pint glass.

He found her eye, his expression moving through interest, desire, confusion, then recognition.

She strode over to the table and leaned down between his two friends.

The man set down his glass, grinned at her. "Ello, 'ello, 'ello.' He tapped the other two men on their shoulders. 'This is a friend of mine. Liv. Hide your stashes, mind. She's a copper.'

'I'm impressed you remembered my name,' said Blackwood. She smiled, hoping it looked vaguely seductive.

The other two shifted their chairs back to watch the show.

'Bet you don't remember mine.'

'Ryan Decker.'

He laughed. 'Nice to know I made an impression.' He held a hand out to shake. 'Pleased to meet you again.'

Blackwood ignored the hand. 'Impression is a strong word for the effect you had on me.'

'I remember you using stronger.'

The other two enjoyed that. One slapped the other's back, laughing.

Blackwood pushed closer, steadying herself on the table. 'I gave you a second chance, remember?'

Decker frowned. 'Oh, yeah.'

'Still time to take it.'

The back-slapper's eyes widened. 'Is this the one who threatened to throw you out of a window?'

'The very same,' said Decker, smirking.

'Oh, she's a keeper, bro.' He shrieked with laughter.

Decker faced Blackwood down. 'So, are you gonna arrest me for ghosting you?'

'Yeah,' said the third man. 'Get your handcuffs out, darling.'

Decker scuffed him across the top of his head, turned back to Blackwood. 'Look. You need to get the message. People disappear for a reason, yeah?'

She stiffened. 'Because they haven't got the balls to say goodbye?'

He pushed his head closer to her. 'Because they've had enough of you. Because you're no use to them anymore.' He hissed into her ear. 'Because they don't want you in their life.'

Blackwood stood upright, took a breath.

Decker raised his eyes at Blackwood in challenge. 'Begging ain't a good look, yeah? You should learn to let go. Lower your standards.'

She picked up a half-full pint glass and splashed the contents in Decker's face.

'Fuck's sake!' said the back-slapper. 'That was my drink.'

'Oh, sorry,' said Blackwood. She checked the table, then snatched up the glass in front of Decker and emptied it over his head. 'There you go.'

She spun, then elbowed her way to a side door that led outside.

Decker shouted after her. 'That's why I don't do mental women.'

Blackwood kept her eyes forward and set off towards Finsbury Park tube station. The night air was dense and muggy, and the tepid drizzle reminded her she needed the toilet. But to go back now would mean passing Decker and cronies.

She kept moving, taking long and purposeful strides, desperate to extend the distance between herself and the pub.

She talked out loud, composing an apology to Lennox.

'Sir... I was out of line. Way out of line. If you gave me another chance...'

A group of passers-by shot her a curious look.

She shook her head. 'No, no. DCI Lennox. Sir. I understand your reservations and I apologise for misspeaking. But I can prove to you I'm ready for this responsibility.'

A couple swerved to avoid her.

Blackwood ignored them, warming to her theme. 'I know I've made mistakes, but isn't that part of learning? You can't expect perfection from the start. Even you must have messed up when you were starting out.'

She reached the station, pausing under the awning as the rain intensified. Her phone buzzed in her pocket.

PC Tom Harris.

Not now.

Blackwood rejected the call and dug the phone deep into her pocket. She stood with her back to the wet wall, trying to compose, reset.

The phone buzzed again.

She answered. 'Hey,' she said sharply. 'It's late. What's up?'

'Liv...' He paused.

'What's going on, Tom?'

'Sophie Lawson. She's in intensive care at North Mid.'

Blackwood dropped her head back, felt the raindrops slide down her cheeks. 'Hartley.'

'Yeah,' said Harris. 'He's being treated in A&E there. She winged him with a rolling pin, of all things. He's claiming self-defence. Says she hit him first.' Harris scoffed. 'It's bollocks, Liv. He nearly fucking killed her.'

The missed call. From the night with Rosie.

Blackwood stared ahead, through the curtain of rain. She squeezed the phone side button, switching it off.

Her knees gave way, and she let herself slide down the wall to the soaking pavement.

She sat there for a while, propped upright.

As the tears came, she gripped the back of her head with both hands and pulled it down between her knees.

PART THREE

HYPERFOCUS

Chapter Forty-Two

He eased the BMW off the unmarked track onto the gravel by the lock-ups. He stopped the car by the end garage and sat for a while, the engine purr an undulating aquamarine that washed away the residue of the city's brittle reds and yellows.

The hunger howled at the pit of his stomach: a feral vacancy. His last attempt had been clumsy, imperfect. This time would be right. He had selected his target with clean logic. This time he would not allow himself to be steered by messy emotion.

He put on the nitrile gloves and approached the wall pad. He swiped the access card, with its familiar double-bleep of lime green, and stepped inside.

As he closed the door behind him, his captive began to roll and writhe inside the boot of the Insignia, kicking against the underside of the lid. With the man's movement restricted by such tight bonds, the thumping sounds were muffled. But an occasional impact in the lid's centre resonated enough to potentially be heard outside. The end garage was set away from the others, but it was still a risk. He told his captives that he was monitoring the noise from afar, and if they weren't quiet, then he would be back to silence them. That usually worked. But this one seemed determined to rebel.

He flicked on the light and opened the boot, reeling at the reek: manifest fear and desperation. He had trussed the man up tightly, with duct tape rolled in multiple layers around his wrists and ankles, and a strip over his mouth. The captive's flushed forehead shone with sweat, and he snorted as he drew rapid hits of the lock-up's stale air in and out of his nostrils, wild eyes staring.

He took the machete from a drawer and leaned in, showing it to the man. He pushed the tip of the blade against his flabby cheek, dimpling the flesh.

'I'm going to close the boot again,' he said in a low, controlled voice. It was the first time he'd spoken since acquiring his latest helper. 'If you make another noise in here, the next time I open it will be to gut you.' He pressed the machete blade onto the man's stomach, just hard enough to depress the skin through his sweat-soaked shirt. 'You will die here, alone, slowly, in terrible pain. Do you understand?'

The man whimpered from behind the gag, then nodded frantically, tears running down his face.

He eased the blade pressure and, with his free hand, smoothed out the man's matted hair. 'It's okay. It'll be okay. You need water.'

His captive nodded again.

He set the machete aside and retrieved a grubby plastic bottle from the Insignia passenger seat. He reached back into the boot, gripped the edge of the tape, and ripped it off with a swift tug.

He tipped the bottle to his captive's cracked lips, taking it away as he swallowed and licked his lips, then applied it again.

'Slowly now.' He smoothed the man's hair as he craned his neck, sucking and slurping at the water.

He tossed the empty bottle aside and took a roll of tape from another drawer. He tore off a fresh strip and approached his captive.

'Thank you,' the man said. 'But I need food. Please.'

He smiled, pressed the tape across the man's mouth, patting and smoothing it in place. 'No. You don't. That will come later. When we're done.'

He reached up to the open boot lid and stared down at his partner in crime. The man had screwed his eyes closed, and his body shook with silent sobs.

'Please don't cry. You'll be free soon.'

He closed the boot.

Chapter Forty-Three

Lennox sat before his computer, staring into the HOLMES log-in screen. Another day had slipped away, and he had scrutinised every dark corner of Operation Ossuary, building an outline for tomorrow's full team brief. Normally, he found it easy to corral his ideas into a compelling causal matrix. But he felt muddled, clumsy. The case was like a wet bar of soap, and he was squeezing too hard.

He pulled up the report on Derek Simmons, the homeless man found in the River Colne. The DNA match to the fingernail fragment from the Harpenden scene had seemed promising, but extensive background checks had revealed no connection to Lara Tanner or Daniel Foster.

He switched to a document he'd created in a specialist app that mapped out the chronology of the killings. First kill in 2017. Second in 2018. Third in 2019. Year-long gaps, and then a five-year stretch to the murders of Lara and Daniel. If the Bones Killer had stuck to his rhythm, he would have scheduled another kill in summer 2020. The Covid pandemic would have constricted his movement and possibly derailed his preparation, but he could have easily picked up the slack in any of the following four years.

They had developed a rudimentary profile and checked prison, hospital and travel records between 2019 and 2024 for potential hits. Whitmore had overseen contact with other police forces, hoping to match up with similar murders that might indicate the killer had moved and was active elsewhere. But nothing stuck.

Victimology had raised no patterns other than the victims' perceived high social status. But even that had been subverted by Lara and Daniel.

He thought back to the Blackwood confrontation, and her idea about accomplices. Could that explain why the killer left no trace? Did it connect to the five-year gap? Had his methods of acquiring the accomplices hit a logistical problem?

In Lennox's long career, there had only been one other case that had proven so unfathomable, no matter how much effort and resource he poured into it.

He navigated to a separate HOLMES portal that required extra verification. This section, invisible to most users, housed the department's cold case files. Only a select few—typically officers of DCI rank or higher—had the clearance to access the archives.

He forced his eyes away from the photo of Jonah and found the file he was looking for.

MP/15/08/2010/AA
OPERATION SONGBIRD
MISSING PERSON INVESTIGATION
ABIGAIL ASHBOURNE

He pulled up the photo of the nineteen-year-old

Abigail, taken a few weeks before her disappearance. Deep green eyes. Lightly tanned. Shoulder-length blonde hair glittering in the sun. Wide, genuine smile with a small gap between her front teeth.

Her mother had said she'd always been an outdoor type.

Plain white blouse with a silver neck chain just visible at the neckline: a gift from her parents.

The photo had been taken in the garden of her family home in Hertford Heath. Lennox magnified the image. There was a treeline—the edge of a wood—visible in the distance behind Abigail.

'We'd get to the trees and she'd see me hesitate and then urge me to follow.'

He stared at the smile, the eyes.

'She had this look. So sure of herself. It was hard to resist.'

There had been no sign of Abigail Ashbourne since a warm August night, fourteen years ago.

Lennox shifted the image to the side and zoomed in closer to the tattoo just visible on the left side of Abigail's head, behind the ear: a small white circle at the bottom surrounded by a curved black teardrop shape.

Yin. Symbolising shadow or darkness. Dark energy. Aloofness. The moon.

Blackwood's tattoo had a small black circle at the top, with the surround in white.

Yang. Positive energy. Active motion. Light. The sun.

He gave a grim smile. *Teenagers.*

Lennox scrolled through the witness statements, timelines, persons of interest. All paths that led nowhere.

Olivia Blackwood, friend. Also nineteen. Interviewed with her mother, Angela. Nothing to work with.

He navigated to the Physical Evidence log and scanned the list until he found what he was looking for.

ITEM AE02010-0037
PERSONAL DIARY/NOTEBOOK.
LEATHER-BOUND. RED.
CENTRAL EVIDENCE STORAGE, LAMBETH.
BOX REF: CES-AA-2010-B3

Lennox accessed the Central Evidence Storage database and entered the box reference. The system quickly returned the information.

AISLE 7, SHELF 4, POSITION 12
LAST INVENTORY DATE: 03/05/2023

A soft knock on the door.

Whitmore.

Lennox held up a hand as he jotted down the details.

He stood up, minimised the case app on his screen and walked over to the Jura.

'Come in,' he called, his back to the door.

Whitmore entered. 'Sir.'

Lennox lifted the lid of the machine, inhaled.

'Have a seat, DI Whitmore.'

He took out the airtight ceramic container and carefully measured out a precise amount of single-origin Yirgacheffe beans.

'Always everything...'

'Coffee?' he asked, not turning.

'No, thank you, sir. I have a small update. The victimology you requested on Simmons and the other drowning victims.'

Lennox closed the lid of the Jura, set his ultraviolet Le Creuset mug into the holder, and tapped the *ESPRESSO* icon. He pondered for a moment, then tapped the *BREW* icon.

He turned, leaned back against the machine shelf, smiled at Whitmore.

'Sir. We've confirmed that the two earlier drowning victims, the ones from 2018 and 2019, were both right-handed. Simmons was left-handed.'

He lowered his gaze.

A nutty aroma percolated around the office.

Whitmore pressed on. 'The slash wounds on the first three Bones Killer victims were left to right, consistent with a right-handed attacker. But on Lara and Daniel—'

'The wounds were right to left,' said Lennox. 'Black-wood flagged this. It was a good call, but she concluded that the killer might have injured his right hand controlling Lara and Daniel and was forced to use his left. But this also backs up her idea about accomplices. The killer might be using the men to carry out the actual killings, then disposing of them afterwards.'

'But why? Why go to all that trouble? Whatever he's getting from the killings, from the bones, why wouldn't he just do the deed himself?'

Lennox brought his coffee over. 'We should ask why he might *not* want to do the killings himself.'

Whitmore threw up her hands. 'It can't just be about avoiding trace evidence, because he devotes a lot of time to forensic-level clean-up.'

Lennox gazed out of the window. 'Or the violence itself doesn't give him the kick he's after. Cabrera noted this.' He blew on his coffee, tapped the handle with his thumb. 'It's something in the bones. In what they represent. In the ritual.'

'What if not touching the victims is integral to that ritual?'

Lennox nodded slowly. 'Using accomplices would explain the efficiency of the killings. The lack of hesitation marks or signs of struggle. If he's using desperate men to do his dirty work, and he's brutalised them, they'd be more likely to follow his instructions to the letter. They'd want it to be quick, brutal. Get it over with.'

'It could also go some way to explaining the gaps between the killings. It would take time to find and groom suitable accomplices.'

Lennox set down his mug and leaned forward, elbows on the desk. 'He's not only meticulous in cleaning up after himself. He's outsourcing the risk. We've been looking for a direct killer. But he's more of a puppet master.'

Chapter Forty-Four

Blackwood stepped up the treadmill pace, feet slamming into the infinite rubber. Her iPad, propped on the machine control panel, played a virtual cycling video from Yosemite National Park. The rider's-view camera glided along a snaking road, framed by towering sequoias with a backdrop of sheer granite cliffs.

She held her phone as she ran, editing her Spotify gym playlist: adding new tracks, deleting old, reworking the sequencing. She propped the phone next to the iPad and switched to a game: a cartoonish building grew taller as multicoloured storeys flew in from either side. Her job was to match the colours to different breeds of giant monsters who ate the storeys and stopped the building toppling.

Blackwood swiped at the building stacks, feeding the monsters, keeping sync with the current playlist song—nice and loud—while the on-screen rider sped along a stream-side path under a hard blue sky.

She chased her *Monsters Ate My Condo* high score,

projected herself into the UNESCO natural splendour, pushed for a 5K personal best.

But her thoughts still found room for Sophie Lawson, for the sting of Lennox's rebuke, and for the gnawing feeling that she'd made a mess of everything: breaking her promise to Sophie, getting distracted by Lennox's personal pain, overstepping boundaries with her theories.

Her mind raced faster than her feet could carry her.

Was there still time to correct her course? Embrace process over intuition?

Her incoming call screen replaced the game.

She slowed the treadmill to a brisk walk and tapped her headphones, silencing the music and connecting the call.

'Hello?'

'Detective Blackwood?' The voice was familiar. 'This is Emma Cook from the New Hope shelter.'

'Ah. Ms Cook. Hello. Sorry... I'm a bit out of breath. Don't worry. It's not what you're thinking.'

Inappropriate.

Cook paused for a moment, then managed a small laugh. 'I'm sorry to interrupt, but after our meeting I asked our night manager, Mark, to enquire about those three unfortunate men you mentioned. Peter Kensington, Jamie Farrell and Derek Simmons. I'm afraid we've come up blank. Nobody really remembers much about them. We have around two hundred guests each week, and the dates are quite a while back. I'm so sorry we couldn't help.'

Blackwood's shoulders sagged. 'That's okay. I appreciate the efforts.'

'I do have something else you might be interested in, though. An ex-guest of ours says he'd be willing to talk about an incident that occurred outside the shelter a few years ago, after he was turned away for a bed.'

'How long ago?'

Cook was quiet for a moment. 'August. 2019.'

Third bones killing.

'Okay,' said Blackwood. 'What sort of incident?'

'He wouldn't say much. Something about an offer he received as he was trying to stake out somewhere to sleep in the park. He said it made him nervous and he'd always planned to report it but never got round to it. He wasn't in a good place at the time, but he's back on his feet now. He says he has some free time today if you're interested. I'd be happy to join you. The Pond Café in Cassiobury Park at 2pm? Would you or Detective Lennox be available?'

Blackwood hesitated.

A tall, older man in a grey-and-black Under Armour track top stepped onto the adjacent treadmill and entered his programme.

She angled away, facing the gym's floor-to-ceiling windows overlooking the street. 'I'll need to check and get back to you. I should clarify something, Ms Cook. I'm actually still a Police Constable, not a detective. I'm in training and hoping to make detective soon. This sounds intriguing, but I'll have to run it past my superiors and get back to you. Sorry for the confusion.'

'I see. That's quite alright. I appreciate the honesty. Let me know as soon as you can.'

Blackwood ended the call and stared out at the morning traffic clamour around the North Harrow crossroads. The urge to chase the lead alone was strong. To show initiative, prove herself, present a breakthrough. If it came to nothing, she could report back to Lennox and Whitmore and claim she could tell it wasn't worth bothering them. But following up without their knowledge could come over as reckless, entitled.

'Between stimulus and response, there is a space. Try to lengthen that space.'

She switched back to music, upped the treadmill pace, and returned to Yosemite.

Chapter Forty-Five

Lennox prowled over to the far side of Dr Alistair Moorcroft's office and peered into the abstract painting hung above the examination couch. Jagged, organic shapes formed by bold brushstrokes in deep reds, blacks and whites. The mood was urgent, chaotic, with shapes and forms pulsing outward. He sensed a struggle for calm amid of some great disorder.

'Hello, hello.' Moorcroft breezed in through the open door, closing it behind him. He beamed at Lennox. 'Ah! Lee Krasner. That piece is called *Imperative*. 1976, I believe.' He flopped into the green leather chair and laid a folder on the desktop. 'It's a print, sadly. Krasner endured a marriage to Jackson Pollock, which perhaps explains the sense of chaos. I'd say she's the more talented, but that's not a popular view.'

Lennox sat in the upholstered patient chair. 'I prefer something more structured. Though I can appreciate the intensity of that kind of abstract.'

Moorcroft gave a pained smile. He opened the folder

and slipped on his circular spectacles. 'Mr Lennox. I've received reports from Dr Amelia Desai, Consultant Neuro-radiologist at The London Clinic, and Mr Charles Hargreaves, Consultant Neurosurgeon at the National Hospital for Neurology and Neurosurgery.' He took a breath, glanced up at Lennox, then back down at the folder. 'I'm afraid the MRI findings show mild cortical atrophy, particularly in the temporal and parietal lobes.' He turned a page and read from the document. *'Slight hippocampal volume loss, more pronounced on the left side. Some white matter hyperintensities in the frontal and parietal regions. Subtle enlargement of the lateral ventricles.'*

He paused, reading to himself. Traffic noise from Harley Street drifted down from the high window behind Lennox.

'These findings could be consistent with normal ageing,' Moorcroft continued, 'but given your symptoms, it's all a little troubling. I feel we need further investigation.'

Lennox nodded. 'The last time I was here, you talked about observations moving towards ideas. So, what are the ideas? What's troubling you? Specifically.'

Moorcroft grimaced. 'Mr Hargreaves notes a similarity to neurodegenerative processes.'

He paused, reading to himself again.

Lennox gazed up at the photograph above Moorcroft: the sea defence poles standing vertically, extending out into still water.

'While not definitive,' Moorcroft continued, reading from the reports, *'the imaging findings, in conjunction with the patient's reported symptoms, suggest the need for a comprehensive cognitive assessment and potential biomarker studies.'*

Lennox sighed. 'Didn't we do a comprehensive cognitive assessment?'

'We certainly did. But the next steps involve more

neuropsychological investigation. Specific blood tests. We need to consider a lumbar puncture to analyse cerebrospinal fluid for neurodegenerative markers.'

Lennox switched his gaze to *Imperative*. He saw the painting's suggestion of a cracked mirror, or a fractured patina, exposing the squirming forms beneath.

Moorcroft's speech became constricted, diffuse.

Something about brain changes that might not be visible on MRI scans.

Something about abnormal protein levels.

'Are you talking about dementia?' said Lennox.

Moorcroft took a long breath, held it, slumped forward as he let it out. 'We're not there yet. But, yes. That is one idea.'

Lennox refocused on Moorcroft. 'I'm fifty-two years old.'

Moorcroft sat back, considered him. 'It would be unusual. Around ninety per cent of dementia cases are diagnosed after the age of sixty-five.'

'So... We're talking about early-onset dementia?'

Moorcroft tried to suppress a nervous laugh, failed. 'The standard term now is young-onset dementia. Less ambiguous. But, yes.'

'That's one idea,' said Lennox, turning back to *Imperative*.

'Indeed.'

A moment of silence.

Moorcroft cleared his throat. 'We would also look at a PET scan. That allows us to observe how the brain functions at a cellular level and it can detect abnormalities in glucose metabolism which is helpful in identifying certain types of dementia.'

Lennox nodded. 'Like?'

'Alzheimer's. Frontotemporal... Alzheimer's is the most common form. It accounts for around seventy per cent of cases.' He held up a hand, palm out. 'But, again. We're speculating. This is a long way from diagnosis. We're gathering information.'

Lennox closed his eyes for a moment.

A bus engine chugged outside. Scaffolding poles clattered.

The world still turning.

He opened his eyes to discover Moorcroft in his chocolate brown waistcoat and cream shirt. Head bowed, as if in mourning.

How much time had passed?

'Next steps?' asked Lennox, his voice steadier than he felt.

Moorcroft jerked his head up and rubbed his hands together. 'I'd suggest starting with neuropsychological testing as soon as possible.' He picked up another paper. 'Mr Hargreaves concludes that, given your occupation and potential impact on your work, we should expedite the diagnostic process. Early intervention could be crucial in managing symptoms and planning for the future.'

'What kind of intervention might we be talking about?'

'In the case of Alzheimer's, inhibiting medication. And there's cognitive rehab, lifestyle change, psychological support, occupational therapy.'

Back up to the poles. The ocean of glass.

'By inhibiting you mean slowing it down?'

'Indeed.'

Eyes on Moorcroft again.

'But not reversing it.'

Moorcroft swept a palm across his forehead. 'Mr Lennox, forgive me. We are racing ahead a little—'

'Is it terminal? If the gathered information supports the idea, what's the life expectancy?'

Moorcroft narrowed his eyes. 'As I say, Mr Lennox, I suggest we move on to the next stage of investigation. I'm not sure it's helpful at this point to—'

'Dr Moorcroft.' Lennox took out his phone. 'I could find out within the next ten seconds by using this. Or you could go some way towards earning your three-hundred-pound consulting fee by giving me the general idea yourself.'

Moorcroft offered the pained smile again. 'Young-onset dementia is progressive, meaning that symptoms worsen. There is no cure. Life expectancy varies depending on the type of dementia and when it's diagnosed.' He paused. 'Some individuals live for up to twenty years, while others decline more quickly. The general range is between five and ten years.'

Chapter Forty-Six

Lennox walked to his office window and took a sip from his ultraviolet mug. The Hendon Police College campus lay before him, simmering in the mid-morning heat. A group of trainees scurried along the path between the low-rise concrete tactical centre and the sleek, glass-and-steel forensic lab. His grip tightened on the mug handle as he raised his eyes to the cobalt sky, lightly streaked with drifting cloud.

And then down and across, to the slate-grey pitched roof of an old admin building with moss clinging to its north-facing edge. He focused on the weathered tiles, catching movement.

A pigeon landed, ruffling its feathers.

He stepped forward, squinting at the edges of the surrounding buildings, scanning the dark corners for the distinctive silhouette.

He spun and strode out of the office, across the busy open-plan floor, weaving through the desks. He turned down a corridor lined with framed commendations and favourable statistics. He gave a polite tap on the door at the end and entered without invitation.

Carla Whitmore's office was compact but airy, with an ajar window above a row of neatly labelled filing cabinets. Her desk was clear apart from a slim laptop and a small snake plant.

She turned from her computer to face him. 'Sir. I was just about to call you. Blackwood had a call from the manager of the New Hope shelter. She wants to meet this afternoon with an ex-guest who might have some information.'

'Did Blackwood call you to tell you this?'

'Yes. Shall I go? Take her with me?'

Lennox took a seat. 'Let's talk about bones.'

Whitmore smoothed the sides of her hair with one hand. 'Okay.'

'The gaps between the killings. I've been obsessed with them from the start. We've explored various options for how he acquires the animal bones. Hunters, fishermen, zoos, wildlife parks, farms, pet owners, animal control centres, taxidermists.'

Whitmore nodded. 'All of which would leave paper trails. Taxidermists would be risky. Their bones would be consistent with specific techniques, methods of preserving.'

'Exactly. The killer is too meticulous to risk that. Maybe he has to gather animals from unofficial sources. That would take time.'

'Roadkill?'

Lennox tapped his thumb on the edge of his mug. 'Or shooting or trapping them himself. Either way, it would be a slow process, given the volume of bones he seems to require.'

'Sir, we explored these angles before and drew a blank.'

'We need to revisit. We can't get comfortable and assume there will be a long gap before the next killing.' He stared down into the coffee. 'I think the shift from high to low status was a mistake. And the two people instead of one… I don't think that was planned.'

Whitmore pulled her chair closer to the desk. 'How so?'

'He's been consistent in targeting high-status individuals. I don't know why yet, but it's true. The external markers from the Harpenden house. The location, the Tesla. They all promised high status. But in the long lay-off since the third killing, something's changed.' His words came faster now, as if hurrying to keep up with his thinking. 'He's still forensically aware, as before, but he's not as meticulous. He's winging it more. Something's thrown him off his axis. He's not on his game.'

'Something big happened during the gap,' said Whitmore.

'Yes. Has he been away? I know we've checked prison records, but did he find another place or situation to quiet his urges? And is that no longer an option?' He shook his head, refocused on Whitmore. 'Whatever it is, he's struggling to find his feet again. He's made mistakes. Target acquisition. Forensic clean-up. The fingernail, the hair in the doorframe…'

'That turned out to be Lara's.'

'Yes, but it shows he's dropped his standards. Or, after a period of stability in his life, his urge has returned but he's—'

'Out of practice?'

Lennox set his mug down on Whitmore's desk. 'The question is, does he know he's made the mistakes?'

Whitmore leaned forward, caught up in Lennox's intensity. 'He's organised. Intelligent. I'd say so.'

'So would I. And given that specifically high-status kills seem to sustain him for long periods...'

'You think he's going to kill again soon.'

'Yes. Whatever the bones do for him psychologically, they take time to collect. I think that's the key to the gaps. Blackwood is right. The high-status kills satisfy him. He's like a python, gorging on an enormous meal and then able to rest for months before the next hunt. A low-status kill means he needs to feed again soon.'

Whitmore pointed. 'And that means he needs to loosen up. Take a risk. Get the bones quickly.'

Lennox smiled, straightened up. 'Go see the shelter manager and her contact. Brief me later. And take Blackwood.'

Chapter Forty-Seven

The Pond Café sat in the centre of Cassiobury Park, a two-hundred-acre green oasis on the western edge of Watford that was once the grounds of a country house. Blackwood and Whitmore approached from the perimeter of the adventure playground, side-stepping the swimsuited children running a gauntlet of water jets that squirted up from a patchwork splash pad.

Inside, the café was busy with a growing lunch crowd gathered around a blackboard menu. Blackwood spotted Emma Cook and a male companion in a claret-and-sky-blue baseball cap at an isolated table on a balcony overlooking an ornamental pond.

'Ms Cook,' said Blackwood. 'Lovely to see you again. This is Detective Inspector Whitmore.'

Cook gave a tight smile and half-stood to shake hands. 'Sorry to drag you out here.'

'No, no,' said Whitmore, pulling over a pair of pastel-blue metal chairs. 'It's beautiful. I've had worse settings for interviews.'

Cook gestured to the man at her side. 'This is Mick Doherty. As I said on the phone, he's an ex-guest of the shelter and is keen to talk to you.'

Blackwood shifted her chair into the shade of an awning and sat down.

Doherty was mid-forties, bandage-white, with a salt-and-pepper goatee and cautious, deep-set eyes. He wore a faded denim jacket over a black Def Leppard T-shirt. A tarnished silver hoop earring glinted in his left ear. He took off his cap with a strange little regal flourish, as if proud to reveal his flyaway greying hair and a scalp pink and peeling from too much sun.

'How are you doin', ladies?' said Doherty.

Brummie.

He took off the jacket and hung it on the back of his seat, then rested his hands on the table, fingers splayed. The skin around his knuckles was scarred and pitted, and his fingernails looked like he'd been digging with his bare hands.

His eyes flicked between Whitmore and Blackwood, lingering a beat too long on the latter.

'Thanks for meeting us, Mr Doherty,' said Whitmore. 'I understand you have something you'd like to share.'

He issued a wheezy laugh and bore his stained teeth. 'It's true what they say. I've done nothing wrong, but I feel so guilty.'

'Can we get you anything?' said Blackwood.

'You're alright. I've got some tea and toast coming. They know me here. I used to come in a lot when I was on the street.' He took out a pouch of Old Holborn and a packet of Rizlas. 'You don't mind if I smoke?'

Blackwood shrugged.

'No problem,' said Whitmore.

'Yeah, so Em's lad, Jenkins, he was asking about them three fellas you're interested in,' said Doherty, working on his roll-up. 'Didn't recognise 'em. But it got me thinking about something that happened a few years ago. Shit me right up.' He flinched. 'Sorry… It put the willies up me.'

He looked to Cook for approval. She nodded.

'Mick's story is complex,' said Cook. 'He was a car salesman in Luton.'

'Lost that 'cos of the gambling.' He whistled. 'It's the worst of the addictions, I reckon. Goes through everything like a dose of salts. Relationships, kids, parents. The house was the last to go. I was eighteen months on the streets. Got into drink, drugs. You name it. Proper little roadman for a while. Nothing too bad, mind. Just a bit of a rogue. Discovered the New Hope and got meself turned around, thanks to the employment programme.'

A young server brought over a tray with a mug of tea and two slices of white toast.

Doherty finished building his roll-up and slipped it behind his ear. 'Got me own flat now. Nice and private.'

'Mick works as a mechanic at Kwik Fit in town,' said Cook.

Doherty raised a finger in the air. 'Two years sober. D'ya fancy a bit?' He pointed to the tray.

'No, thank you,' said Blackwood. Whitmore shook her head.

He unpeeled a single serving of butter. 'Surprised they let you in the bobbies with colour in your hair, love. No offence.' He looked up. 'Don't get me wrong. I like girls with personality. Most of 'em look the same, these days. Do you know what I mean? All the filler. Them big lips.'

Blackwood exchanged a glance with Whitmore. 'Can you tell us what happened in August 2019, Mick?'

He smiled as he dug his knife into a mini pot of jam and scraped it on the toast. 'Am I under arrest?'

'You will be if you put butter on top of that jam,' said Blackwood.

Doherty looked up, gave her the stained teeth again. 'Nah. I'm doing this slice with only butter and the other with jam.' He took a bite, his eyes widening as he chewed. 'So, that night, I get the knock-back from New Hope. They were full up. Couldn't do much about that. I head back down to Cass. Find a spot under a tree, behind bushes. It was getting on, so I knew I probably wouldn't get a bench near the canal where it's safer and quieter.' He took a slurp of tea. 'I get to the bottom of the road, and there's a car I haven't seen before at the end of Park Avenue, sitting in the shade. Fella comes over from the car and says he might be able to help us out.'

'In what way?' said Whitmore.

Doherty took another crunch of toast, chewed for a moment. 'Says he's got a property he's turning into a halfway house, out in Holywell. He offers me a place to kip. Food. Even work. Helping him do the place up.' He took another slug of tea, eyes gleaming over the rim of the mug. 'When you're on the street, an offer like that is tempting, you know? You'll take any kind of respite while you plan your next move.'

'What did the man look like?' said Blackwood.

Doherty sloshed the tea around in his mug. 'A plain Jane, really, you know? Nothing that'd make you look twice. It was dark, mind. Average height. Brownish hair. Neat. Side parting. Early thirties, I reckon. Tall fella. Lean and mean.' He took another drink. 'Sharp eyes. Proper focused. Felt like he was looking into you.'

Whitmore took out a pad and made a few notes. 'What was he wearing?'

'Blue shirt, I think. No tie. Looked like he'd just come from an office job or summat.'

'Would you recognise him if you saw him again?' said Whitmore.

Doherty whistled. 'It's been a while, but I reckon I could.'

Small, fading tattoo of a lion crest on his left forearm.

Lion facing left, tail curled at the back.

'You an Aston Villa fan, Mick?' said Blackwood.

'Till I die, yeah. Is it the cap?'

'Tattoo.'

He looked down at his arm. 'Bloody hell. You don't miss much, eh? What's your team then, darling?'

'I don't have one, really. There's a thing for Stevenage FC on my mother's side of the family, but it's never interested me.'

Doherty wheezed out another laugh. 'I'm not bloody surprised, supporting Stevenage.'

She smiled. 'So, what made you uncomfortable about this man, Mick?'

'First-name terms, love. Like it.' He smiled and pulled the roll-up from his ear, lit it with a Zippo. He took a drag and tilted back his head, exhaling the smoke vertically upwards. 'Thing is, you see. People think that because you're homeless, you must be stupid. The halfway house, the work and food… Felt like bollocks to me. I used to buy used cars to sell on. So I know what bullshit smells like. I made a few bad calls early on. Burned a few bridges. But I got better at spotting a dodgy offer. Something that didn't add up.'

Left eye twitch.

Doherty leaned forward, elbows on the table. 'So, this bloke's well dressed. Nice and smart. But he's driving a silver-grey Insignia. Vauxhall. I'd say 2015 model. Alloys were eighteen-inch, ten-spoke. And he had a dent on the rear bumper. So... The cuffs didn't match the collar. That's a right old banger for his look. So, I told him I'd leave it. Never saw him again.'

'Just to confirm,' said Cook, 'we've had no reports of such a halfway house in that area.'

Doherty took another puff of his roll-up. 'I know this probably doesn't sound like much, but it spooked me. There was something off about him. Listen. Why don't I give you my address and number, love? In case anything comes of it, you know.'

Blackwood glanced at Whitmore again. 'Okay, that'd be fine.' She took a yellow Post-it note from her shoulder bag.

Doherty slipped a pen from his inside pocket. He looked up as he wrote. 'Oh! And the other thing was, while we were talking, a fella comes out of one house near the park entrance and sparks up his strimmer, starts cutting his hedge. Not a nice noise, but not that loud. And the bloke with the Vauxhall practically doubles over, sticking his fingers in his ears, screwing his face up like he's in pain. Then he just turns away and gets off. Back to his car. No thank-yous or goodbyes. Some funny people about, ain't there?'

Chapter Forty-Eight

'So,' said Lennox, getting up from his desk. 'Our potential witness is a reformed gambler with a love of classic rock and the charm of a chimpanzee.'

'Can't fault his car knowledge, though,' said Whitmore, sitting alongside Blackwood. 'He was pretty specific about the make and model.'

Lennox hitched up onto the coffee machine shelf and gazed out of the window at the activity in the office outside.

Blackwood's knee bounced. She had been in the room with Whitmore for five minutes and Lennox hadn't looked at her directly.

A silence settled as he placed his palms together, as if in prayer, and ran the edges of his fingers up and down his grey-stubbled chin.

Lennox hopped off the shelf and walked back to his desk. Late afternoon sun blazed through the window, painting the room in slanted shadows. He sat down.

More silence. He held this one for so long it startled Blackwood when he finally spoke.

'What do you think?' he said, eyes down, head tilted towards Blackwood.

It took her a couple of seconds to realise he was talking to her. 'Doherty was pretty old-school, sir.'

'That's what you feel you should say. Tell me what you think.'

She held his eye. 'He was unreconstructed.'

Lennox raised an eyebrow.

Blackwood glanced at Whitmore; she had lowered her head. 'Okay. He was a sexist wanker. A mess of microaggressions. A negative reference to my hair colouring. Called me "love" and "darling". Also, lots of little power plays. The only bloke with three women and he ate while we talked. Performative disrespect, possibly based on past dealings with the police. Or it could have been a way of emphasising he was the one in charge, as he had something we wanted to know. He didn't ask us if we minded him smoking. He said, "You don't mind if I smoke." It was an assumption. More statement than a question. If we'd objected, it would have made us seem churlish. He also insisted on giving me his phone number on a flimsy pretence, after earlier clarifying that he had a "nice and private" flat. He didn't ask for my number, because I might have rejected him. The usual shit women get from entitled men all the time. Sir.'

Lennox smiled. 'Did you believe him? As a witness.'

'I did.'

He propped his elbows on the desk, rubbed his hands together. 'Recommendations?'

Blackwood hesitated. 'Keep his number on file. Ask other New Hope guests if they encountered the man with the Insignia and been offered something similar. Emma Cook said there had been no evidence of such a halfway house existing, so we could check that...' She faltered. 'Trace the car?'

Lennox leaned forward. 'Why?'

'Find the registered owner. Rule him out.'

He nodded, pondering. 'DI Whitmore. Retrospective ANPR, five-mile radius around each crime scene and cross-reffed with Simmons' last movements. Focus on silver-grey Insignias, especially 2015 models. Forty-eight-hour window around each incident. Cross-ref with DVLA database, stolen vehicle reports, traffic camera footage. Go back to witnesses and show them photos. Parking tickets or moving violations. Social media and online marketplaces. He might have bought the car second-hand to avoid a paper trail. Taxi and ride-share companies. The Insignia is a popular model for private hire. A driver might have noticed a similar car acting suspiciously. Local garages. Service history. Offers of overpayment to stay off the books. CCTV near the New Hope and other shelters. We're not just looking for the car. We're looking for patterns. Repeated sightings. Reoccurring routes.'

Whitmore took out her pad and made some notes.

Blackwood steeled herself. 'Sir. The halfway house sounds like a lure story. He wanted to tempt Doherty into the car, possibly to use him as a forced accomplice. Think of the slash wound anomaly. I know it sounds—'

'I agree,' said Lennox, smiling again. 'Simmons was the only left-hander among the drowning victims. His DNA was at the Harpenden scene. Your theory is starting to work for me. So let's play it out. If he's using vulnerable men to commit the murders for him, then disposing of them, making their deaths look like accidental drownings, that raises a lot of questions. Why? How does he convince them to kill for him?'

Whitmore looked up. 'The killings are straightforward enough. Quick and efficient. Executions. No sexual sadism.'

'He doesn't want to touch the victims,' said Blackwood. 'Only the bones. Like Dr Cabrera said, it's the bones that give him what he needs, not the killings.'

'Keep going,' said Lennox.

'Maybe that explains the long gaps. He needs time to find the bones. Time to acquire the forced accomplices. Time to... brutalise them. Threaten them. Break them down.'

'He conditions them,' said Whitmore. 'Grooms them. Convinces them they'll die if they don't do as he says.'

Lennox looked between them both. 'It sounds outlandish, but it's terrifyingly easy to force desperate people to perform acts against their conscience. He could withhold food, water, sleep.'

'He could offer money,' said Whitmore.

Lennox got up and strolled to the window. 'The Harpenden accomplice was left-handed, unlike the others. For such a scrupulous killer, it's sloppy. And it fits with my feeling that he's not quite up to speed after the long break.'

Blackwood frowned. 'It bothers me that there's no drowning victim that correlates with the 2017 kill.'

'Maybe the first kill was solo and he realised he needed to adjust,' said Whitmore. 'Distance himself. Serials often learn most from their first, then refine their methods.'

'Okay,' said Blackmore. 'If he is using forced accomplices, why wouldn't they just attack the Bones Killer with the weapon they used to kill the victims? After all he's put them through.'

Lennox peered out towards the dark corners of the rooftops. 'He has security. A long-range method of controlling them. Gun. Taser.'

'DI Whitmore told me you're worried he might kill again soon,' said Blackwood. 'He knows he's made mistakes. Lara and Daniel haven't satisfied him.'

'Which means he may make more mistakes,' said Lennox. 'We know he needs the bones, for whatever reason. He might not feel he has the time to acquire them safely. He could be forced to cut corners. Use outlets that leave a trail.' Lennox turned again, paced back to his desk. 'DI Whitmore. Cross-check the car search with places that might be useful for acquiring animal remains or bones. Zoos, wildlife parks, farms, pet sanctuaries, animal control centres. CCTV and ANPR. Get started.'

Whitmore made a final note.

Lennox sat down. 'Give us a second.'

'Sir.' Whitmore got up and walked out, closing the door quietly behind her.

Lennox drew in a deep breath through his nose, exhaled through pursed lips.

Here it comes.

He angled his head. 'Let's go for a walk.'

Chapter Forty-Nine

Lennox and Blackwood followed the flat, broad track that encircled Sunny Hill Park. The path-side land sloped gently upward, past manicured flowerbeds loaded with late summer blooms. Blackwood slowed to survey a cluster of basking couples, then switched her attention to the shouts from a crowded football game at the top of the hill. She sidestepped to avoid a toddler on a tricycle, and turned back to Lennox, who was power-walking into the shade beneath a dense canopy of oaks.

She jogged to catch him up. 'I swear you're testing my fitness on these little outings. Do you not believe in stopping to smell the flowers?'

He took a seat on a bench before a pond flecked with algae. 'This is business, not leisure.'

Blackwood nodded to the rusting plaque on the bench backrest: *IN LOVING MEMORY of ARTHUR THOMAS FIELDING 1932-2018*. 'Do you think Arthur will mind us talking shop?'

Lennox leaned back. 'It's what he would have wanted.'

He cupped a hand above his eyes and gazed up at the football. 'Do you play sport?'

She sat, keeping a couple of body widths between them. 'I run a bit. Mainly at the gym. Not often enough. I hate it, though.'

'Maybe find something you enjoy?'

Blackwood took out her hair tie, restrung her curls. 'The things I enjoy tend not to be good for me.' She pointed. 'Coots!' A pair of black birds with white foreheads and beaks drifted across the pond surface. 'They have lobed feet. Great for swimming, but they look stupid on land. That white shield on their heads gets bigger and brighter during breeding season. It's nature's own dating app profile picture. You should see their chicks. They look like punk rockers. They hatch with bright red bald patches and spiky tufts of orange down. Abi and I used to say they look like they've had an electric shock.'

They shared a few seconds of silence, listening to the sloshing water at the pond edge.

Blackwood shifted around on the bench, angling herself towards him. 'Sir...'

'No need.'

'Sorry?'

'To apologise.'

She nodded, looked up the hill, at the distant city skyline visible through gaps in the treeline. 'Whitmore briefed me. About Simmons being left-handed. And the latest thinking.'

'We have a few days left in our...'

'Arrangement.'

'If you like. So, we should make the most of the time.'

Blackwood smiled. 'Draw a line under it?'

He grimaced. 'I hate that expression.'

'Sorry. Yes. It means, "I'm right and I'm tired of this conversation."'

Lennox laughed. 'Since you were injudicious in your comments, I think it buys me a pass to ask a personal question.'

She squinted at him. 'Go on.'

'Tell me about the tattoo.'

She shrugged, ran a hand over the symbol behind her ear. 'Just something I had done a few years ago.'

'Try again.'

'It's a Yang symbol.'

He smiled. 'Getting there.'

'Oh. You've had a look at Abi's file.' She watched the coots as they bobbed their heads and fluffed their features, before settling back into their serene glide, leaving V-shaped ripples in their wake. 'We had them done together. She was a year younger, but definitely the mature one. I think she indulged me.'

'Interesting that I had to coax out the connection. It tells me how much she meant to you. The bond is something you instinctively protect.'

She looked at him. 'Okay...'

He met her eye. 'Remember what Cabrera said? About how we hold on tightest to the things we love the most. Out of fear of losing them.'

'Even when the holding tight is counterproductive.' She started to say more, stopped, started again. 'We were young. Experimenting. It grew into something more. For me, at least.'

'But not for Abi?'

Blackwood shook her head. 'I tested the water once, not long before she disappeared.' She turned away, wincing.

'Sorry. Over-share. Anyway. It didn't go well. I never had the chance to put it right.'

The coots climbed out of the pond and waddled over to a patch of shade.

'Jonah preferred birds to big cats,' said Lennox. 'He had a major phase of being into tropical birds.'

'I bet he told his mates all about that.'

Lennox smiled. 'Of course. I believe most teenage boys harbour a private passion for bowerbirds.'

Her eyes widened. 'Oh my god. Bowerbirds. Don't get me started. They're fabulous. They're like interior designers. They build elaborate shag pads to impress the ladies, then decorate them with all kinds of stuff. Bottle caps, straws, stolen laundry pegs.'

'The most shocking thing,' said Lennox, 'was that I had no idea it might be coming. You'd think a parent would see unhappiness in their child. Depression. Pain.' He shook his head. 'I didn't see any of that in Jonah. If it was there, I was too busy to notice.'

'It's not your fault you didn't see it. Some people get good at masking. Disguising their feelings to get through the day. To cope with whatever's going on with them.' She looked back up to the hill. 'It's a full-time job with me. It's exhausting.'

Lennox bowed his head. 'Jonah is the mystery of my life. Like Abigail is yours, I suppose.'

He was silent and still for a long time. Blackwood tuned in to the shouts from the football game, the chimes of an ice-cream van arriving at the park entrance.

'Some people just get lost,' she said.

Cringe. Too much?

She pushed on. 'It's human to think you can save people. To want to save them. I had a recent case at Wood

Green. A young woman who was clearly being coercively controlled over in Hale Wharf. Sophie Lawson. I gave her my private number.' Lennox winced. 'I know. And she called, but I was busy. Then I found out she was in hospital. Her partner beat her up, claimed he was defending himself.'

'Is she okay?'

'Just about. If I'd answered the call...'

'I can put her in touch with a domestic violence advocate I know,' said Lennox. 'She could help Sophie navigate the system. Particularly if the partner is playing dirty.'

'Thank you, sir.'

'In the meantime, knuckle down with Whitmore on those lines. The car. Places he might get animal remains quickly...'

Lennox stood up and walked away, back towards the unit. Blackwood followed.

'You'll need to follow process to survive,' he continued. 'But not at the expense of your other qualities. I want you to use your authentic self to your advantage. Don't hide it.' He sighed, glanced over. 'And here's an over-share of my own. I'm not sure how much longer I can stay at the top of my game. So I need you to help me catch this killer.'

Chapter Fifty

Blackwood joined a short queue at the MIT cafeteria. The late shift always left her craving tea and something sweet, but the afternoon rush had left the display cupboards looking bare.

She had never been good at waiting her turn. Her first driving examiner had failed her on moving off before he'd finished giving instructions; the second on pulling away at the opposite red-amber signal, before her own light had turned green.

She juggled the coins in her pocket, counting and recounting, switching her attention from the conversations in the queue to the overhead menu board with its flickering LED prices, to the stream of staff filing in from the afternoon shift change. She looked out across the cafeteria and spotted Dom at the window table where she'd seen him before. But this time he was alone, hunched in close to his laptop.

At last, the queue shuffled forward and Blackwood

ordered a mint tea and a stale-looking Portuguese custard tart.

She took her tray and headed straight over to Dom's table. He looked up and guided her in with a broad smile.

'Hello again,' said Blackwood, setting her tray down.

He nodded to the tart. 'You shouldn't have.'

She laughed. 'I need the energy boost, traipsing round after Lennox.'

Dom shook his head. 'Traipsing?'

Blackwood took a sip of tea. 'What? It's a good word.' She crunched into the tart: bland filling, tasteless filo, over-baked. Dom gazed across the table at her, head slightly angled. 'Oh. Sorry. Mind if I join you?'

'Yeah, I do. I'm busy.' He smiled. 'Nah, it's fine. You still here, then?'

'Not for much longer, I think. I've learned a lot, though. Noticed a lot.'

'Like?'

She chewed, pointed a wagging finger at him. 'I might be wrong, but I think you've been watching me.'

Flash of concern, quickly styled into an incredulous smile.

'At first,' Blackwood continued, 'I thought, "He couldn't be. He's married".' She pointed to the silver wedding ring. 'But then I heard you were separated.'

She took another bite, raised her eyebrows at him, goading for a response.

He lowered his head, flustered, then looked up. 'Are you always this direct?'

'Yeah.'

'Okay... You're right. My marriage ended last year. Mutual.' He shrugged. 'It happens.'

Blackwood took more tea. 'It does. Around half of UK marriages end in separation or divorce.'

He gave a soft laugh. 'Is this your usual approach?'

'I admit this is direct, even for me. So, do you work here on staff?'

'No. Agency. We do IT services for New Scotland Yard and various MITs across London.' Dom closed his laptop. 'I quite like not having a single base. Keeps things interesting.'

Blackwood abandoned the tart, half-eaten. 'You don't feel like a Londoner to me.'

Dom narrowed his eyes. 'Have you been stalking me?'

'No. You probably feel the same about me. Us small-towners can sniff each other out.'

He held up his hands in mock surrender. 'You got me. I'm from Holme-next-the-Sea.'

'Not next *to* the sea?'

'I know. It's annoying. Something to do with the Vikings. Next-the-Sea. Near Hunstanton.'

She nodded. 'Population?'

'About two hundred.'

'Oh, Christ. I'm a Metropolitan elite compared to you. I'm from Ware in Hertfordshire. About twenty thousand people. Not the greatest place to grow up mixed race. So, what do your parents do?'

'Farm. Started as dairy, then wheat, sugar beet. My dad got me involved from a pretty early age. I hated it. The stink, the muck. Luckily, I had a head for computers.'

Blackwood gave a mock shudder. 'I think I have a slight farm phobia. It's the machinery. The stories about people carrying their severed arms to the local hospital to have them stitched back on.'

He laughed. 'That really doesn't happen that often. Most accidents are from fatigue. Or trying to fix machinery yourself because you can't afford the call-out fees. The main thing I remember is this constant worry about weather and market prices. Dead batteries in tractors. Blocked irrigation pipes.'

Blackwood leaned forward, elbows on the table. 'Can I ask you a question?'

'Go on.'

'How do you find working with DCI Lennox? When we first met, you said you thought he was "up himself".'

Dom took a breath, his gaze shifting to the window and the view across the campus. 'He is, but with good reason. He's brilliant.' He looked at her. 'I've been doing this for a while now. I've seen briefings and cases at many other units, including the big boys at the Yard. Lennox is something different. He just has that... thing.'

Blackwood wrinkled her nose. 'Not X factor?'

He laughed. 'Well, that phrase is ruined now. It's more like…'

'Aura?'

'Yeah.'

There was a loud crash as a catering assistant cleaning an adjacent table dropped an empty metal tray on the hard floor. Blackwood startled and turned.

Dom's hands flew up to his ears, and his face contorted, as if in physical pain.

Blackwood frowned. 'You okay?'

He took a breath. 'Yeah. Hangover. Had a late one last night.'

She rummaged in her shoulder bag. 'I've got drugs for that. Paracetamol. Aspirin...'

Dom checked his watch. 'Thank you.' He leapt to his feet. 'But I'm late for a meeting.' He winced again, steadying himself on the edge of the table.

Blackwood got up and walked alongside him as he hurried to the adjoining doors. 'You should get on the electrolytes. Not the sports drinks, though. They're just sugar. Coconut water is great.' She raised a finger. 'Or dissolve a pinch of salt and sugar in water. Squeeze of lime. That's what they give you in hospitals, basically.' He pushed through the doors; she followed. 'Or eggs. They have an amino acid that breaks down the alcohol toxins. Well... Actually, the whole toxin thing is a myth. It's more about inflammation and dehydration. And your brain is trying to compensate for the depressive effects...'

Dom stopped at the ajar door of a meeting room, already full of milling detectives. He smiled sheepishly, pointed into the room. 'This is me.'

She held up a hand. 'Sorry. Brain dump. Hey! We should have a drink soon. Low-alcohol beer.' She grinned. 'For lightweights.'

But he was already inside and closing the door.

Chapter Fifty-One

Lennox stood before the curved desk in the Monro Room, one hand resting on a large sketchpad mounted on an easel. The projector screen remained dark behind him. Khokhar sat in her usual spot, beside DCI Rafferty.

He turned to face the gathering. Blackwood had arrived early, and taken a spot alongside Whitmore, three rows from the front, amid a cluster of solemn DIs. She turned to look up to the top tier of seating. The female admin assistant who normally worked with Dom sat alone in the corner, tapping at her tablet.

'So... We have DNA evidence that connects one of our drowning victims to the Bones Killer scenes. But it's the pattern of the killing blows that's painting a clearer picture.'

He turned to the pad and wrote *BONES* in thick black marker at the centre. 'After seven years, our investigative lines have yielded very little. So, I'd like to try a different approach, alongside the current fine work being done by DI Whitmore and the Intelligence Cell.' He drew a circle around the word on the pad. 'I feel certain the Bones Killer knows he's made a mistake with Lara and Daniel, who would, to his mind, be low-status victims compared to the others. This change in victim profile suggests that something has compromised his routine, his obsessive attention to detail. I suggest he needs to kill again, much sooner than we might expect, based on his offending pattern so far.'

Murmurs rippled through the audience.

Khokhar clasped her fingers together on the surface of the curved desk and regarded Lennox with a curious squint.

'We have the drownings,' he continued. 'Three deaths by water, each following a Bones Killer attack. Three individuals linked to the same homeless shelter in Watford. Two right-handers which tally with the direction of the wounds in the second and third killing. One left-hander, which matches the fourth. Given the DNA link to the Harpenden scene, I'm confident that all these factors are not coincidence.'

He drew a series of straight lines outward from the circle.

Slight tremor in the right hand.

'Are you saying there's no single Bones Killer?' said Rafferty.

'No. I submit these crimes are the work of an overseer. A single individual who plans and arranges the killings and is present at the scenes, but does not perform the murders himself.'

'Accomplices,' said Khokhar.

'Yes. We've interviewed a witness who was approached by a man with a silver-grey Vauxhall Insignia, just before the third killing. I believe this was the Bones Killer. He has acquired his accomplices by abducting individuals who have been turned away from overnight beds at the Watford shelter. He tempts them into his car with offers of work and housing. He then brutalises and conditions them to deliver the killing blows while he observes.' Lennox paced a little in front of the easel. 'We have a retrospective ANPR hit on a silver-grey Insignia near the Harpenden scene. Plates lead to a legally registered Insignia in Birmingham. This car has an alibi for the night of the latest bones killing.'

'Cloned plates,' said someone behind Blackwood.

'Exactly. This strengthens the lead. We're looking at CCTV from near the other scenes and at locations where the killer might quickly gather bones. I believe that the gaps between the killings are partially because the Bones Killer has followed a safe but lengthy process to acquire the animal remains and bones. But now he's made a mistake with the Harpenden targets, and he will need to kill again soon and therefore speed up this process. So, we're looking into road-kill collection services, pet crematoriums, butcher's shops for larger bones, taxidermists, wildlife rehabilitation centres. Also, break-ins or thefts at these locations, in case he takes an unofficial route.'

Louder murmurs.

Khokhar suppressed a scoff. 'But, Oz... Why on earth would he go to all the trouble to find accomplices when he could just do the killing himself?'

Lennox tapped the pad with the cap of the marker. 'That's what I'd like to find out. I believe the answer lies in the killer's relationship to the animal bones. There is a deep connection there. Possibly spiritual.'

Rafferty leaned over and whispered something into Khokhar's ear.

'Is this Cabrera, Oz?' said Khokhar.

He ignored her and wrote *RITUAL* at the end of one

line. 'We've dug deep into the hard evidence. The victimology. Forensics. Witnesses. I'm now asking you all to pool your knowledge and head down into the cellar with me. Help me understand what might be going on in this killer's head.' He tapped the word *RITUAL*. 'What does the killer get from the bones at the scenes? We know from imprints that he chooses a pair of bones to hold tightly. But he distances himself from the act of killing.'

Rafferty twirled a pen in the air. 'Could it just be that he has his hands full? He can't physically hold the bones and perform the killings.'

'And there's the obvious advantage of not leaving his own DNA on the victims,' said Khokhar. 'Although he's diligent about clean-up, anyway. So that doesn't really work.'

'No,' said Lennox. 'Focus on the bones. His deep connection. The tight grip. The bones mean something to him.' He beckoned. 'Give me practices that incorporate animal bones.'

After a short silence, Rafferty spoke up. 'Shamanism? Bones in tribal rituals.'

Lennox scribbled this onto the mind map. 'Okay. What else?'

'Divination?' called a DI from the middle row. 'Fortune telling with bones.'

'Relics?' said Whitmore. 'Like saints' bones in churches.'

Lennox wrote the suggestions on the pad, adding others as they arose: totems, spirit animals, ancestral connections. The mind map grew more complex, with lines encircling and intersecting.

Khokhar leaned forward in her seat. 'In Hinduism, cows are sacred. Could there be a religious element?'

'Life force,' said another voice. 'The idea that bones themselves contain power.'

Lennox added more to the pad.

'Or they're conduits,' Blackwood said. 'Like conductors.'

'Yes,' said Rafferty. 'What if he needs to hold them to connect with their... power, as he sees it? To draw something from them?'

Lennox wrote *TRANSFORMATION* and underlined it. 'There are many killers in history for whom the act of killing isn't satisfying in its own right. It doesn't fuel sadism or sexual gratification. It's a means to a greater end. Something about the murder serves a higher purpose in the murderer's damaged mind. US killer and grave-robber Ed Gein believed that through his rituals he could absorb the essence of his victims and transform himself. The Bones Killer might be driven by something similar. The human victims are mere sacrifices, and direct contact with them might compromise his process.'

'Richard Chase,' said Rafferty, pointing a finger into the air. 'American spree killer. Believed that drinking his victims' blood would stop his heart from shrinking.'

'And Herbert Mullin,' said a DI a few seats along from Blackwood. 'He actually believed his murders would stop earthquakes.'

Scattered laughter.

Lennox's marker squeaked as he added notes to the mind map. 'So, we may be dealing with someone who's interested in anthropology, with a firm grasp of comparative religion or occult practices.' He turned. 'Someone who believes he can channel a kind of higher energy through a connection with primal animal essence... Bones.'

A moment of silence.

'This is pretty out there, Oz,' said Khokhar, her voice gentle.

Lennox put the cap back onto the marker. 'We've had to go out there to get here. We're closer than we've been in seven years.' His eyes swept the room. 'After a long period of hopeful casting, we finally have a fish on the line. We either land him now before his next kill or watch him slip back into the depths.'

Chapter Fifty-Two

He steered the white Skoda Estate off the A1 at Stirling Corner, aiming for the northern suburbs of Radlett and Borehamwood. As he drifted further from the human hustle, the engine settled into a steady aquamarine purr, rippled by the crimson flares of passing traffic.

He kept the windows closed, swaddled in the tight evening air.

As usual, he controlled the new car with a pathological caution. Always a comfortable distance from the speed limit. Always giving way. Subservient. More absence than presence.

Tall hedgerows gathered around him as he left the arterial roads behind and pushed through to the unlit single tracks of rural Hertfordshire.

Nature's guard of honour.

The hunger spiked inside him, crazed and urgent now. Like some unspeakable creature, cast into a deep pit, leaping for the rim.

He held back the craving, nullifying his mind with

promises of the peace to come. It was easier now, with prime sustenance so close.

He turned into a broad connecting track flanked by dim streetlamps and slid past detached houses with landscaped gardens, set back from the road behind double gates and stone walls topped with wrought-iron railings.

He pulled into a lay-by beneath a handsome horse chestnut and killed the engine. The target house was a short distance up the road: thankfully unfortified, with no gates and fronted only by low hedges. But it was substantial: red brick, with a hipped roof and bay windows. A gravel drive curved past a small lawn to a garage at the side. No lights on. No sign of activity. No second car.

He lowered his head and waited, cocooned in the stillness.

An indigo wash rose behind his eyes, stirring him. Car engine: later than he'd expected.

The vehicle pulled into the drive and a tall man got out, silhouetted against the porch light. The man let himself into the house and turned on soft hall lighting.

He lowered the driver's side window a few inches, flinching at the mint-green pulse.

No welcoming voice called out. No lights came on elsewhere in the house.

He watched as the hall light extinguished, replaced by a distant glow near the back of the house.

Kitchen.

He lowered his head, closed his eyes.

When he looked again, the edge of the curtains covering a window at the side of the house leaked a light-blue flicker that sent a roll of nausea up from his stomach into the base of his throat.

Television.

Each pulse of shifting light built a discordant symphony of flinty yellows and greens that forced him to look off to the side until his peripheral vision had processed and nullified the visual.

He lingered there for a long time, lowering his head for respite, then raising it again, until the blue light went out, replaced by low lighting upstairs, and shortly after, darkness.

He started the engine, stirring a rich violet pulse that reflected his mood, his anticipation.

Everything was in place.

He would take his nourishment.

Chapter Fifty-Three

'Resting your eyes again?'

Blackwood awoke at the gentle shake on her shoulder. She lifted her head off her arms, blinking at the mess of multicoloured Post-it notes around her desk. Some were stuck to her monitor, others arranged in colour groups across the top of her keyboard. Two empty Costa Coffee cups teetered at the top of her overflowing wastebasket.

Lennox gazed down at her. 'Been down a rabbit hole?' He strode away across the deserted MIT floor.

She jumped to her feet and gathered up the Post-its, then caught up with Lennox as he approached his office.

The wall clock read 7:15am.

He eyed her as he unlocked the door. 'What time did you get in?'

'I didn't.' She followed him inside.

Lennox closed the door behind them, opened his blinds. 'You've been here all night?'

She shrugged. 'Twenty-four-hour office. You said we should make the most of our time left.'

He nodded, walked to the Jura. 'I know you did a later shift yesterday. But that didn't extend into the small hours.' He raised the sky-blue mug and waggled it in the air. 'Can your heart take another hit?'

Blackwood nodded. 'Yes, please.' She sat down and scattered the Post-its over the desk.

She watched as he prepared the coffee in silence.

Lift the lid. Inhale.

Measure out the precise quantity of Yirgacheffe beans.

Pour them into the machine.

Mug into holder.

Tap the ESPRESSO *icon.*

Tap the BREW *icon.*

'I'm ready to open the envelope,' said Blackwood.

Lennox nodded. 'As in Cluedo?'

'Yes.'

The scent of coffee wafted over as the machine ground and hissed. Lennox stood with his back to her, preparing his own mug.

He squashed the lid back onto the ceramic container and put it back in its place.

She wanted to wait.

Window.

Misty out.

Muffled laughter as a pair of detectives entered the office floor.

She waited some more.

He knows this is hard for me.

It's a test.

'We need to revoke Dominic Marlow's HOLMES access,' said Blackwood.

Lennox brought the coffee over. 'The IT guy?'

'Yes. From the agency.'

'Why?'

'Because I think he's the Bones Killer.'

Brace for the laughter.

The speech about trying too hard.

He sat down, eyebrows raised, nodding. 'Talk me through it.'

'A few things have bothered me since I first met him.'

He sipped. 'You sound like Columbo.'

'Who?'

'Never mind. Keep talking.'

Blackwood took a breath, steeling herself. 'In the Monro Room, when you presented following the Harpenden murders, I was fidgeting in my seat and it made the backrest squeak loudly. Nothing too horrible, but Marlow's reaction seemed really extreme. Wincing, covering his ears. At first, I thought he was doing it as a joke. But he wasn't.' She blew on her coffee, tried a sip. Too hot. 'Misophonia is a common ADHD trait. So, I can empathise when I see someone's irritation at a specific noise. But this felt different. And then, yesterday, I spoke to Marlow in the cafeteria. A server dropped a metal tray and he reacted like a bomb had gone off.'

Lennox frowned. 'So, maybe he has problems with his hearing?'

She shook her head. 'He has synaesthesia. It's a neuro-logical condition where stimulation of one sensory or cogni-tive pathway leads to involuntary experiences in another. A muddling of the senses. You might see sounds as colours, or vice versa. You might taste words, associate numbers or time periods with personalities. There's a type called grapheme-colour synaesthesia, where letters or numbers are coloured. And there's a type called sound-to-colour synaes-thesia, where different sounds evoke colours or shapes. Sometimes that reaction is so extreme it can be distressing or even painful.' She reached forward and lifted a yellow Post-it note with the words *DOHERTY* and *STRIMMER* written on it. She waved it in the air. 'When we spoke to the guy from the New Hope, he said that the man who had offered him work and shelter had an extreme reaction to the sound of a garden tool. He said he doubled over, stuck his fingers in his ears.'

She took a breath, tried a tentative sip of coffee, flexed the big toes on her feet alternately.

One left, one right.

Two left, two right.

Three left, three right.

Back to one.

Lennox placed his hands on the edge of the desk and drummed his fingers. 'Okay. First...'

'How do I know Marlow has synaesthesia? I did some online stalking. Legal. He wrote a post about workplace inclusivity on LinkedIn when he was at his previous job, before he joined his current agency. He mentioned his own synaesthesia as an example of neurodiversity. He's also posted several times in a Facebook group for synaesthetes. He talks about how he struggles with extreme reactions to discordant sound and sees colours as a response to audio and tactile stimuli.'

She paused. Lennox leaned back in his chair. 'Go on.'

Blackwood took another hit of coffee and sifted through the Post-its. She pushed on. 'He used to post abstract paintings on an Instagram account that's been inactive for ten years. The captions refer to the paintings as visual representations of how he experiences certain sounds and colours. I also found posts from Marlow on a synaesthesia subreddit, and a couple of answers he gave to Quora questions.'

Lennox held up a hand. 'Why do you see the synaesthesia as so significant?'

'A muddle of his senses might help explain why he needs to touch the bones, but not the victims. Is there something about the proximity to a live murder that gives him a specific heightened sensory reaction?' Lennox made a sour face. 'I know. It sounds strange. But I'm just trying to connect the dots and get into his head.'

'I've never really noticed Marlow as behaving particularly oddly,' said Lennox. 'As if he's experiencing sensory overload or whatever. He's always seemed pretty personable and competent.'

'Masking again. He probably only experiences the extremes when he's in a heightened state. Stressed or tense or aroused. I'm sure he has good strategies for everyday life, as long as he can manage his surroundings and keep things predictable. But when something is a shock to him, he can't just ride it without an obvious reaction.'

Lennox picked up an orange Post-it with the word *FARM?* in large, bold letters. 'What's this?'

'Marlow grew up on his parents' farm near to a small town in Norfolk. The details he gave me made it easy to narrow it down.' She took a few of the orange Post-its and read the scrawls of notes. 'Back when Marlow would have been six years old, there was an outbreak of foot-and-mouth disease in Norfolk. I found a record from his family farm that documents a mass slaughter of livestock because of infection or potential exposure. It was horrendous. Officials from the Ministry of Agriculture came in and effectively commandeered the farm. They had a team of vets, supported by military personnel to ward off resistance or protest, who herded the farm's cows and calves into a temporary structure and killed them, one by one, with bolt guns.' She checked the notes. 'They killed calves with lethal injection. Then they exsanguinated all the animals and burned the bodies in burial pits to prevent spread.'

Lennox flattened his palms against his face and massaged his eyes. 'Jesus Christ. And Marlow would have been six? Surely his parents would have kept him from seeing any of this.'

'You would hope so. But they could have been distracted. Imagine the chaos and the anger. The government turns up with soldiers and murders your livelihood before your eyes. They were compensated, but the emotional and economic fallout would have been intense. And if Marlow saw some of this...'

'It could warp his ideas around death, humans, animals. Perhaps he saw the remains being bled and burned. It would be tough to process, relating those remains to the living creatures. Did you find contacts for his parents?'

She shook her head. 'Both deceased. But I suppose we could dig deeper into family connections to find out exactly what happened.'

He waved a hand, nodded to the notes. 'Is there more?'

'Yes.' She took another drink, held up the mug. 'This is really, really good, by the way. It's helping.'

'Carry on.'

'Marlow studied a combined degree in Archaeology and Anthropology at Cambridge. Which aligns with the ideas about an interest in bones and ritualistic practices. I looked at a few niche forums on shamanic rituals and animal spirituality, but I couldn't find his usual nicknames or avatars. Maybe that's one he likes to keep to himself.' Blackwood set down the coffee and stood up. 'Sorry. I've got to move around.' She gathered up the Post-its and walked to the window, patting at the base of her neck with a hand. 'Marlow's agency job gives him access to police databases, including HOLMES. It might explain his forensic awareness and how he monitors the investigation.'

'Did you look at his work history?'

'Of course.' She browsed through her notes. 'After university, he was a junior curator at a small anthropological museum in East Anglia. That would have given him early access to skeletal remains, knowledge of preservation techniques. Then, he moved to London and took IT courses and worked at a city bank as a support technician. After that, he was promoted to IT Specialist and, a few years later, began working in IT at Homicide and Major Crime Command. Scotland Yard.'

'Giving him access to police databases, investigation details, forensic techniques.'

'Yes. Teaching him how to avoid leaving footprints, both digital and in the real world.'

Blackwood paced at the window. 'Then he joined the agency he's with now. Oh, and the city bank was—'

'Handelsbanken?'

'Yes. He could have used his position to research his first kills.' She walked back to the desk, shuffling through the Post-its. 'We're nearly there... Oh. The gaps. He was married in 2019. Just after the third kill. Yesterday, he told me they separated last year, which aligns with the long gap between the third kill and Harpenden.'

'Right. The marriage might have blunted his urges.'

'But the separation could have triggered a need to kill again.'

Blackwood scattered the Post-its on Lennox's desk, then navigated to something on her phone. 'One last thing. I took Marlow's current image and used AI to de-age him five years. He doesn't look that different, but it might help jog

Doherty's memory if we ask him to ID. I could produce a few other images in a similar vein, using different people. Show him all of them. To protect against accusations of leading.'

'An AI-dentity parade,' said Lennox, smiling.

Blackwood rolled her eyes. 'If you must. He gave me his address and number so I could drop in. Ah. Nearly forgot... Marlow is also a member of a local wildlife photography club. I checked their socials. They do regular meets in rural areas. That would give him plenty of opportunity to collect roadkill or other dead animals.'

'Or even trap them himself, then prepare and store the bones. Taking his time.'

'Yes. Another explanation for the gaps.' Blackwood picked up her mug, finished the coffee. She looked at Lennox with wide eyes. 'What do you think?'

He pondered for a moment. 'It's interesting.'

She scoffed. 'Does that qualify as praise from you?'

'There's a lot of connectivity, but we need to solidify it. What about the Insignia?'

'Oh, yeah. DVLA shows he owns a black BMW 3 Series. Maybe he once owned an Insignia and ditched it when he got married, or after the encounter with Doherty?'

'Okay. Let's bring Whitmore in and get her started on this. Full DVLA search on Marlow's registered vehicle history. Warrants for bank records, to look for spending patterns in the run-up to the killings.' Blackwood sat down, which seemed to prompt Lennox to stand and do his own pacing. 'Monitor his home. Discreet surveillance. Track his movements. Get phone records for the periods surrounding each killing. Check for patterns in calls or messages. Show Doherty that photo line-up. Re-interview witnesses from previous scenes with Marlow's description. Maybe get a warrant to search his home and other properties linked to him. Look for evidence of animal remains or bones.' He pointed. 'Might have to hold that one back until we feel confident enough to arrest. Talk to former colleagues and ex-wife about behaviour and interests. Travel records that correlate with the killings. CCTV looking for Marlow or the Insignia in the areas near the scenes.'

'Sir, can we do all this without alerting Marlow?'

'We'll have to. We're nowhere near an arrest threshold yet. Did you check if Marlow is working here today?'

She nodded. 'I did. He isn't.'

Lennox sat down again, drummed on the desk. 'Not a good idea to revoke his HOLMES access. That'll alert him. But we can keep this intelligence work off HOLMES for now until we have some clarity. You can start with that ID from Doherty. I need Whitmore here, and that's good solo field work experience for you.'

She sprang to her feet. 'There is one positive thing about Marlow.'

'What?'

'He speaks highly of you.'

Chapter Fifty-Four

Mick Doherty lived in a converted Victorian semi on a quiet residential street in North Watford. The house had been carved into four flats, with little evidence of ongoing maintenance: paint peeled from the window frames, and an unloved communal garden sprouted weeds through cracked paving stones.

Blackwood pressed the button for Flat 2B. A distant buzz echoed through the building and, after a moment, she heard heavy footsteps descending bare wooden stairs.

The door creaked open to reveal Doherty in baggy grey joggers and a faded Aston Villa kit top.

He surveyed her with woozy eyes, then grinned and headed back into the flat, leaving the door open. 'What took you so long, eh?'

Blackwood hesitated.

Doherty looked back and swept his arm towards the interior. '*Mi casa es su casa,* darling.'

She stepped inside. The flat was small but surprisingly tidy, with functional furniture. A galley kitchen opened onto a living space overlooked by a wall-mounted TV beside a grubby sash window. The air was laden with stale tobacco smoke and the acidic tang of cheap air freshener: the kind that made the smell worse rather than better. A few framed football programmes hung crooked on magnolia walls.

The morning sun filtered through nicotine-stained net curtains, shedding a sickly half-light across the worn laminate floor.

Doherty filled a white plastic kettle with water. 'Bit of an ungodly hour. Is it my magnetic personality or are you arresting me?'

'Neither. I wanted to show you something.'

'My morning's getting better by the minute.'

She scowled. 'We've done some work on your encounter with the man at the New Hope and I'd like to see if you can pick him out from a few images.'

Doherty slipped two slices of bread into an ageing toaster and took a couple of mugs from a wall cupboard. 'No worries, bab. Brew and toast first?' He wheezed out a laugh. 'Mixed up, this, eh? Normally it's the lady making breakfast the morning after.'

Blackwood moved further into the living space and stood beside a coffee table strewn with racing papers, smoking paraphernalia and empty Red Bull cans. 'I appreciate the offer, Mr Doherty. But I don't have a lot of time.'

Doherty pushed the bread down into the toaster and switched on the kettle. He headed over and flopped down on a musty-looking sofa in front of the coffee table, then patted the seat next to him.

She forced a smile. 'Like I said, I don't have much time.'

He looked confused. 'You are into blokes, aren't ya?'

'Not all of them.'

Blackwood took out her phone, navigated to a set of five

head-and-shoulders shots created with an AI image genera-tor, using a head shot of Marlow as a base. The poses and tones were all similar, but she had modified the individual looks to make them all distinct.

She flipped through to the start of the gallery—the orig-inal image of Marlow—and offered the phone to Doherty. 'Please take a look at these five individuals and tell me if you recognise any as the man who approached you at the New Hope.'

Doherty gathered together his tobacco and Rizlas. 'A piece of advice for you, yeah? I know you're just doing your job, but you might get more out of people if you're nicer to them, eh? I dunno. I invite you into my home. You turn down my offer of hospitality. You won't even sit next to me. And then you ask me to help you out. You must have heard of *quid pro quo*? Something for something.' He looked up as he rolled his cigarette and grinned again.

Roaring kettle.

Toasting bread.

Greasy teeth.

Blackwood set the phone down on the coffee table and took a bright yellow Post-it from her shoulder bag. 'Mr Doherty. In our last meeting, you described yourself as "a bit of a rogue".' She smiled. 'I looked into that.' She read from the note. 'Three arrests for receiving stolen goods. One for possession. A caution for common assault. Several debt-related county court judgements. And an intriguing connection to a cannabis farm raid in Rickmansworth last year.'

He sneered. 'Nowt to do with me.'

'Maybe not. But a broader investigation might reveal more than nowt.'

The toast popped up.

He laughed, a little nervous. 'I get it. So, we're bad cop now.'

'I just want to make myself clear. Despite your obvious hopes, sexual favours are off the table. But I could do you the courtesy of not looking more deeply into your roguish tendencies. Look. Things went wrong for you, Mick. And now you're getting your life back together. Like you said, you were homeless, but you're not stupid.' She nodded to the racing papers on the coffee table. 'Although your reading material isn't a good sign, given your gambling difficulties. So, why don't you drop the Lothario bullshit and do the not-stupid thing? Have a quick look at those pictures and tell me if you recognise the man with the Insignia.'

Steam billowed out into the living space as the kettle clicked off.

Doherty shook his head, grin wavering. He abandoned the roll-up and reached for the phone. He sat back on the sofa and swiped through the images.

First image. Brief glance. Slight head shake. Shift of position.

Second. Longer look. Solid head shake. Shoulders relaxed.

Third: Marlow. Breath held. Fingers squeezing the sofa cushion.

Fourth. Dismissive wave. Regular breathing resumed.

Fifth. Barely a look. Lounging. Performatively casual.

Doherty shoved the phone back along the coffee table. 'Sorry, darling. Can't be sure about any of them.'

Blackwood picked up the phone, turned it so the screen faced Doherty. 'Have one more look for me.' She swiped through the images slowly, watching him.

He kept his eyes on the screen, shaking his head.

As she reached the Marlow image, Doherty's eyes flicked away to look at her, then shifted back to the phone as she moved on to the fourth picture.

She swiped back to the image of Marlow, compelling him to look. 'It was this man, wasn't it, Mick?'

He squinted into the screen. 'Like I said, darling. It was years ago.' He pointed, looked up at her. 'But I'm pretty sure he's the one.'

Blackwood pocketed the phone. 'Thanks for your time, Mr Doherty.'

As she headed out, he got up and walked back to the kitchen. 'That's my reward, then? Gratitude?'

'It's all you're getting from me, yes.'

'Can't blame a fella for trying, right?'

Blackwood paused at the door. 'A piece of advice for you. *Yeah?* Update those seduction techniques. In the twenty-first century, women wait for mutual attraction before they submit to male charms.'

Chapter Fifty-Five

Blackwood laid her phone on Lennox's desk. On-screen, Dominic Marlow's de-aged image stared up at them, his features subtly altered but his sharp eyes unchanged.

She looked at Whitmore, standing on the other side of the desk. 'The first time I showed Doherty this photo, he held his breath and squeezed a sofa cushion. The second time, he actually looked away.'

'Not a great poker player, then,' said Lennox.

'But he ID'd him?' said Whitmore.

Blackwood retrieved the phone and took a seat. 'He said he was "pretty sure" it was the man who tried to tempt him into his Insignia.'

Whitmore moved around and stood by the closed door. 'Was he as charming as he was in the park café?'

'In his head, yeah. I've dealt with plenty of men like Doherty. They make everything about power, control. And when they feel like they don't have either, their tells are obvious. He didn't want to look at the image again because he knew I'd see the recognition in his face. But then I think he realised he might have more to gain by just giving me the ID.'

'You did well,' said Lennox. 'But it's shaky. We need to build the other work on top.'

'We might have something.' Whitmore sat at the round table by the coffee machine and took out her laptop. 'The Intelligence Cell has trawled CCTV from the original scenes. But we're going back a few years. It'll take time.' She turned the screen towards them. 'But we have a recent ANPR hit on the Insignia. It was caught near the approach road to the Riverside Industrial Estate outside St Albans. One business there is Wilde's Taxidermy and Natural History. Completely legit. In the UK, taxidermists who wish to sell protected species need to be registered with the Department for Environment and the Animal and Plant Health Agency. The owner, Neville Wilde, is fully compliant, with plenty of evidence of ethical sourcing, and he's a member of the UK Guild of Taxidermists.'

'That must be a fun dinner-dance,' said Blackwood.

'The bad news,' continued Whitmore, 'is that he doesn't answer his phone. At least not the number on his website and paperwork.'

Lennox drummed on the desk. 'What other businesses operate out of the estate?'

Whitmore checked her laptop. 'Agricultural supplies. Small-scale manufacturer workshops. Machinery repair shop. Couple of building material specialists. The Insignia was tagged two evenings ago, approaching closing time, according to the website.'

'False plates?' asked Blackwood.

'Yes. Same ones he's used before. Cloned from the legitimate car in Birmingham.'

'And Marlow himself?' Lennox set down his mug.

'No response to calls. His flat's empty. His agency manager says he's taken a few days off. Confirmed by our IT Director.' Whitmore navigated to her emails. 'Also, Sarah Chapman just sent this over.' She looked up. 'She's the IT admin with the braided hair. I asked her to monitor Marlow's HOLMES activity, but not to tell him. Obviously. Looks like he's accessed the Operation Ossuary file multiple times over the past fortnight. Including this morning, when he's not even here.'

Blackwood got up and looked over Whitmore's shoulder. 'Is he using a VPN to mask his location?'

'Sarah says it looks that way, yes.'

Blackwood leaned in and read from Chapman's report. 'IP mismatch. Known VPN IP ranges. High latency connection. Obfuscated server.'

'She says she could confirm the VPN with more time,' said Whitmore. 'But it seems clear.'

Lennox stood up, paced. 'Marlow now knows we're onto the Insignia. But there's no reason to believe he thinks we're onto him specifically. And it doesn't mean he won't try for another kill. If anything, it might speed up his schedule.'

'We need the taxidermist to ID him,' said Blackwood.

Lennox nodded, pondered for a moment. 'Carla, get to work on the warrant to arrest Marlow. Go through DSI Khokhar. She has several favoured magistrates and judges. She should be able to get it through today. Meanwhile, all hands on tracking him down. Phone, financials. Monitor transport hubs. Usual haunts. Friends. Socials. Get it on the PNC.'

'Marlow has the black BMW registered,' said Blackwood.

'Track it,' said Lennox.

Whitmore made a note. 'I'll keep the Intelligence Cell

focused on the Insignia, but look for the BMW, too. Cross-reference known addresses, previous sightings. We might catch a pattern now we know what we're looking for.'

Lennox strode to the door. 'You run the show here, Carla. I know that St Albans estate. PC Blackwood and I can be there in half an hour.'

He crashed out of the office.

Whitmore angled her head towards the door and Blackwood hurried after him.

Chapter Fifty-Six

Twilight mist swirled around Lennox's Volvo as it juddered along the potholed access road. The Riverside Industrial Estate was a patchwork of prefab steel and corrugated metal low-rise units, all shuttered for the night. At the back of the site, they crawled past vacant loading bays, rows of skips overflowing with building waste, and an abandoned burger van, its serving hatch sealed with an ageing padlock. Beyond, farmland rolled away towards the A414, its rape-seed glowing yellow in the fading light.

Blackwood pointed to an outbuilding set back from the loading bays. A neat, hand-painted sign read *WILDE'S TAXIDERMY & NATURAL HISTORY* above smaller text: *BY APPOINTMENT ONLY*. The single-storey unit was clad in dark timber with a slate-tiled pitched roof and was distinguished from its neighbours by traditional sash windows, all dark except for a faint fluorescent glimmer dappling through a blind at the rear.

Lennox slotted the Volvo between two skips and looked across at Blackwood. 'Somebody home?'

Blackwood leaned forward and peered out at the light from the blind. 'Why wouldn't they answer the phone?'

He nodded. 'Go on.'

'Maybe nobody's home and they leave the light on to make potential intruders think twice. Or it's from some kind of display cabinet. Or they're here but only respond to calls at certain times. I'm also thinking this is like a horror film. They'll find us here stuffed in the morning.'

Lennox laughed. 'Let's have a look.'

He got out and walked to the unit entrance; Blackwood followed. A light rain shower doused them as they reached the door.

A grubby white plastic doorbell sat below a fading sign, hand-printed in large block capitals: *RING FOR ATTEN-TION. SPECIMENS LEFT WITHOUT PRIOR ARRANGE-MENT WILL DISPOSED.*

Blackwood looked at Lennox. 'Will disposed?'

'Thoughts?'

'Proofreading isn't a priority for taxidermists.'

He pressed the button. A loud buzz sounded through the building.

They waited.

Lennox tried again.

Nothing.

'Is it locked?' said Blackwood.

Lennox tried the handle; the door opened. He looked at her. 'PACE considerations?'

She thought for a moment. 'Section 17? Entry to save life or limb.'

'What's our reasonable belief?'

'Premises are unlocked during closed hours. Internal lighting suggests occupancy. No response to bell. Given our suspicions, risk to life outweighs breach of privacy.'

Lennox pushed the door. They walked through into a narrow corridor that stank of vinegar and bleach.

Blackwood gagged.

'Formaldehyde,' said Lennox.

Blackwood took out her phone and aimed the light at the glass cabinets that lined one side of the corridor. She startled, stepped back. 'Dead badger.'

'Have you ever seen a live one?' Lennox peered in at the displays: a fox frozen mid-leap; stern owls, hawks, game birds; the badger, mounted on a plinth, eternally startled.

'Who the fuck likes this stuff?' said Blackwood.

'I suppose it's the next step up from a memorial. The embodiment of the dead thing, preserved as if it's still alive.' He walked on. 'I agree, though. It's just—'

'Creepy,' she finished. 'Animals turned into ornaments. Does anybody do it for humans?'

'You mean Grandad in his favourite armchair? I hope not.'

They moved deeper into the building, where the scents grew stronger: medicinal tang, stale fur, a sickly-sweet undertone of decay.

The glow visible from outside came from an ajar door near the back.

'Hello?' Lennox called out and eased the door open, exposing a fug of acetone, lacquer, glue, and the musk of decomposing animal matter.

They stepped into a large workshop area, with several benches cluttered with tools—scalpels, needles, brushes—and jars filled with curious substances. On the far side of the room, sturdy metal tables held the partial remains of several animals, presumably in mid-process, with their fur slicked and their skin stretched into impossible contortions.

Rows of lamps hung from the ceiling, spotlighting the grotesque forms.

A connecting door led to a small office; Blackwood leaned over to look inside.

A man lay face down on the floor.

'Oh!' She staggered back. 'Jesus Christ.'

Lennox stepped in and crouched beside the body. 'Single gunshot. Back of the head.' He touched the man's neck. 'Cold.'

Blackwood steadied herself against the wall, her breath coming in shallow gasps.

He got up and faced her, eye to eye. 'You okay?'

'No. I've never…'

'Just breathe through it. Focus on the details. We're doing a job.'

'What if—'

'He's not fresh. Killer's long gone.' He looked around. 'Not the kind of place anyone would want to linger.'

Blackwood stepped to the side, getting a clear eyeline on the body. 'Wilde?'

'Probably. Take your time, Liv. Let it process.'

She slowed her breathing. 'Don't say the first one is the hardest.'

He gave a grim smile. 'It's true. If this is Marlow, the gun explains how he controls his accomplices.'

She nodded, frantic. 'He's rushing. Needs materials quickly.'

'Yes. And he'd rather kill than risk leaving a trail.'

Lennox's phone rang: a long, loud jangling bell.

Blackwood startled, gripped his sleeve. 'Oh, my god. Who leaves their ringer on?'

He answered. 'Lennox.'

Blackwood carefully approached the body as he spoke. She crouched, looked over the scene.

Blood matted in Wilde's thinning grey hair.
Fists clenched.
One leg bent at the knee. The other straight.
One shoe half off.

It felt surreal. Unreal. Like one of the displays in the corridor. As if at any moment, Wilde might stand up and adjust his pose, reset himself.

Lennox ended the call. 'Whitmore. They've traced the Birmingham Vauxhall Insignia. The one whose plates Marlow cloned. He bought the car with cash from an elderly seller in Essex last year. Private sale. Looks like he convinced the man to delay notifying the DVLA, claiming he was between addresses. Then he found the Birmingham car. Same model, colour, year. Probably through DVLA database searches, given his IT skills, then he made false plates matching the Birmingham reg. He's been using the Insignia with cloned plates for the kills and keeping his BMW for everyday use.'

Blackwood got up, faced Lennox. She stared into space for a moment, then looked up at him. 'What?'

He frowned. 'Which part didn't you catch?'

'All of it. Something about the Insignia and BMW.'

'Short version... He switched in cloned plates from a second Insignia. Whitmore's team is tracking both cars and hunting for Marlow. We'll pick him up soon.'

Blackwood looked back at Wilde. 'What about this?'

'There's a crime scene team on the way. We can wait for them in here, surrounded by dead things, or we can go back to the car.'

They sat in the Volvo, as the gloaming blended to full dark. Blackwood gazed out at the vague shape of the taxidermist building, lit only by the tepid workshop lamps.

Lennox was silent, scrolling through his phone.

'Didn't we just make it harder for the forensic team?' said Blackwood.

He looked up from the phone. 'It's fine. We logged entry verbally, stuck to a single path, kept to the edges of rooms where possible. And it'll be easy enough to eliminate our prints.' He sighed, tossed the phone onto the back seat. 'Sometimes you have to contaminate to investigate. The team will work around us. ETA five minutes for the SSV.'

'SSV?'

'Scientific Services Van. Forensics.'

Lennox opened his window and leaned his head out.

Petrichor from the cooling tarmac.

The distant rumble of the A414.

A fox's wail, echoing off the metal units.

'Back in the Hendon park,' said Blackwood, 'you said something about staying top of your game. I thought you were being facetious.'

'I wasn't. I'm just monitoring a health issue. Stress-related, most likely. Newsflash from the future… This is the youngest and healthiest you'll ever be.'

She puffed out a sigh. 'Is this your idea of a motivational speech?'

Lennox turned. 'It's exactly that. Liv... You're exceptional.' He smiled. 'I think you know that. But keep sight of how this work can grind that out of you. You can get obsessed. Lose yourself in self-importance. Dine out on the successes. Become detached from the things that really matter. Remember to reserve a safe place for yourself.'

Blue lights strobed above the buildings behind, from the access road.

'Your hand trembles sometimes,' said Blackwood.

He nodded. The police vehicles parked up behind. Blue-and-red light cycled over Lennox's face. 'I know you want to stay and watch the action here. But Whitmore is on this. I'll brief her, then drop you home. We'll find Marlow. But whatever happens, I'll be strongly recommending you for CID. Mallory has a big say in it. But he's an arsehole, and DSI Khokhar listens to me. You'll be fine.'

Lennox opened his door.

'Sir,' said Blackwood. 'I mean...'

He held up a hand. 'I'm not great with thank-yous.'

'Okay. So, you drop me home. Then what will you do?'

He frowned. 'I think wild mushroom risotto.'

Chapter Fifty-Seven

Lennox lifted each piece of porcini from their soaking liquid, laying them carefully on a sheet of kitchen roll. The mushrooms had bloomed in the hot water, transforming from brittle fragments to velvet-soft flesh. He'd already diced the fresh chestnut mushrooms to precise cubes, measured the Arborio rice into a clean bowl, prepared the simmering vegetable stock. Before him on the granite worktop, ingredients waited in measured portions: minced shallots, pasted garlic, fresh thyme.

The sombre and stately sound of The Cure's 'Faith' album blanketed the kitchen, as Lennox heated olive oil in a midnight-blue Le Creuset pan. He added the shallots, garlic, rice, and a generous splash of Verdicchio wine that sizzled as it released notes of citrus and almond.

The evening was hot and airless, and Lennox caught the scent of night-blooming jasmine through the open kitchen window, mingling with the earthy aroma of the mushrooms.

The rice grains gleamed like mother-of-pearl. He settled the risotto to a gentle simmer and headed through a heavy oak door down stone steps to the blissfully cool cellar. Steel wine racks lined the walls. Wine had been Martha's thing, and the racks now lay mostly empty.

He found the bottle of Brunello di Montalcino they'd bought on their last holiday together in Tuscany. It had survived a Christmas party, Jonah's death, the separation. It was time to let it go.

Lennox took dinner on his lap, switching between channels, unable to settle on anything: a documentary about deep sea creatures; a BBC2 period drama with Timothy Dalton; an episode of *Coast* about Northumberland. He ate too much of the creamy, yielding risotto, drank too much of the full-bodied wine.

He reclined on the sofa and closed his eyes for a moment, then sprang up, turned off the television, and took the bottle and glass upstairs to his office. The Brunello had loosened something in him, and he sat down heavily at his desk and took a manila envelope stamped with *CENTRAL EVIDENCE STORAGE, LAMBETH* from a shelf above the computer. He slid out the red leather-bound journal and flipped through a few pages.

But the heat pressed down on him and he steadily sank into the chair, succumbing to the tug of sleep.

He jerked awake, dry-mouthed and stiff-necked. The computer showed a screensaver of blending cityscapes in high-definition: New York, Rome, London. The clock in the screen corner read five minutes past midnight.

Lennox hauled himself out of the chair, picked up the bottle, and toured round the first-floor rooms in a drowsy stupor, closing windows.

He headed back down to the sitting room, double-checked he'd turned off the television.

Double-check the stove next. Windows, lights.

Maybe a nightcap decaf.

He walked through into the kitchen.

A figure stood by the sink, barely more than a shadow, illuminated by the soft uplighting at the base of the wall cupboards. He was young, skinny, and wore nitrile gloves and a surgical mask. His eyes blazed with a terror that reached deeper than the moment. Heavy patches of sweat stained his tatty T-shirt. Lennox winced at his foul body odour.

He looked down at the man's feet.

Blue forensic overshoes.

Lennox tested the reassuring weight of the wine bottle, but scanned the room for a more lethal, enduring weapon.

Heavy pan still on the stove. Too far.

Knife block. Too close to the man.

Cast iron frying pan hanging from a rack. Within arm's reach, but awkward to unhook.

There was a large marble pestle in the cupboard near the door. But he didn't know exactly where, and he would need to crouch to dig it out.

He held up his hands in surrender. 'Whatever he's told you, he can't let you live after this. I know he's hurt you. Work with me now and you can survive it.' He craned his neck, trying to see behind the man, out of the open window. 'I'm a detective. I can help you.'

'Put the bottle down,' the man hissed. But his voice was hollow, reedy, and it sounded more like a plea than a demand.

He raised a heavy-looking brown leather cosh and shuffled forward.

Lennox placed the bottle on the worktop, then ran to the rack. He lunged for the frying pan.

But the man moved in fast and struck him across the back of the head with the cosh.

His legs buckled, and he dropped to the floor, into black.

Chapter Fifty-Eight

Blackwood lay on her bed in her underwear, starfished and wide awake. The open window delivered an occasional zephyr of baked air across her skin.

The crumpled body at the taxidermist office had been confirmed as Wilde. The image had branded onto her retinas, and her plan to overload herself to tiredness had failed. She'd started with *Monsters Ate My Condo* on her phone, while half-watching a tabloidy true crime doc on Netflix. Then she'd pulled out her laptop and fallen deep into a doomscroll hole, switching between social platforms, then browsing taxidermy websites, medical journals about sound-to-colour synaesthesia, a Reddit thread about Victorian bone collectors.

She shuffled over to the window and looked down on the silent street. A bronze Polestar 2 glided past, its engine a polite drone.

Blackwood tapped out a rhythm across the back of her hand with her fingertips: three from right to left, three left to right.

The bent leg.
Clenched fists.

How had Wilde's life led him to that moment? How had he developed his interest in taxidermy? Had his domestic clients wanted to pretend their pets were still alive or just see them presented as if they were, in that ghastly parody of aliveness?

Her mind scampered around, buffeting against random thoughts. Had Wilde been single? If not, had he met his partner through his profession? Could he have been in on the killings from the start? Had his work made it more or less likely that he was vegetarian? More or less likely that he had loved animals? Was there an animal fetish? How much had he charged? What had his typical day looked like? How had he got to work?

And Dom... Marlow. She circled back to their conversation in the cafeteria. What squirmed beneath that mask of normality? What had he seen of the mass slaughter on his parents' farm? Did it relate to the killings? The bones? Had he married because he thought he'd flushed the trauma from his system, or was it an act of extreme distraction? An attempt to sideline his urges.

She reached for her phone and called Whitmore. It rang and rang, and she was about to give up when it connected.

'Liv. It's very late. I'm coordinating the scene team at Wilde's place. What is it?'

'Sorry, ma'am. I couldn't sleep. I knew you'd still be at the scene. I wanted to ask... The ANPR hit on the Insignia near Wilde's. Did it register twice with some delay between? Did we catch it arriving and leaving?'

Silence on the line. Commotion in the background.

'I'll check,' said Whitmore. 'But it's not—'

'What about Wilde? Did he have a car? Is it parked nearby? Are there car keys in his workshop?'

Whitmore sighed. 'We're still processing the scene. Luminol sweep. Spatter. Fingerprints. Trace evidence. We've got people taking soil samples. Photographing and casting tyre tracks. Surrounding searches. It's going to be a long night, Liv. Victimology is way down the list.'

'I'm worried about DCI Lennox.'

'Why?'

Blackwood put the phone on speaker and rolled off the bed. 'High-status family background. Senior detective. His father was a prominent barrister.'

'Right. So?'

'He's Marlow's type. High status. I know Marlow has an admiration for him. He told me himself. And as you said, Lennox's recent struggles have been noted at Hendon. Marlow could see him as vulnerable.'

More commotion at Whitmore's end. 'I can see your thinking, but I have a scene to work. Call him if you're obsessing. You'll get a rocket at this hour, though. I've got to go. I'll look into the car thing.'

She hung up.

Blackwood tried Lennox's number; the call rang a few times then went to Voicemail.

Back seat of the Volvo.

He threw it there. He might have forgotten about it.

She finished dressing, then went back to her laptop and navigated to the familiar blue-grey interface of the HOLMES remote hub on her laptop, recalling Dom's mention of personal files being held in there somewhere. In the Administrative portal, she found the Human Resources database.

Current Deployments... Active Officers... Senior Management Team...

She entered 'lennox' in a searchable directory of officer profiles and found his details: line manager, phone number, address.

If she could do this, so could Marlow.

She picked up her phone again, typed the address into Uber.

Chapter Fifty-Nine

Cold tile against Lennox's cheek.

Kitchen floor.

Thudding headache. Fuzzed vision. Taste of blood.

His mouth was covered by a strip of heavy duct tape. He tried to draw in air quietly through his nose, but he spluttered, spraying bloodied snot that ran down the gag and dribbled off his chin.

Movement and voices through in the sitting room.

Lennox tried to wriggle onto his back to get a better view, but his wrists and ankles were bound by multiple layers of tape.

The young man who'd struck him came into view. He stood over Lennox, sighed, then grabbed him by the ankles and dragged him through into the sitting room, over the polished oak floorboards. The furniture had been pushed back against the walls, creating a circular space in the centre. The man dumped Lennox by the far wall.

'*Step away.*'

Lennox raised his head. Dominic Marlow stood by the

Georgian fireplace, holding a Glock 19 handgun raised oddly high, at head level. He was stooped, as if burdened, and wore a sweat-darkened white T-shirt and saggy black jogging trousers. He regarded his assistant with a tilted head and a detached, unfocused gaze: zoning into his essence but not his physical form. Like his accomplice, he wore nitrile gloves, surgical mask, forensic overshoes.

A canvas holdall sat at his feet.

As the young man moved away from Lennox, he bumped into a side table and a photo frame clattered to the floor.

Marlow's body jerked and clenched. He doubled over, semi-foetal. 'Quiet, quiet!'

The man glared at him. 'We're in the middle of fucking nowhere. What does it matter?'

Marlow sprang forward with startling speed and pressed the gun under the man's chin. 'Do you want to go back in the car?'

Lennox shifted onto his other side.

A hunting machete with a worn leather grip lay on a wingback chair near the door. Too far. Not an option. And his bonds were too tight, anyway.

The man craned his head away from the gun. 'I need food,' said the young man, defiant but wavering. 'Water at least. I'm not doing this unless I get something now.'

Marlow kept the gun on the man as he backpedalled to the holdall and with his free hand took out a half-empty water bottle. He threw it to the man, who drained the bottle in seconds.

He held it out. 'More.'

Marlow took the empty bottle, slipped it back into the holdall. 'After the ritual.'

He took out two pairs of handcuffs and slid them across

the floor to the man. 'Ankles, then wrists. Hands behind back.'

The man hesitated. Marlow raised the gun again, and he clicked the first pair of cuffs around his own ankles, then drew his wrists together behind his back and snapped the second pair into place.

Marlow stepped forwards and checked the cuffs.

He retreated and laid the gun on the floorboards near the front window, then crouched beside the holdall, unzipping it wide open.

Lennox watched, more in fascination than fear, as Marlow removed the contents: a bird skull, no bigger than a marble; the curved sweep of a fox's jaw; the chalky white skull of a weasel or ferret, split lengthwise; the lattice of a ribcage from something larger; delicate wing structures that may have been bat or small bird; a perfect row of teeth; vertebrae from various small mammals; sharp incisors still anchored in a fragment of jaw.

Marlow's breathing was shallow and rapid behind the mask, as he slowly and steadily laid the bones out over the floorboards in separate groups, forming a complex tableau.

Lennox writhed into a new position, drawing the gaze of the handcuffed man. He widened his eyes, imploring, but the man's shoulders slumped and he looked away.

Lennox shuffled himself up against the wall and surveyed the patterns as Marlow continued to work, slow and methodical, lost in his ceremony. The bones formed ever more elaborate geometries: spokes radiating outward, crescents, spirals. He laid out a group of one type, stepped back to admire the altered picture, rearranged, then returned to the holdall for more.

As the display grew more elaborate, Marlow had to pause more often, lowering his head and pressing his fingers to his temples, massaging vigorously before resuming his work.

And he had started to mutter to himself. Lennox couldn't catch anything intelligible, but now, as part of the Bones Killer's captive audience, he saw the picture. They had investigated the scenes as signature presentation. Essential backdrop to Marlow's fantasies.

But it was all an extravagant hallucination. As Marlow's mingled senses threatened to overwhelm him, he had reframed his trauma into an empowering delusion.

As a young child, he had surely seen the government executioners systematically snuffing out those beautiful creatures he had known and loved. Humans sacrificing animals to save themselves.

For Marlow, the bones were symbolic of life, not death.

They were both filter and amplifier, channelling potent but toxic human energy and alchemising it into something pure and nourishing.

The murders could not be performed by his own hand, as that would corrupt the transfer.

Marlow wasn't a killer; he was a conductor.

Lennox let himself slide back down the wall and recalled Moorcroft's words on life expectancy should his symptoms lead to a dementia diagnosis.

Between five and ten years.

The timeline had been drastically revised.

But at least now his death would be quick.

Chapter Sixty

Blackwood cupped her hands against the window of the Uber Tesla, squinting out at the tree-lined road. She checked her Google Maps app; Lennox's house was minutes away.

Her phone charge had slipped into the red, drained by monitoring their position on the app.

She leaned forward from the back seat. 'Excuse me, Amrit. Do you have an iPhone charger?'

The driver—a middle-aged Sikh man with kind, watchful eyes—dropped his speed to a steady crawl. The Tesla's hushed engine made the silence more acute.

'Sorry,' he said. 'I have a Pixel.'

'Okay. Could you slow down here, please?'

Her phone vibrated with a call. She answered.

'I thought you'd still be up,' said Whitmore. 'You're on a roll, Liv. The Insignia didn't leave here. David Pearson's deputy SOCO found it parked in a wood at the back of the site. I've called in a vehicle team.'

'What about the taxidermist? Did he have a car?'

A pause on the line. 'Yes. White Skoda Estate. It's not here. Marlow must have dumped the Insignia, knowing we were onto it, and taken Wilde's Skoda. We'll track it, but there's a lot of moving parts now.'

'Lennox isn't answering his phone. I'm near his house.'

'His house? Liv. It's late. He probably doesn't—'

She hung up, checked Google Maps. 'Amrit, could you let me out here, please?'

He checked her in his rear-view mirror. 'Really? It's pitch black.'

She showed her warrant card.

Amrit pulled the car into a shallow passing place and Blackwood got out. The night air was still and close. She crouched. Through a gap in the trees on the far side, she could make out Lennox's substantial detached house, set back from the road behind a low brick wall.

Lights on. First and ground floor.

Curtains drawn.

She leaned into the open window. 'I'm just going to check on someone. Can you please wait here? I'll be back in ten minutes and you can take me back home. If I'm not back in ten minutes, please call 999.' He grimaced. 'Please. It's a win-win. You get a bigger fee if I come back. I'll tell my next of kin to make sure you get a five-star review if I don't.'

Blackwood walked along a narrow path that had been lightly scored into the roadside verge. She navigated by her phone light, keeping the device low to the ground. The verge thinned at the approach to Lennox's drive, and she crouched, then hugged the stone wall as she stepped round onto a paved section that ran alongside the gravel.

From this angle, she had a clear view of the house front. The ground-floor light was a soft glow behind the closed curtains of the room facing the road.

Sitting room?

Overhead, a brighter light burned in a first-floor window.

Shadows moved behind the ground-floor curtains.

Impossible to tell how many people.

She checked her phone. 1:45am.

Charge down to three per cent.

Blackwood crossed over the paved section onto the edge of the drive and slowly, silently, edged up to the driver's door of Lennox's Volvo V60.

His phone sat on the back seat, its long edge tucked into the base of the backrest.

She turned, headed back down the paved section, and stood behind the stone wall, gazing into the blackness as the road sloped up, then flattened towards a broad expanse of open ground.

Golf course.

Blackwood rejoined the roadside path and continued around the house perimeter, crouched and close to the wall.

Her phone light caught a glint of metal up ahead. She slowed to a creep, holding the device even lower, navigating by the faintest glimmer from the grass below.

She stumbled, as her leading foot scuffed against harder ground where the verge gave way to a deep-set lay-by. She raised her phone light and a streak of ice shot through her.

A white Skoda Estate had been wedged in, as far from the road as possible.

She turned again, headed back to the front entrance

and walked up the paved path beside the drive, hurrying now.

Think it through.

With each murder, the killer had accessed via an open window on a warm night.

Blackwood looked back at the entrance, traced her eyes up the paved path, past the Volvo...

She checked the phone charge—two per cent—then aimed it at the ground and followed a flagstone path that curved around the side of the house, through an open wooden gate into a sheltered back garden with trimmed grass.

She squatted down, listening.

Nothing.

As her eyes adjusted, she spotted a low light leaking through a half-open sash window at the back of the house.

She checked the phone again; the screen had dropped to black.

Her heart drummed hard.

The options swirled and sorted through her mind.

Go back to Amrit. Ask him to call Whitmore.

She didn't know the number.

Would he call 999?

It was late, so traffic would be light. Despatch would be from Borehamwood or Watford. He'd seen her warrant card, so a police officer in trouble would escalate. But even a Category One call could mean a fifteen-minute response time.

The Skoda had sealed it. Marlow was here. By the time she had got back to Amrit, made the call if he hadn't...

Blackwood scurried across the back lawn and squatted beneath the open window. She drew in a slow breath, then raised herself just high enough to peer inside.

The kitchen was modern: granite worktops and chrome appliances. Glass-fronted wall units with uplighting.

Half-empty bottle of wine on the worktop.

She hauled herself up and over the sill, staying low.

Movement through in the room beyond.

Boots on wooden floor.

Door ajar.

She moved further into the kitchen and picked up the bottle by the neck, then edged to the door and looked through the gap.

Dominic Marlow stood with his head down in the centre of an intricate array of animal bones, laid over the floor in clusters and patterns.

Is he praying?

He turned and paced away, towards the curtained window, revealing a handgun laid on the floor beside a canvas holdall.

Blackwood needed a wider aspect on the room. She inched the door open just a touch and shuffled over to get a new perspective.

Lennox lay against the wall at the far end of a grand fireplace, bound and gagged with duct tape, eyes half closed, eyelids flickering.

A gaunt, dishevelled man stood beside him, feet and hands cuffed.

Her breath caught.

Her heart beat so hard she could feel it in her fingertips.

Attack?

Look for another phone and call for back-up?

Cause a distraction somewhere and draw them out?

Marlow picked up the gun, then walked over to the man and unlocked his cuffs, keeping the weapon trained on him but out of his reach. He headed back to the holdall and sank to his knees amid the bones.

'Take it,' said Marlow.

He sounded dreamy, detached. It was impossible to equate the appealing, personable character she'd first encountered at Hendon with the creature a few feet away.

The gaunt man cautiously moved to a point out of Blackwood's sightline, then went back to his spot, carrying an evil-looking machete.

Gun too close to risk an attack.

His accomplice looks weak.

Blackwood's hands trembled on the bottleneck. The edges of her vision blurred.

Marlow set down the gun again and took out two long bones, raising them out in front of him. They were clean and smooth, like porcelain.

Idling engine noise on the road outside.

Car door slamming.

Amrit?

Blackwood's fingers tightened on the bottle. The option suddenly felt absurdly feeble, like a last resort in a combat video game.

Get a knife from the block?

The one thing she had on her side was surprise.

If they had got it all right, the thin man had been controlled and brutalised. If she could incapacitate his tormentor, the man might not attack her.

Marlow carefully set down the bones and picked up the gun. He stood up and walked to the sitting-room window, inching open the edge of the curtain to get a look outside.

Blackwood shifted her position, and her foot bumped against the door frame.

The gaunt man looked over, spotted her. 'What the fuck?'

Marlow spun round, saw Blackwood.

She sprang to her feet and shouldered into the room, then raised the wine bottle and threw it to the floor with maximum force. It shattered, launching a shower of wine and glass fragments across the floor, over the bones.

Marlow cried out at the sound. He stumbled back into the curtain, ducking his head, hands covering his ears.

The man with the machete lunged for him. But Marlow raised his head, catching the movement.

He raised the gun and fired, illuminating the room with a microsecond of muzzle flash. The shot was impossibly loud in the constricted space, and Blackwood instinctively dropped low as the bullet punched into the ceiling.

The gaunt man startled, checking his stride. He tried to lunge at Marlow again, but his foot rolled across one of the long bones and he crashed to the floor, dropping the machete, which spun away under the sofa.

He scrambled to his feet, dived for Marlow, pinning him to the wall beside the curtains, holding the arm with the gun, trying to force it away.

Blackwood heaved herself upright, watching the man wrestle with Marlow.

Help him.

Find the machete. No time.

Find something else to hit Marlow with.

But the air seemed to coalesce around her and she stood there, poised but frozen in place. Suspended between attack and defence.

She looked across to the trussed Lennox and found his gaze.

He jerked his head towards the kitchen, eyes wide.

He wants me to go. To run.

She looked back to Marlow and the gaunt man.

Marlow drew back his head and butted the side of his assailant's face.

The accomplice roared, let go of Marlow's arm, held his hand to his cheek.

Blackwood charged at Marlow, head down.

She caught him off-centre, but strong enough to force him to grip the fireplace with his free hand, preventing himself from toppling to the side.

The front door exploded inward.

'Armed police! Stand still!'

Three black-clad figures in ballistic vests and helmets swarmed the room, automatic rifles raised.

The lead officer aimed at Marlow. 'Drop the weapon. Hands above your head. Now!'

His colleagues held their rifles on the gaunt man and Blackwood, who both raised their arms.

Marlow lowered his head but stared down the officer. He kept the gun low, beneath hip level, pointed down.

The officer kept his aim rigid. He raised the volume. 'Drop the gun now or I will shoot. This is your final warning.'

Marlow crouched and set the gun down on the floor.

'Cross your ankles. Put your hands on your head. Interlock your fingers.'

Marlow complied. Two more officers moved in from opposite angles, rifles trained. The lead officer maintained his aim as his colleagues approached.

'Do not move! Cover.'

The officer on Marlow's left holstered his rifle and drew his Taser. The other kept his weapon raised. The Taser officer gripped Marlow's hands, forced him face-down, and secured his wrists with rigid cuffs.

'One detained,' he called out. 'Weapon secure.'

The lead officer lowered his rifle. 'Clear.'

'I'm a PC,' said Blackwood to the armed-response lead. She nodded to Lennox. 'He is a senior detective. Oswald Lennox. DCI.'

'We know who he is,' said the man. 'Show me your ID.'

She gave a pained smile. 'I think I left it in the car.'

The lead officer looked at Lennox, who was nodding vigorously.

He angled his head and another officer walked over and peeled the tape from Lennox's mouth. He pulled out a multi-tool from his vest pocket, flicked open the safety blade, and carefully cut through the layers of tape binding Lennox's wrists and ankles. Lennox steadied himself, then got to his feet, helped by the officer.

He took a few steadying breaths and walked over to Marlow, staring him out for a moment.

He turned to Blackwood, gave her a slight nod, and angled his head towards Marlow.

Blackwood took a moment to study him.

Eyes narrowed.

Body angled away, giving her space.

Hint of a smile at the corner of his mouth.

She stepped forward. 'Dominic Marlow. I am arresting you for the murders of Daniel Foster and Lara Tanner.' She hesitated. 'I am also arresting you for the murders of... Christian Kerrigan, Duncan Langford, and Robert Sinclair. I am further arresting you for the murders of Peter Kensington, Jamie Farrell, and Derek Simmons, and for the murder of Neville Wilde.' She glanced at Lennox, who raised his eyebrows. 'I am also arresting you for false imprisonment and attempted murder.'

Blackwood paused, drew in a breath. 'You do not have to say anything. But it may harm your defence if you do not mention when questioned something which you later rely on in court. Anything you do say may be given in evidence.'

Lennox nodded to the lead officer, who ushered Marlow out through the front door. His colleague tried to do the same with the accomplice, but Lennox put a hand on his shoulder. 'This man is innocent. Please give him some water.'

The officer followed the gaunt man back into the kitchen.

Lennox turned to face Blackwood.

'You left your phone in the car,' she said.

'You left your ID.'

She looked around at the scattered bones, the broken glass, the spilled wine. 'Sorry about the mess.'

Chapter Sixty-One

THREE DAYS LATER

DSI Aisha Khokhar's office baked in the glare of the morning sun, washing her glass-topped desk in deep amber. She half-closed the blind slats and walked to a recessed shelf with a tall water jug.

Lennox watched in silence as she prepared two glasses. Her silver bracelet slipped down her wrist as she poured.

'There's a lot to process, Oz,' said Khokhar, bringing over the water. 'Most importantly, how are you feeling?'

'Like I've been interviewed by half the Met's counselling service.' He touched the fading bruise at the base of his skull. 'The Medical Examiner cleared me physically. Just soft tissue damage. But Occupational Health wants me to complete six mandatory sessions with the Trauma Risk Management team before signing me back to full duties.'

'You know the standard.' Khokhar passed him a glass. 'The TRiM practitioners are there to make sure the pieces get put back together with no missing bits.'

He took a sip, smiled. 'I can't guarantee that, ma'am. They say I need to complete a personal risk assessment. Document my lived experience of the incident. Prove I'm not suffering acute stress reaction or showing signs of PTS.'

She took her seat, adjusting her hijab. 'And are you?'

'No. But they'll want to monitor for delayed onset. Weekly check-ins for the first month. Then monthly for six months.'

Khokhar fixed him with her probing brown eyes. 'Don't go all alpha on me, Oz. There's no shame in taking the support. You were assaulted in your own home. Bound and held at gunpoint. That's not a typical evening.'

'It's not the worst thing that's happened to me. And I'm still here.'

She sat back. 'The wellness team also mentioned cognitive testing.'

Lennox adjusted his tie. 'That isn't necessary.'

Khokhar's eyes narrowed slightly. 'Still. You should ease yourself back in. Tell me about Marlow. I've read the statements, but I'd like to hear it from you unfiltered.'

'CPS is pushing for a whole life order. His legal team will probably advise a guilty plea, given the evidence.' He shifted in his chair. 'The man he brought to my house, Jordan Walsh, says Marlow kept him in the boot of the Insignia with minimal food and water and promised to release him once he'd completed the task. He recruited Walsh from a homeless shelter in Hemel Hempstead with the same story he told Doherty. Offers of food, shelter, work. Walsh wasn't fully under his spell, though. I think Marlow took more time over the grooming on previous kills, but he had to rush this one. Probably because of his mistake in killing Lara and Daniel, whom he saw as lower status.'

Khokhar nodded. 'Which also explains why he felt he

had to acquire the animal remains quickly from the taxidermist but kill him to avoid leaving a paper trail.'

Lennox leaned back into the slatted lighting from the window. 'It's going to take time to unpack the psychopathology. We'll probably get nothing coherent from Marlow himself. We might learn more if he submits to psychiatric evaluation. I believe the trauma we think he experienced during a cull at his family farm blended with his mingled senses, creating a toxic compulsion and some pretty intense delusions. I think he saw animals as pure in some sense, and humans as polluted. And so the clean bones of the untainted animals, their essence, somehow transfigured the potent but impure human energy, set loose by the killing, into a force that fulfilled him. Nourished him.'

Khokhar closed her eyes for a moment, opened them again. 'And is this your assessment or Dr Cabrera's?'

Lennox gave a half-smile. 'A bit of both. We had coffee yesterday. He thinks Marlow's synaesthesia solidified this pathological need to transform death into something pure. Something beautiful.'

'And Walsh?'

'He'll be treated as a victim. Whitmore's handling the wrap-up. CPS is confident on all counts, given the links to the previous murders, the drownings. And by dumping the Insignia at Wilde's, Marlow strengthened our case. We can also draw a solid line from the first three targets to Marlow's IT access at the Handelsbanken private bank.'

Khokhar took a long drink of water, then brightened. 'So, let's talk about Blackwood.'

'She did well.'

Khokhar scoffed. 'She certainly did. Fine instinct from DI Whitmore, too. Blackwood called her from outside your house and she called in the AR team. I'm nominating

Blackwood for the Chief Constable's Commendation. The Honours Committee will review it, but I'm confident.'

'She deserves it.'

'I'm also recommending her for promotion to Detective Constable, citing your report. Since this is where she was mentored, I also want her based with us during her probation. I've no doubt she'll integrate well. DCI Mallory is insisting she complete her outstanding training requirements, but after my award commendation and her work on this case, the assessment board should fast-track the promotion.' Khokhar tapped her pen on the desk. 'There's admin, budget allocation, team restructuring. Nothing insurmountable. I've already met with the DCS and Specialist Crime Assistant Commissioner.' She frowned. 'Your involvement in this case ended with your life at serious risk, Oz. But your work was vital, as was your mentoring. It's all been noted.'

Lennox nodded. 'Plenty of magic left in the wand.'

Khokhar leaned forward, smiling. 'You should take a break. Happy to sign you off.'

'I don't need a break, ma'am. But I would like something not so urgent to keep me busy while I ease myself back in. I want to heat up a cold case.'

Chapter Sixty-Two

Blackwood swerved away from the midday crowds on the sloping central lawn of Sunny Hill Park and ducked into the shade beneath the canopy of oaks. She hopped over a flowerbed of purple salvias and headed for the algae-strewn pond. Lennox sat on the Arthur Fielding bench, with his back to her approach.

'This feels like a bad spy film,' she said, flopping down beside him.

He glanced over. 'Did you not get the memo about having a *Financial Times* tucked under your arm?'

She nodded to the orange-and-grey backpack sitting at his feet. 'Have you brought a picnic?'

He grimaced. 'I hate picnics. Wasps and dogshit. Have they finished probing?'

'Medical Examiner gave me the all-clear. Had my TRiM assessment yesterday. Counselling next week.' She shrugged. 'This will be my fifth therapist. My last one ended in a nasty argument because I felt like he wasn't really listening. I needed a counsellor to get over the counselling.'

Lennox laughed and gazed out at the pond. A shaft of sunlight caught the rising vapour from the water's surface. 'Congratulations, by the way.'

'For saving your life?'

'I assume it wasn't personal. You would have done it for anyone.'

She angled her head from side to side. 'Maybe not Mallory.'

'I meant congratulations on the change in letter. PC to DC.' He paused. She turned to him, primed for a thank-you, but he held up a hand. 'How is Sophie Lawson?'

'Oh. Yes. The advocate contact you passed on... She's in touch with her. I'm trying to stay out of it.' She cried out, pointed. 'It's our coots!'

The pair of velvet-black birds with their distinctive white shields drifted into view, their heads bobbing gently as they crossed the water. An elderly woman with two young children approached the pond from the opposite edge. The woman gave the children a bread wrapper fashioned into a bag, and they took it in turns throwing handfuls of crumbs into the water.

'Shouldn't do that,' Blackwood said, keeping her voice low. 'Bread is bird junk food. High carb, low nutrients. Doesn't help their foraging instincts, either.'

'I don't think it's an arrestable offence, though.'

She gathered herself. 'So, what now?'

'Are you working notice at Wood Green?'

'Yes. My mum was delighted. My boss was not.' She thought for a moment, knee bouncing. 'You know what? I haven't seen much about the Bones Killer case in the news.'

'Khokhar doesn't want to shout too loud about it.'

'Because of Marlow being under her nose for so long? Walsh will sell his story, though, right?'

Lennox puffed out a sigh. 'Probably. But he'll have to wait until after sentencing.' He angled himself towards her. 'Here's a nasty little postscript. We got a hit on Marlow's BMW near to your Harrow home address, a few days before Marlow attacked Wilde.'

Blackwood sat back on the bench, eyes wide. 'Yes. Was he targeting me, too?'

'At first, maybe. Then he probably felt the shared house would make it too difficult, realised I lived alone...' He raised an eyebrow. 'Higher status.' He held her eye, smiling.

'Hey. I'm catching up now.'

Lennox looked back to the pond. 'Average time from DC to DS is five years. Another three to DI. You'll get there in half that.'

She stared at the ground, scuffed her heels. 'I quite fancied Marlow. I thought he fancied me, too.' She gave a bitter laugh. 'Sums up my luck with men. Dickheads or murderers.'

'How about women?'

'Not much better lately, either.' She stared up into the cloudless sky. 'I think I'll stick to birds.'

Lennox picked up the backpack and set it on his lap. 'Every relationship will fail until one doesn't.'

She turned to him sharply. 'Crazy to think that Marlow fetishised animals and killed Wilde surrounded by all those horrible stuffed creatures... Oh. I meant to ask. How's your health thing?' She winced. 'Sorry. Inappropriate. I was also going to compliment you on your house. Whitmore said...'

Slow down.

She took a breath. 'I had lunch with DI Whitmore. She said you must have been terrified, knowing what Marlow was planning. Knowing the case history so well.' She glanced at the pond, back to Lennox. 'Were you? Scared?'

Lennox smiled and unzipped the backpack. 'I remember a glorious summer day like this, back when Jonah was small. We were in the garden. Martha was inside, unwell with hay fever. A little blue-and-yellow bird hopped up to us.'

'Blue tit.'

'Jonah held out his hand. Unbelievably, it flew onto his finger and perched there.'

'That's wonderful.'

He nodded. 'Those moments seem trivial and fleeting, but you come to realise how important they are. How the small things are the big things. I'm more afraid of losing those memories, of living without them, than I am of losing my life.'

'Is this about the health issue? I've noticed a few things.'

He found her eye. 'Like what?'

Blackwood hesitated. 'Can I be totally honest?' She barrelled on, without waiting for an answer. 'Your hand shaking. Little moments of blankness and hesitation.' She twisted round on the bench, fully facing him. 'Sir... Leaving your phone in the car. Who doesn't notice their phone is missing?' She shuffled closer. 'I know all about masking. The last time we were in this park, you told me not to hide my authentic self. I think I know what you're worried about. I saw those things with my grandma.'

Lennox was silent for a long time. 'I'm having tests. They're monitoring. It could be nothing. It probably is nothing. But in my job, once the blood gets into the water, the sharks get busy. Khokhar is setting me up for early retirement.' He took a manila envelope from the backpack. 'But I'm doubling down. I want to revitalise my mind. Keep it active. That's how you fight this kind of decline, isn't it?' He set the envelope down on the bench between them. 'You can help me do that.'

She pointed. 'What's this?'

'Have a look. It's a 2010 diary we took from Abigail Ashbourne's home soon after her disappearance.' Blackwood picked up the envelope. 'Don't get too excited. She doesn't document her innermost thoughts. Most of it is pretty mundane. Appointments, birthdays.'

Blackwood took a red leather-bound notebook diary from the envelope. Each week of the year had its own page, divided into seven daily blocks. Her breath caught at the sight of Abigail's handwriting: the circular flourishes that formed the 'i' dots; the curlicues on the tails of her long 'g', 'j' and 'y' tails. 'I remember she had these diaries when we were kids. Same style.' Her voice was thin and distant. She looked at Lennox. 'Her mum bought them for her every year.'

'It's the only one we found.' He shrugged. 'Makes sense, as it's a diary. She probably threw the old ones away. There are some entries in a sort of gobbledygook language. Is that the secret code you used to share?'

'Yes, when we had our detective agency. It wasn't a very sophisticated code, though.'

Lennox smiled. 'Move the first letter back one place in the alphabet, the second back two, repeat.'

Blackwood turned the pages. 'Yes. But there's only a few coded entries. And they don't look very interesting. Just things she might not want her mum to know about.' She squinted at the faded writing. 'This one's about smoking a spliff and feeling sick... Something about a boy she met at Bev Payne's party.' She looked up briefly. 'I remember it... Another about a trip to the cinema with girlfriends. I don't remember that, but I was probably there.'

'Look at 12th April.'

Blackwood flipped to the page. Abigail had filled the day with multiple lines made up of the same two initials—JP—stacked on top of each other.

The elderly woman and the children moved away from the pond, leaving Lennox and Blackwood alone.

'Primrose Hill,' said Lennox. 'Ivory Room. White Lion. Mr Shade...'

Blackwood looked up at him, wide-eyed. 'It didn't occur to me.'

'The code?'

'Yes. Move back one place from "L" and it becomes "J". Move two places back from "S" and it becomes "P".'

Lennox nodded. 'So, "LS" becomes "JP". But why not write the whole note in your code, though?'

'That was part of the secret. Mixing it up. We had stupid rules about the code. Names get coded, but places stayed. So, if someone intercepted our messages, they'd know where to look but not who to look for. We thought we were so clever.' Blackwood flicked through the pages again. 'The other entries don't really stick to that, though.' She looked up, smiling. 'The technique we invented as children confused me as an adult.'

Lennox gently took the diary from Blackwood, slipped it back into the envelope. 'I find it interesting that she didn't write any of the other details in here. Just the initials, coded. And I assume the other parts of the note are either cryptic or references to places or real people. But we have actual initials to work with now. "JP". We just have to work out what the rest of the note refers to.'

Blackwood looked back to the central lawn. 'We?'

Lennox leaned forward, head down. He smoothed out his hair with both hands. 'I used to see this case as cursed. It obsessed me. It became all I could see. Whatever angle or approach I took, I could never get anything to make sense. It was like trying to find the end of a rainbow.' He sat up. 'The deeper I fell into the hole, the less attention I gave to Jonah. For a long time, I blamed the case for his death. And in therapy, I realised how it's a sign of poor mental health to hold on to familiar pain rather than let it go and risk the unfamiliar. When something needs to die, but you keep it alive, it can end up killing you. Then, once Jonah ended his life, my obsession shifted to trying to understand why. It finished my marriage. It nearly finished me.'

Blackwood watched, frowning, as Lennox spoke. She sighed. 'So, why would you want to go back to it?'

He looked over at her. 'Because now there's you. One degree of separation. You knew her. It gives us context.'

'And two messed-up heads are better than one.'

He laughed. 'I think so. Plus, we have a fresh angle. Something new. It gives me an excuse to reopen the case.'

'Two letters?'

'It might be enough.'

'I promised her mum.'

Lennox flinched. 'So did I.'

They sat in silence for a moment, tainted by the whine of a light aircraft descending towards Elstree.

'Okay,' said Lennox. 'To answer your question...'

'What question?'

He raised an eyebrow. '"So, what now?"'

'Ah.'

'Let's find out what happened to Abigail Ashbourne.'

Also By Andrew Lowe

Love builds the strongest cages.

A young boy vanishes from his London home—no forced entry, no witnesses, just terrified parents and an empty house. A horrific discovery beneath a derelict mansion links the case to a methodical predator. As DCI Lennox and DC Blackwood close in, the killer makes a bold move, turning the hunt into a deadly battle of wills.

Turn the page for a free preview…

The Vanishing Room: Prologue

Adrian Gale checked the feeding tube, ensuring the site around his wife's abdomen showed no signs of redness, swelling or unusual discharge. He dabbed the area with a sterile chlorhexidine wipe.

The January half-light peered through the window, casting Gale's precise choreography onto the pastel-green walls.

There had been nineteen years of marriage: the first ten in the same bed, the next three a steady decoupling as the hospital-grade equipment overran their shared space and Gale installed himself in the smaller spare room. For the past six years, he had completed his transformation from lover to husband to nurse.

'There we go, my love.' His voice carried the soft burr of rural Dorset. 'Fresh as a daisy.' He checked the supplemental feeding pump's display—400ml delivered overnight—before disconnecting the empty nutrient bag. The PEG tube was an essential back-up, though they both pretended it was temporary. 'Did you sleep well? Is the new drug helping?'

Victoria's fingers twitched against the Egyptian cotton sheets: four hundred thread count, changed daily. She raised herself a little, silver hair fanned across the pillows. Her face held an asymmetrical droop: left eye slightly lower than the right. The disease had stolen her muscle tone in patches—cording her neck, hollowing her cheeks—but her eyes stayed sharp, tracking her husband's movements with an almost eerie clarity, as if her condition were a clumsy suit she was forced to wear while her essence functioned perfectly beneath.

She cranked out a smile and her voice emerged, thin but steady. 'I don't think it's doing much. The spasms kept me up for a while. Around three, I think. I didn't want to wake you.'

At fifty-eight, Victoria was four years Adrian's junior, though the illness had aged her beyond mathematics.

'They said it might take a week or two to find the optimal dose,' said Gale, checking his watch.

8:15am. Medication time.

He browsed the blister packs, arranged in neat rows on the bedside table: baclofen for the muscle spasms, gabapentin for nerve pain, amitriptyline for sleep.

The morning pills had to be taken with food. He reached for the specialist beaker with a curved spout and helped Victoria take small sips of the nutritional shake he'd prepared earlier. Each swallow required concentration from them both. When she'd managed 50ml, he dropped a baclofen and a gabapentin into a small china bowl and crushed them partially, before helping her take them with careful sips of thickened water.

Gale kept his manner brisk and breezy, reminding

himself that he was a giver of relief, not attending a deathbed. He kissed his wife's forehead, gazed out at the monochrome sky. 'I wish I could say it's a nice day.'

She turned her head to the window. 'It's a day.'

He smiled, took a digital thermometer from the bedside table drawer. Victoria held the tip under her tongue as he reached for the notepad and pen, behind the pile of paperbacks.

The thermometer beeped: 36.8°C. Gale logged it in the pad and reached for the mobile hoist tucked against the wall. He guided it forward on silent castors, positioning it exactly parallel to the bed. The spreader bar clicked as he attached the sling straps, checking each connection twice.

'All aboard!'

With one hand on the control pendant, he activated the electric actuator, watching the boom arm rise in smooth increments until Victoria was suspended above the mattress.

He shifted her position, checking for pressure sores around her sacrum and hips. The skin felt smooth, unbroken. The alternating-pressure mattress did most of the work, but he would turn her again mid-morning, just as he did every few hours.

She watched him. 'Are you getting enough rest?'

He reversed the hoist procedure, each movement muscle-mapped through thousands of repetitions. The actuator hummed as he lowered her back down, the sling's tension releasing in perfect symmetry.

He detached the straps in his usual sequence—right shoulder, left shoulder, right leg, left leg—before rolling the hoist back to its designated space.

'I rest when you rest,' he said.

He smoothed her hair, adjusted the pillows to support

her neck, then moisturised her hands with calendula cream, working it into the stiffened joints.

A whine from the doorway made them both look up. Ziggy, their elderly black Labrador, stood with his head tilted. He pawed at the wooden floor.

Gale helped the dog up onto the ramp he'd built beside the bed. Ziggy's tail wagged as Victoria stroked his ears. The grey muzzle and clouded eyes betrayed his age.

'Lovely boy,' said Victoria, scratching Ziggy under his chin. 'Still like a puppy for his walk.'

Gale checked Victoria's emergency button was within reach and headed for the door, closely followed by Ziggy. 'Back soon, my love. Treat yourself to a doze. I'll wake you with some proper breakfast. I just have to check on some business.'

When Gale returned from the walk, Victoria's breathing had deepened into sleep. He adjusted her pillows without waking her, checked the position of the emergency call button.

Ziggy settled into his bed in the corner of the room, nose tucked under his tail.

Gale slowly climbed the steep staircase at the end of the upstairs hall. Each step took him further from the gentle routines of the day, every footfall advancing a steady transformation.

Once inside the converted attic space, he locked the door and settled into his ergonomic chair, adjusting the height until his feet sat flat on the thinning rug.

He pulled up close to the desk and nudged the mouse, waking the three monitors. Each displayed a different room, viewed from a high angle. Two were identical modern kitchens with glossy white units and quartz worktops. The other was a sitting room with bifold doors opening onto a postage-stamp front garden. All three bore the same designer's fingerprints: ambient downlighting, integrated appliances, engineered oak flooring.

The central monitor showed the only occupied room. A woman in her late thirties stood at the kitchen island, phone pressed to her ear. She wore leggings and a loose T-shirt, and her long blonde hair was tied into a scruffy ponytail. Behind her, a boy of around eight played on a tablet at the breakfast bar, legs swinging against his stool.

Gale slipped on a pair of noise-cancelling headphones and clicked on a corner icon, unmuting the feed audio. He leaned forward, adjusting his rimless glasses.

The woman had ended the phone call and was talking to the boy.

'I'm taking Luna in at five on Monday, babes. The vet said it won't take long and it's nothing to worry about.'

The boy kept focus on the tablet. She shuffled closer.

'But, listen. Dad has a game and he won't be back until later. I won't be gone much longer than half an hour, and—'

'I'll be fine, Mum.' He looked up. 'I'm not a baby.'

She smiled, kissed him on the forehead, and walked out of the kitchen.

Gale listened to her footsteps thumping up the stairs, then muted the audio and retrieved a ring-bound notebook from the desk drawer.

Hannah and Ben Rushton. He had watched them and the father, Chris, for three weeks now.

Hannah always checked the front door was locked twice.

347

Ben hummed theme tunes from his video games.

Chris swore in front of Ben when Hannah wasn't around.

Chris and Hannah got through a bottle of wine every week night: she had a large glass, he finished the rest.

Once Ben had gone to bed, they squabbled about money, extended family politics, sex, sport. She loved F1, he didn't.

Ben left his football boots in the hall every Tuesday and Thursday, despite Hannah's repeated requests to put them in the utility room.

Chris watched *Match of the Day* every Saturday evening with a glass of Hoegaarden but usually fell asleep midway.

Together, Hannah and Chris watched true crime dramas. On evenings when Chris wasn't around, Hannah watched *Selling Sunset* and *Married at First Sight* with their ginger tabby Luna on her lap. It had been off its food for a few days.

Gale sat back in his seat, listening to Ziggy's claws tapping on the hallway floor below, patrolling in his old-dog way, keeping watch on Victoria in her medicated sleep.

He allowed himself a small smile.

Thirty minutes would be enough.

The Vanishing Room: Chapter One

DCI Oswald Lennox found a spare spot against a marble pillar with a clear view of the podium. He rested the back of his head on the cool stone and surveyed the municipal grandeur. Church House sat somewhere between a grand railway hotel and a well-funded university hall, with ornate coving, converted brass chandeliers, and a broad oak staircase that swept up to a mezzanine gallery.

Framed portrait photographs lined the walls between the high windows: former commissioners glowering out at the thirty round tables, each with a centrepiece vase of white chrysanthemums. A small platform at the far end supported the podium, flanked by Met Police Federation banners and a projection screen showing the force crest.

Lennox sipped from his glass of Château Lynch-Bages, tasting blackcurrant, cedar, truffle. This, along with an earlier sample of the gruesome coffee, confirmed his palate was still functioning. He could still make connections with the flavours. Blackcurrant: his grandmother's jam tarts. Cedar: the scent of pencil shavings from the class sharpener fixed to his English teacher's desk. Truffle: an omelette from a small bistro in Rue des Rosiers during a New Year trip to Paris with Martha in the mid-2000s.

He watched the young catering staff in black waistcoats weaving between the tables, serving coffee to the scrubbed-up detectives and dress-uniformed brass. The higher ranks —mostly male—stuck to dark tones, with primaries reserved for junior female detectives. The room's proportions created odd acoustic pockets, bouncing fragments of conversation between the pillars: shift patterns, arrest war stories, football chat.

Lennox studied the faces. The surnames connected instantly, but he had to ponder for the ranks, grope for the first names.

A woman in her early fifties stepped up to the podium microphone. DSI Aisha Khokhar wore a black silk tunic that fell to mid-thigh over tailored trousers, and a deep burgundy hijab with a subtle geometric pattern.

'Thank you.' Khokhar smiled and waited as the conversation ebbed into murmur, then silence. 'Six months ago, a trainee demonstrated the sort of courage and investigative insight more common to a detective deep into their career.'

Lennox turned back to his table, where his colleagues had all pivoted to face Khokhar, except for a young woman in a charcoal trouser suit with a streak of purple through her pinned-up black curls. Lennox caught her eye and she sighed, then shifted her chair round to face the podium, scraping the legs loudly on the parquet floor.

Khokhar continued. 'Working closely with senior officers, this PC displayed remarkable analytical skills and unprecedented initiative. Her actions directly led to the arrest of a dangerous multiple killer and saved the life of a senior officer.'

Lennox glanced down at the young woman's right leg. She leaned forward, both hands flat on her right knee which bounced rapidly. She shifted a hand to her thigh, drumming out a repeating pattern with her fingertips.

Khokar continued. 'The officer showed exceptional bravery and commitment, and I'm certain she has a bright future ahead of her.' She paused, her expression darkening. 'It's no secret that the Service has been under intense scrutiny in recent years, particularly for its perceived gender bias. So, this kind of success serves as both an inspiration to other new detectives and shows that our recruitment processes and professional standards are moving in the right direction.' She took out a framed certificate from behind the podium. 'It gives me great pleasure to present the Chief Constable's Commendation for Outstanding Bravery to Detective Constable Olivia Blackwood.'

Khokhar stepped to the side as Blackwood sprang from her chair and hopped up onto the platform, to loud applause.

Lennox smiled at the giveaway sharp creases in Blackwood's brand-new trouser suit. He rested his glass on the floor at his feet and raised his arms high as he clapped.

Blackwood retrieved the framed certificate from Khokhar, shifted to move in for an embrace, then checked herself and accepted the DSI's fulsome handshake. She held the frame out in front with both hands, as if testing its weight, unsure whether to raise it above her head.

She leaned into the microphone, too close, then turned to Khokhar. 'Uh... Thank you. Ma'am.' She lowered her head, as if deferring to royalty, then turned back to the room. 'It's a great honour to be recognised in this way and I'm truly humbled...' Blackwood hesitated, turned to Khokhar again, then back to the room. She reached down to her heeled shoe, took it off, and pulled out a yellow Post-it note, then consulted the note as she wriggled her leg, getting the shoe back on. 'I want to dedicate this to my mum. She always said I should never rest on my laurels. Actually, I don't really know what resting on laurels would look like, but we all know what it means, right?' She grimaced. 'Is it something to do with laurels worn on the head? Anyway. So, I don't do that. Rest on my laurels. In fact, I was looking at the other public service gongs I could shoot for.' She checked the note. 'Up at the top, there's the King's Police Medal, various orders of the British Empire, the George Medal, George Cross. But my mum also said to not get ideas above my station. So I'll just work on being the best version of myself. Then, hopefully the awards will be a by-product of that.' She waved the frame in the air. 'Not that this particular award doesn't mean a lot to me. It does. But... Erm...'

Lennox closed his eyes, willing her to change tack. He looked out at the faces; the grins were slipping.

Blackwood took a breath. 'I was warned to keep this brief. You can probably see why.' Light laughter. 'Uh... I... I've always been told I'm a bit of an acquired taste. I've also heard *difficult, hard work*, and from the less kind people, *mental*.' She thought for a few seconds. 'But I'm neurodiverse. I have ADHD. Compared to some people's burdens, it's one of the lighter loads. But, yes, I suppose it does make me difficult sometimes. Occasionally hard work. And, okay, I'll own it... Maybe veering on mental from time to time.' Louder laughter rippled through the room. 'But it also gives me positive qualities. And I just want to say that I wouldn't be standing up here if it hadn't been for the guidance and patience of DCI Oswald Lennox.' Blackwood shielded her eyes against the podium spotlight and pointed in Lennox's direction. He grinned and raised a hand. 'He showed me that being different doesn't have to be a weakness. It can also be a strength. So...' She raised the frame in the air. 'Here's to the power of diversity. To difference.'

Khokhar started to clap, and the rest of the room joined her. She reached out a hand to Blackwood, ushering her off the platform.

Blackwood turned to go but then leaned back into the microphone: too close, too loud. 'Listen. Believe me. It's not easy being different.' She held up the award again. 'But I suppose this is a good start.'

After the presentations, Lennox parked himself near a radiator at the edge of the reception room. Rain battered the tall windows, rendering the January evening an impressionist blur. The mood had loosened, with detectives gathered in small, over-refreshed cliques.

The heat from the radiator seeped through Lennox's suit jacket. He swirled his wine, then drained the glass, watching Blackwood thread through the crowd beside an older female detective with close-cropped brown hair.

His phone buzzed with a reminder: *SATURDAY SECURITY RESET.*

'Anything exciting?' said Blackwood, appearing beside him with a champagne flute in one hand and the framed commendation in the other.

'Just spam,' he said, too quickly. 'Getting a lot of it lately.'

DI Carla Whitmore settled in between them. 'The spammers are outsourcing to AI now. At least the spelling has improved.'

Lennox slipped his phone into his pocket. 'Maybe I've triggered the algorithms because I've got a birthday coming up.'

Blackwood grinned. 'Nice hint.' She took a slurp of champagne, eyelids lolling.

Lennox waved a hand. 'I ask for nothing.'

Blackwood spluttered on the champagne. 'And you will receive it.' She raised a hand in a flourish. 'In abundance.'

Lennox shared a blank look with Whitmore.

'It's from *The Rocky Horror Show*,' said Blackwood, shaking her head. 'A production came to the theatre in Ware once. It was the most exciting thing to happen in my home town in years. It played for three nights and I went to them all.' She took another gulp of champagne. 'I didn't dress up, though. So, can I ask about the damage, sir?'

He shrugged. 'Fifty-three.'

'Still on the right side of the decade,' said Whitmore. She half-turned, appraising the room. 'The food was almost edible. The last one of these I attended was all rubbery chicken and soft-boiled greens.'

Lennox checked his watch. 'More efficient, too. They used to drag on until midnight.' He looked at Blackwood. 'You were fine. Nice confessional.'

She screwed up her face. 'It went better in my head.'

'Blackwood!' A male voice roared across the room, loud enough to draw glances from nearby groups. All three turned to face a stocky, neckless man with a ruddy complexion and an even layer of short grey hair. An under-sized shirt strained against his frame.

The man strode over, detaching from a group of younger colleagues, all watching with interest. He reached out for Blackwood and drew her into a one-sided hug. 'Congratulations. Quite a night for Wood Green, eh? One of our own.'

Blackwood straightened up. 'Thank you, sir. DI Whitmore, DCI Lennox. This is my old DI, Greg Pollard.'

Pollard gave Blackwood a prod on the shoulder. 'Oi! Less of the old.' He beat his chest with the other hand. 'I taught her all she knows, of course.'

'I doubt that,' said Whitmore.

Pollard frowned, then gave a brittle laugh. 'Thing is, though. It was all there in your gaffer's speech, right?'

'What do you mean?' said Lennox.

Pollard raised his head, glanced at Blackwood and Whitmore, then addressed Lennox. 'Met politics, eh? All those diversity quotas. Don't get me wrong, mind. Blackwood's got the chops. But there are a lot of female officers being fast-tracked to CID, these days.'

Blackwood scoffed. 'Your congratulations are sounding a tiny bit qualified, sir.'

Pollard offered a theatrical shrug and looked at the three of them in turn, in a fruitless search for solidarity.

'DC Blackwood.' Lennox took a step forward and faced her, angling his body away from Pollard. His voice was quiet but clear, slicing through the tension. 'In an informal setting like this, you're under no obligation to call a senior "sir". It's discretionary. A mark of respect.' He turned, fixing Pollard with eyes like Arctic ice. 'And if you want respect, you give respect.'

The Vanishing Room: Chapter Two

Blackwood scurried across Station Road, head down against the swooping wind. The broad thoroughfare traced the edge of Harrow town centre, its weekday gridlock yielding to a few Sunday morning cyclists. To the north, past the shopping centre and cafés, the Victorian terraces of North Harrow rose against a pewter-grey sky.

She flipped up the extravagant fake-fur hood of the burgundy parka bought on impulse in the AllSaints Boxing Day sale. She had been drawn to the abundance of pockets and the military surplus styling but hadn't counted on the hood's overstimulating trim. The synthetic black fluff formed a mini hedge around her eyelashes, tickling her nose every time she turned her head. It would be on eBay come March.

Beneath, she wore black jeans and cherry-red Doc Martens, scuffed at the toes. Her warrant card sat in the breast pocket of a grey wool jumper she'd stolen from her brother a few years ago.

Blackwood ducked under the awning of the tiny café on the corner opposite Waterstones. She'd chosen the spot because it was far enough from both Hendon and Wood Green to avoid running into anyone she knew.

The bell tinkled as she pushed through the door. The windows had steamed opaque and she caught a first sight of a display of Portuguese custard tarts, their pastry shells scored in precise concentric circles. She leaned in, admiring the aesthetic, counting the layers.

'I can move tables if you need to watch the door.'

The voice made Blackwood startle. She'd been so fixated on the pastries she hadn't noticed her contact was already sitting at an alcove table beside the window.

'Sorry.' She flipped back the parka hood.

Heidi Clarke stood and embraced Blackwood. She was tall and athletic, in running gear: leggings and a half-zip thermal top. 'It's okay. I didn't recognise you in your winter wear.'

Blackwood grimaced. 'It's a bit much. More suited to a polar expedition than a London winter. Are you running or have you ran?'

'Ran. Northwick Park, 10K. Thought I'd double up work and play.'

Blackwood looked around.

A few student types hunched over laptops.

Middle-aged couple in matching North Face jackets communing with their phones.

Broken floor tile near the counter, patched with grey cement that didn't quite match.

Female barista with forearm tattoos. She would.

'I got you a black coffee,' said Clarke, gesturing to a mug on the table.

'Thanks, Heidi. That's kind of you.'

'You're only ten minutes late. I'd accounted for at least fifteen.'

Blackwood laughed. 'Must be my improvement mindset.'

Clarke took an iPad from a shoulder bag hung on her chair. 'How is Lennox?'

They sat. Blackwood's head throbbed gently as she sipped the coffee. 'Very well. This is nice. Even he might tolerate it. We went to a police awards do last night. I got my commendation. Drank too much. Saw my old boss from Wood Green.'

Clarke nodded to the pastry rack. 'Anything to eat?'

'I won't linger. This is an illicit encounter, remember?'

'You make it sound so seedy.' She held Blackwood's eye for a second. 'I shouldn't really be here, either, but I wanted to flag a few things. Sophie Lawson is well. A good distance from the fallout, over at her sister's in Sydney. It's a place near the water. Double Bay. She says she swims every morning because it helps with her shoulder.'

Blackwood drank more coffee. 'Of course. It's summer over there.'

'It certainly is. In the high twenties right now.' Clarke pulled something up on the iPad. 'It's good for her. She has physio twice a week. The bruises from the assault have faded. But Mr Lewis Hartley isn't taking it well.'

'In what way?'

The barista came over and added a tray of croissants to the display, then wiped down the windows.

Clarke waited until she'd moved away. 'He's been erratic. Making things as difficult as possible. Showing up at Sophie's old workplace. Trying to access their joint accounts.'

Blackwood's leg bounced. 'That's pretty standard, though, right? He's a controller. They hate being denied access to anything.'

'Yes, but it's the account activity that bothers me. When Lennox asked me to help Sophie, I focused on her safety first, then the financial mess from the separation. Last week, a senior partner from Hartley's firm Clifford Chance got involved. An old-school big beast called Edgar Grantham. He's challenging the non-mol order. Claiming it was obtained under false pretences.' Clarke's fingers tightened around her cup. 'They're pushing extra hard on Hartley's story that Sophie attacked him first. That he was defending himself.'

'That's ridiculous. I saw her injuries. The hospital photos.'

Clarke nodded. 'Yes, but they've got some GP records showing Sophie had anxiety issues last year. They're using that to suggest she was unstable. The move to Australia proves it, of course.'

'But she only went because—'

'She was terrified, yes.' Clarke leaned forward. 'What really spooks me is the lawyer, Grantham.'

Blackwood took an empty sugar packet and began folding it into triangles. 'Clifford Chance is a corporate, right?'

'Very. These guys rarely touch domestic cases. The money's pocket change for them. They mainly deal with corporate mergers and offshore tax arrangements. So, why has one of their top partners made it his business to run interference on a domestic violence case? Feels like more than a colleague's professional courtesy.'

Blackwood folded the sugar packet, pondering. 'Maybe Hartley has friends in high places.'

'Exactly. The kind of places where money moves quietly. I've seen Lewis's statements. He has far more than a property lawyer should have floating around.'

'Maybe he's better with money than relationships.' Blackwood's sugar packet origami had yielded a tiny crane. She propped it on the table and started on another.

Clarke continued. 'Their joint accounts are frozen but somehow Lewis has money flowing through offshore territories. Seven figures.' She lowered her voice. 'Sophie mentioned something to me before she headed to Australia. Lewis was drunk one night, boasting about people he knew who could "make problems go away". She thought he was just showing off, but if this Grantham is one of those people and Hartley is frustrated about being shut out of Sophie's affairs, there might be trouble ahead for her. No matter how much distance she puts between herself and him.'

Blackwood abandoned the origami and twisted the packet into a long coil. She shrugged. 'I'll have a nose into Grantham.'

Clarke sat back and surveyed her. 'Be careful with this, Liv. I acknowledge your philanthropy but this isn't officially your case anymore.'

Blackwood shrugged. 'Extra-curricular. Things are quiet at Hendon.'

Clarke smiled. 'My sister works at St Mary's A&E—'

'I know, I know. You're asking for trouble when you say it's quiet. But that's just confirmation bias. If you look for patterns, you'll find them whether they're there or not. Faces in clouds.'

'Well… That's what Hartley's lawyers are saying about Sophie. That she's paranoid. Seeing things that don't exist. Making up threats. You know it rarely ends well when you let your emotions guide you, rather than cold logic.'

'Gut instinct is a real thing.'

'I'm just saying…' Clarke slid her iPad back into the bag. 'Some doors might be better left closed. Especially if you're planning to go through them alone.'

The Vanishing Room: Chapter Three

Lennox gazed up at the gilt cornicing and coffered ceiling of Wigmore Hall, a jewel box of Edwardian acoustical engineering, as the final notes of Max Richter's 'Sleep' resonated through the wood-panelled chamber. The pianist's hands hovered above the keys, waiting for the reverberations to fade completely.

He turned to the woman at his side: Imogen Winters, early fifties. In the subdued lighting from the crystal sconces he could just make out her profile: the slight tilt of her head, the way she leaned forward in reverent appreciation, her fingers moving slightly as if settling the final decaying notes. His ex-wife Martha had always sat back in her seat, head raised, hands still in her lap like a judge awaiting evidence. They had been apart for eight years now, but her emotional presence lingered like a retinal scar.

Winters linked Lennox's arm as they filed out with the rest of the audience, their shuffling footsteps bouncing off the marble pillars of the vestibule. Outside on Wigmore

Street, the luxury boutiques stood dark and shuttered. Black cabs prowled in the fine evening rain.

Lennox popped up an umbrella and Winters huddled under with him as they walked to his car, her silver-threaded dark hair spilling over his arm.

'Did you know Wigmore Hall is about twenty-three metres long and twelve wide?' said Winters. 'The ceiling height is calibrated precisely for chamber music. It creates the perfect resonance time of 1.5 seconds.'

He did.

'I didn't. Have you worked there a lot?'

Winters laughed. 'I used to practically live there. I guest-conducted the Nash Ensemble for three seasons. Had to learn every corner of that room. How sound behaves in different temperatures. The different humidity levels. The way a full house alters the acoustic profile. Did you enjoy the performance?'

He glanced over. 'That sounds like a trick question.'

'Christ, no. I'm not that formal. I can turn off professional appreciation mode and just get into something. How about you? Are you always on high alert, assessing body language, spotting people who look out of place?'

'I'm a detective, Imogen. Not a bodyguard. I loved the performance. I know his work well. I like minimalism. Ambient. Contemporary classical. I have colleagues who think it's empty. Nothingy. But I like the way it lets you fill the space in your own way. And I love the precision, the formality.'

'Yes,' said Winters dreamily. 'The exactness of minimalism. It's almost mathematical.'

They reached his Volvo V60 Estate, parked at the end of Wellbeck Street. Lennox gave her the umbrella while he unlocked the car and opened the passenger door.

She shook out the umbrella. 'Christ almighty. Is it ever going to stop raining?'

They headed north, through Marylebone, past the rarefied clinics of Harley Street, including the surgery of Lennox's private doctor, Moorcroft. The rain intensified, refracting the headlamps and streetlights in scattered patterns, creating false depth perceptions at street corners. Lennox kept it steady: changing gear at optimal revs, transitioning smoothly, holding a three-second gap to the vehicle ahead. The wipers swished at maximum frequency.

As a younger man, driving had felt expressive, instinctive. Now, it was mechanical. Checks and processes.

Winters held her face close to her window, peering out at the squall. 'While classical composers tend to go straight for the heart, I find the minimalists seem to be all about time perception. Philip Glass writes in circles. John Adams in waves.'

Lennox glanced at her. 'As artists age, I find they become more about what they leave out than what they put in.'

She nodded. 'Refinement. Doing the simple things well rather than over-reaching, showing off that you know how to do everything.'

They drove along Outer Circle on the edge of Regent's Park. A vicious side wind swept horizontal sheets of rain across the windscreen.

'Lovely evening,' said Lennox.

His phone sat in a dashboard mount, Google Maps steering them to Winters' flat in Cannon Lane, ten minutes away.

'We should have taken Albany Street,' she said. 'This is too narrow. It's always claggy.'

He checked the route. 'Sorry, yes. Turned too early. It merges with Albany in a second.'

Lennox's phone buzzed. He glanced over, read the banner notification: *EVENING MEDS AT TEN.*

He grabbed at the device, hoping to unhitch it and drop it into his jacket pocket before Winters could read the message.

But he fumbled, had to try again.

The momentary distraction was enough.

A Deliveroo cyclist materialised out of the rain, high-vis jacket flaring in the Volvo headlights. The cyclist had slipped between the two-way traffic and drifted out in front.

Lennox braked, harder than necessary. The ABS engaged with a mechanical stutter.

Winters gasped as the car skidded to a stop.

A car behind pulled up suddenly behind, sounding its horn.

The wipers maintained their metronomic rhythm: left-right, left-right. Lennox closed his eyes, counting five complete cycles before speaking. As ever, he consoled himself with a convenient culprit: his medications' effect on reaction time.

'I'm sorry, Imogen. He came from nowhere. Are you okay?'

He moved off carefully, then reached over, resting his hand on hers.

She took a juddering breath, withdrew her hand. 'It's fine. I'm fine. Please take me home.'

The Vanishing Room: Chapter Four

The security light snapped on as Lennox scurried through the rain across the gravel drive, jacket pulled over his head. Three new CCTV cameras tracked his progress: one above the front door of his substantial detached house, two at opposing ends of the guttering above the deep-set bay windows. He paused on the portico, beneath a moth battering itself against the lamp's protective casing, then turned to watch the automated security gates clang shut. He had gone for substance over taste in the gate design: diagonal cross bracing with spiked finials; dual-technology sensors with encrypted wireless protocols that required biometric authentication via an app to grant access.

He had set up a location-specific reminder on his smart watch to make sure he never left the house without his phone and wallet, and had the security company override number taped on the inside sole of his shoe.

Lennox took out his phone, checked the daily reset code, and entered it into a pad beside the solid oak door. The latch released and he stepped into the entrance hall.

He performed his nightly checks.

Front door security engaged.

Window catches tested.

Motion sensors active.

His hand tremored as he reached for the hallway light switch, and he pressed his palm flat against the wall until it passed.

The high-ceilinged sitting room lay in wait, exactly as he'd left it that morning: everything aligned, measured, ordered. His gaze lingered at the maroon-and-black Rothko on the far wall, above the spot where Marlow had bound and dumped him. The memory was still jagged: the metallic taste of fear, the cable ties cutting into his wrists, Marlow's methodical movements as he arranged the bones.

Lennox eyed the wingback chair by the door, where Marlow had placed his machete as he went about his work. It was ornamental now.

He walked over and sat in the worn leather Eames lounge chair near the window, then closed his eyes, listening to the house settle into its evening sounds.

The low hum of the heating system entering Night Mode.

The ticking of cooling pipes.

High above, rain pummelled the slate-tiled roof with its newly reinforced rafters.

He was safe here. His abode was his watcher, his keeper. He had transformed it from a spacious family home into a customised fortress.

Lennox took the book of cryptic crossword puzzles from a side table, and zoned in to the clues, deducing the principles. Pattern recognition. Sequential thinking. Mental agility maintenance. Frequent, multi-layered deep thinking to rewire his synapses, retrain his ailing brain.

Meds at ten, then wind-down.

He climbed the stairs to his office and sat at the glass-topped desk between a wall of law textbooks and an over-sized Ansel Adams print of Yosemite's Half Dome. He set down his phone and opened his laptop, then navigated to the day's chess puzzle, resolving it quickly: knight to F7, bishop sacrifice, forced mate in four moves.

He entered the solution and opened a drawer beneath the desk. The Flow headset remained boxed, its sleek white packaging promising 'advanced neurostimulation therapy'. A diagram beneath the box image showed two hydrogel-coated electrodes designed to deliver precise microamp currents to targeted regions of the prefrontal cortex.

Not yet.

At ten, he headed into the bathroom and surveyed his meds and supplements arranged in neat rows along the left side of the shelf above the sink. His current focus was the phospholipid phosphatidylserine and the coline compound Alpha-GPC, due to the strong clinical evidence for support of brain function. Also: Omega-3, Ginkgo biloba for blood flow, Bacopa monnieri for memory support, Lion's Mane mushroom extract for cognitive enhancement, and a high dose of B vitamins. Lennox had recently received an order of Acetyl-L-carnitine, an amino acid claimed to support brain cell function, but he wanted to do more research before adding it to his regime.

This was all self-prescribed, ordered online.

On the right side of the shelf sat the medication sanctioned by Moorcroft: donepezil and its enhancer, memantine, to inhibit breakdown of the chemical that smoothed the transfer of messages around his brain cells; rivastigmine, another inhibitor; modafinil for focus; a low dose of propranolol for the tremors.

A few days ago, Lennox had watched—and then wished he could unwatch—a YouTube video showing the build-up of protein plaques across the frontal and temporal lobes, like limescale inside a kettle.

He would not sit and wait for his healthy brain to erode and hollow out. He would fight the emptying with a discipline of mental agility, clinically proven slowing agents and a smattering of fringe techniques. His natural sense of critical thinking scoffed at the pseudoscience, but if a tiny part of it had a positive benefit, it was worth a place in the arsenal.

Despite it all, he knew there was no escape. No cure. Just delay. If his memories and perceptions were the measure of who he was, of what he was, then he was shifting steadily from awareness to nullness. Becoming nothing.

He had to do something.

Lennox slapped his fist against his forehead in frustration. Had Imogen seen the message about meds? Would it even matter if she had? He was keeping so much hidden. Perhaps it was time to open up to her.

His phone buzzed in his pocket with a call.

He took it out, noted the caller ID with a sigh, then connected.

'Sunday evening, Carla. I'm not holding out for good news.'

DI Whitmore took a breath, puffed it out slowly. 'Sir. We have something in Mill Hill. A battered old manor called Thornfield House. I thought of leaving it until the morning, but it can't wait.'

'Murder?'

She hesitated. 'I'm not sure what it is.'

The Vanishing Room: Chapter Five

The wipers strained against the deluge as Lennox pulled up behind the cordon tape, slotting the Volvo between an incident support vehicle and the Scientific Services Van. The support vehicle's blue lights carved through the darkness, throwing leaping shadows across the overgrown front garden of Thornfield House.

He killed the engine and reached for his phone, muscle memory leading him to the carefully crafted checklist in his Notes app.

SCENE PROTOCOLS
> *Property type/layout verification*
> *Risk assessment review*
> *PPE requirements*
> *Evidence preservation notes*
> *Command structure reminders*
> *Witness identification procedure*
> *Media protocol if required*

Resource allocation checklist

He digested them carefully, one by one, visualising the actions and comments, then noted the time: 22:47.

Through the windscreen, Thornfield House loomed like a haunted house cliché: a three-storey pile of redbrick and white stone detailing. Most windows were boarded, though original glass remained in some of the upper frames. An elaborate turret feature rose from the right wing, its decorative stonework gnawed away by decades of neglect. Mobile units lit up the facade, exposing patches of weathered render and climbing ivy.

DI Whitmore waited at the tape, lurking beneath an oversized umbrella. She held out a set of protective gear as Lennox approached: paper suit, overshoes, nitrile gloves. He took the items and joined her under the umbrella.

'Sorry about the timing, sir,' said Whitmore, raising her voice above the wind.

He looked up at the house. 'I take it Ghostbusters were busy.'

They headed up what had once been a sweeping carriage drive, now a maze of fractured stone and colonising weeds. Secondary succession was taking hold: buddleja sprouting from mortar joints, moss-cushioned flag-stones tilting at precise angles by decades of freeze-thaw cycles. Nature's arithmetic laid bare.

'What's the green van?' said Lennox, gesturing to the vehicle parked near the front gates.

A beefy character jumped down from the van's back doors carrying a stack of yellow hard hats.

'Council structural engineers,' said Whitmore. 'We'll

need to wear head protection. Partial roof collapse in the east side of the building.'

'Talk me through it,' said Lennox, walking slightly ahead and forcing Whitmore to pick up the pace to keep the umbrella over them both. They stopped under the shelter of the porch, flanked by vast bay windows with ornate surrounds that were still intact despite the dereliction.

Whitmore closed the umbrella and propped it against the wall. They put on the protective gear and hard hats and stepped inside. 'The place was built in 1873 for a railway magnate who went bankrupt in '78. Since then, it's been a prep school, a wartime hospital, and most recently, a care home that closed in 2008. It was bought by Meridian Heritage six months ago. The council ordered a structural survey after complaints about urban explorers. Engineers accessed the basement this morning and found something that wasn't on the original plans.'

They walked through into the expansive entrance hall. Mobile lights sat at regular intervals along the walls, their LED arrays slicing through decades of accumulated dust. Whitmore ran a torch beam upwards over the crumbling grand staircase, then raised it to the ceiling, revealing dark patches of damp gathered around the elaborate cornicing. The plasterwork was mostly intact, but rainwater dripped steadily from above, pooling in puddles on the marble floor.

Lennox followed Whitmore to a door beneath the staircase, its tarnished frame adorned with decorative side columns. She turned the brass handle and pushed. The hinges squealed as the door opened.

Lennox peered around her shoulder to a descending stone staircase, lit from mobile lighting below. 'Okay. So, we're literally going down to the cellar?'

Whitmore led the way, through the cold and chalky air.

'The engineers were checking load-bearing walls, looking for subsidence in the foundations. Standard stuff. It was originally a coal cellar down here, later converted to a laundry room during the building's institutional phase. The plans show a simple Victorian basement. But there's been some recent unauthorised modification.'

Lennox inhaled a dose of dust and coughed, as they emerged into a vaulted chamber: six metres by eight, with walls rising to meet segmented brick arches that spanned between cast-iron beams designed to support the weight above. A rectangular opening had been dug out in the precise centre of the concrete floor, around one and a half metres square. Mobile lights surrounded the hole, trained down at the interior, revealing precision-cut edges and contemporary concrete, its dark grey surface unsullied against the aged substrate. An aluminium extension ladder was hooked over the edge, secured to steel anchor points with carabiners.

Three forensic officers in white Tyvek suits conferred around a mobile evidence processing station. The tallest figure detached himself from the group and walked over to Lennox and Whitmore. Down here, chief SOCO David Pearson's short silver hair rendered him luminescent and ghostly under the industrial spotlights.

Pearson took off his spectacles and nodded to Lennox. 'Good evening, sir.'

'So far, so bad, David. I assume what's down in the pit isn't going to improve things?'

'You'll want to see for yourself.' Pearson handed over a small LED torch with an ultra-bright beam. He gestured to the hole. 'The new concrete looks polymer-modified. Probably with silica fume additives. Whoever dug this out didn't skimp on quality. It'll take time to analyse the aggregate composition and extraction methodology, map the tool signatures, determine the precise construction timeline. But, judging by the tool marks alone, we're a long way past amateur hour. The angles look exact, with every surface deliberately finished. Someone took their time here. We've documented the upper structure, but the real story is down below.' He slipped his glasses back on and looked between Lennox and Whitmore. 'I can give you the how, but the why is all yours. The ladder's rated for one-fifty kilos. Anchors are all tested.'

Lennox walked over to the pit and crouched at the side, above the ladder.

Whitmore followed him. 'Sir...'

He held up a hand. 'I need to see it unfiltered.'

Lennox aimed the beam down into the pit. The aperture was tapered: wide at the top, barely half a metre square at the base, around four metres deep. The walls were lined with nursery-style wallpaper—pink and blue alternate panels featuring fluttering butterflies and prancing lambs—now grimy with age.

A white sheet lay at the bottom, draped over a small form.

'That's our covering,' said Pearson. 'This is all pretty sophisticated work. The top of the pit was sealed with a fresh concrete panel, perfectly matched to the original flooring. You'd never know it was here unless you were looking for it.' He indicated three small fixtures in the corners. 'Camera mounts here and here. Microphone housing. There's even a ventilation system using low-speed fans. It's minimal, but precise. Intake port at floor level, exhaust near the top, with acoustic baffling in the conduits to minimise sound transmission. Just enough air exchange to maintain viable oxygen levels without any detectible sound or power signature. The walls are lined, beneath the wallpaper, with dense mineral wool, and the top panel is probably a composite, with the concrete bonded to vibration-dampening material. Even if someone had screamed down here, the sound attenuation would have rendered it inaudible.'

Lennox's beam caught scuff marks at the top of the opposite pit wall. 'Access?'

'Extension ladder, most likely,' said Pearson. 'We found microscopic rubber transfer on the concrete at impact points, consistent with industrial-grade ladder feet. You'd see them on any building site.'

Lennox handed the torch to Whitmore. 'Light my way, Carla.' He grasped the ladder and lowered himself down. The metal was cold even through his gloved palms, and the wallpaper closed in as he descended and the dimensions narrowed. At the bottom, the paper was shredded and scored with fingernail scratch marks.

He crouched beside the sheet and carefully peeled away the corner.

Whitmore's torch beam illuminated the partially mummified remains of a child, the body positioned in a foetal curve against the narrowed base of the pit. Desiccation had drawn the skin tight across the orbital bones, with the lips retracted to reveal small teeth. Dark hair still clung to the skull in patches. The hands were drawn up to the chest, fingers contracted into rigid claws. The body wore blue pyjamas with a faded Spider-Man motif, the fabric bunched and twisted. Partial adipocere formation had created a waxy whiteness across the exposed skin.

'Male?' Lennox spoke quietly, but Pearson still caught it.

'Yes. From pelvic morphology, mandibular angle, orbital characteristics.'

'Age? TOD?'

'Based on skeletal development and dentition, I'd say no more than ten years old. I'd call TOD around four months ago, judging by the advanced state of desiccation in such a controlled environment. But we'll need full pathology work-up to confirm everything.'

Lennox looked over the corpse. No signs of physical trauma or bindings. The pit itself had been the restraint.

He looked up to the rim, shielding his eyes from the torch beam. 'How long would the ventilation system have run?'

Pearson tilted his head from side to side. 'Basic twelve-volt. Two small DC fans powered by a sealed battery rated for around three weeks of juice. After that, the air exchange would gradually fail.'

'And the cameras and microphones were removed at some point, then the top repaired?'

'It looks that way, yes,' said Pearson.

Lennox gently relaid the sheet over the remains and stood up, gazing down at the shape. 'Whoever put the boy here either deprived him of food and watched him starve to death or left him enough to live on for a few weeks then watched him suffocate.'

Grab your copy...
vinci-books.com/LennoxBlackwood

About the Author

Andrew Lowe was born in the north of England. He has written for *The Guardian* and *The Sunday Times* and contributed to numerous books and magazines on films, music, TV, video games, sex, and shin splints.

He lives in the south of England, where he writes, edits other people's writing, and shepherds his two sons down the path of righteousness.

Acknowledgments

Many thanks to the remarkable *Detective Constable Daley Jones* of the ADHD Alliance for his generous advice on ADHD and policing. It's a good job I set a time limit on our Zoom call. :)

Inspiration strikes in strange places, and a randomly Googled article by *Stephen Moss* on the peregrine falcon and other London birds sparked ideas that begin in this book and will continue through the series.

I'm infinitely grateful to *Linda Clare*, Professor of Clinical Psychology of Ageing and Dementia at Exeter University, for her clear-eyed insight into cognitive impairment and young-onset dementia. Also, *Katelin* at the *Alzheimer's Society* went above and beyond with her educational calls and emails.

Andrew Lowe
London, 2025